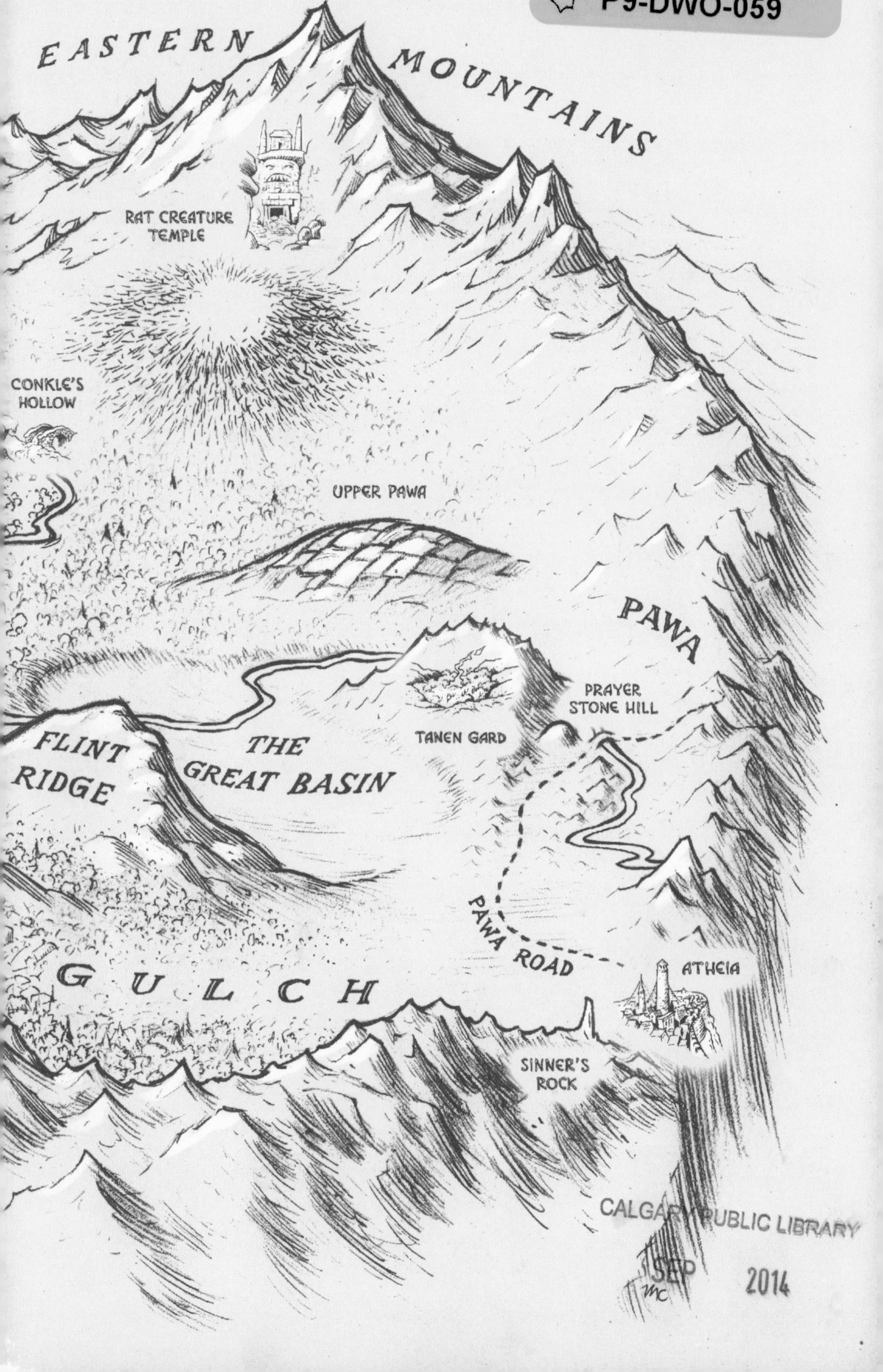
EASTERN MOUNTAINS
RAT CREATURE TEMPLE
CONKLE'S HOLLOW
UPPER PAWA
PAWA
PRAYER STONE HILL
TANEN GARD
FLINT RIDGE
THE GREAT BASIN
PAWA ROAD
ATHEIA
GULCH
SINNER'S ROCK

Dreaming of Harvestar

BONE

THE DRAGONSLAYER

BY JEFF SMITH

WITH COLOR BY STEVE HAMAKER

graphix

An Imprint of

◼SCHOLASTIC

Library of Congress Catalog Card Number 95068403.

ISBN-13: 978-0-439-70626-1 — ISBN-10: 0-439-70626-2 (hardcover)

ISBN 0-439-70637-8 (paperback)

ACKNOWLEDGMENTS

Harvestar Family Crest designed by Charles Vess

Map of *The Valley* by Mark Crilley

Color by Steve Hamaker

20 19 18 17 16 15 14 13   14 15

First Scholastic edition, August 2006

Book design by David Saylor

Printed in Singapore 46

This book is for Irene Kilty

for inspiring her grandson's imagination

CONTENTS

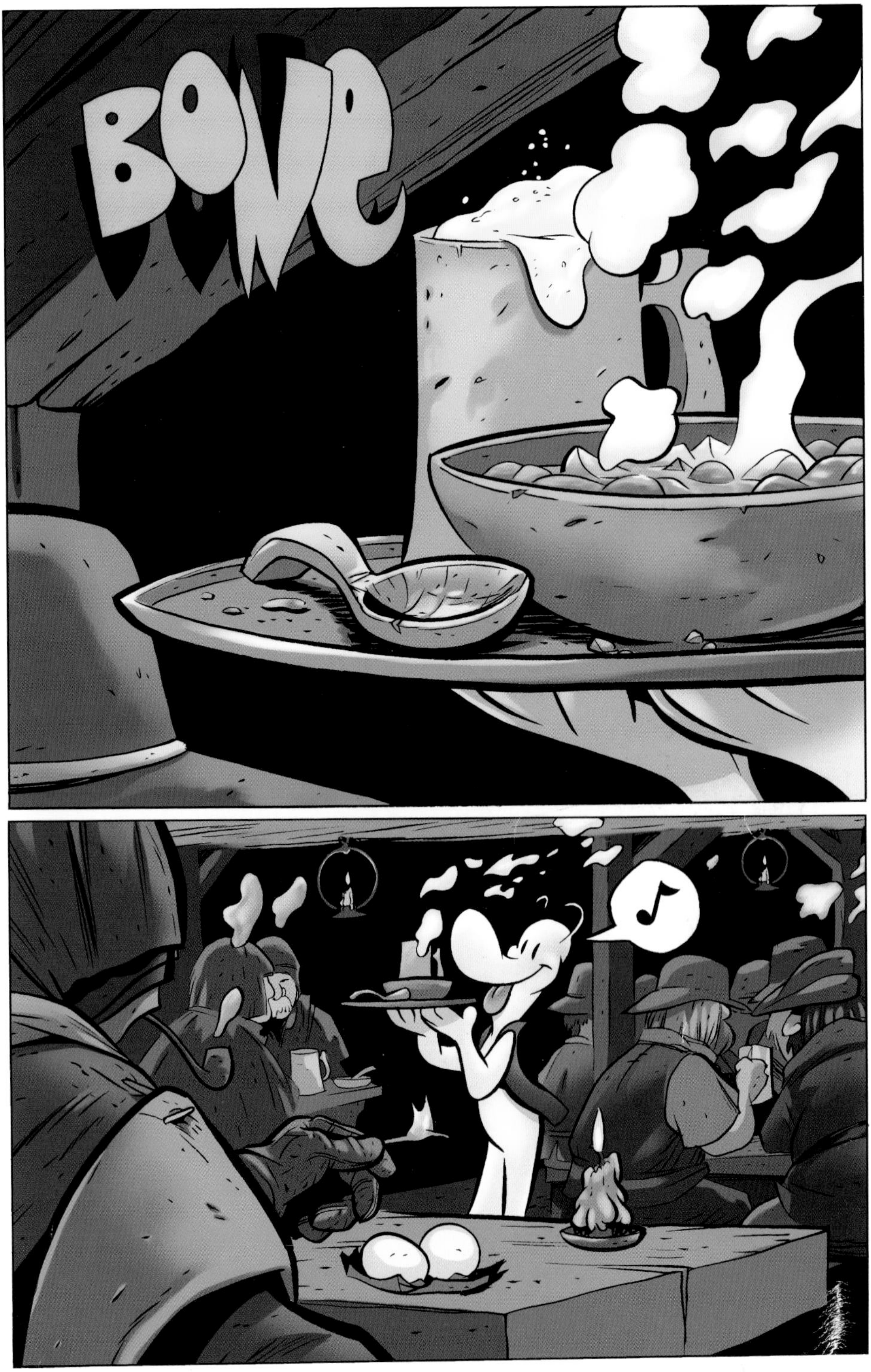
BONE

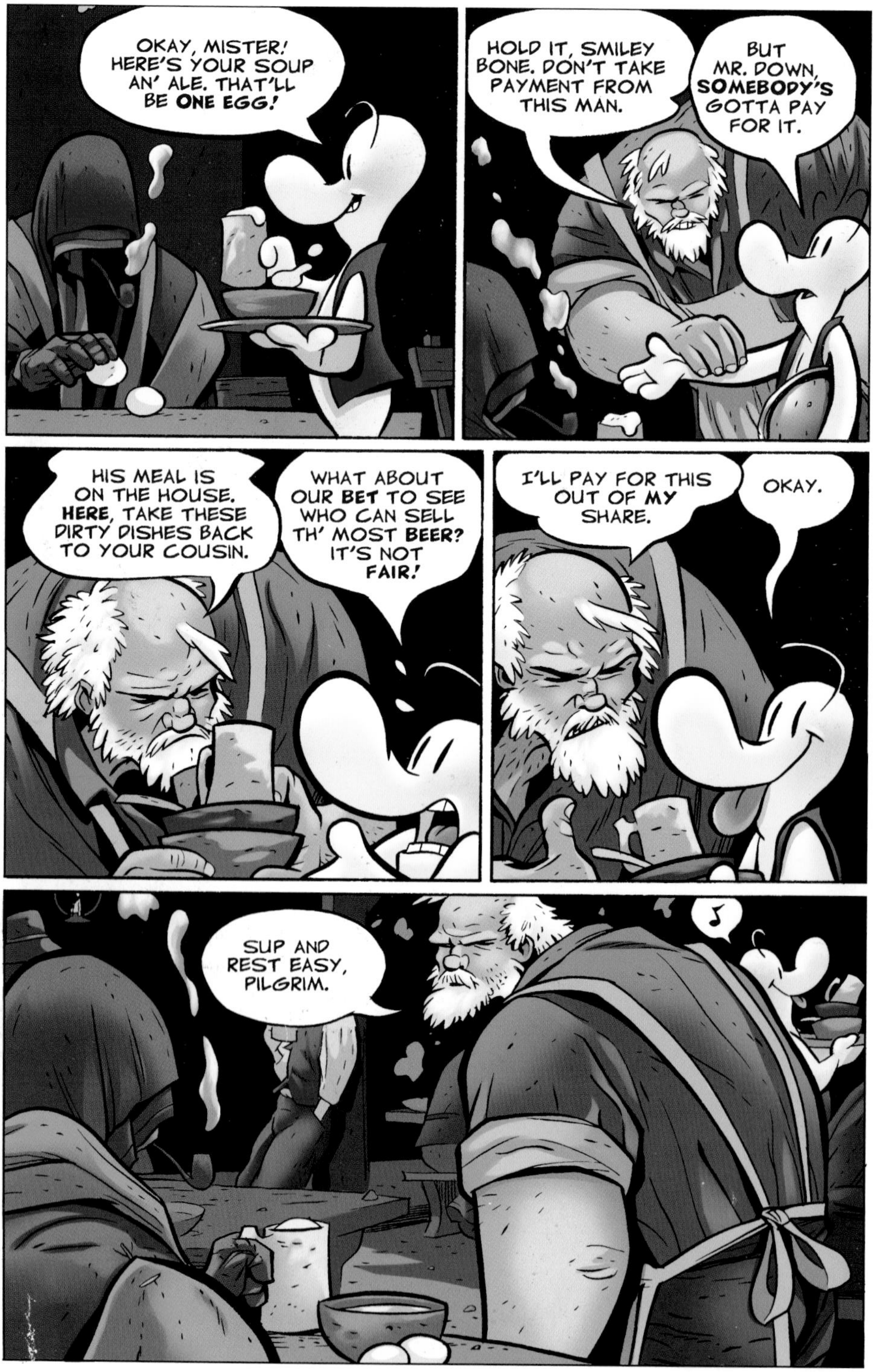
OKAY, MISTER! HERE'S YOUR SOUP AN' ALE. THAT'LL BE **ONE EGG**!
HOLD IT, SMILEY BONE. DON'T TAKE PAYMENT FROM THIS MAN.
BUT MR. DOWN, **SOMEBODY'S** GOTTA PAY FOR IT.
HIS MEAL IS ON THE HOUSE. **HERE**, TAKE THESE DIRTY DISHES BACK TO YOUR COUSIN.
WHAT ABOUT OUR **BET** TO SEE WHO CAN SELL TH' MOST **BEER**? IT'S NOT **FAIR**!
I'LL PAY FOR THIS OUT OF **MY** SHARE.
OKAY.
SUP AND REST EASY, PILGRIM.
♪

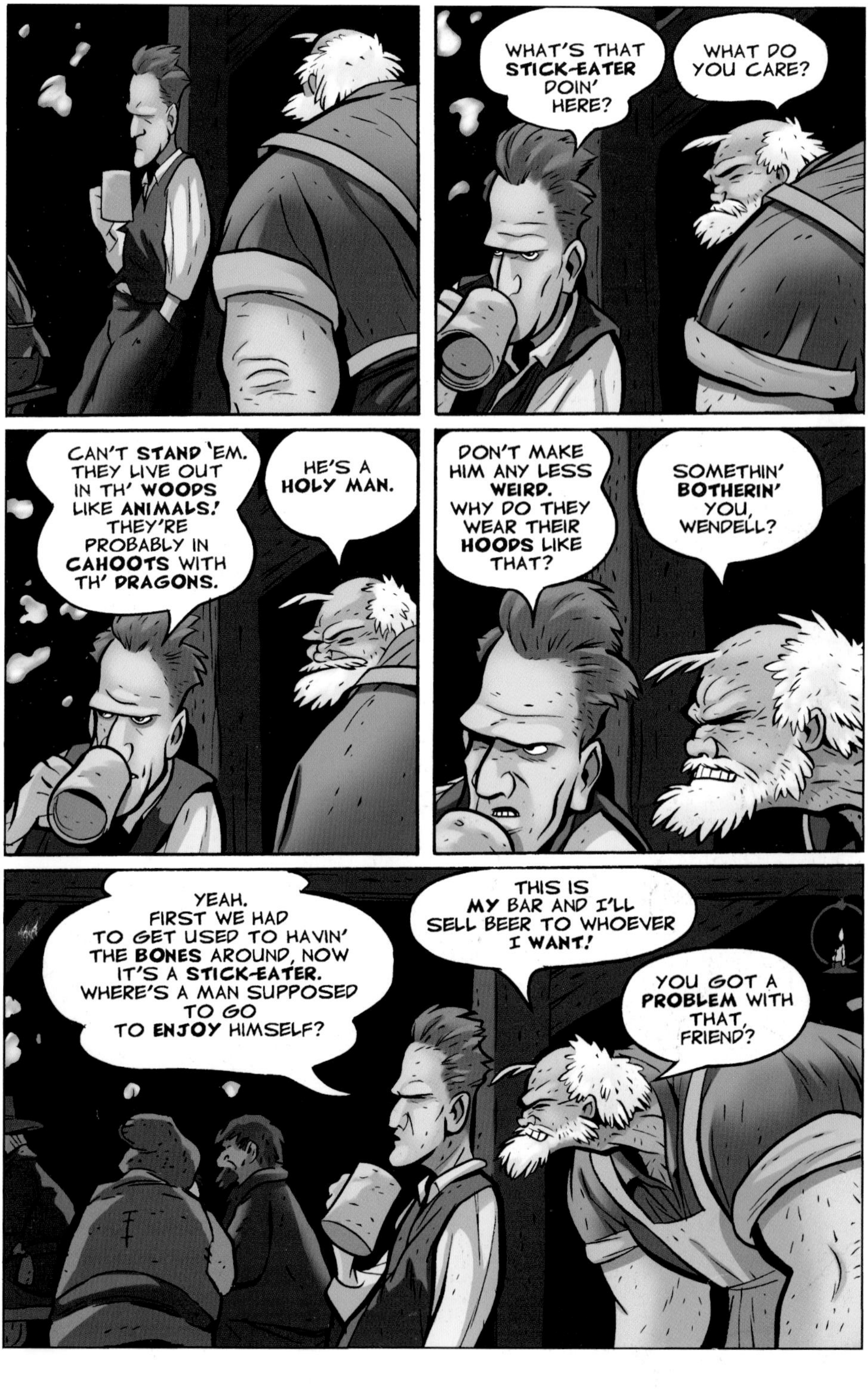
WHAT'S THAT STICK-EATER DOIN' HERE?
WHAT DO YOU CARE?
CAN'T STAND 'EM. THEY LIVE OUT IN TH' WOODS LIKE ANIMALS! THEY'RE PROBABLY IN CAHOOTS WITH TH' DRAGONS.
HE'S A HOLY MAN.
DON'T MAKE HIM ANY LESS WEIRD. WHY DO THEY WEAR THEIR HOODS LIKE THAT?
SOMETHIN' BOTHERIN' YOU, WENDELL?
YEAH. FIRST WE HAD TO GET USED TO HAVIN' THE BONES AROUND, NOW IT'S A STICK-EATER. WHERE'S A MAN SUPPOSED TO GO TO ENJOY HIMSELF?
THIS IS MY BAR AND I'LL SELL BEER TO WHOEVER I WANT!
YOU GOT A PROBLEM WITH THAT, FRIEND?

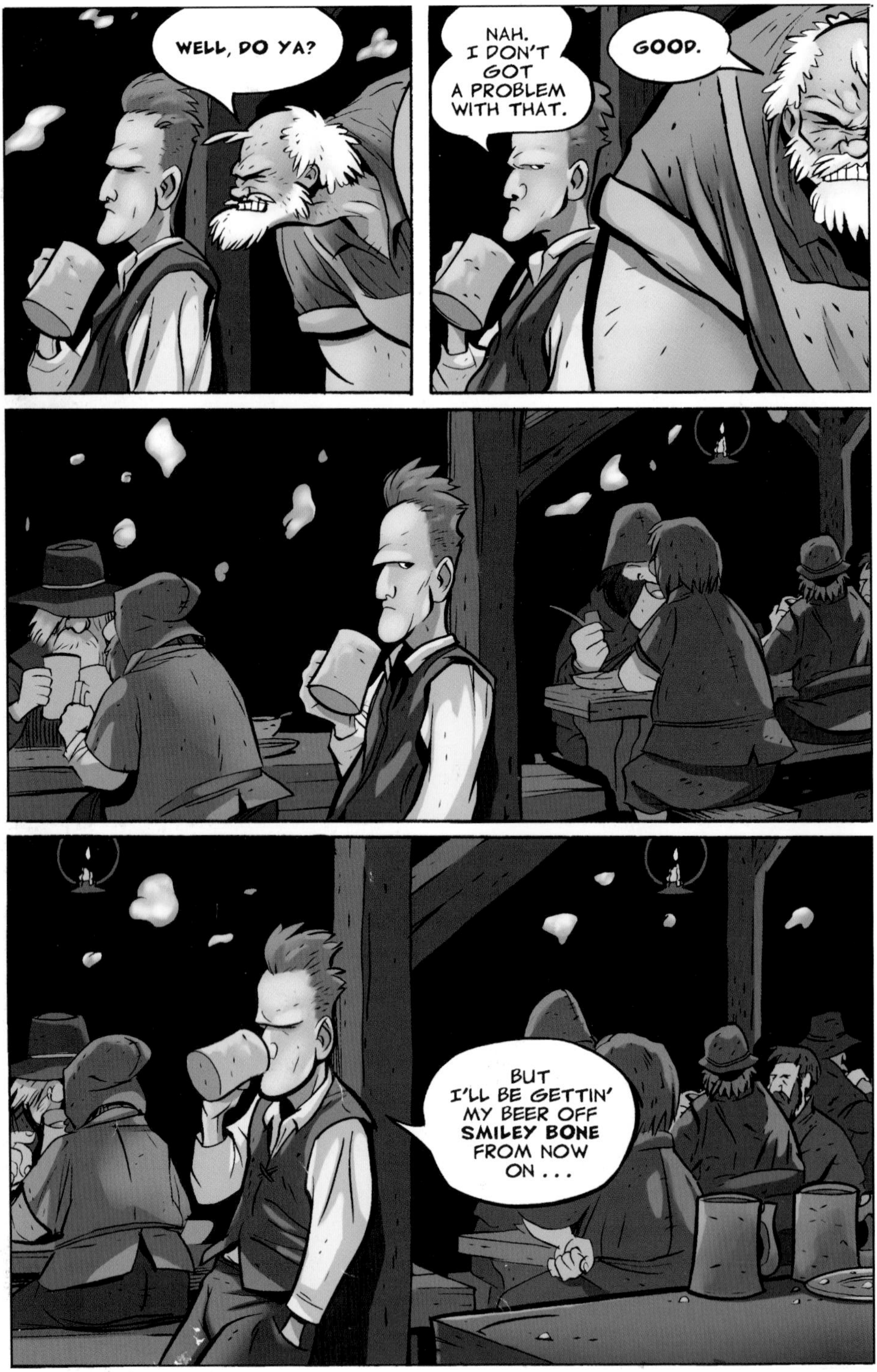
WELL, DO YA?
NAH. I DON'T GOT A PROBLEM WITH THAT.
GOOD.
BUT I'LL BE GETTIN' MY BEER OFF **SMILEY BONE** FROM NOW ON . . .

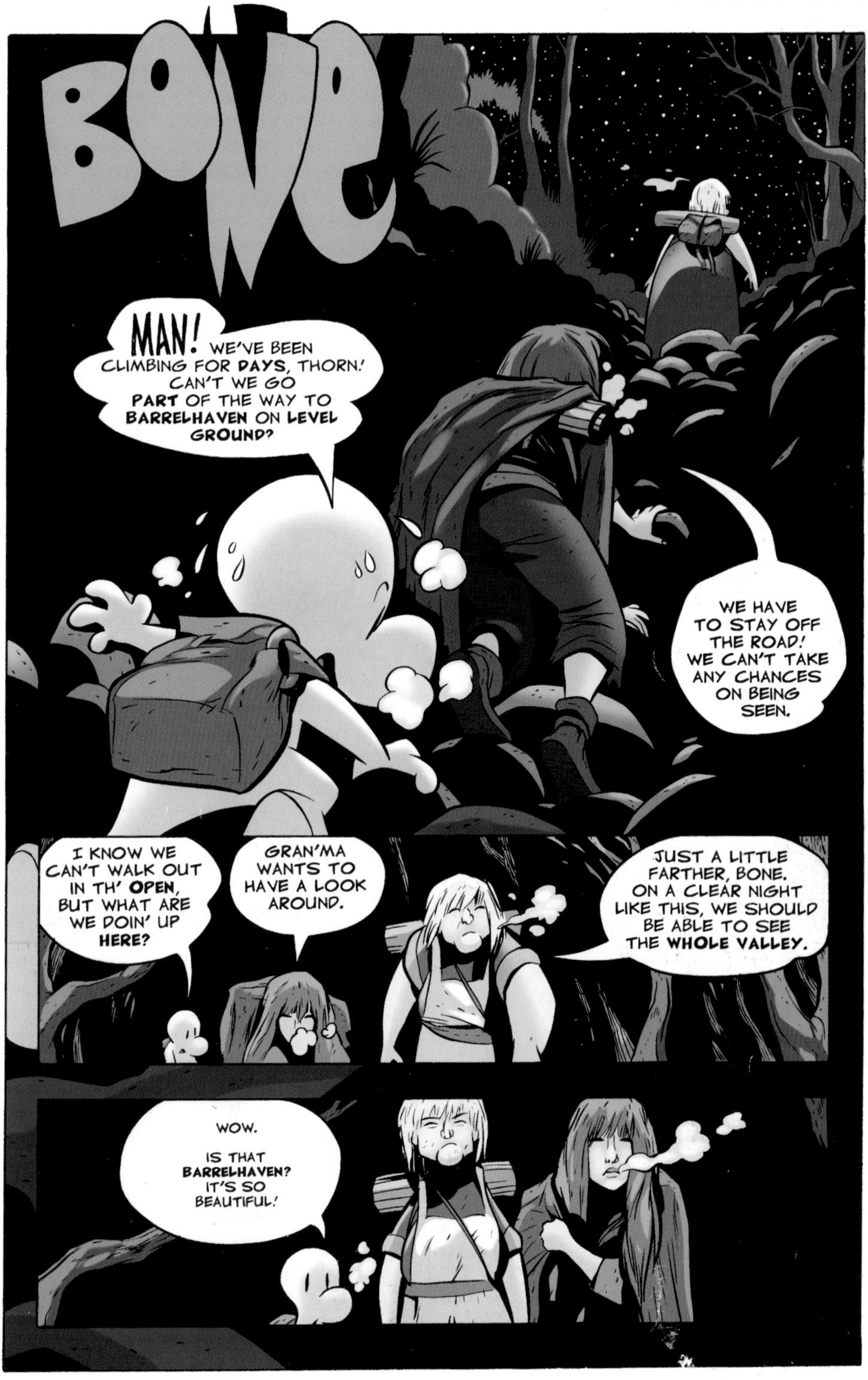
BONE
MAN! WE'VE BEEN CLIMBING FOR DAYS, THORN! CAN'T WE GO PART OF THE WAY TO BARRELHAVEN ON LEVEL GROUND?
WE HAVE TO STAY OFF THE ROAD! WE CAN'T TAKE ANY CHANCES ON BEING SEEN.
I KNOW WE CAN'T WALK OUT IN TH' OPEN, BUT WHAT ARE WE DOIN' UP HERE?
GRAN'MA WANTS TO HAVE A LOOK AROUND.
JUST A LITTLE FARTHER, BONE. ON A CLEAR NIGHT LIKE THIS, WE SHOULD BE ABLE TO SEE THE WHOLE VALLEY.
WOW.
IS THAT BARRELHAVEN? IT'S SO BEAUTIFUL!

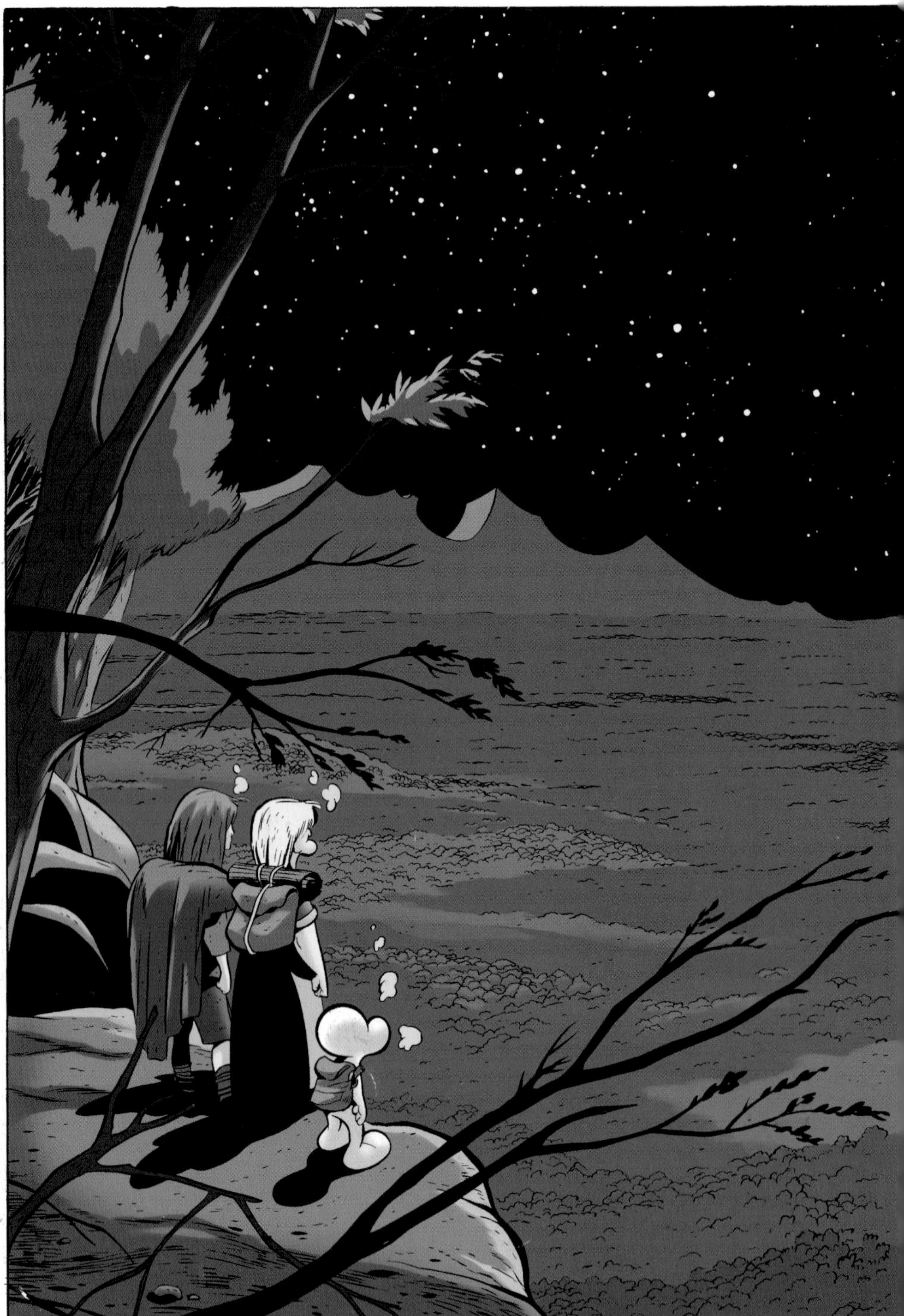

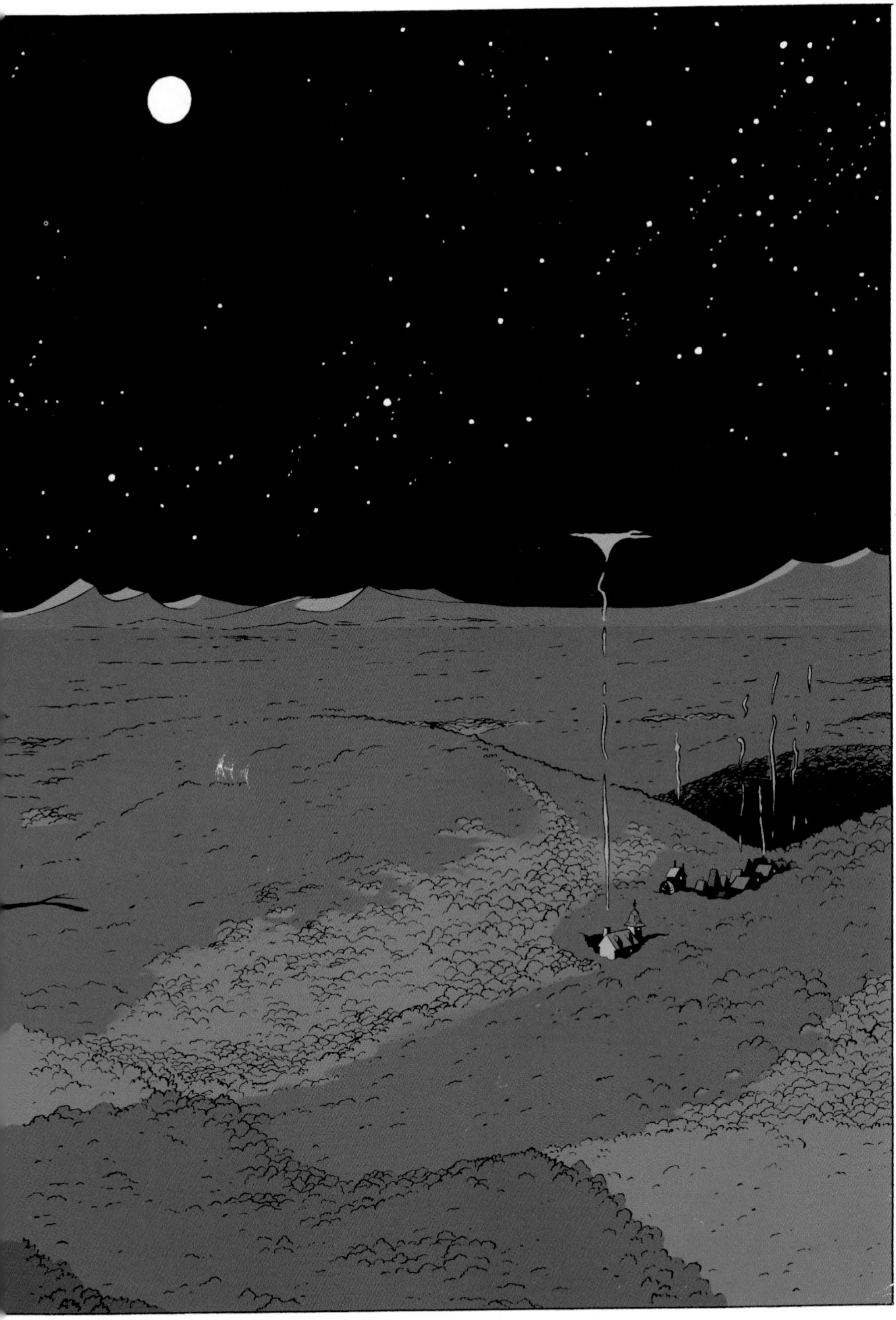

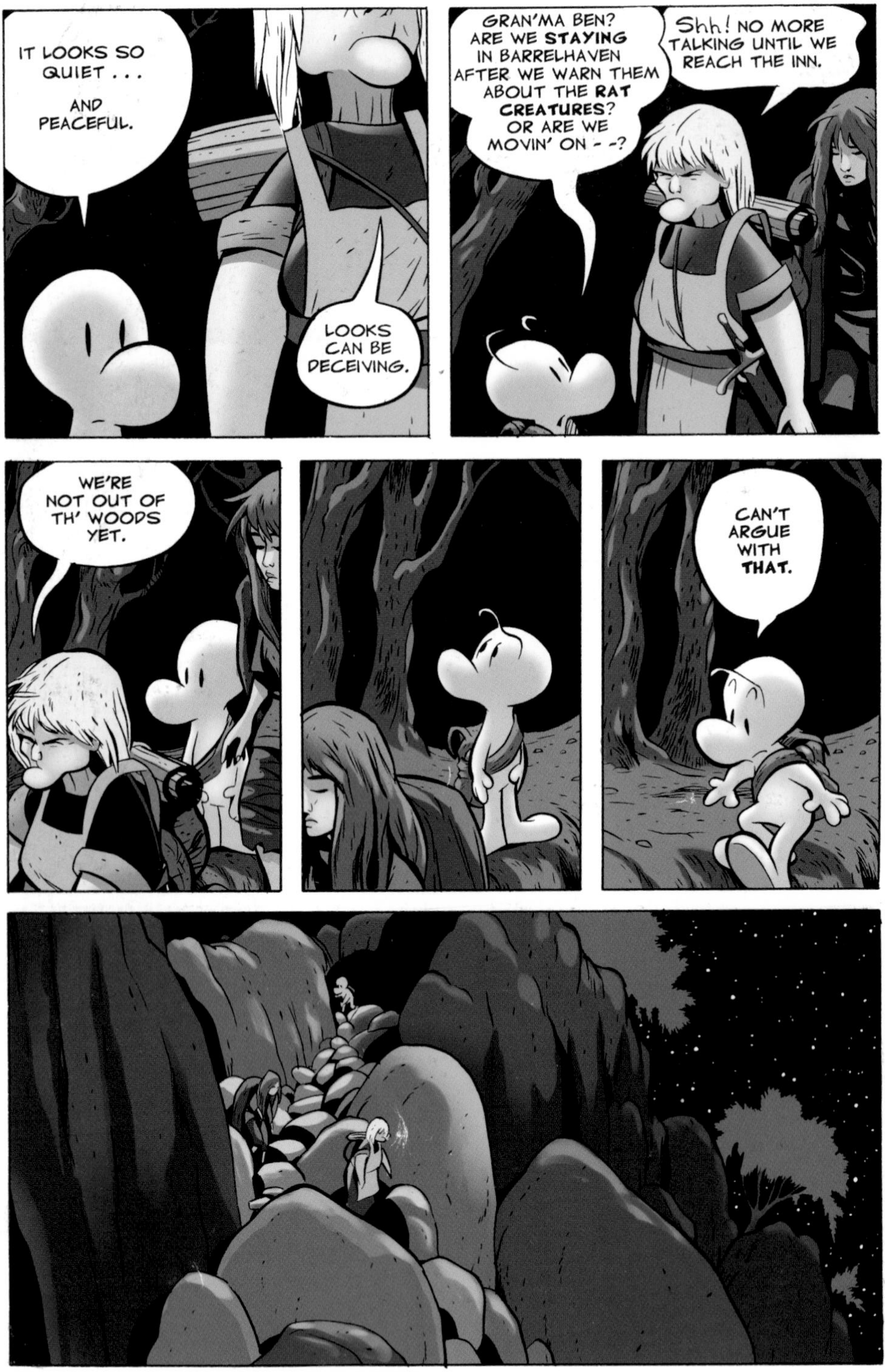
IT LOOKS SO QUIET . . . AND PEACEFUL.
LOOKS CAN BE DECEIVING.
GRAN'MA BEN? ARE WE STAYING IN BARRELHAVEN AFTER WE WARN THEM ABOUT THE RAT CREATURES? OR ARE WE MOVIN' ON - -?
Shh! NO MORE TALKING UNTIL WE REACH THE INN.
WE'RE NOT OUT OF TH' WOODS YET.
CAN'T ARGUE WITH THAT.

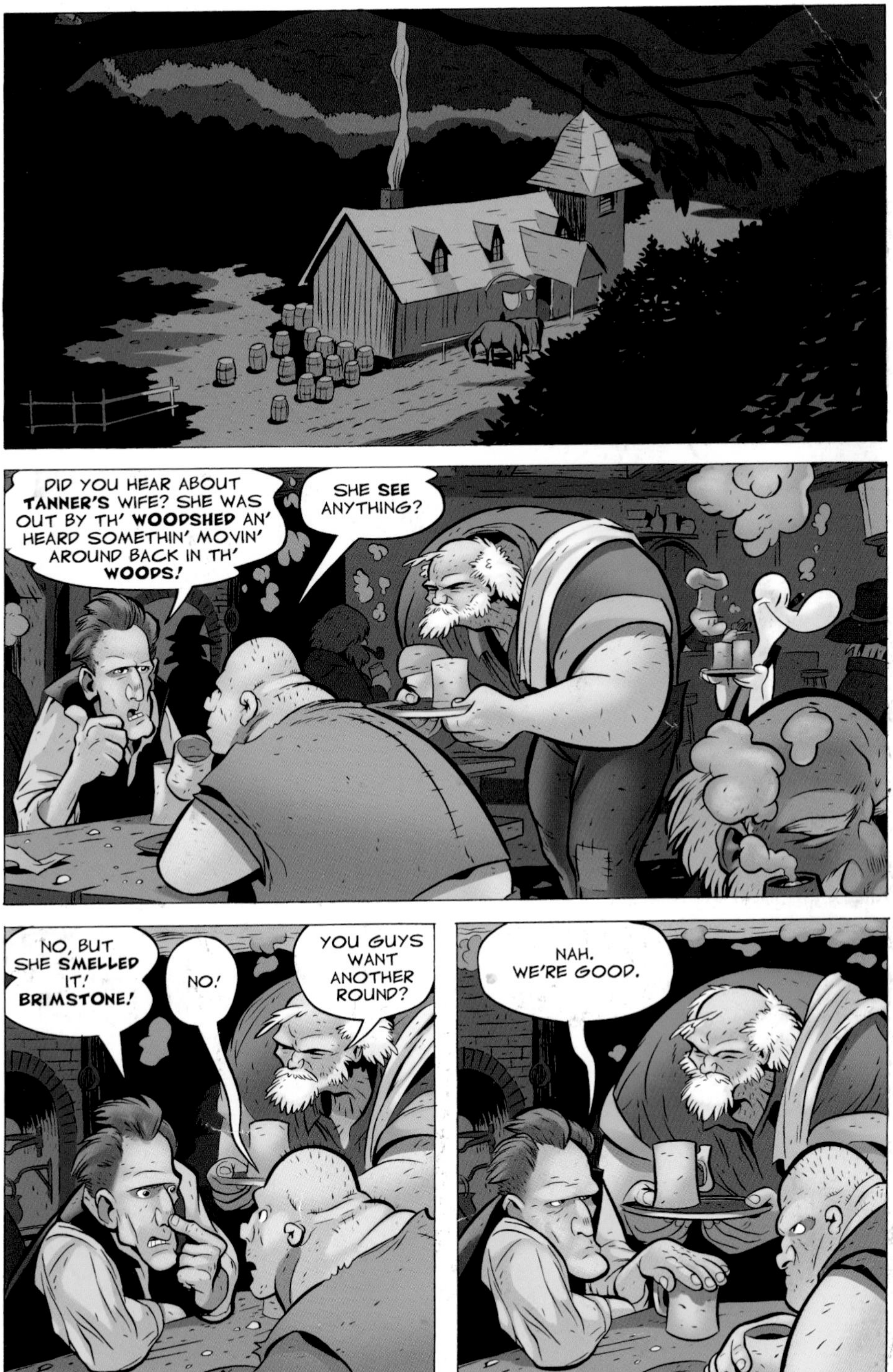
DID YOU HEAR ABOUT TANNER'S WIFE? SHE WAS OUT BY TH' WOODSHED AN' HEARD SOMETHIN' MOVIN' AROUND BACK IN TH' WOODS!
SHE SEE ANYTHING?
NO, BUT SHE SMELLED IT! BRIMSTONE!
NO!
YOU GUYS WANT ANOTHER ROUND?
NAH. WE'RE GOOD.

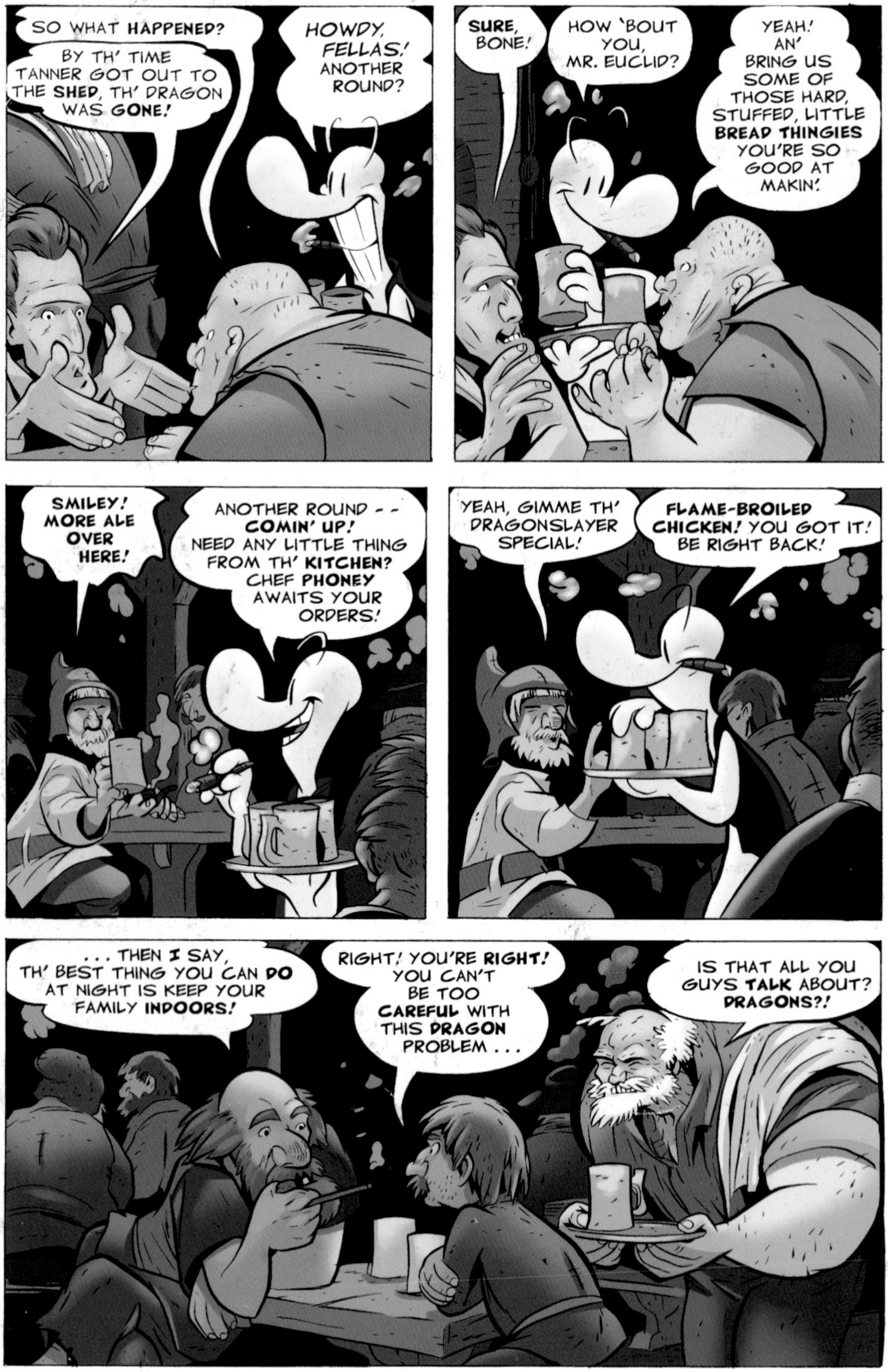
SO WHAT HAPPENED?
BY TH' TIME TANNER GOT OUT TO THE SHED, TH' DRAGON WAS GONE!
HOWDY, FELLAS! ANOTHER ROUND?
SURE, BONE!
HOW 'BOUT YOU, MR. EUCLID?
YEAH! AN' BRING US SOME OF THOSE HARD, STUFFED, LITTLE BREAD THINGIES YOU'RE SO GOOD AT MAKIN'!
SMILEY! MORE ALE OVER HERE!
ANOTHER ROUND -- COMIN' UP! NEED ANY LITTLE THING FROM TH' KITCHEN? CHEF PHONEY AWAITS YOUR ORDERS!
YEAH, GIMME TH' DRAGONSLAYER SPECIAL!
FLAME-BROILED CHICKEN! YOU GOT IT! BE RIGHT BACK!
... THEN I SAY, TH' BEST THING YOU CAN DO AT NIGHT IS KEEP YOUR FAMILY INDOORS!
RIGHT! YOU'RE RIGHT! YOU CAN'T BE TOO CAREFUL WITH THIS DRAGON PROBLEM ...
IS THAT ALL YOU GUYS TALK ABOUT? DRAGONS?!

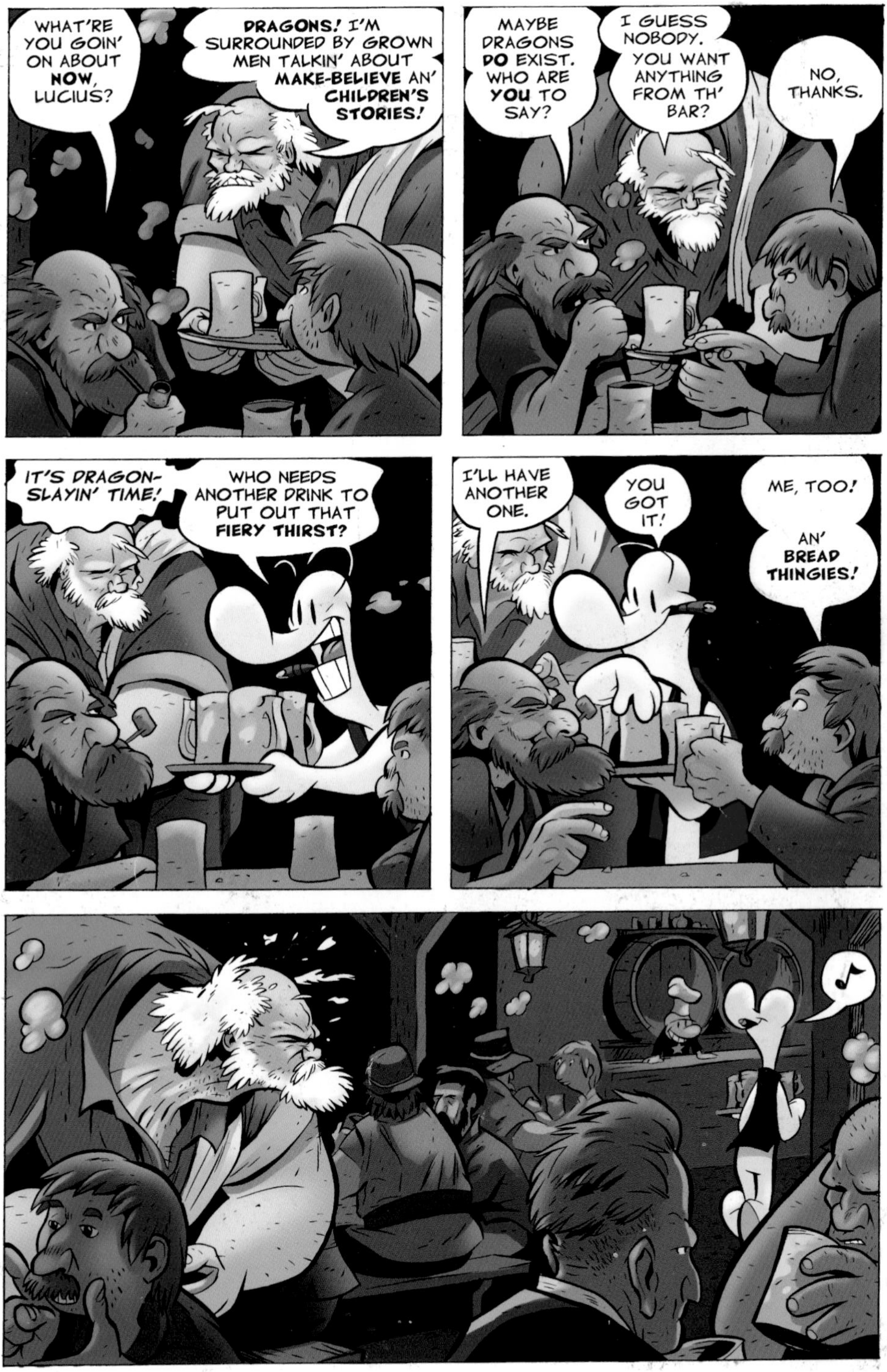
WHAT'RE YOU GOIN' ON ABOUT NOW, LUCIUS?
DRAGONS! I'M SURROUNDED BY GROWN MEN TALKIN' ABOUT MAKE-BELIEVE AN' CHILDREN'S STORIES!
MAYBE DRAGONS DO EXIST. WHO ARE YOU TO SAY?
I GUESS NOBODY. YOU WANT ANYTHING FROM TH' BAR?
NO, THANKS.
IT'S DRAGON-SLAYIN' TIME!
WHO NEEDS ANOTHER DRINK TO PUT OUT THAT FIERY THIRST?
I'LL HAVE ANOTHER ONE.
YOU GOT IT!
ME, TOO!
AN' BREAD THINGIES!

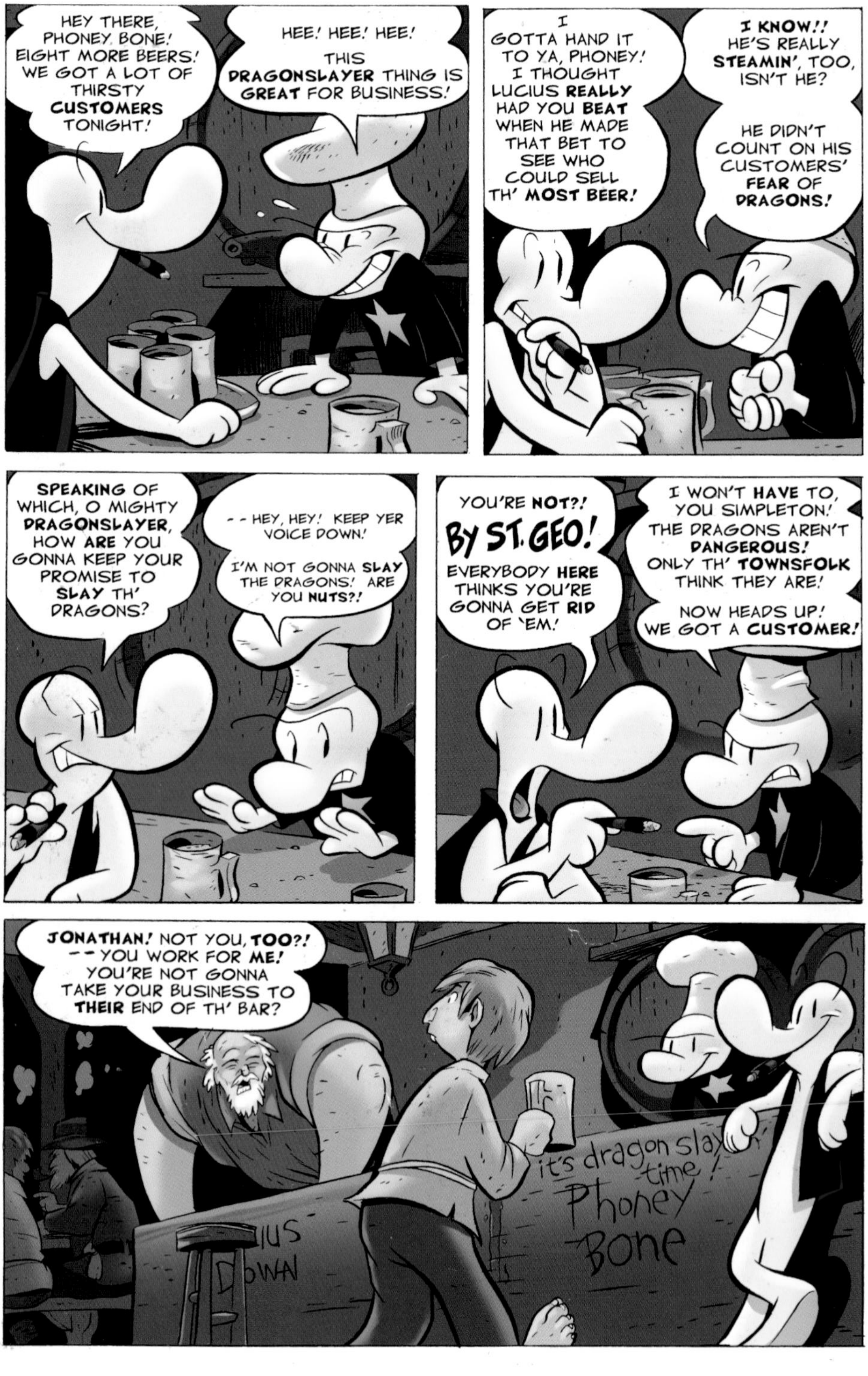
HEY THERE, PHONEY BONE! EIGHT MORE BEERS! WE GOT A LOT OF THIRSTY CUSTOMERS TONIGHT!
HEE! HEE! HEE! THIS DRAGONSLAYER THING IS GREAT FOR BUSINESS!
I GOTTA HAND IT TO YA, PHONEY! I THOUGHT LUCIUS REALLY HAD YOU BEAT WHEN HE MADE THAT BET TO SEE WHO COULD SELL TH' MOST BEER!
I KNOW!! HE'S REALLY STEAMIN', TOO, ISN'T HE?
HE DIDN'T COUNT ON HIS CUSTOMERS' FEAR OF DRAGONS!
SPEAKING OF WHICH, O MIGHTY DRAGONSLAYER, HOW ARE YOU GONNA KEEP YOUR PROMISE TO SLAY TH' DRAGONS?
-- HEY, HEY! KEEP YER VOICE DOWN!
I'M NOT GONNA SLAY THE DRAGONS! ARE YOU NUTS?!
YOU'RE NOT?!
BY ST. GEO!
EVERYBODY HERE THINKS YOU'RE GONNA GET RID OF 'EM!
I WON'T HAVE TO, YOU SIMPLETON! THE DRAGONS AREN'T DANGEROUS! ONLY TH' TOWNSFOLK THINK THEY ARE!
NOW HEADS UP! WE GOT A CUSTOMER!
JONATHAN! NOT YOU, TOO?! -- YOU WORK FOR ME! YOU'RE NOT GONNA TAKE YOUR BUSINESS TO THEIR END OF TH' BAR?
it's dragon slay time!
Phoney Bone

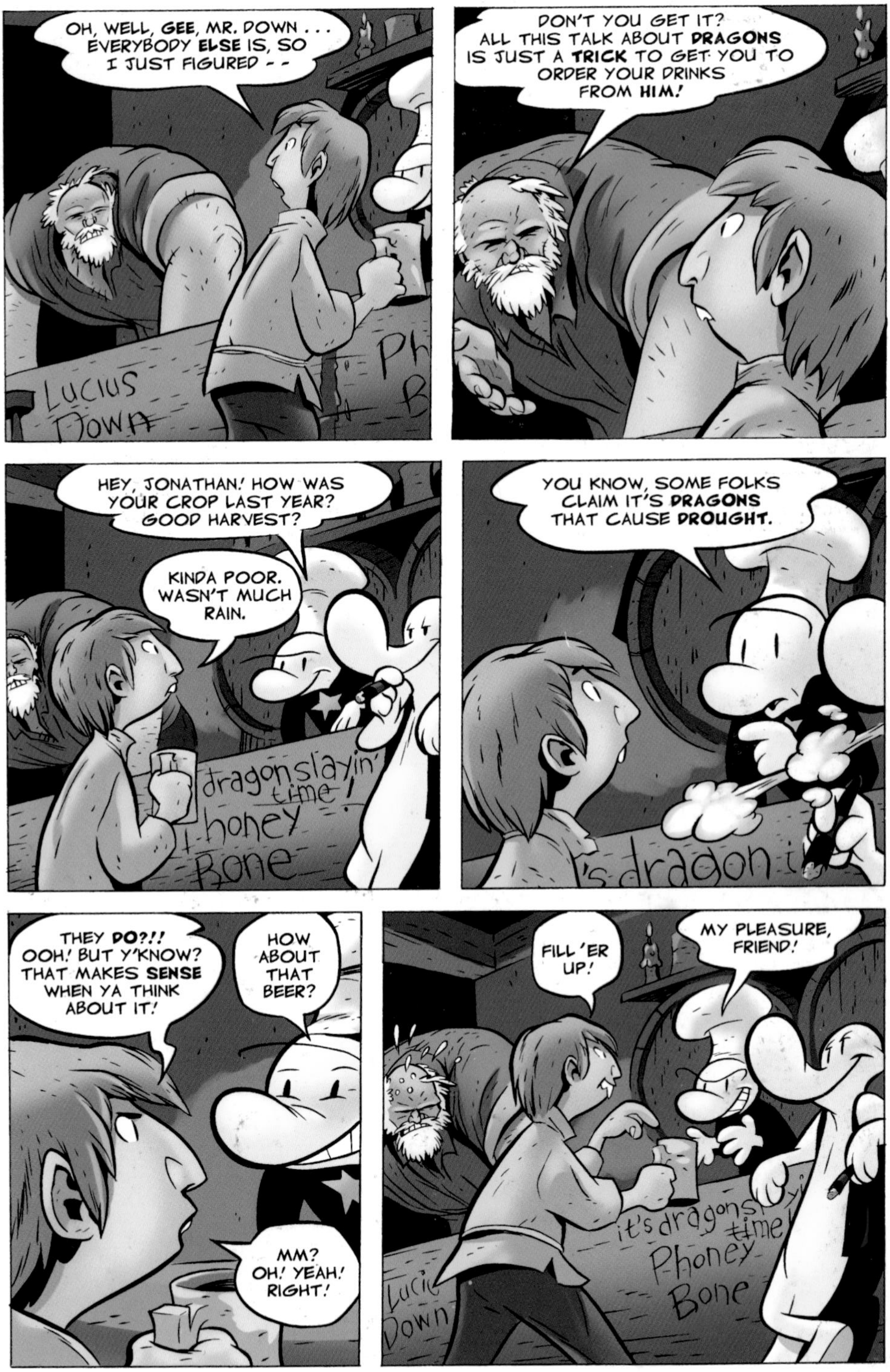
OH, WELL, GEE, MR. DOWN . . . EVERYBODY ELSE IS, SO I JUST FIGURED - -
Lucius Down
DON'T YOU GET IT? ALL THIS TALK ABOUT DRAGONS IS JUST A TRICK TO GET YOU TO ORDER YOUR DRINKS FROM HIM!
HEY, JONATHAN! HOW WAS YOUR CROP LAST YEAR? GOOD HARVEST?
KINDA POOR. WASN'T MUCH RAIN.
dragonslayin' time! honey Bone
YOU KNOW, SOME FOLKS CLAIM IT'S DRAGONS THAT CAUSE DROUGHT.
THEY DO?!! OOH! BUT Y'KNOW? THAT MAKES SENSE WHEN YA THINK ABOUT IT!
HOW ABOUT THAT BEER?
MM? OH! YEAH! RIGHT!
FILL 'ER UP!
MY PLEASURE, FRIEND!
it's dragonslayin' time! Phoney Bone
Lucius Down

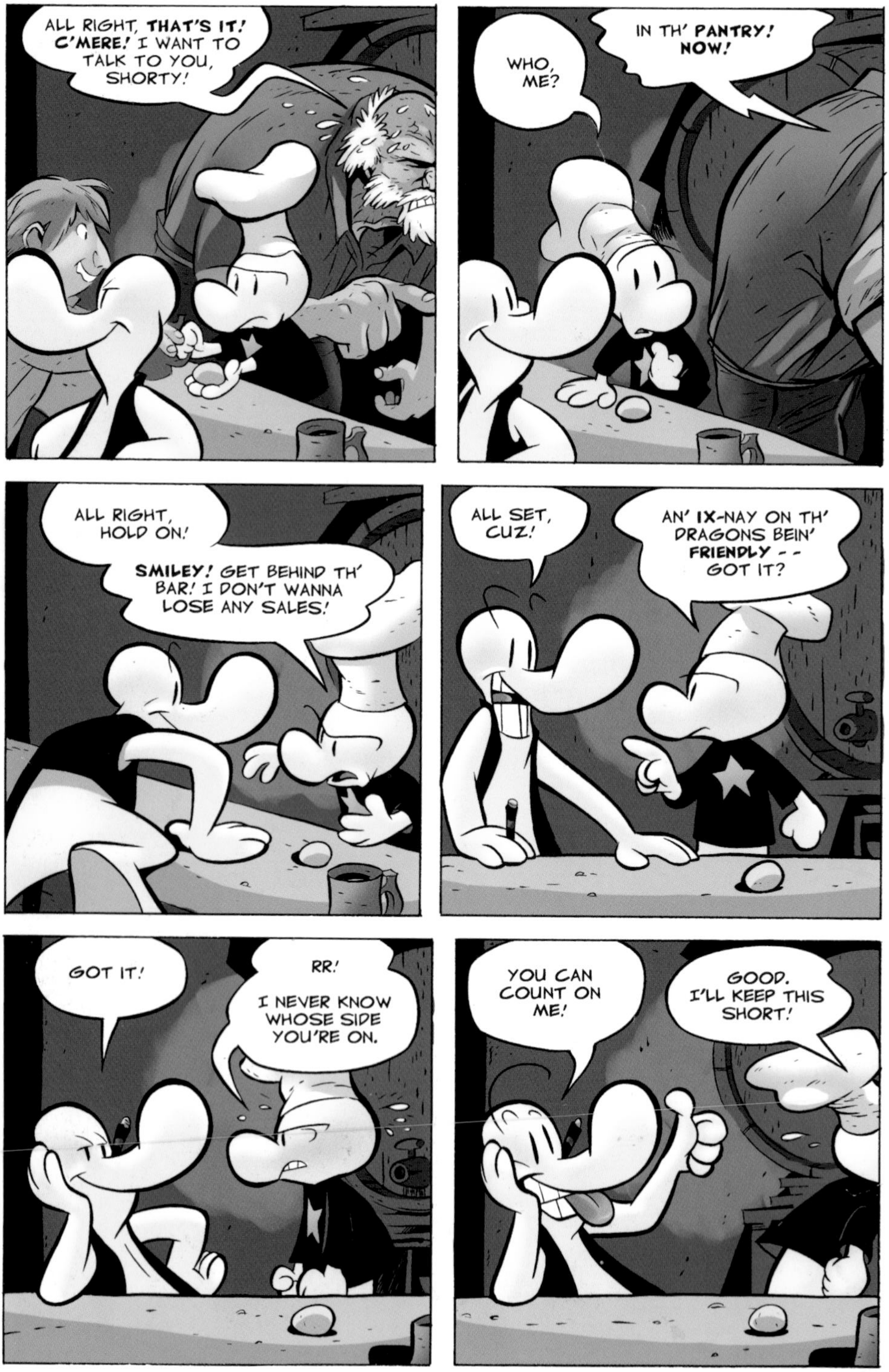
ALL RIGHT, THAT'S IT! C'MERE! I WANT TO TALK TO YOU, SHORTY!
WHO, ME?
IN TH' PANTRY! NOW!
ALL RIGHT, HOLD ON!
SMILEY! GET BEHIND TH' BAR! I DON'T WANNA LOSE ANY SALES!
ALL SET, CUZ!
AN' IX-NAY ON TH' DRAGONS BEIN' FRIENDLY - - GOT IT?
GOT IT!
RR!
I NEVER KNOW WHOSE SIDE YOU'RE ON.
YOU CAN COUNT ON ME!
GOOD. I'LL KEEP THIS SHORT!

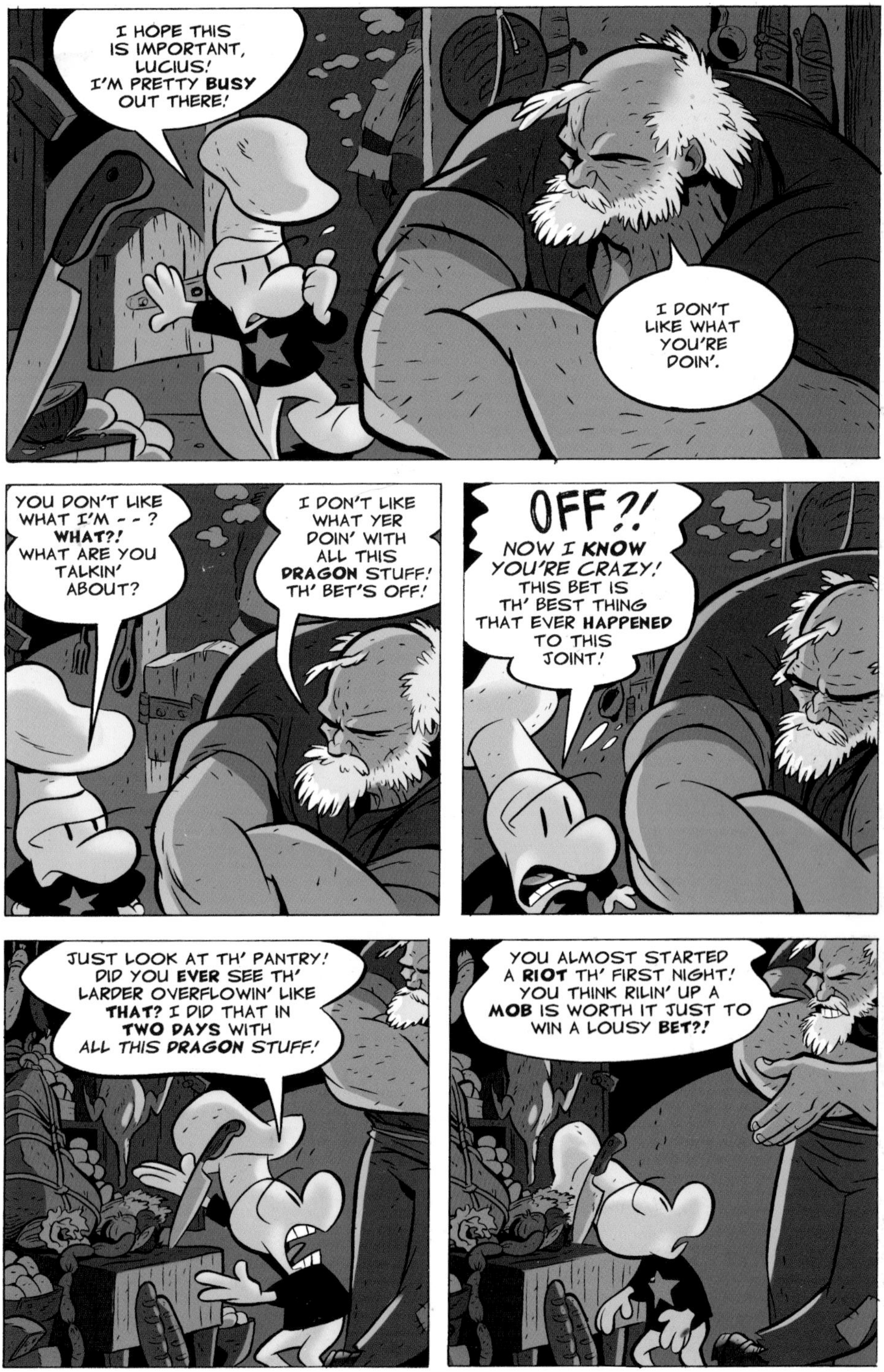
I HOPE THIS IS IMPORTANT, LUCIUS! I'M PRETTY BUSY OUT THERE!
I DON'T LIKE WHAT YOU'RE DOIN'.
YOU DON'T LIKE WHAT I'M - - ? WHAT?! WHAT ARE YOU TALKIN' ABOUT?
I DON'T LIKE WHAT YER DOIN' WITH ALL THIS DRAGON STUFF! TH' BET'S OFF!
OFF?!
NOW I KNOW YOU'RE CRAZY! THIS BET IS TH' BEST THING THAT EVER HAPPENED TO THIS JOINT!
JUST LOOK AT TH' PANTRY! DID YOU EVER SEE TH' LARDER OVERFLOWIN' LIKE THAT? I DID THAT IN TWO DAYS WITH ALL THIS DRAGON STUFF!
YOU ALMOST STARTED A RIOT TH' FIRST NIGHT! YOU THINK RILIN' UP A MOB IS WORTH IT JUST TO WIN A LOUSY BET?!

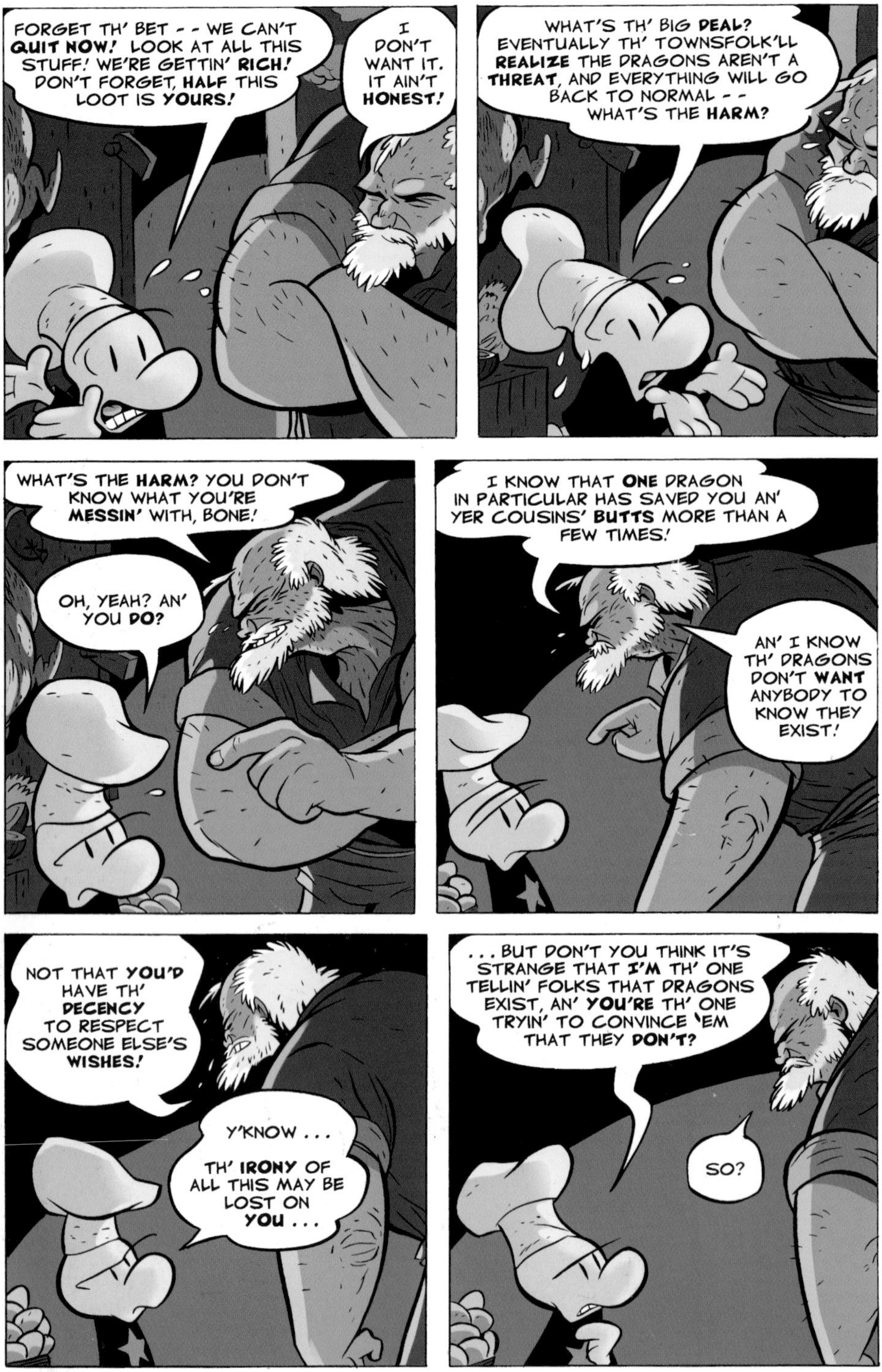
FORGET TH' BET - - WE CAN'T QUIT NOW! LOOK AT ALL THIS STUFF! WE'RE GETTIN' RICH! DON'T FORGET, HALF THIS LOOT IS YOURS!
I DON'T WANT IT. IT AIN'T HONEST!
WHAT'S TH' BIG DEAL? EVENTUALLY TH' TOWNSFOLK'LL REALIZE THE DRAGONS AREN'T A THREAT, AND EVERYTHING WILL GO BACK TO NORMAL - - WHAT'S THE HARM?
WHAT'S THE HARM? YOU DON'T KNOW WHAT YOU'RE MESSIN' WITH, BONE!
OH, YEAH? AN' YOU DO?
I KNOW THAT ONE DRAGON IN PARTICULAR HAS SAVED YOU AN' YER COUSINS' BUTTS MORE THAN A FEW TIMES!
AN' I KNOW TH' DRAGONS DON'T WANT ANYBODY TO KNOW THEY EXIST!
NOT THAT YOU'D HAVE TH' DECENCY TO RESPECT SOMEONE ELSE'S WISHES!
Y'KNOW . . .
TH' IRONY OF ALL THIS MAY BE LOST ON YOU . . .
. . . BUT DON'T YOU THINK IT'S STRANGE THAT I'M TH' ONE TELLIN' FOLKS THAT DRAGONS EXIST, AN' YOU'RE TH' ONE TRYIN' TO CONVINCE 'EM THAT THEY DON'T?
SO?

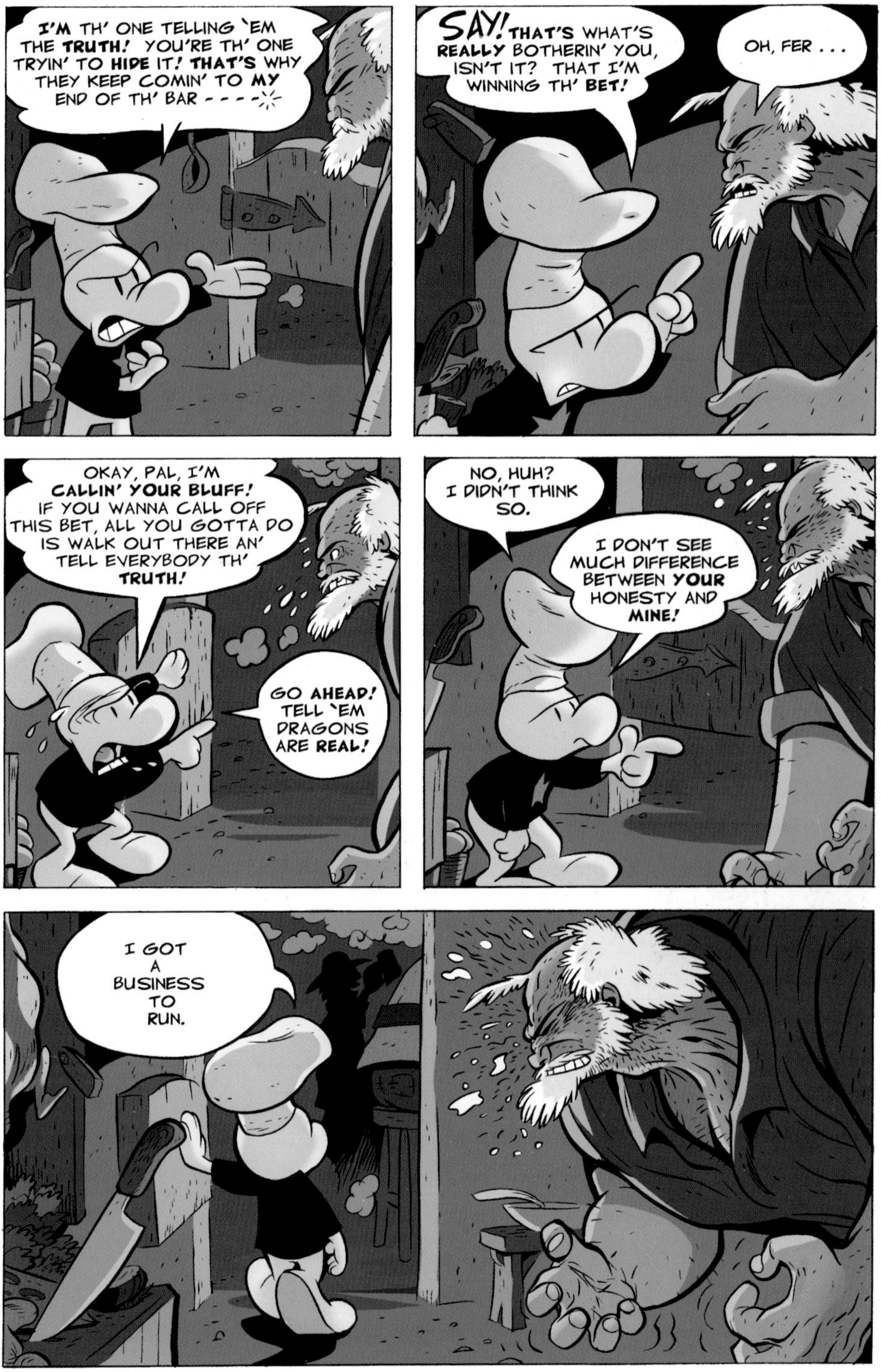
I'M TH' ONE TELLING 'EM THE TRUTH! YOU'RE TH' ONE TRYIN' TO HIDE IT! THAT'S WHY THEY KEEP COMIN' TO MY END OF TH' BAR - - - -
SAY! THAT'S WHAT'S REALLY BOTHERIN' YOU, ISN'T IT? THAT I'M WINNING TH' BET!
OH, FER . . .
OKAY, PAL, I'M CALLIN' YOUR BLUFF! IF YOU WANNA CALL OFF THIS BET, ALL YOU GOTTA DO IS WALK OUT THERE AN' TELL EVERYBODY TH' TRUTH!
GO AHEAD! TELL 'EM DRAGONS ARE REAL!
NO, HUH? I DIDN'T THINK SO.
I DON'T SEE MUCH DIFFERENCE BETWEEN YOUR HONESTY AND MINE!
I GOT A BUSINESS TO RUN.

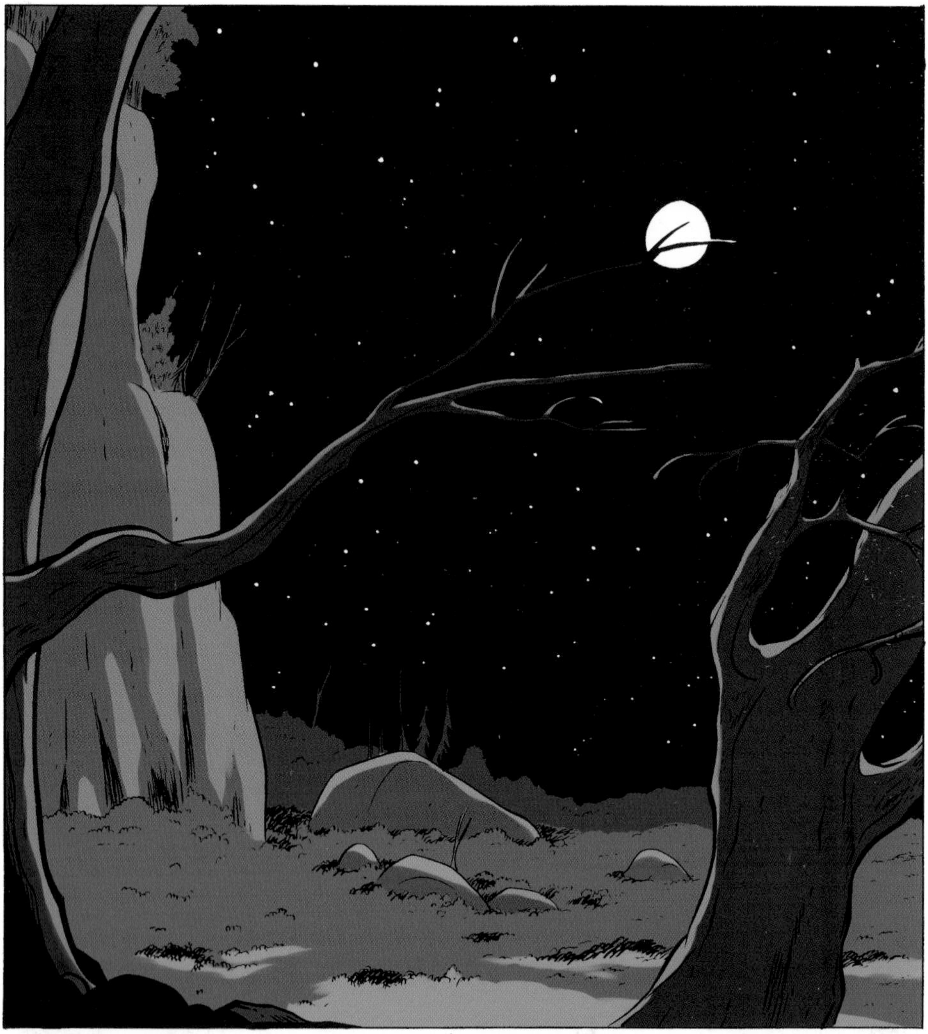

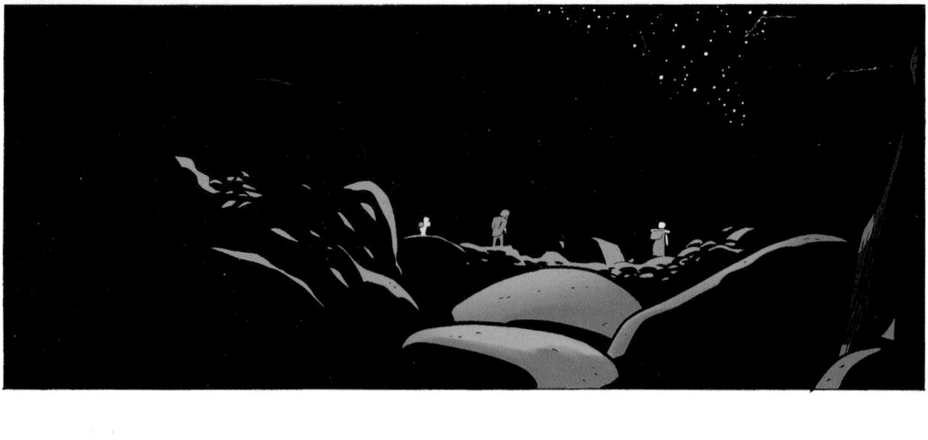

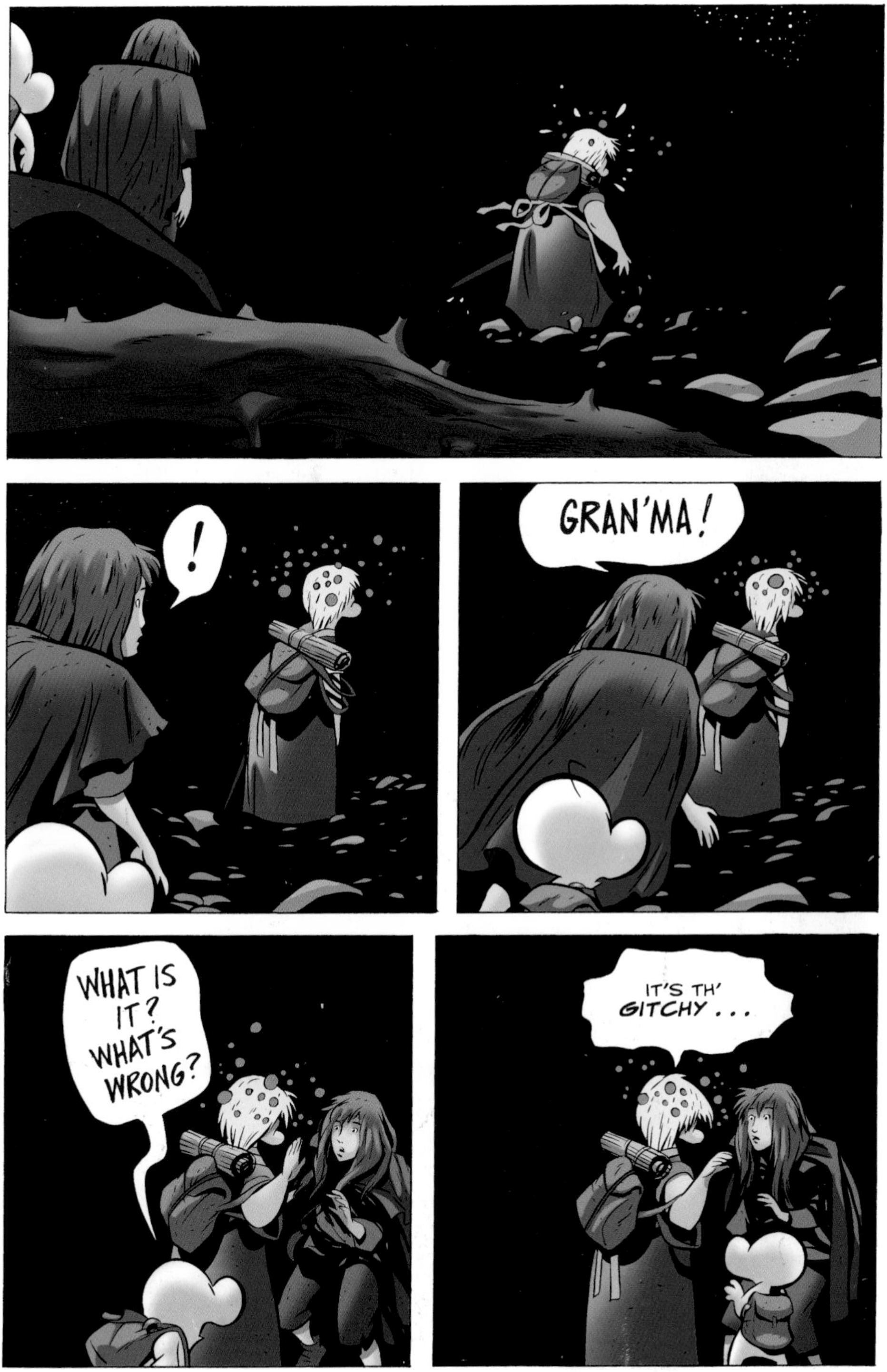
!
GRAN'MA!
WHAT IS IT? WHAT'S WRONG?
IT'S TH' GITCHY...

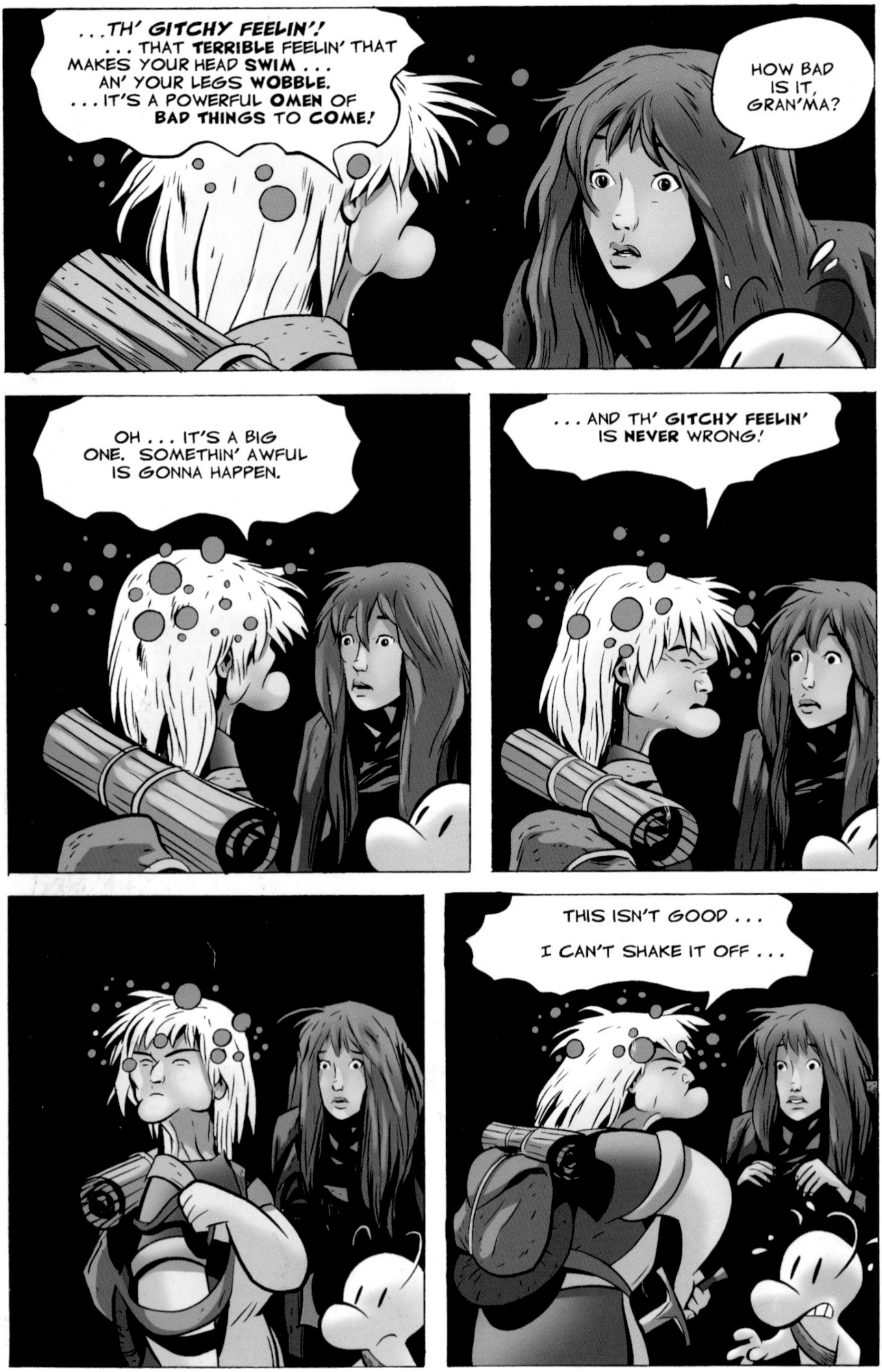
...TH' GITCHY FEELIN'!
...THAT TERRIBLE FEELIN' THAT MAKES YOUR HEAD SWIM... AN' YOUR LEGS WOBBLE. ...IT'S A POWERFUL OMEN OF BAD THINGS TO COME!
HOW BAD IS IT, GRAN'MA?
OH... IT'S A BIG ONE. SOMETHIN' AWFUL IS GONNA HAPPEN.
...AND TH' GITCHY FEELIN' IS NEVER WRONG!
THIS ISN'T GOOD...
I CAN'T SHAKE IT OFF...

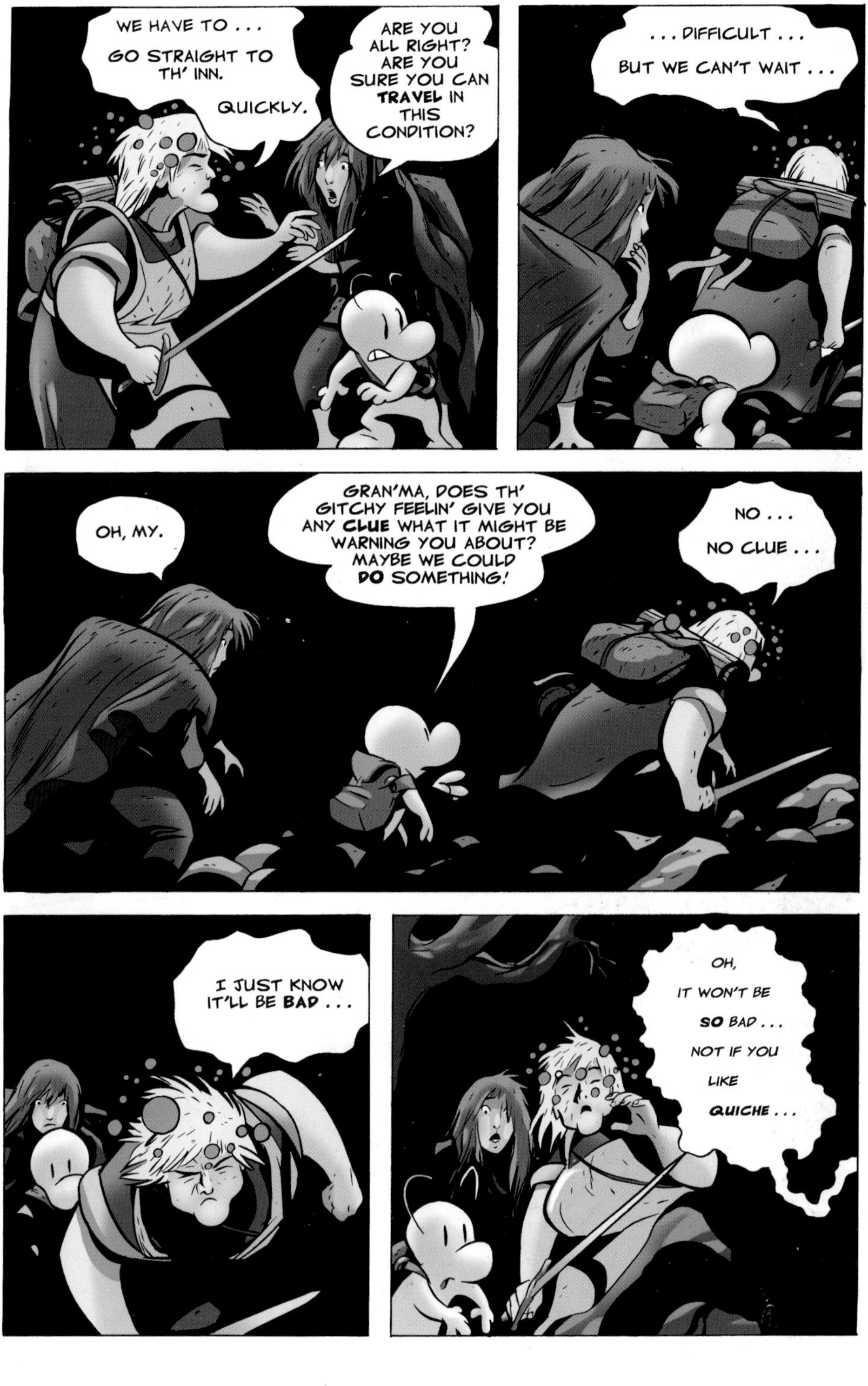
WE HAVE TO . . .
GO STRAIGHT TO TH' INN.
QUICKLY.
ARE YOU ALL RIGHT? ARE YOU SURE YOU CAN TRAVEL IN THIS CONDITION?
. . . DIFFICULT . . .
BUT WE CAN'T WAIT . . .
OH, MY.
GRAN'MA, DOES TH' GITCHY FEELIN' GIVE YOU ANY CLUE WHAT IT MIGHT BE WARNING YOU ABOUT? MAYBE WE COULD DO SOMETHING!
NO . . .
NO CLUE . . .
I JUST KNOW IT'LL BE BAD . . .
OH,
IT WON'T BE
SO BAD . . .
NOT IF YOU
LIKE
QUICHE . . .

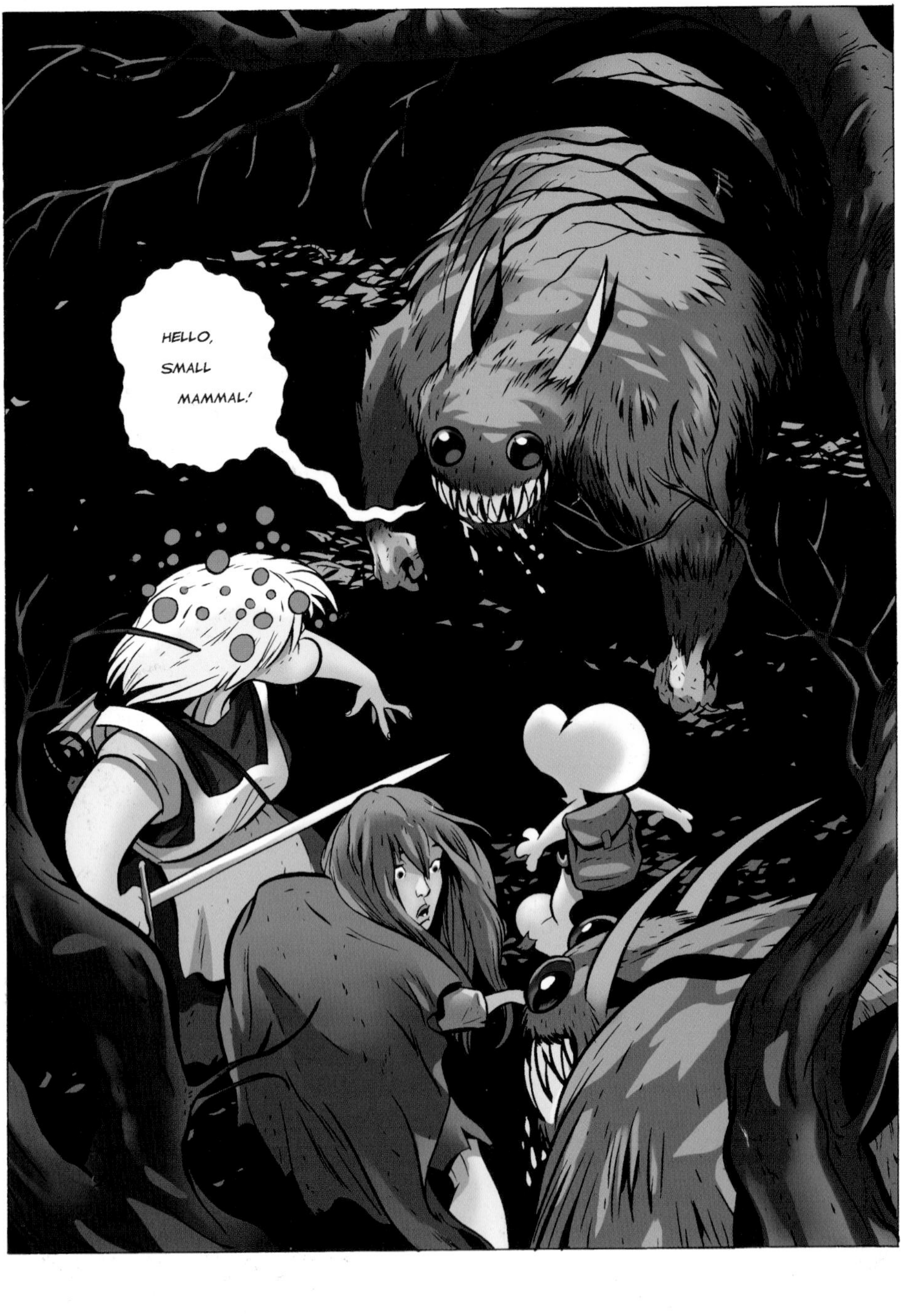
HELLO, SMALL MAMMAL!

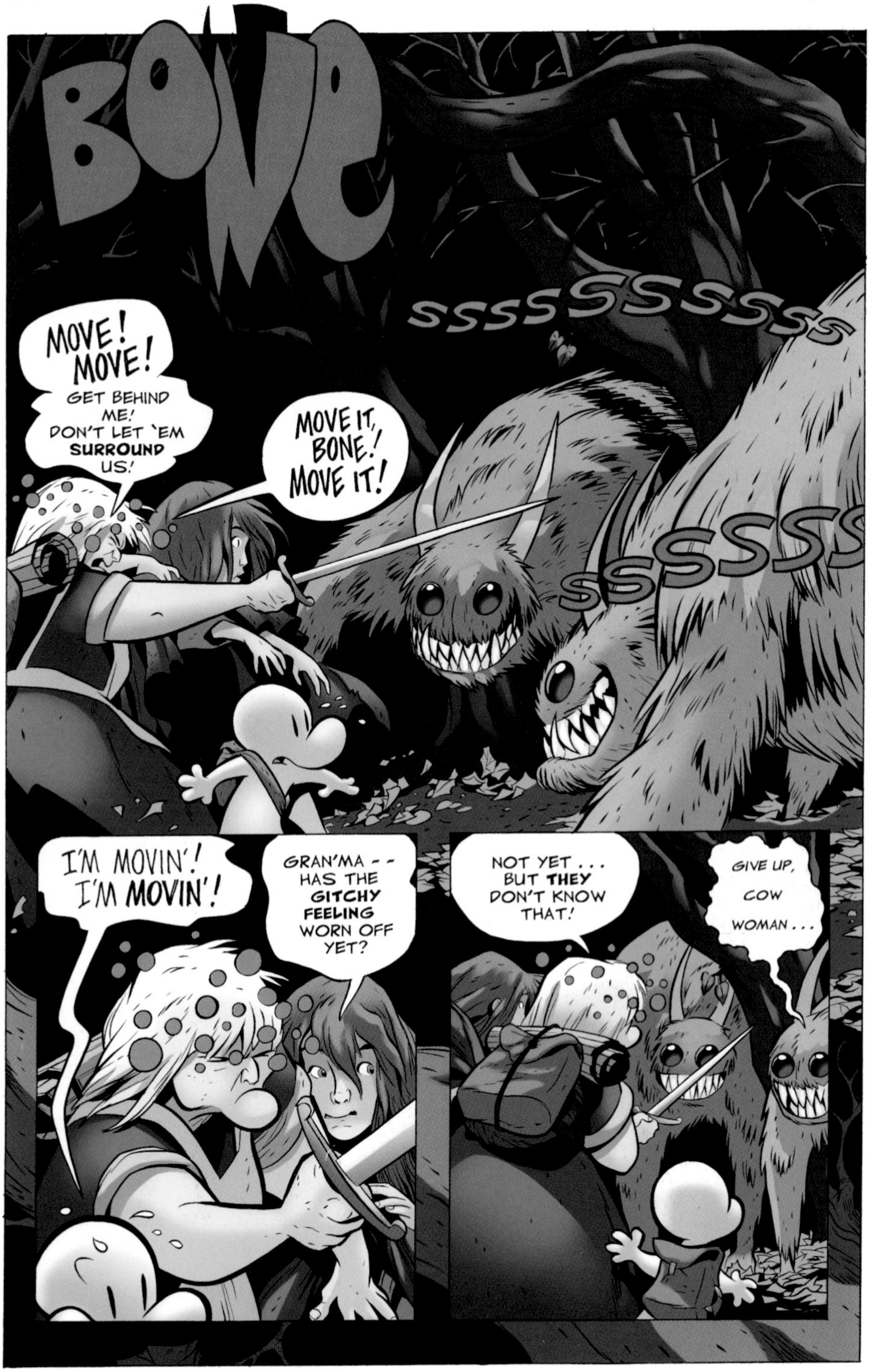
BONE
SSSSSSSSSSSSS
MOVE! MOVE! GET BEHIND ME! DON'T LET 'EM SURROUND US!
MOVE IT, BONE! MOVE IT!
SSSSSSS
I'M MOVIN'! I'M MOVIN'!
GRAN'MA -- HAS THE GITCHY FEELING WORN OFF YET?
NOT YET ... BUT THEY DON'T KNOW THAT!
GIVE UP, COW WOMAN ...

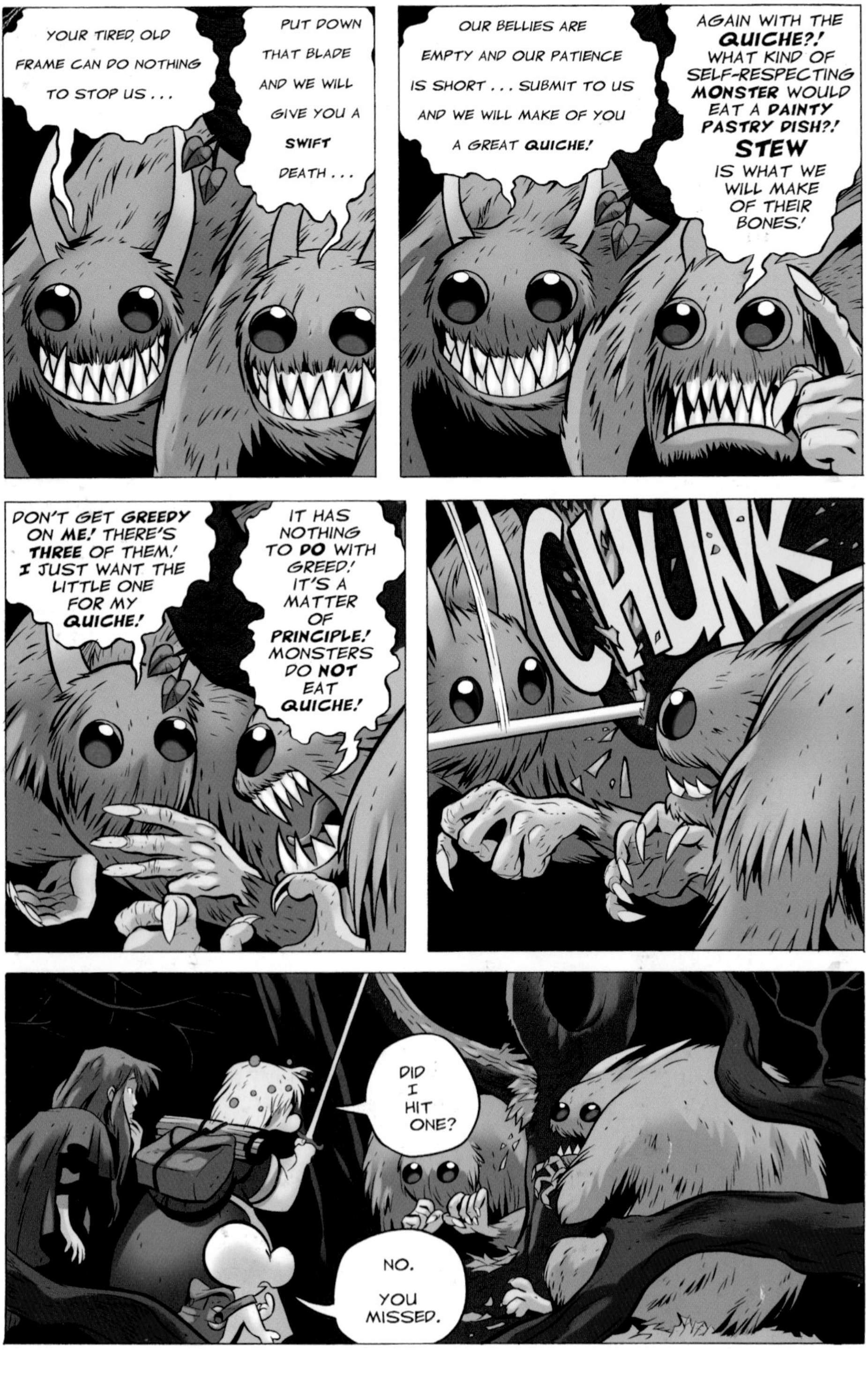
YOUR TIRED, OLD FRAME CAN DO NOTHING TO STOP US . . .
PUT DOWN THAT BLADE AND WE WILL GIVE YOU A SWIFT DEATH . . .
OUR BELLIES ARE EMPTY AND OUR PATIENCE IS SHORT . . . SUBMIT TO US AND WE WILL MAKE OF YOU A GREAT QUICHE!
AGAIN WITH THE QUICHE?! WHAT KIND OF SELF-RESPECTING MONSTER WOULD EAT A DAINTY PASTRY DISH?! STEW IS WHAT WE WILL MAKE OF THEIR BONES!
DON'T GET GREEDY ON ME! THERE'S THREE OF THEM! I JUST WANT THE LITTLE ONE FOR MY QUICHE!
IT HAS NOTHING TO DO WITH GREED! IT'S A MATTER OF PRINCIPLE! MONSTERS DO NOT EAT QUICHE!
CHUNK
DID I HIT ONE?
NO.
YOU MISSED.

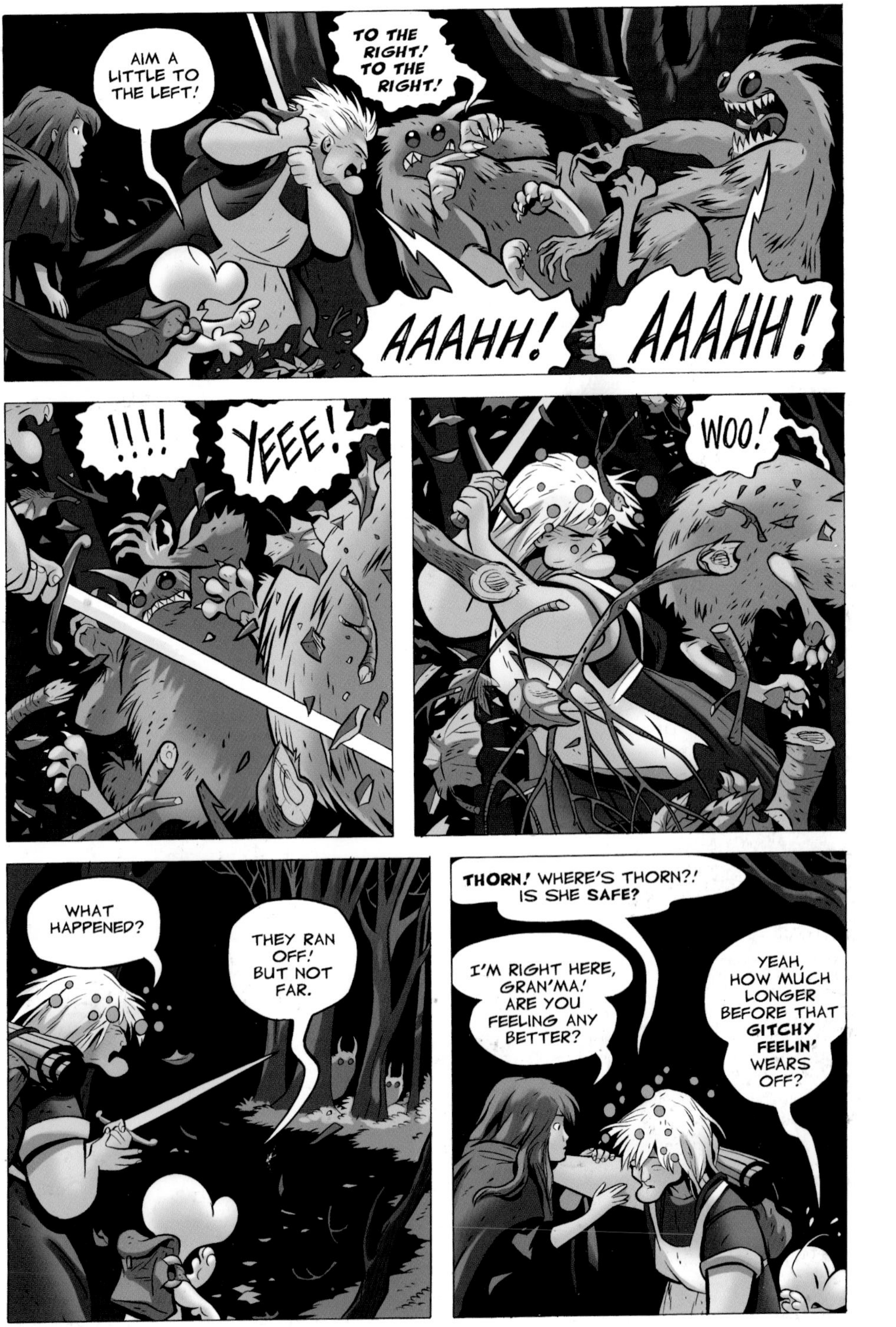
AIM A LITTLE TO THE LEFT!
TO THE RIGHT! TO THE RIGHT!
AAAHH!
AAAHH!
!!!!
YEEE!
WOO!
WHAT HAPPENED?
THEY RAN OFF! BUT NOT FAR.
THORN! WHERE'S THORN?! IS SHE SAFE?
I'M RIGHT HERE, GRAN'MA! ARE YOU FEELING ANY BETTER?
YEAH, HOW MUCH LONGER BEFORE THAT GITCHY FEELIN' WEARS OFF?

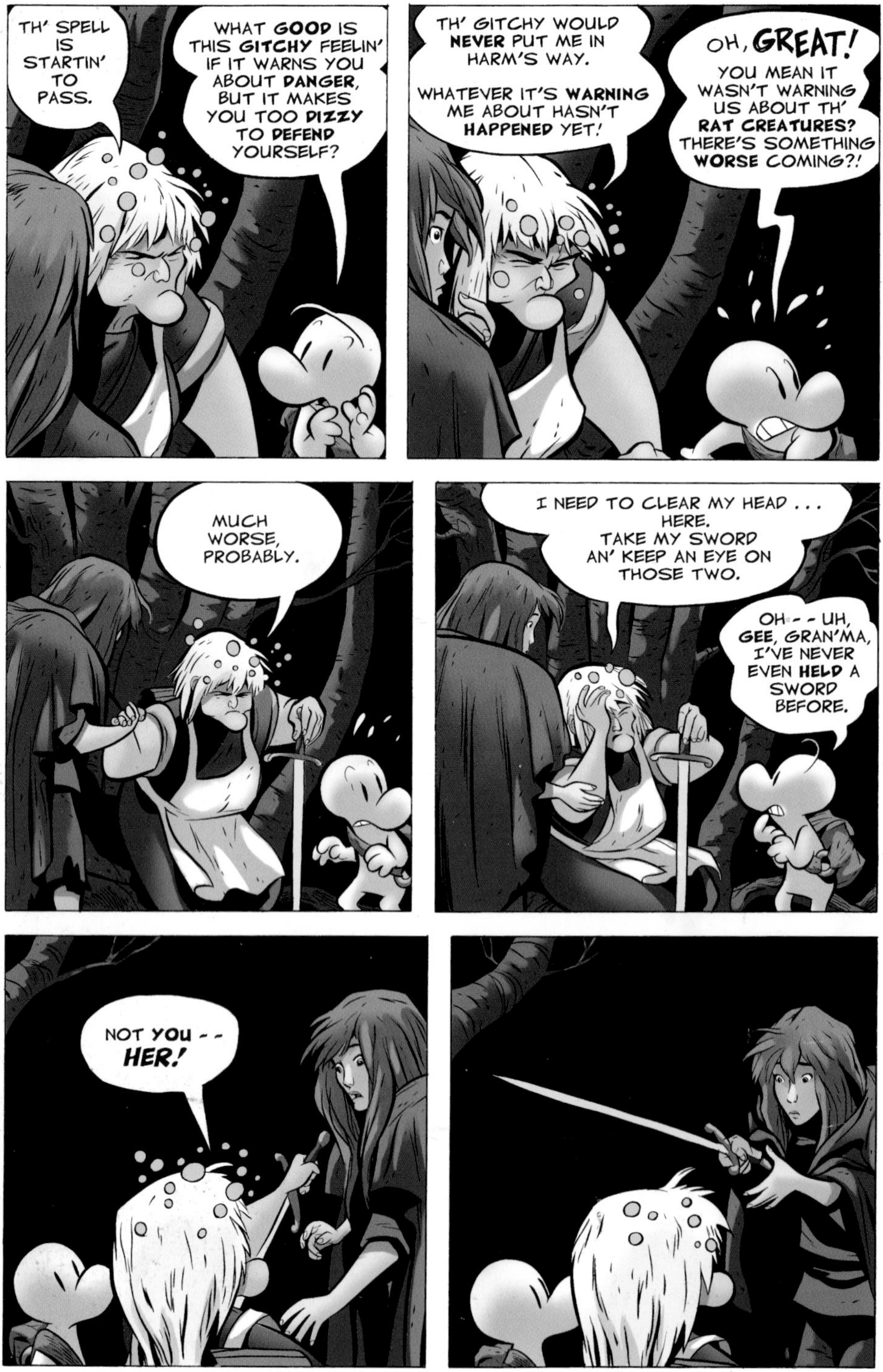
TH' SPELL IS STARTIN' TO PASS.
WHAT GOOD IS THIS GITCHY FEELIN' IF IT WARNS YOU ABOUT DANGER, BUT IT MAKES YOU TOO DIZZY TO DEFEND YOURSELF?
TH' GITCHY WOULD NEVER PUT ME IN HARM'S WAY.
WHATEVER IT'S WARNING ME ABOUT HASN'T HAPPENED YET!
OH, GREAT!
YOU MEAN IT WASN'T WARNING US ABOUT TH' RAT CREATURES? THERE'S SOMETHING WORSE COMING?!
MUCH WORSE, PROBABLY.
I NEED TO CLEAR MY HEAD . . . HERE. TAKE MY SWORD AN' KEEP AN EYE ON THOSE TWO.
OH- - UH, GEE, GRAN'MA, I'VE NEVER EVEN HELD A SWORD BEFORE.
NOT YOU - - HER!

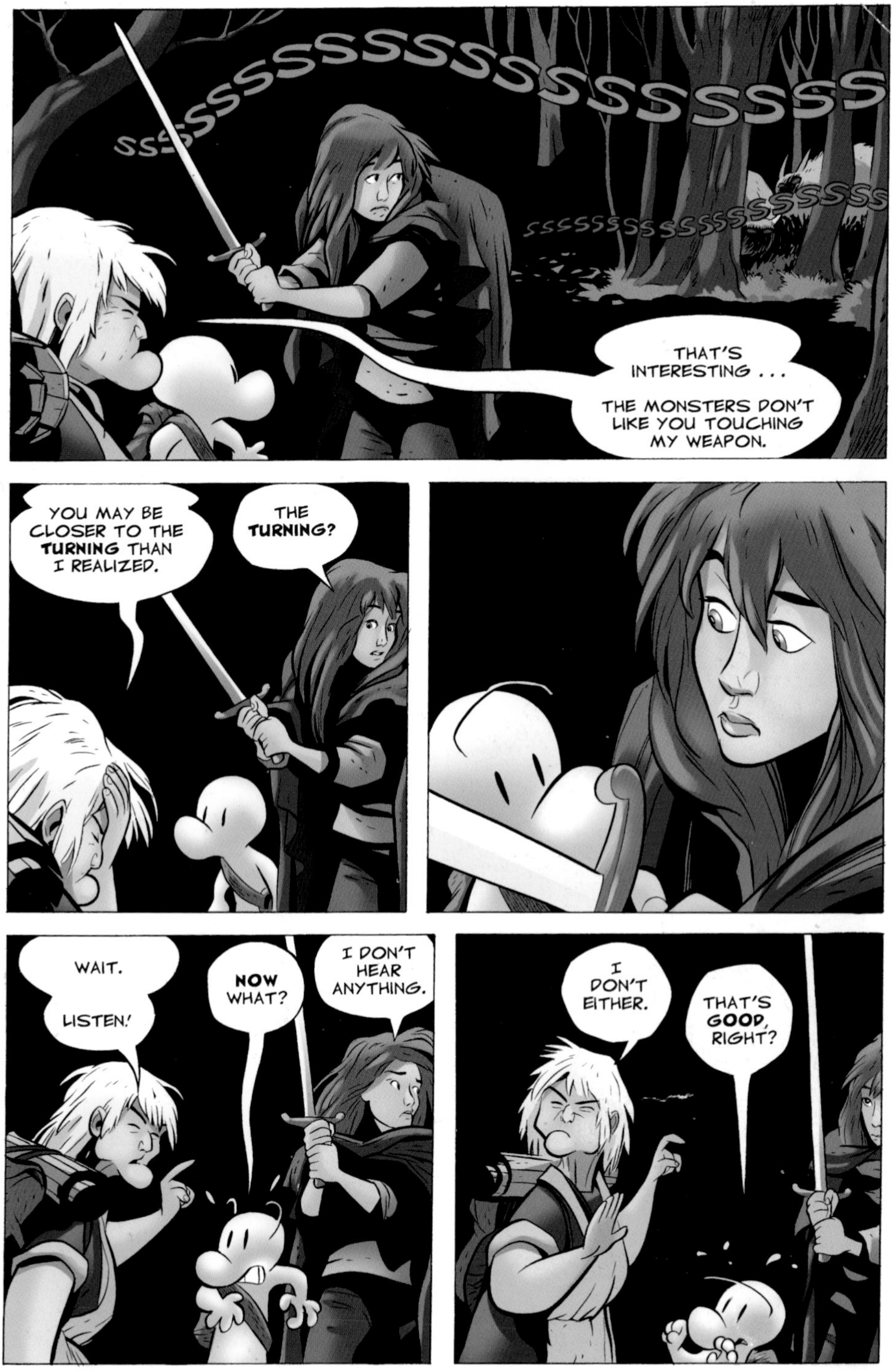
SSSSSSSSSSSSSSSSSSSSSSS
SSSSSSSSSSSSSSSSSSSSS
THAT'S INTERESTING . . .
THE MONSTERS DON'T LIKE YOU TOUCHING MY WEAPON.
YOU MAY BE CLOSER TO THE TURNING THAN I REALIZED.
THE TURNING?
WAIT.
LISTEN!
NOW WHAT?
I DON'T HEAR ANYTHING.
I DON'T EITHER.
THAT'S GOOD, RIGHT?

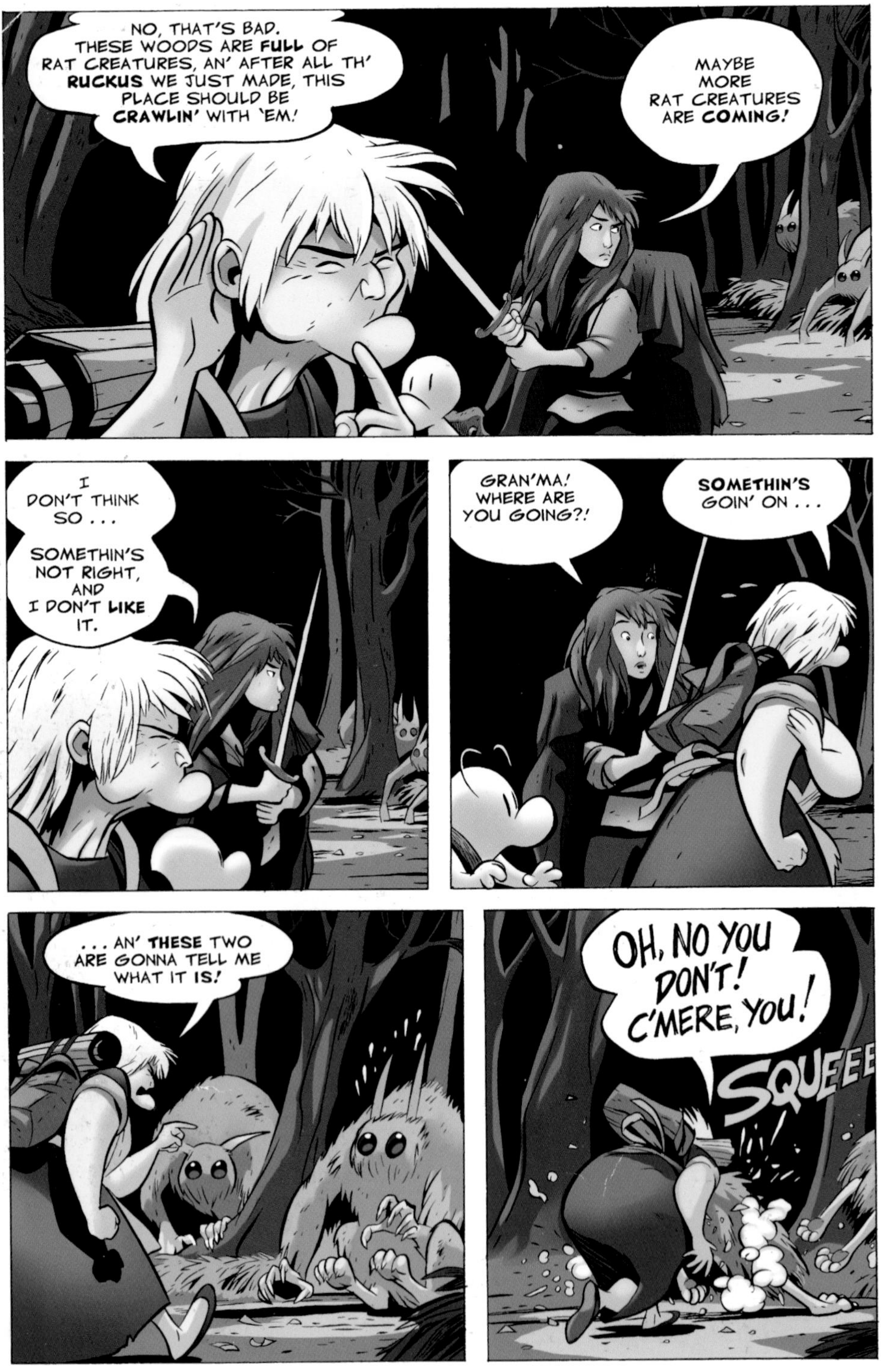
NO, THAT'S BAD. THESE WOODS ARE **FULL** OF RAT CREATURES, AN' AFTER ALL TH' **RUCKUS** WE JUST MADE, THIS PLACE SHOULD BE **CRAWLIN'** WITH 'EM!
MAYBE MORE RAT CREATURES ARE **COMING!**
I DON'T THINK SO . . .
SOMETHIN'S NOT RIGHT, AND I DON'T **LIKE** IT.
GRAN'MA! WHERE ARE YOU GOING?!
SOMETHIN'S GOIN' ON . . .
. . . AN' **THESE** TWO ARE GONNA TELL ME WHAT IT **IS!**
OH, NO YOU DON'T! C'MERE, YOU!
SQUEEE

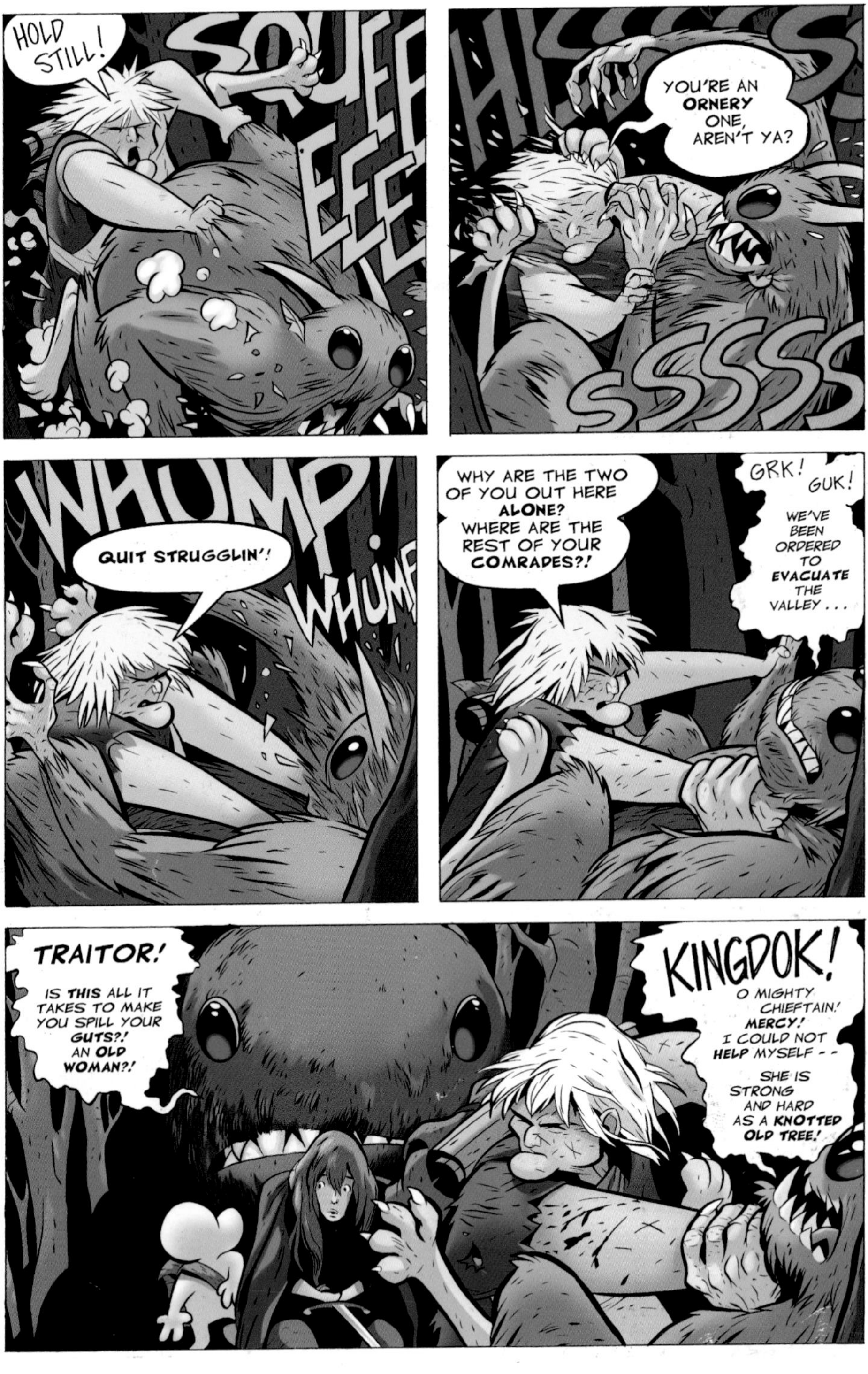
HOLD STILL!
YOU'RE AN ORNERY ONE, AREN'T YA?
WHUMP!
QUIT STRUGGLIN'!
WHY ARE THE TWO OF YOU OUT HERE ALONE? WHERE ARE THE REST OF YOUR COMRADES?!
GRK! GUK!
WE'VE BEEN ORDERED TO EVACUATE THE VALLEY . . .
TRAITOR!
IS THIS ALL IT TAKES TO MAKE YOU SPILL YOUR GUTS?! AN OLD WOMAN?!
KINGDOK!
O MIGHTY CHIEFTAIN! MERCY! I COULD NOT HELP MYSELF - -
SHE IS STRONG AND HARD AS A KNOTTED OLD TREE!

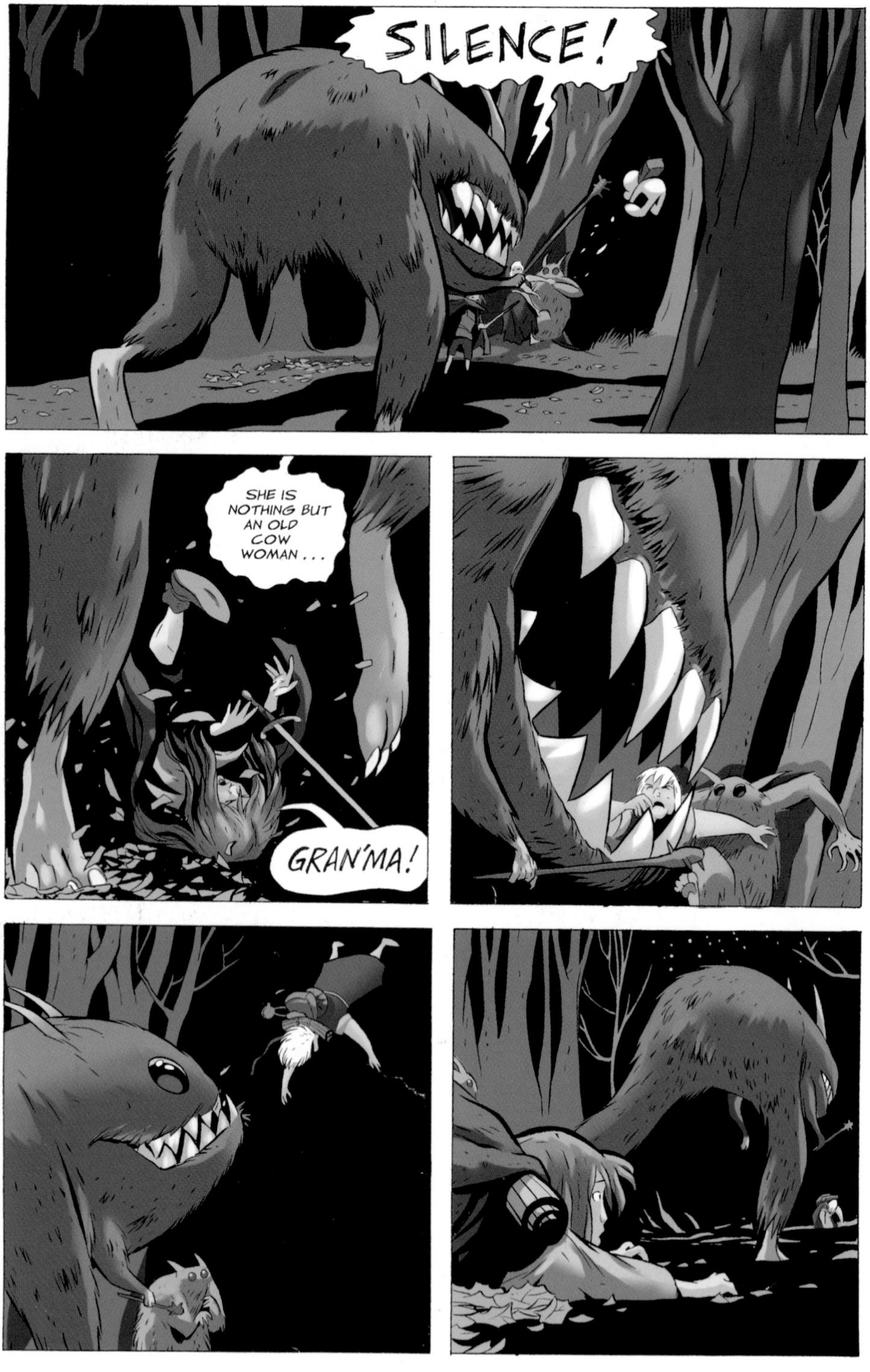
SILENCE!
SHE IS NOTHING BUT AN OLD COW WOMAN . . .
GRAN'MA!

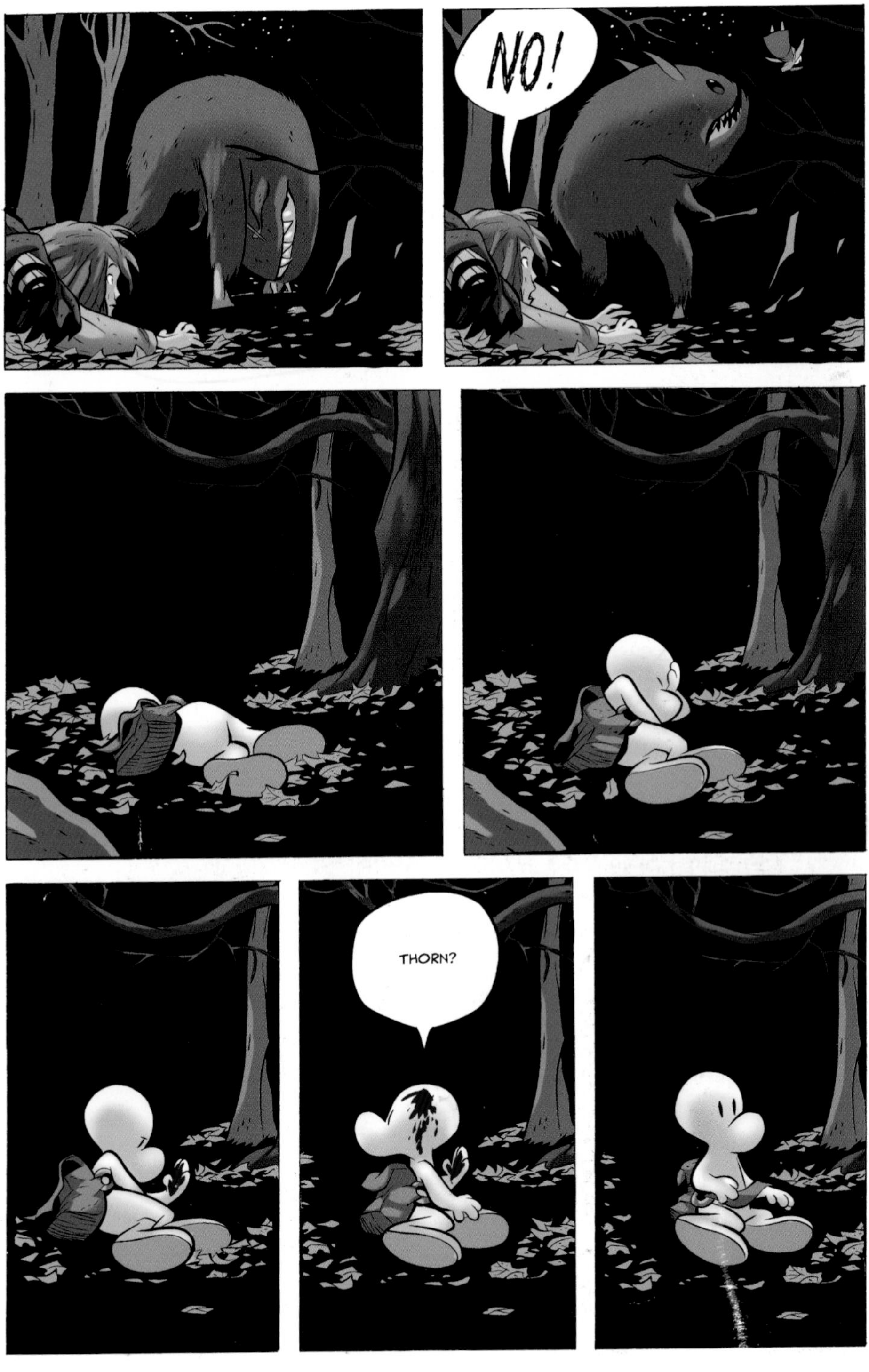
NO!
THORN?

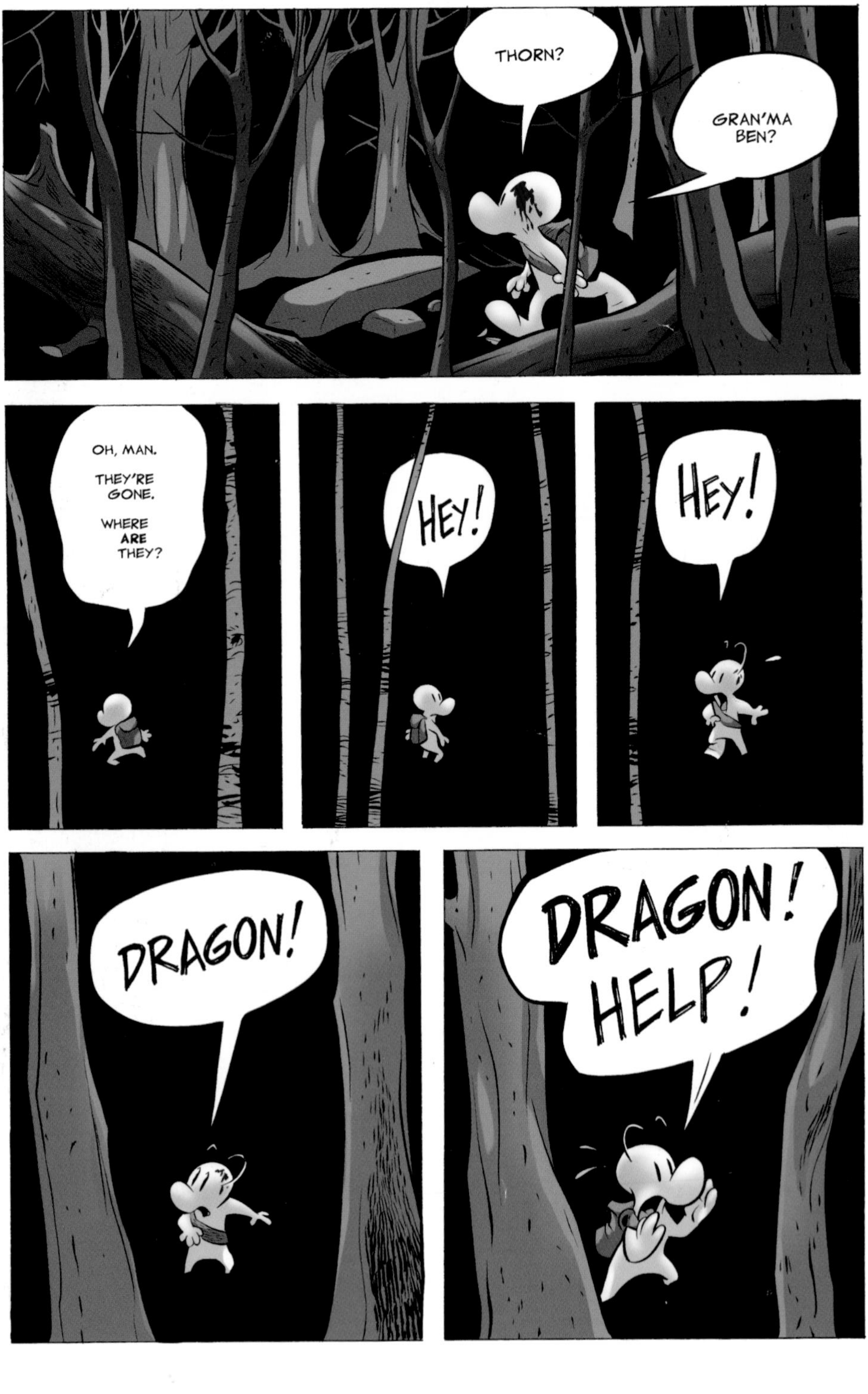
THORN?
GRAN'MA BEN?
OH, MAN. THEY'RE GONE. WHERE ARE THEY?
HEY!
HEY!
DRAGON!
DRAGON! HELP!

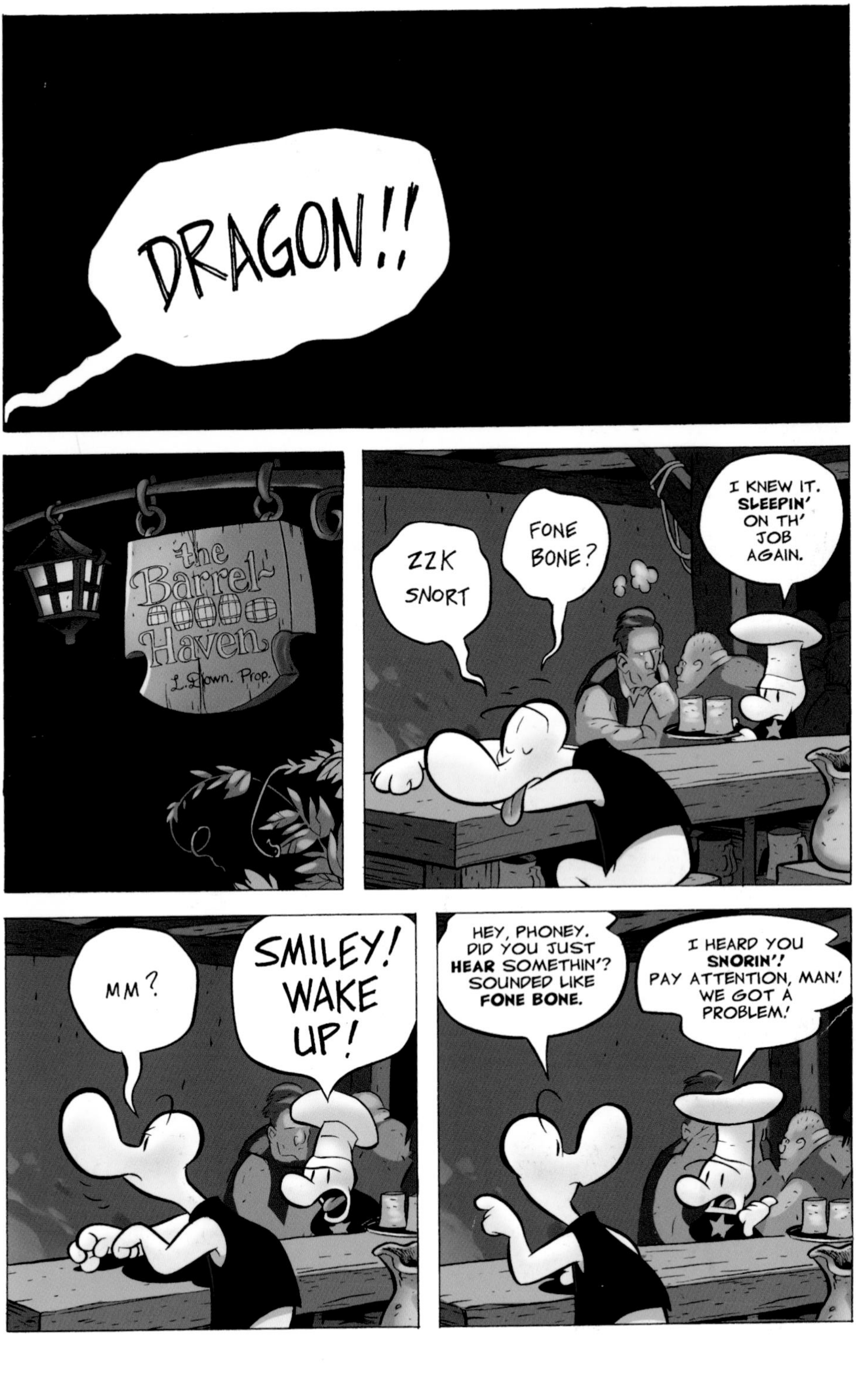
DRAGON!!
the Barrel Haven
L. Down. Prop.
ZZK SNORT
FONE BONE?
I KNEW IT. SLEEPIN' ON TH' JOB AGAIN.
MM?
SMILEY! WAKE UP!
HEY, PHONEY. DID YOU JUST HEAR SOMETHIN'? SOUNDED LIKE FONE BONE.
I HEARD YOU SNORIN'! PAY ATTENTION, MAN! WE GOT A PROBLEM!

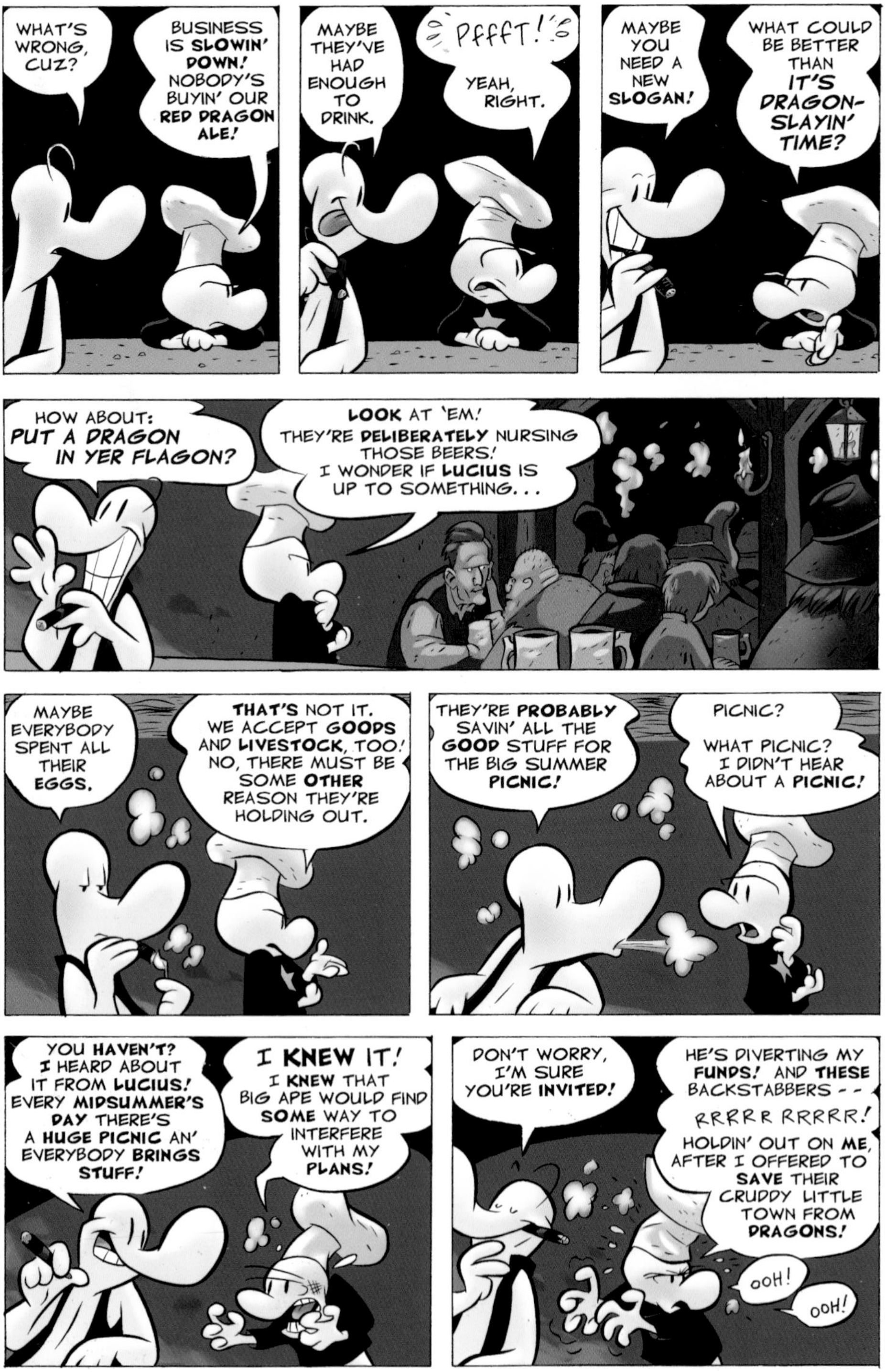
WHAT'S WRONG, CUZ?
BUSINESS IS SLOWIN' DOWN! NOBODY'S BUYIN' OUR RED DRAGON ALE!
MAYBE THEY'VE HAD ENOUGH TO DRINK.
PFFFT!
YEAH, RIGHT.
MAYBE YOU NEED A NEW SLOGAN!
WHAT COULD BE BETTER THAN IT'S DRAGON-SLAYIN' TIME?
HOW ABOUT: PUT A DRAGON IN YER FLAGON?
LOOK AT 'EM! THEY'RE DELIBERATELY NURSING THOSE BEERS! I WONDER IF LUCIUS IS UP TO SOMETHING...
MAYBE EVERYBODY SPENT ALL THEIR EGGS.
THAT'S NOT IT. WE ACCEPT GOODS AND LIVESTOCK, TOO! NO, THERE MUST BE SOME OTHER REASON THEY'RE HOLDING OUT.
THEY'RE PROBABLY SAVIN' ALL THE GOOD STUFF FOR THE BIG SUMMER PICNIC!
PICNIC?
WHAT PICNIC? I DIDN'T HEAR ABOUT A PICNIC!
YOU HAVEN'T? I HEARD ABOUT IT FROM LUCIUS! EVERY MIDSUMMER'S DAY THERE'S A HUGE PICNIC AN' EVERYBODY BRINGS STUFF!
I KNEW IT! I KNEW THAT BIG APE WOULD FIND SOME WAY TO INTERFERE WITH MY PLANS!
DON'T WORRY, I'M SURE YOU'RE INVITED!
HE'S DIVERTING MY FUNDS! AND THESE BACKSTABBERS --
RRRRR RRRRR!
HOLDIN' OUT ON ME, AFTER I OFFERED TO SAVE THEIR CRUDDY LITTLE TOWN FROM DRAGONS!
OOH!
OOH!

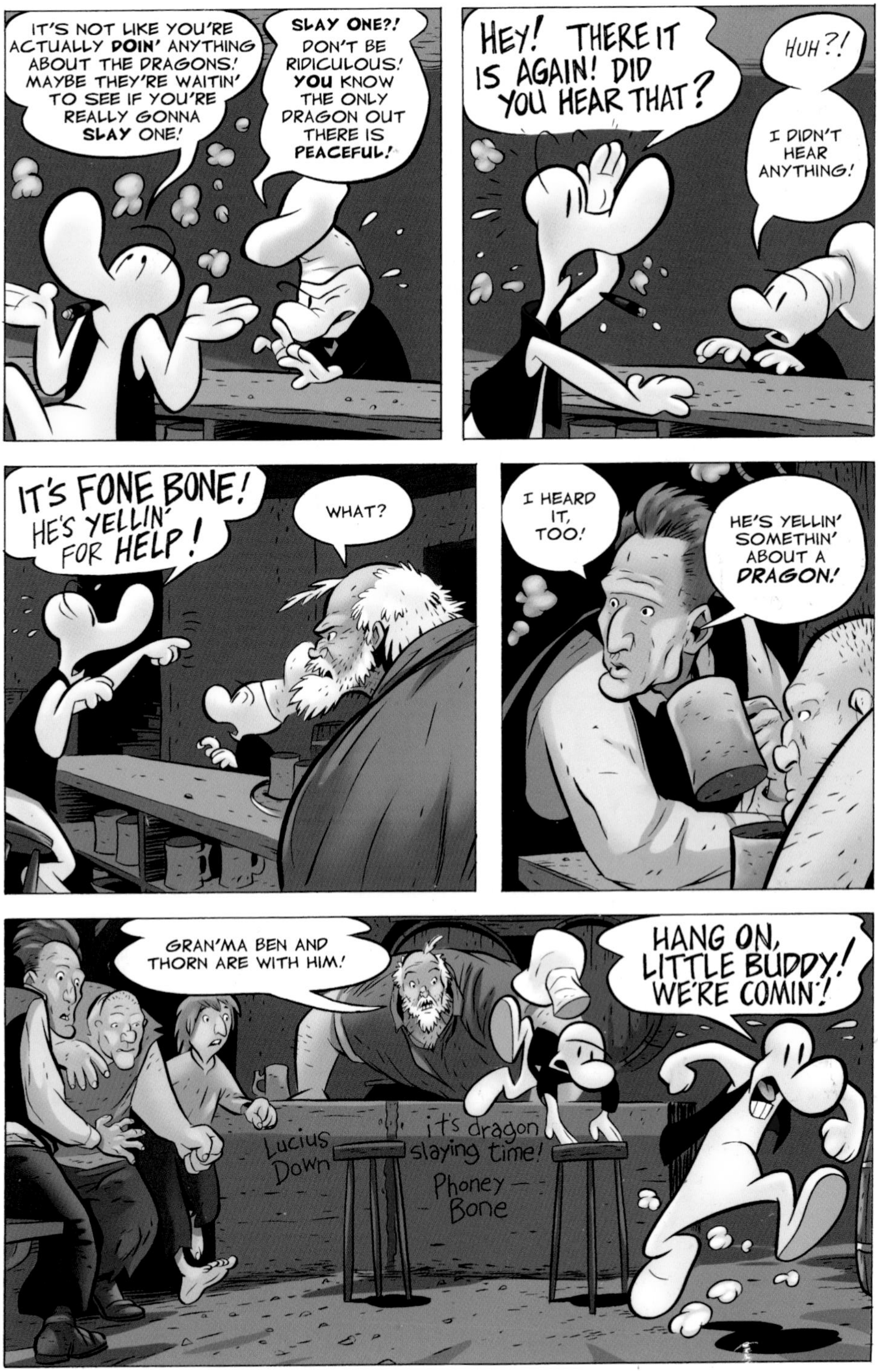
IT'S NOT LIKE YOU'RE ACTUALLY DOIN' ANYTHING ABOUT THE DRAGONS! MAYBE THEY'RE WAITIN' TO SEE IF YOU'RE REALLY GONNA SLAY ONE!
SLAY ONE?! DON'T BE RIDICULOUS! YOU KNOW THE ONLY DRAGON OUT THERE IS PEACEFUL!
HEY! THERE IT IS AGAIN! DID YOU HEAR THAT?
HUH?!
I DIDN'T HEAR ANYTHING!
IT'S FONE BONE! HE'S YELLIN' FOR HELP!
WHAT?
I HEARD IT, TOO!
HE'S YELLIN' SOMETHIN' ABOUT A DRAGON!
GRAN'MA BEN AND THORN ARE WITH HIM!
HANG ON, LITTLE BUDDY! WE'RE COMIN'!
Lucius Down
it's dragon slaying time!
Phoney Bone

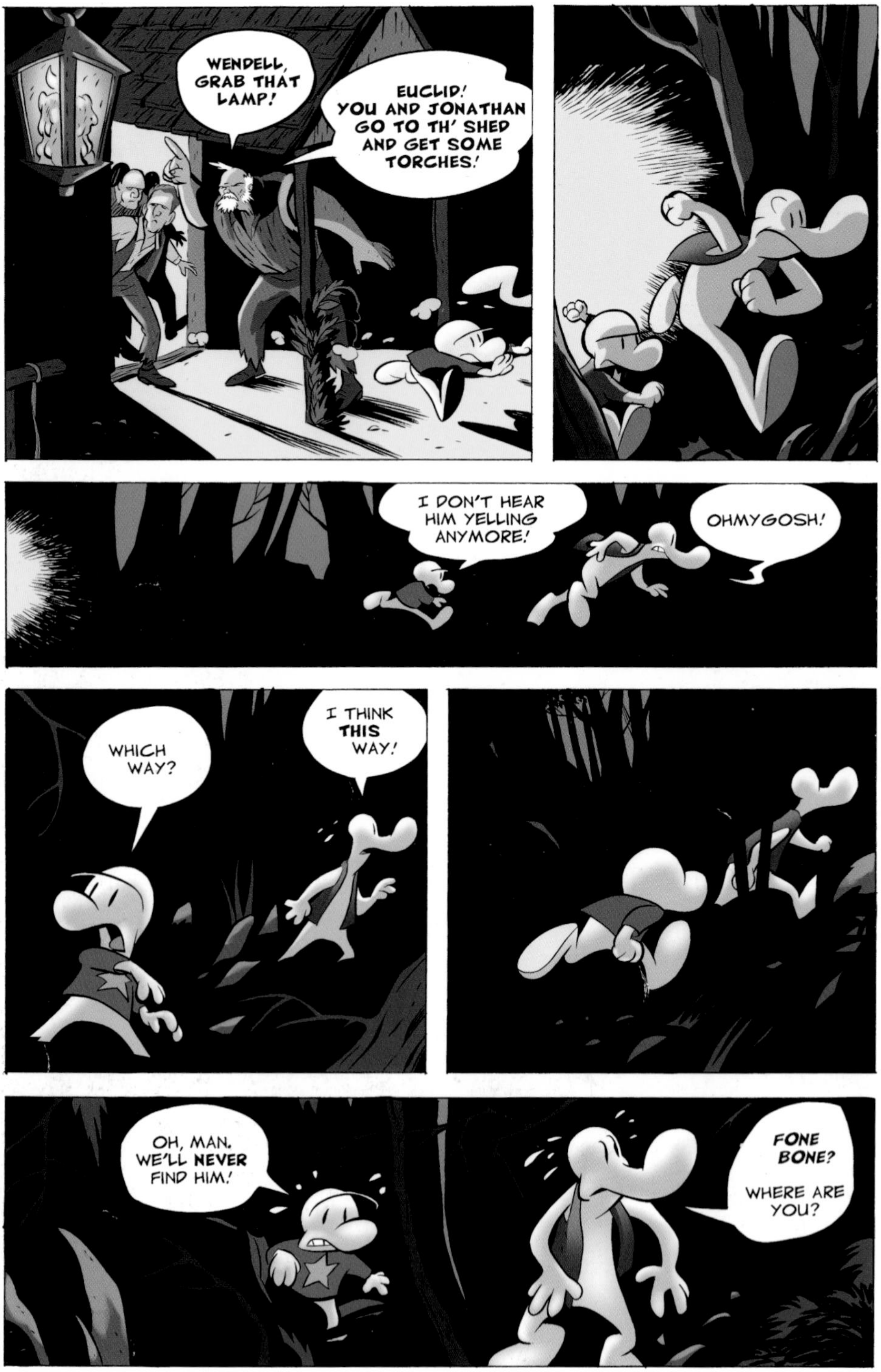
WENDELL, GRAB THAT LAMP!
EUCLID! YOU AND JONATHAN GO TO TH' SHED AND GET SOME TORCHES!
I DON'T HEAR HIM YELLING ANYMORE!
OHMYGOSH!
WHICH WAY?
I THINK THIS WAY!
OH, MAN. WE'LL NEVER FIND HIM!
FONE BONE?
WHERE ARE YOU?

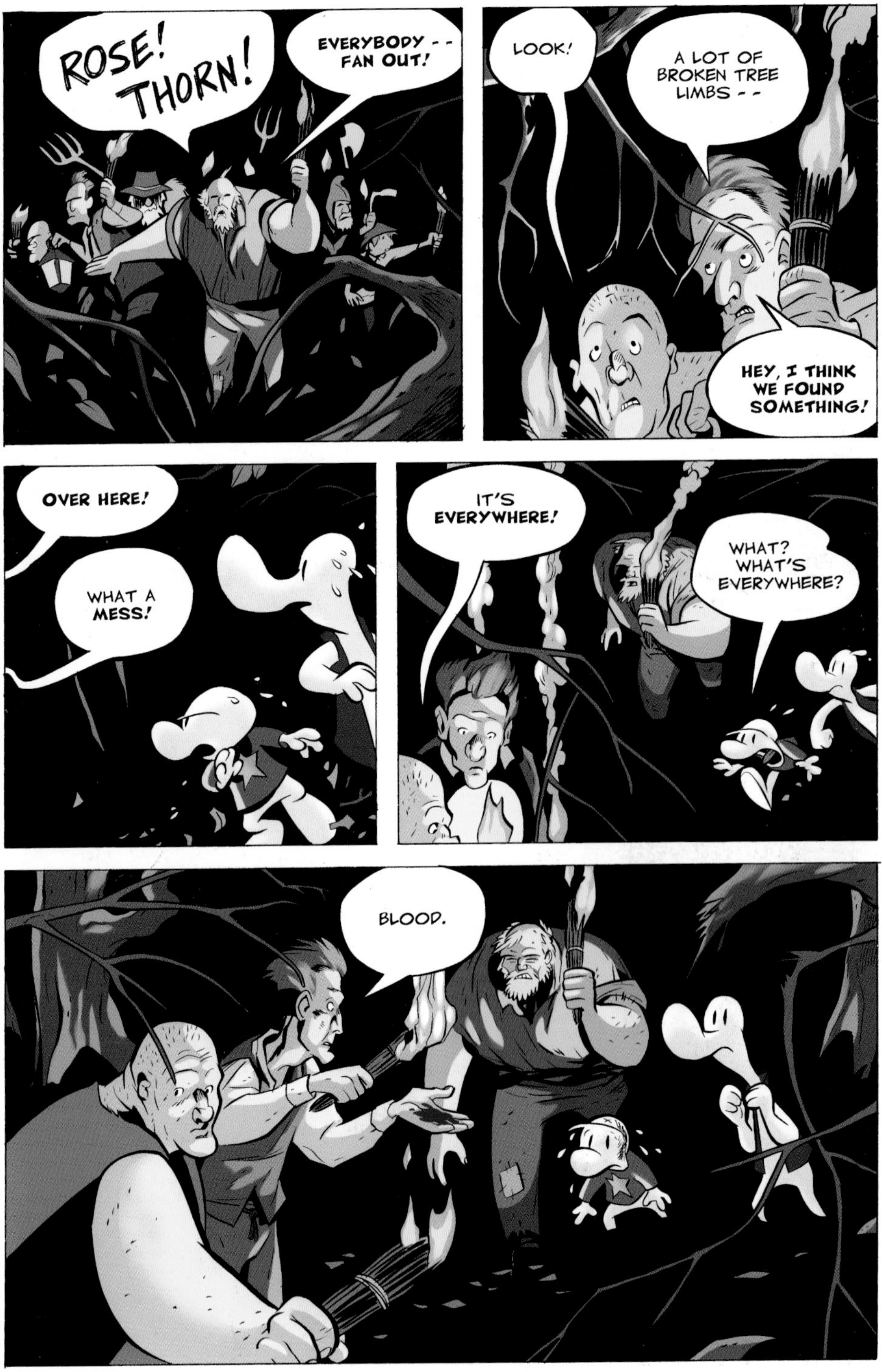
ROSE! THORN!
EVERYBODY - - FAN OUT!
LOOK!
A LOT OF BROKEN TREE LIMBS - -
HEY, I THINK WE FOUND SOMETHING!
OVER HERE!
WHAT A MESS!
IT'S EVERYWHERE!
WHAT? WHAT'S EVERYWHERE?
BLOOD.

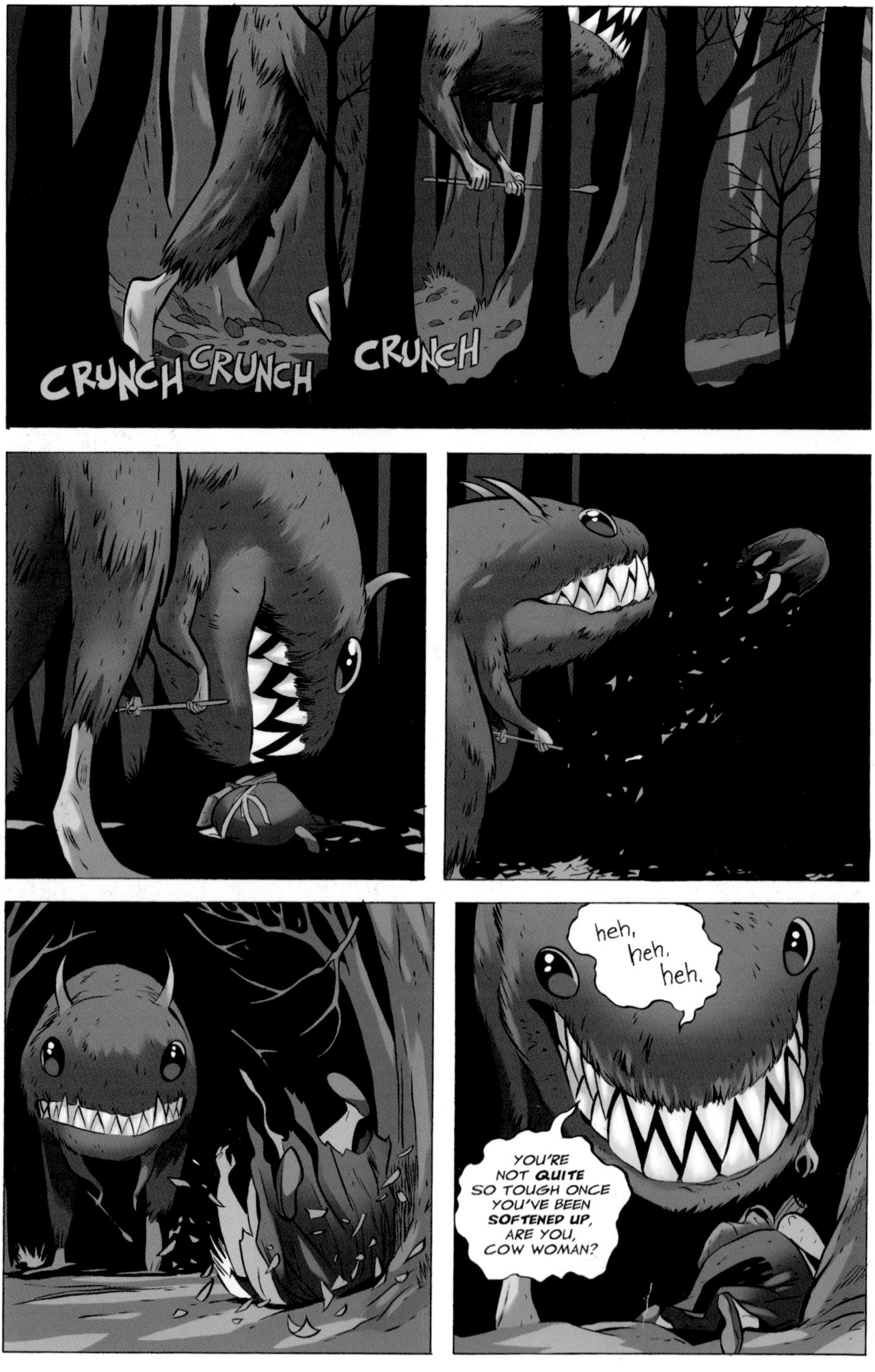
CRUNCH CRUNCH CRUNCH
heh, heh, heh.
YOU'RE NOT **QUITE** SO TOUGH ONCE YOU'VE BEEN **SOFTENED UP**, ARE YOU, COW WOMAN?

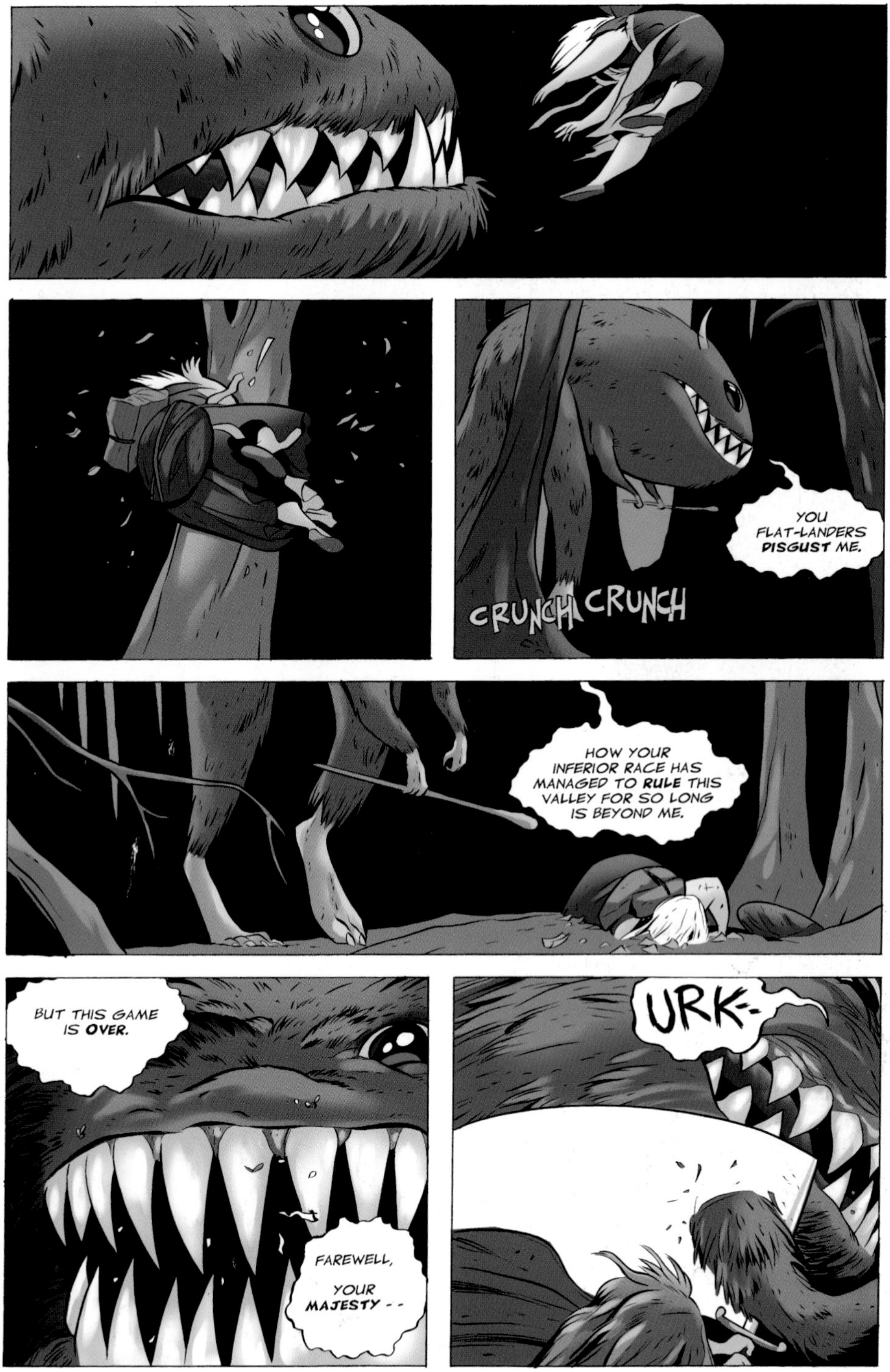
YOU FLAT-LANDERS **DISGUST** ME.
CRUNCH CRUNCH
HOW YOUR INFERIOR RACE HAS MANAGED TO **RULE** THIS VALLEY FOR SO LONG IS BEYOND ME.
BUT THIS GAME IS **OVER.**
FAREWELL, YOUR **MAJESTY** - -
URK-

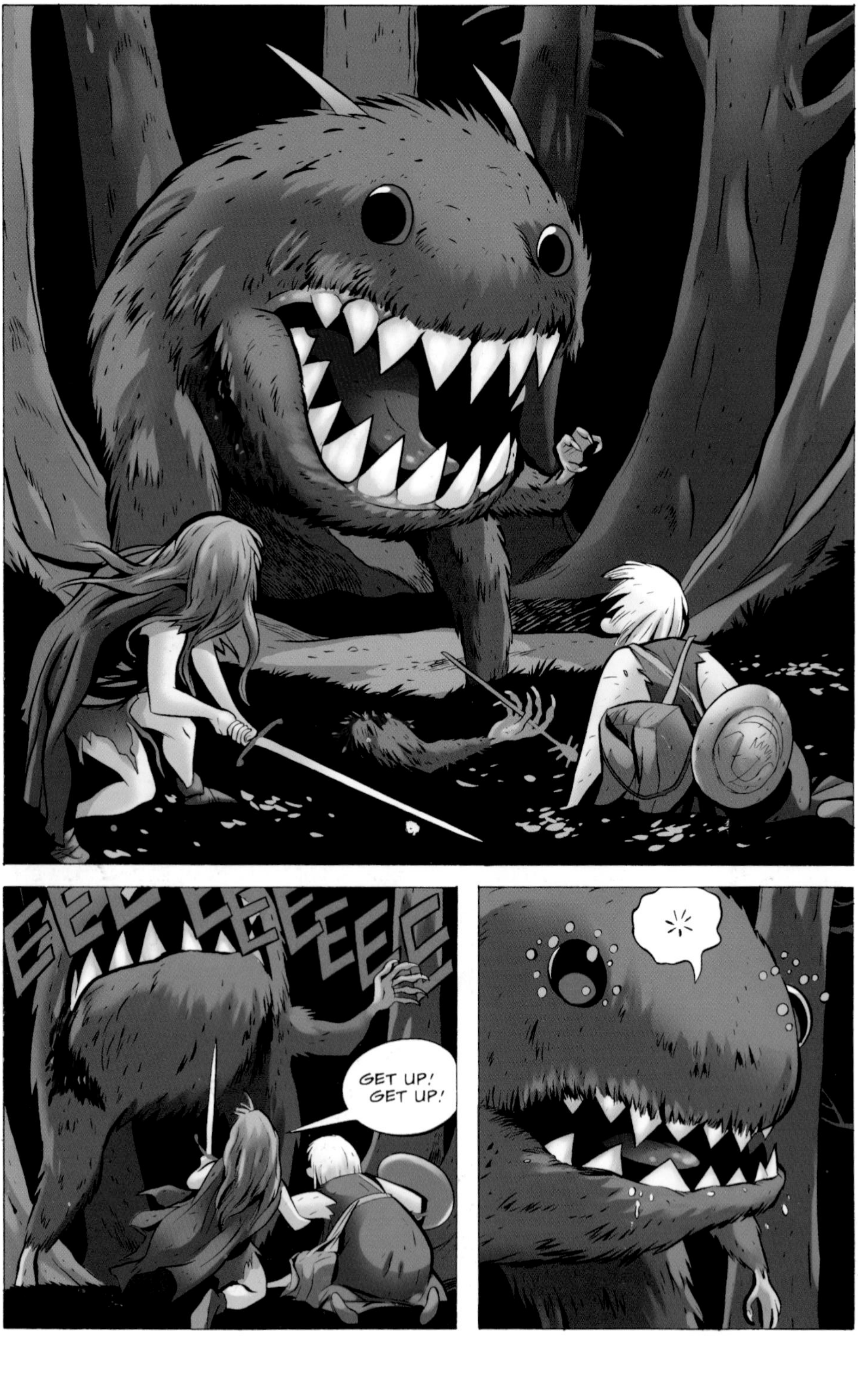
EEEEEEEEE
GET UP! GET UP!

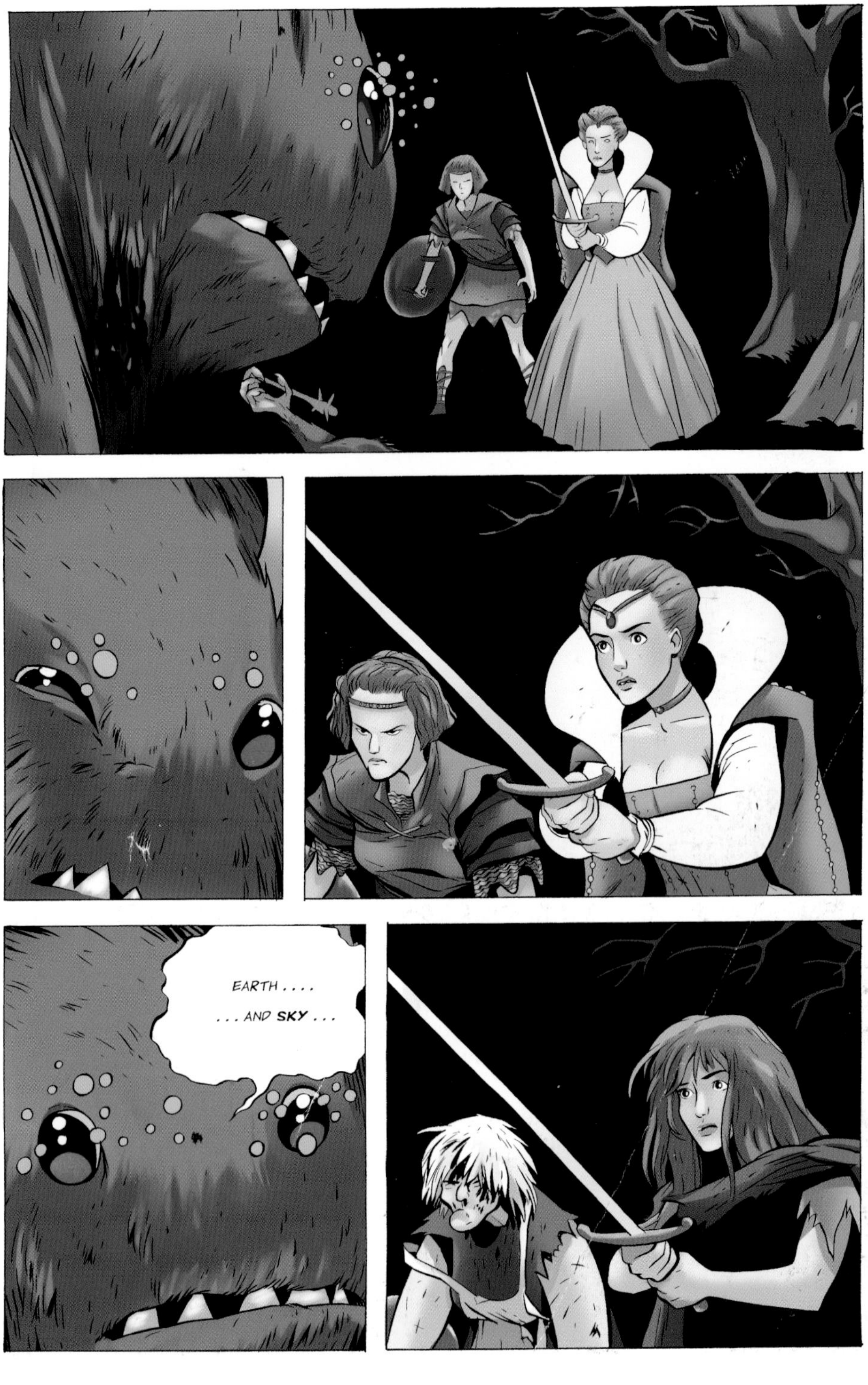
EARTH . . . .
. . . AND SKY . . .

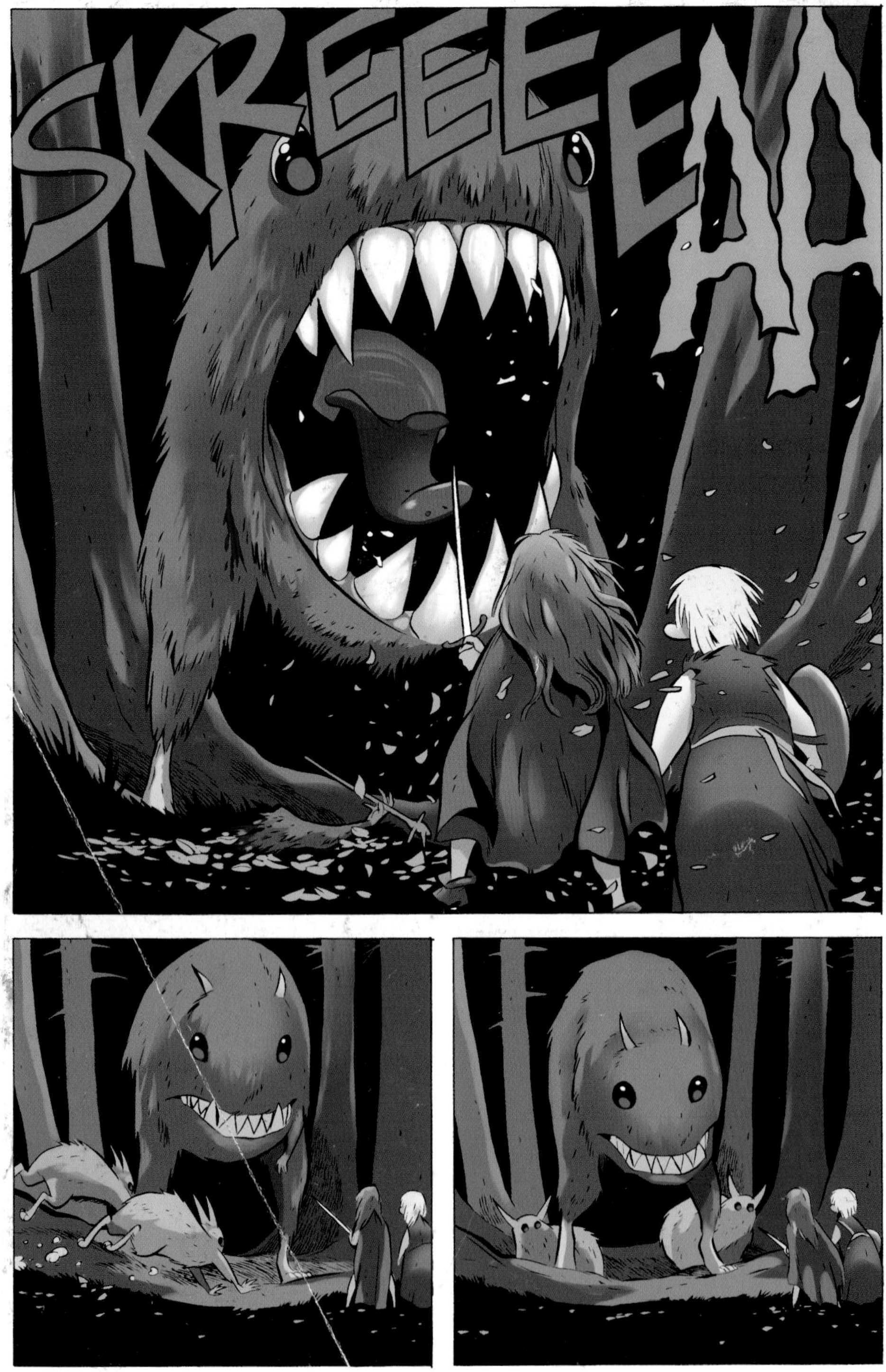
SKREEEEAA

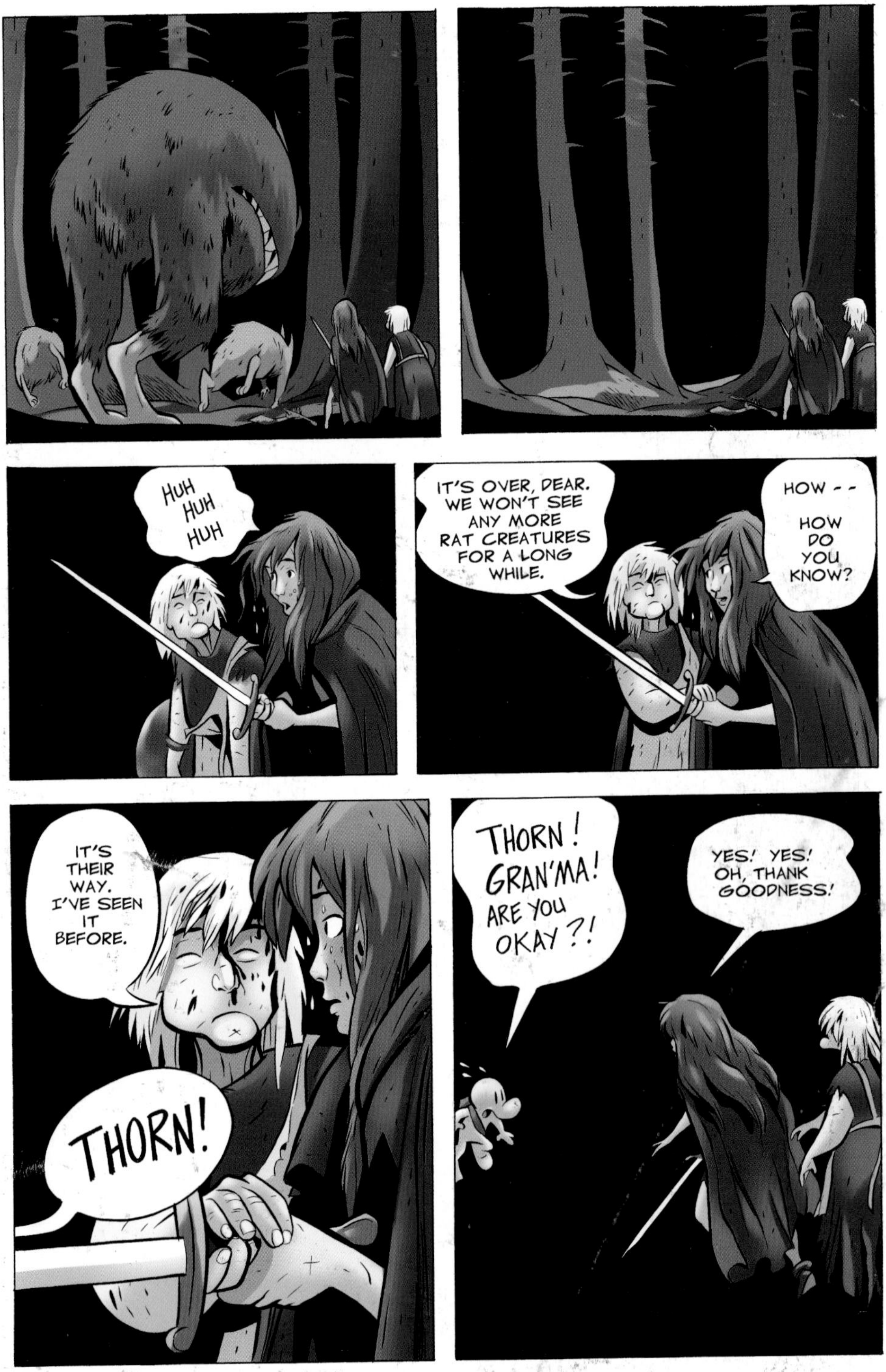
HUH
HUH
HUH
IT'S OVER, DEAR. WE WON'T SEE ANY MORE RAT CREATURES FOR A LONG WHILE.
HOW - -
HOW DO YOU KNOW?
IT'S THEIR WAY. I'VE SEEN IT BEFORE.
THORN!
THORN! GRAN'MA! ARE YOU OKAY?!
YES! YES! OH, THANK GOODNESS!

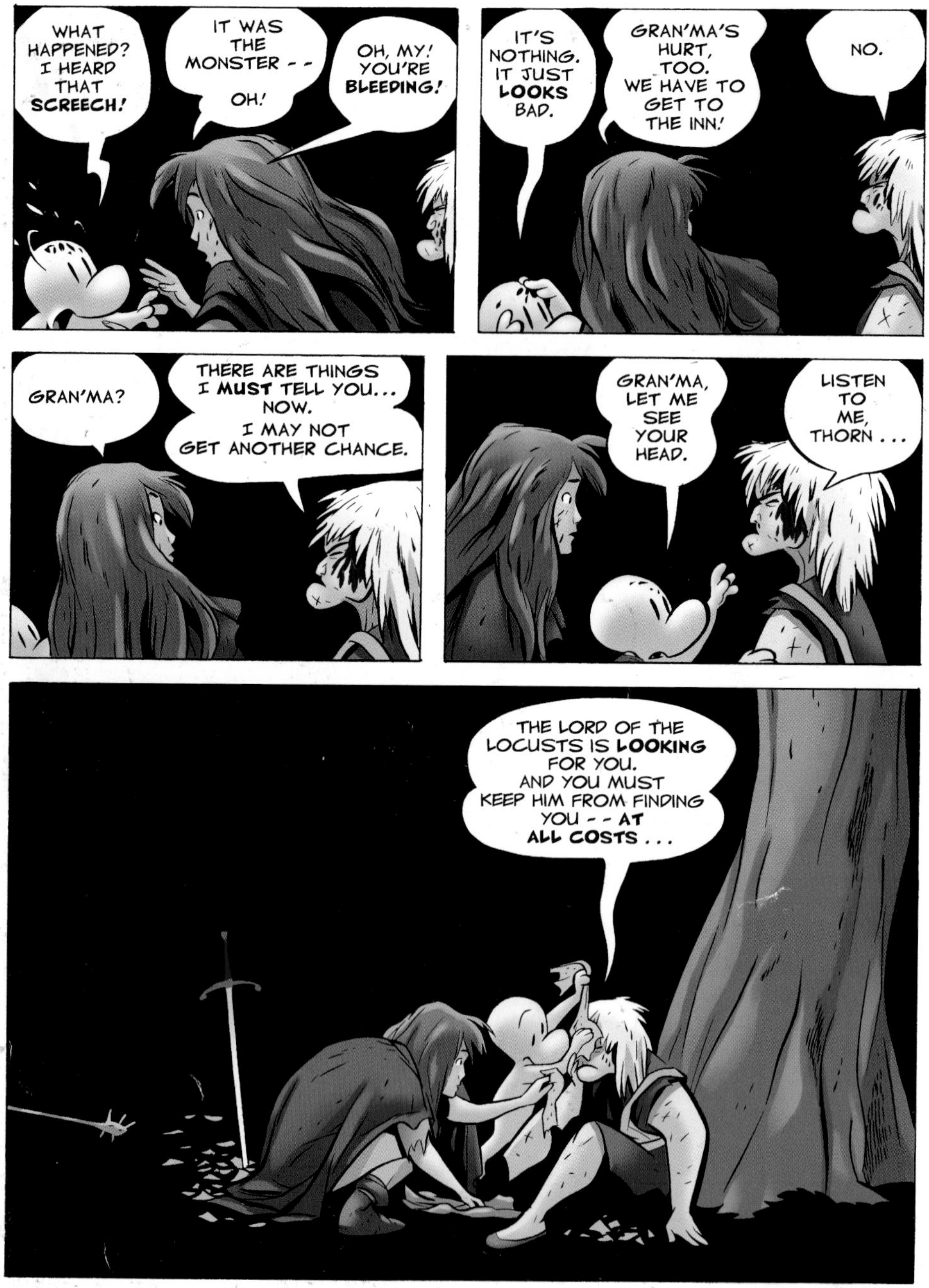
WHAT HAPPENED? I HEARD THAT SCREECH!
IT WAS THE MONSTER - -
OH!
OH, MY! YOU'RE BLEEDING!
IT'S NOTHING. IT JUST LOOKS BAD.
GRAN'MA'S HURT, TOO. WE HAVE TO GET TO THE INN!
NO.
GRAN'MA?
THERE ARE THINGS I MUST TELL YOU... NOW. I MAY NOT GET ANOTHER CHANCE.
GRAN'MA, LET ME SEE YOUR HEAD.
LISTEN TO ME, THORN ...
THE LORD OF THE LOCUSTS IS LOOKING FOR YOU. AND YOU MUST KEEP HIM FROM FINDING YOU - - AT ALL COSTS ...

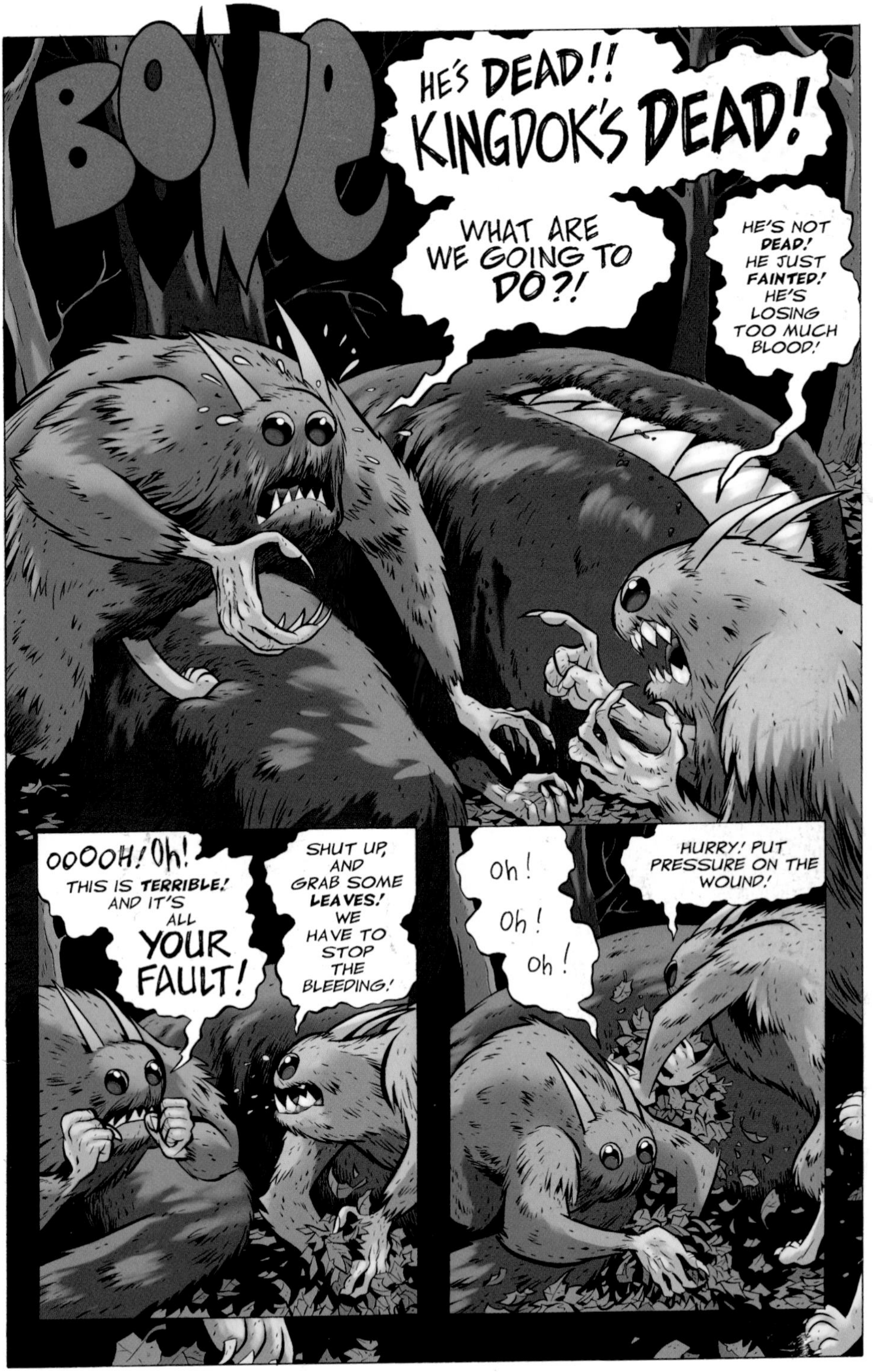
BONE
HE'S DEAD!! KINGDOK'S DEAD!
WHAT ARE WE GOING TO DO?!
HE'S NOT DEAD! HE JUST FAINTED! HE'S LOSING TOO MUCH BLOOD!
OOOOH! Oh! THIS IS TERRIBLE! AND IT'S ALL YOUR FAULT!
SHUT UP, AND GRAB SOME LEAVES! WE HAVE TO STOP THE BLEEDING!
Oh!
Oh!
Oh!
HURRY! PUT PRESSURE ON THE WOUND!

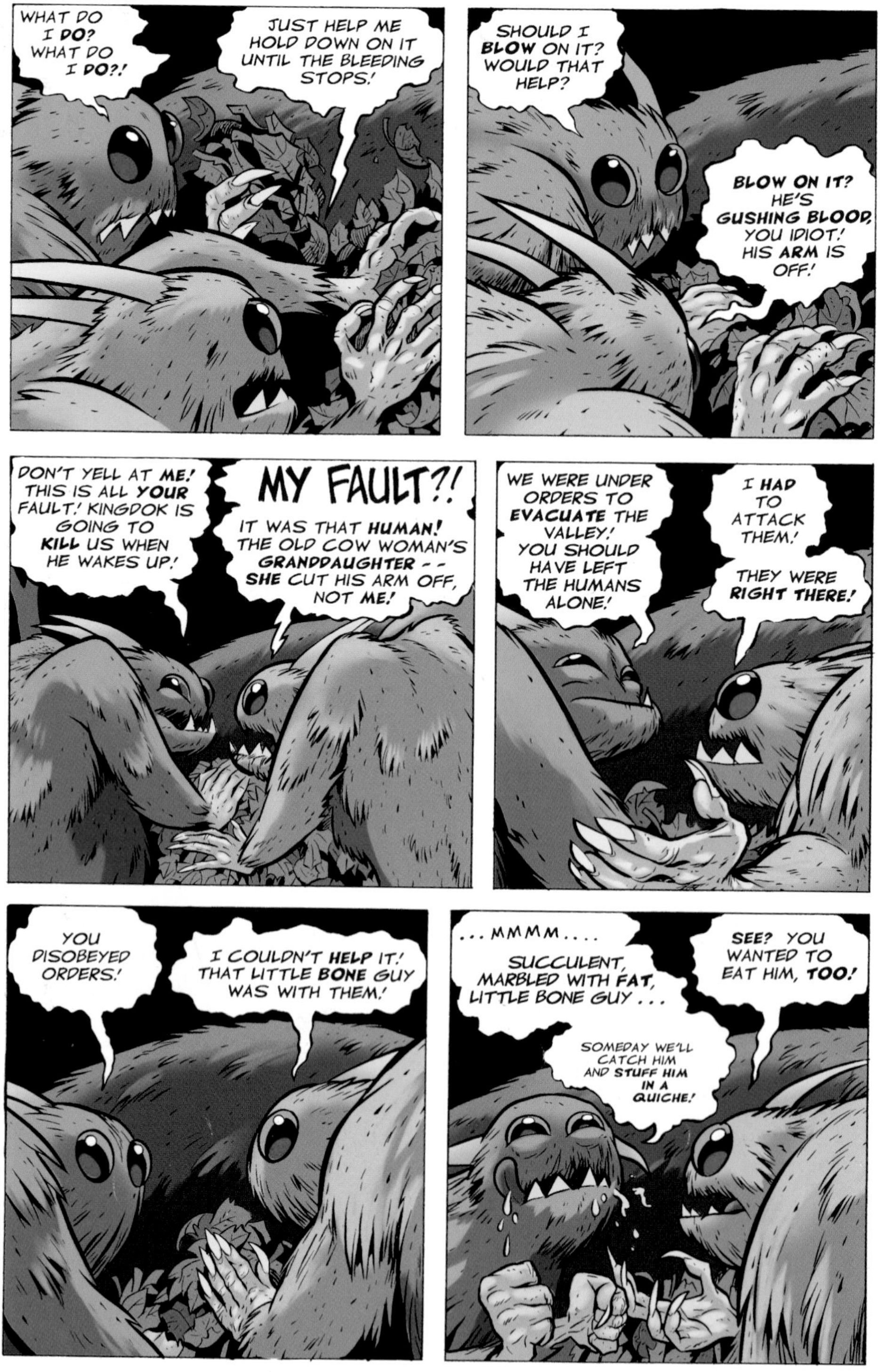
WHAT DO I DO? WHAT DO I DO?!
JUST HELP ME HOLD DOWN ON IT UNTIL THE BLEEDING STOPS!
SHOULD I BLOW ON IT? WOULD THAT HELP?
BLOW ON IT? HE'S GUSHING BLOOD, YOU IDIOT! HIS ARM IS OFF!
DON'T YELL AT ME! THIS IS ALL YOUR FAULT! KINGDOK IS GOING TO KILL US WHEN HE WAKES UP!
MY FAULT?!
IT WAS THAT HUMAN! THE OLD COW WOMAN'S GRANDDAUGHTER -- SHE CUT HIS ARM OFF, NOT ME!
WE WERE UNDER ORDERS TO EVACUATE THE VALLEY! YOU SHOULD HAVE LEFT THE HUMANS ALONE!
I HAD TO ATTACK THEM!
THEY WERE RIGHT THERE!
YOU DISOBEYED ORDERS!
I COULDN'T HELP IT! THAT LITTLE BONE GUY WAS WITH THEM!
... MMMM....
SUCCULENT, MARBLED WITH FAT, LITTLE BONE GUY ...
SEE? YOU WANTED TO EAT HIM, TOO!
SOMEDAY WE'LL CATCH HIM AND STUFF HIM IN A QUICHE!

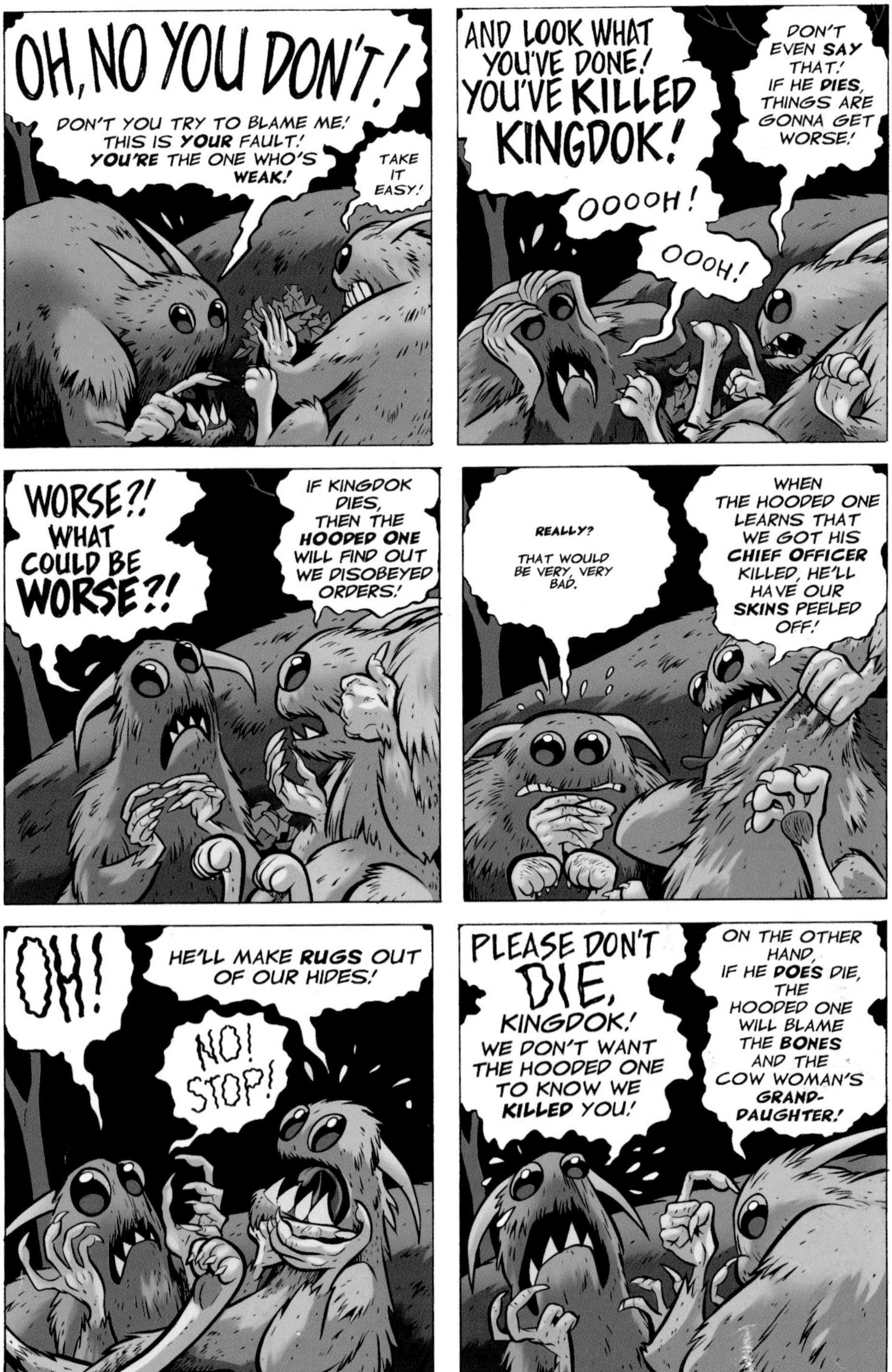
OH, NO YOU DON'T!
DON'T YOU TRY TO BLAME ME! THIS IS YOUR FAULT! YOU'RE THE ONE WHO'S WEAK!
TAKE IT EASY!
AND LOOK WHAT YOU'VE DONE! YOU'VE KILLED KINGDOK!
DON'T EVEN SAY THAT! IF HE DIES, THINGS ARE GONNA GET WORSE!
OOOOH!
OOOH!
WORSE?! WHAT COULD BE WORSE?!
IF KINGDOK DIES, THEN THE HOODED ONE WILL FIND OUT WE DISOBEYED ORDERS!
REALLY?
THAT WOULD BE VERY, VERY BAD.
WHEN THE HOODED ONE LEARNS THAT WE GOT HIS CHIEF OFFICER KILLED, HE'LL HAVE OUR SKINS PEELED OFF!
OH!
HE'LL MAKE RUGS OUT OF OUR HIDES!
NO! STOP!
PLEASE DON'T DIE, KINGDOK! WE DON'T WANT THE HOODED ONE TO KNOW WE KILLED YOU!
ON THE OTHER HAND, IF HE DOES DIE, THE HOODED ONE WILL BLAME THE BONES AND THE COW WOMAN'S GRAND-DAUGHTER!

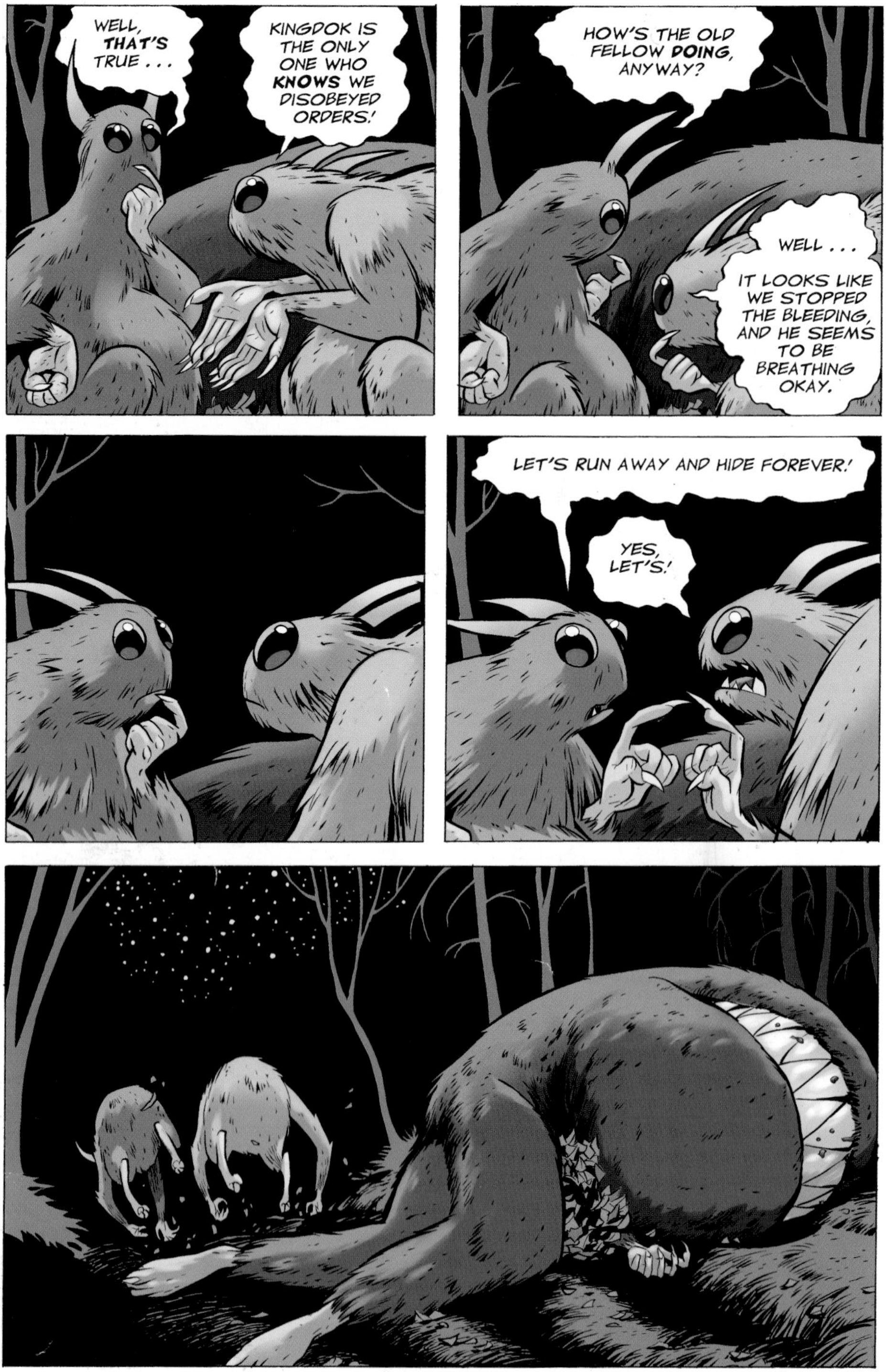
WELL, THAT'S TRUE . . .
KINGDOK IS THE ONLY ONE WHO KNOWS WE DISOBEYED ORDERS!
HOW'S THE OLD FELLOW DOING, ANYWAY?
WELL . . .
IT LOOKS LIKE WE STOPPED THE BLEEDING, AND HE SEEMS TO BE BREATHING OKAY.
LET'S RUN AWAY AND HIDE FOREVER!
YES, LET'S!

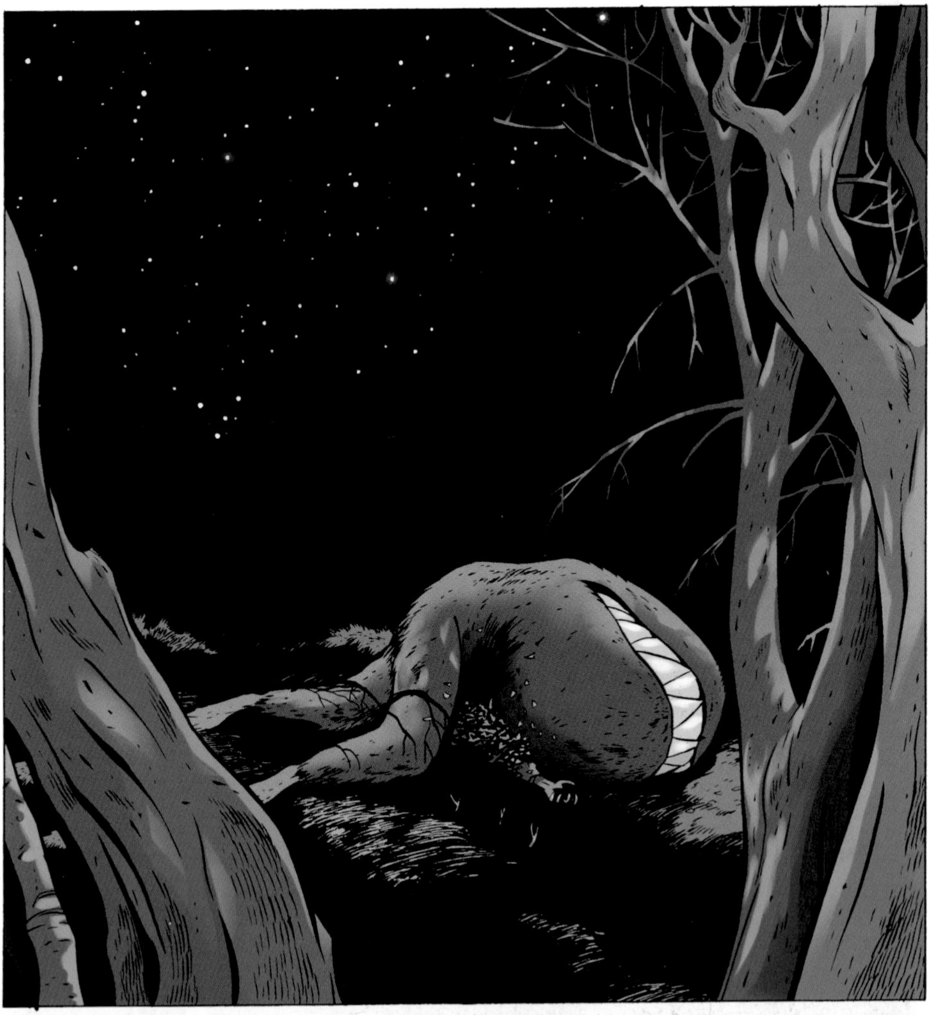

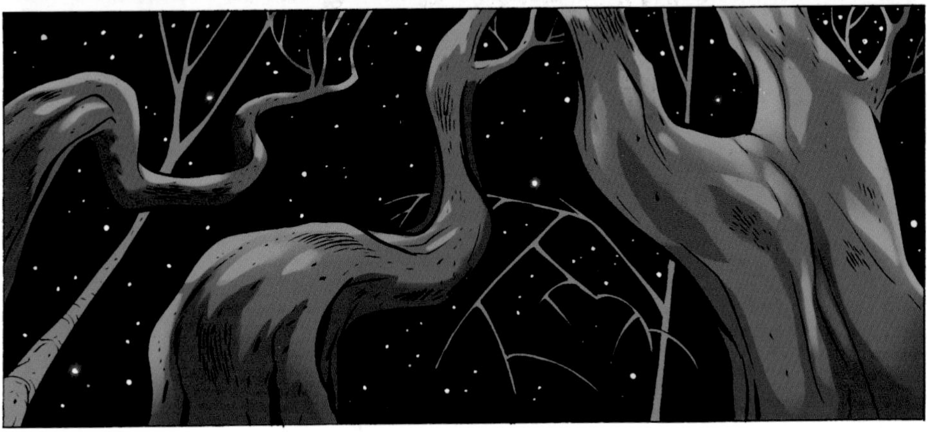

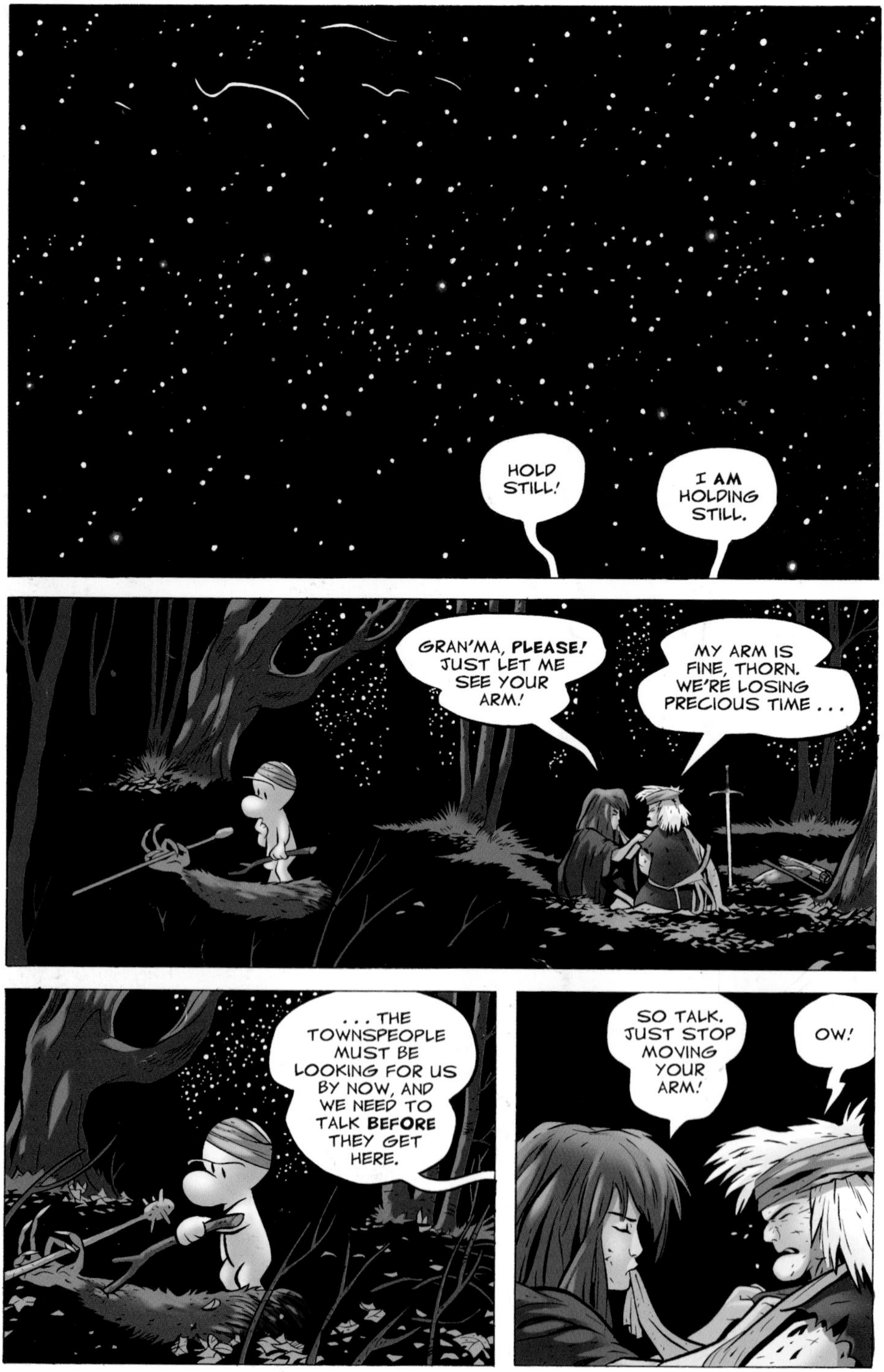
HOLD STILL!
I AM HOLDING STILL.
GRAN'MA, PLEASE! JUST LET ME SEE YOUR ARM!
MY ARM IS FINE, THORN. WE'RE LOSING PRECIOUS TIME . . .
. . . THE TOWNSPEOPLE MUST BE LOOKING FOR US BY NOW, AND WE NEED TO TALK BEFORE THEY GET HERE.
SO TALK. JUST STOP MOVING YOUR ARM!
OW!

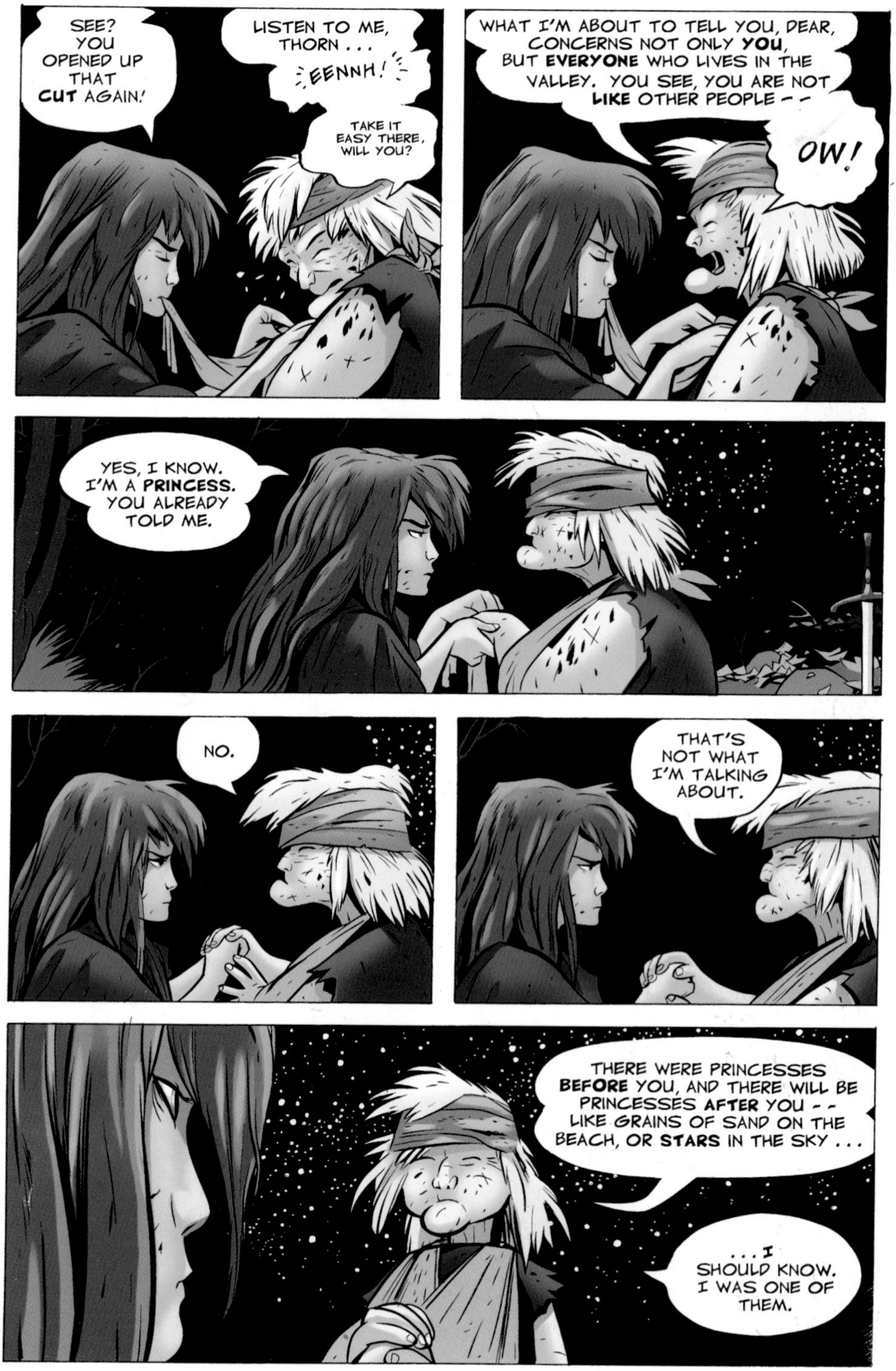
SEE? YOU OPENED UP THAT CUT AGAIN!
LISTEN TO ME, THORN . . .
EENNH!
TAKE IT EASY THERE, WILL YOU?
WHAT I'M ABOUT TO TELL YOU, DEAR, CONCERNS NOT ONLY YOU, BUT EVERYONE WHO LIVES IN THE VALLEY. YOU SEE, YOU ARE NOT LIKE OTHER PEOPLE - -
OW!
YES, I KNOW. I'M A PRINCESS. YOU ALREADY TOLD ME.
NO.
THAT'S NOT WHAT I'M TALKING ABOUT.
THERE WERE PRINCESSES BEFORE YOU, AND THERE WILL BE PRINCESSES AFTER YOU - - LIKE GRAINS OF SAND ON THE BEACH, OR STARS IN THE SKY . . .
. . . I SHOULD KNOW. I WAS ONE OF THEM.

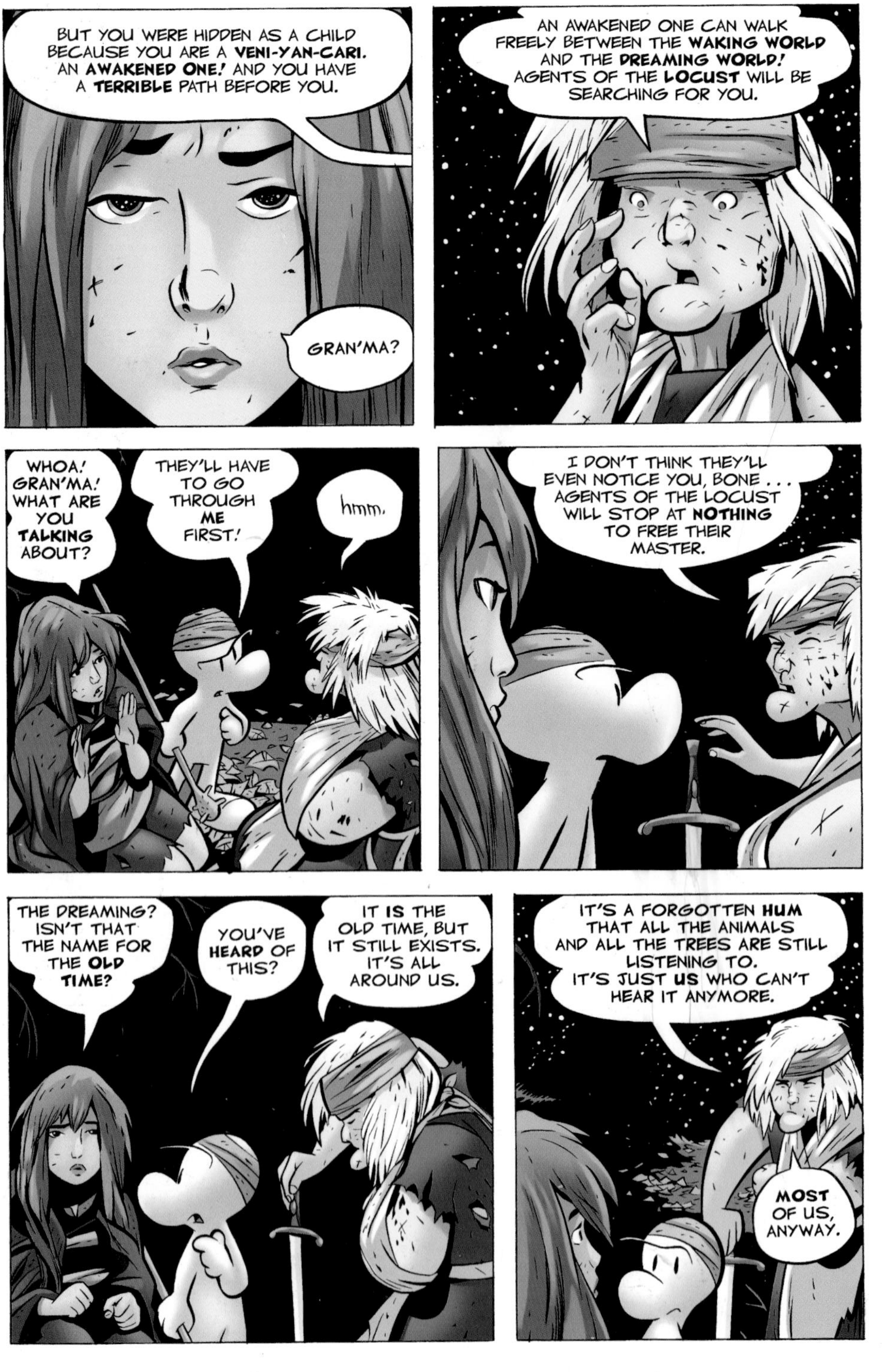
BUT YOU WERE HIDDEN AS A CHILD BECAUSE YOU ARE A **VENI-YAN-CARI.** AN **AWAKENED ONE!** AND YOU HAVE A **TERRIBLE** PATH BEFORE YOU.
GRAN'MA?
AN AWAKENED ONE CAN WALK FREELY BETWEEN THE **WAKING WORLD** AND THE **DREAMING WORLD!** AGENTS OF THE **LOCUST** WILL BE SEARCHING FOR YOU.
WHOA! GRAN'MA! WHAT ARE YOU **TALKING** ABOUT?
THEY'LL HAVE TO GO THROUGH **ME** FIRST!
hmm.
I DON'T THINK THEY'LL EVEN NOTICE YOU, BONE . . . AGENTS OF THE LOCUST WILL STOP AT **NOTHING** TO FREE THEIR MASTER.
THE DREAMING? ISN'T THAT THE NAME FOR THE **OLD TIME?**
YOU'VE **HEARD** OF THIS?
IT **IS** THE OLD TIME, BUT IT STILL EXISTS. IT'S ALL AROUND US.
IT'S A FORGOTTEN **HUM** THAT ALL THE ANIMALS AND ALL THE TREES ARE STILL LISTENING TO. IT'S JUST **US** WHO CAN'T HEAR IT ANYMORE.
MOST OF US, ANYWAY.

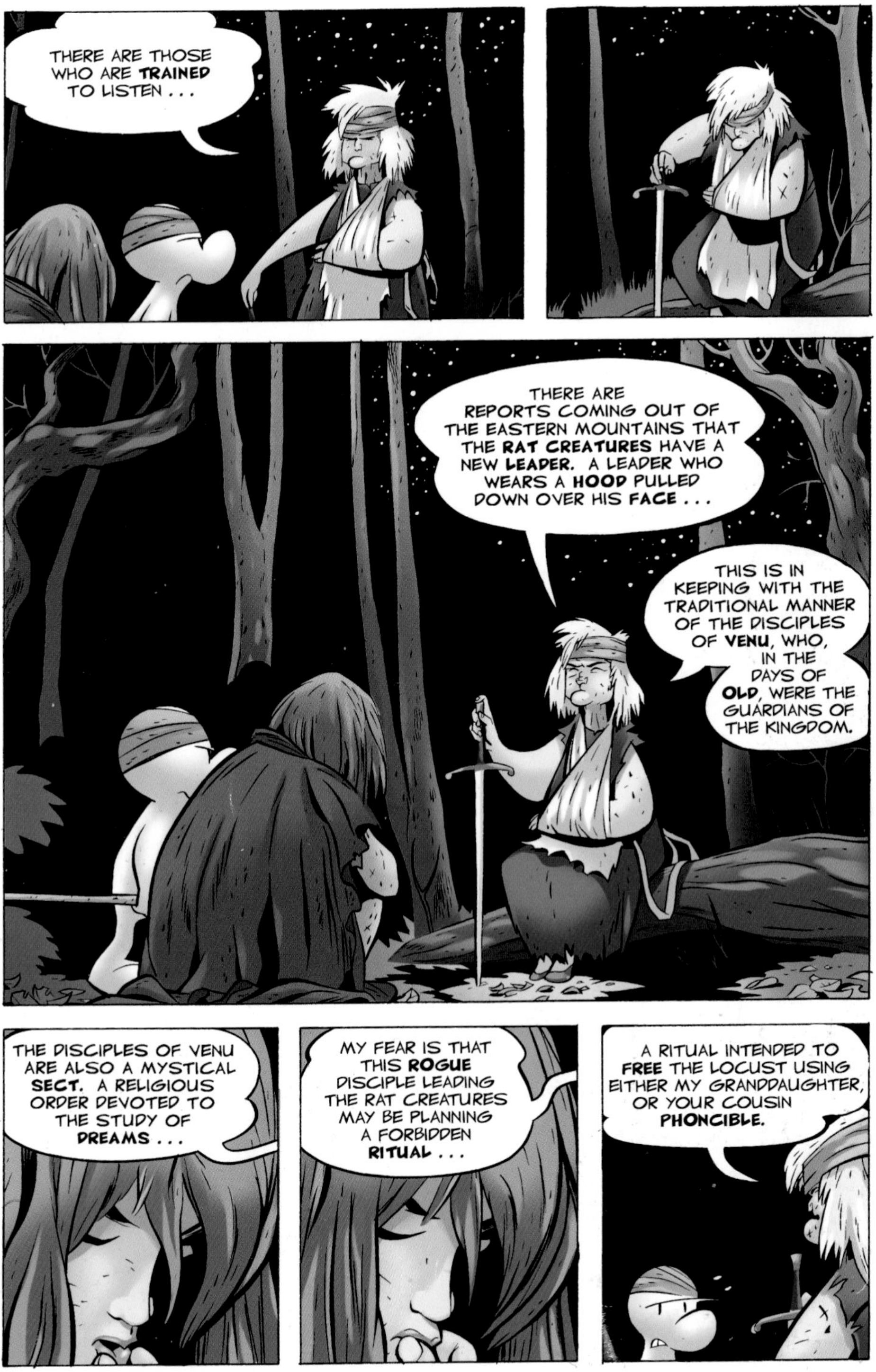
THERE ARE THOSE WHO ARE TRAINED TO LISTEN . . .
THERE ARE REPORTS COMING OUT OF THE EASTERN MOUNTAINS THAT THE RAT CREATURES HAVE A NEW LEADER. A LEADER WHO WEARS A HOOD PULLED DOWN OVER HIS FACE . . .
THIS IS IN KEEPING WITH THE TRADITIONAL MANNER OF THE DISCIPLES OF VENU, WHO, IN THE DAYS OF OLD, WERE THE GUARDIANS OF THE KINGDOM.
THE DISCIPLES OF VENU ARE ALSO A MYSTICAL SECT. A RELIGIOUS ORDER DEVOTED TO THE STUDY OF DREAMS . . .
MY FEAR IS THAT THIS ROGUE DISCIPLE LEADING THE RAT CREATURES MAY BE PLANNING A FORBIDDEN RITUAL . . .
A RITUAL INTENDED TO FREE THE LOCUST USING EITHER MY GRANDDAUGHTER, OR YOUR COUSIN PHONCIBLE.

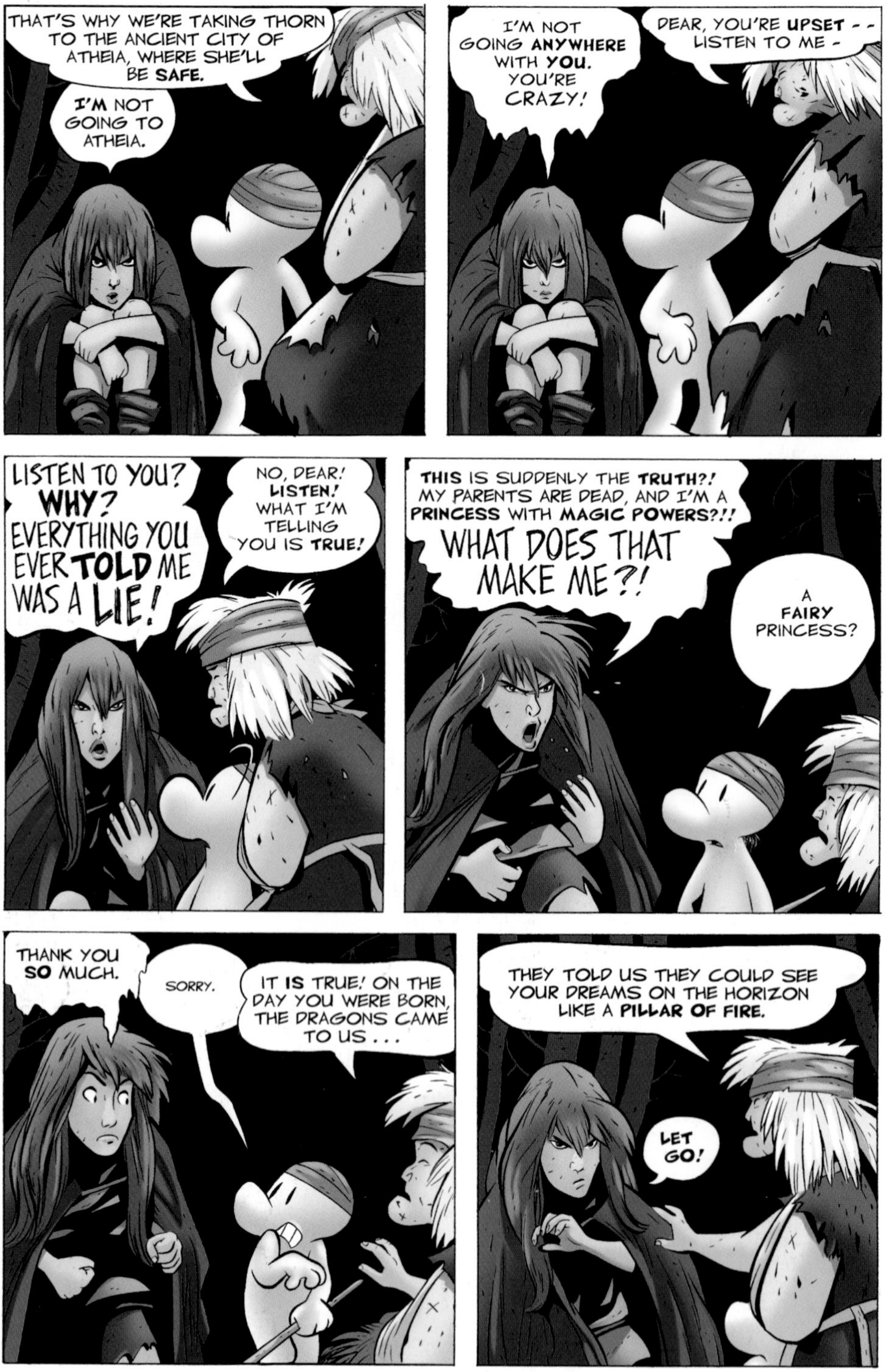
THAT'S WHY WE'RE TAKING THORN TO THE ANCIENT CITY OF ATHEIA, WHERE SHE'LL BE SAFE.
I'M NOT GOING TO ATHEIA.
I'M NOT GOING ANYWHERE WITH YOU. YOU'RE CRAZY!
DEAR, YOU'RE UPSET -- LISTEN TO ME -
LISTEN TO YOU? WHY? EVERYTHING YOU EVER TOLD ME WAS A LIE!
NO, DEAR! LISTEN! WHAT I'M TELLING YOU IS TRUE!
THIS IS SUDDENLY THE TRUTH?! MY PARENTS ARE DEAD, AND I'M A PRINCESS WITH MAGIC POWERS?!! WHAT DOES THAT MAKE ME?!
A FAIRY PRINCESS?
THANK YOU SO MUCH.
SORRY.
IT IS TRUE! ON THE DAY YOU WERE BORN, THE DRAGONS CAME TO US . . .
THEY TOLD US THEY COULD SEE YOUR DREAMS ON THE HORIZON LIKE A PILLAR OF FIRE.
LET GO!

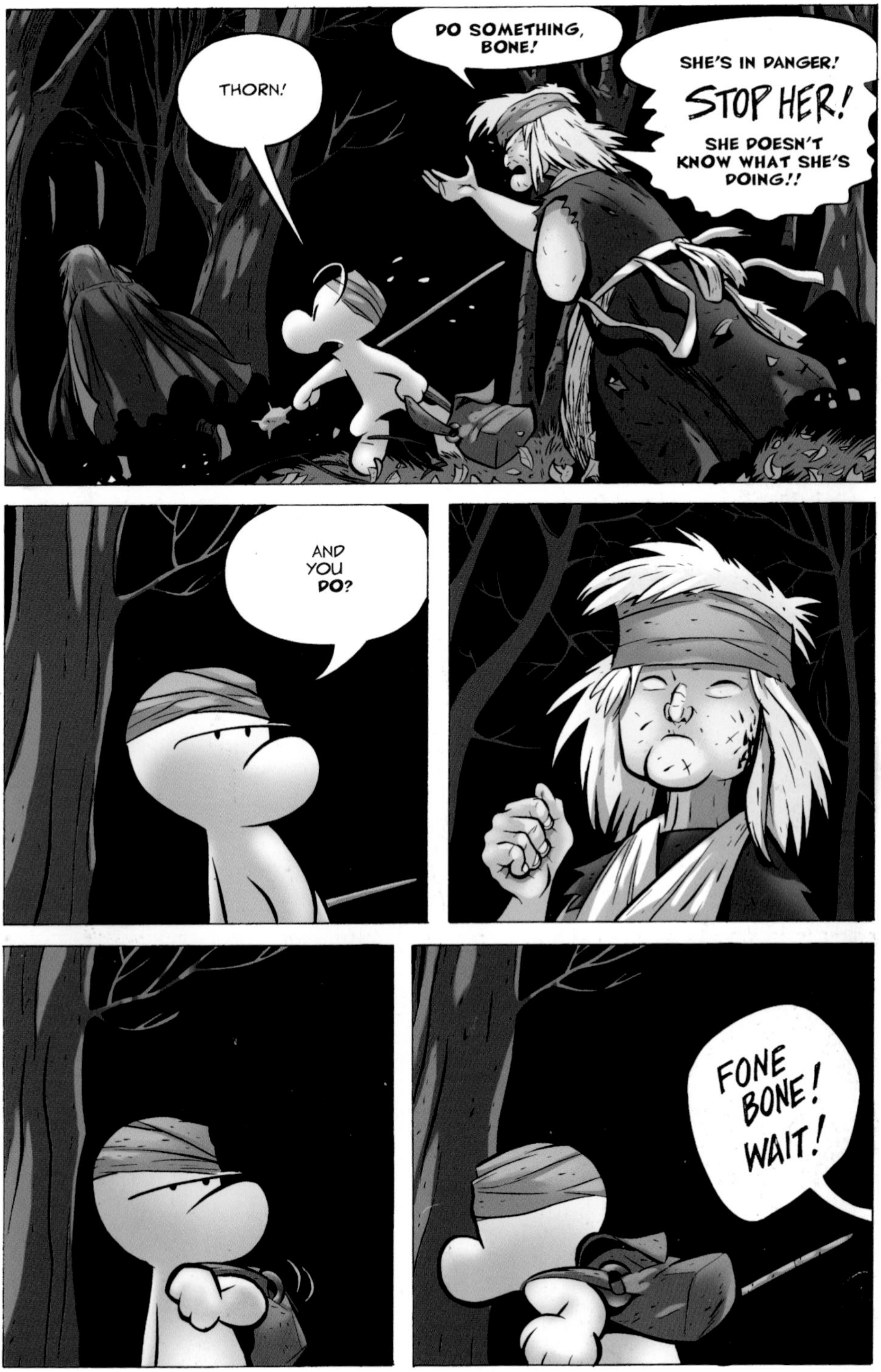
THORN!
DO SOMETHING, BONE!
SHE'S IN DANGER!
STOP HER!
SHE DOESN'T KNOW WHAT SHE'S DOING!!
AND YOU DO?
FONE BONE! WAIT!

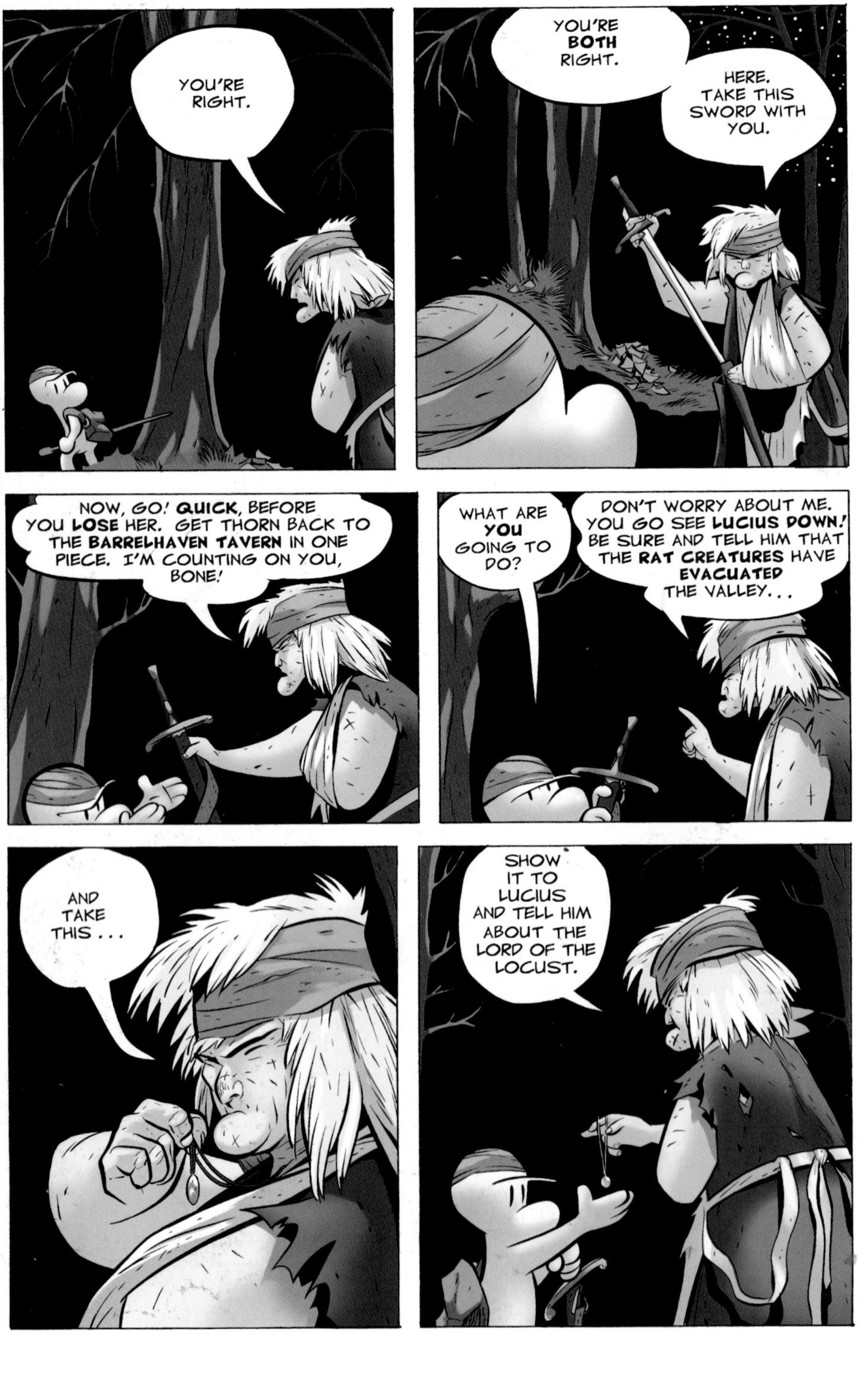
YOU'RE RIGHT.
YOU'RE **BOTH** RIGHT.
HERE. TAKE THIS SWORD WITH YOU.
NOW, GO! **QUICK**, BEFORE YOU **LOSE** HER. GET THORN BACK TO THE **BARRELHAVEN TAVERN** IN ONE PIECE. I'M COUNTING ON YOU, BONE!
WHAT ARE **YOU** GOING TO DO?
DON'T WORRY ABOUT ME. YOU GO SEE **LUCIUS DOWN!** BE SURE AND TELL HIM THAT THE **RAT CREATURES** HAVE **EVACUATED** THE VALLEY...
AND TAKE THIS...
SHOW IT TO LUCIUS AND TELL HIM ABOUT THE LORD OF THE LOCUST.

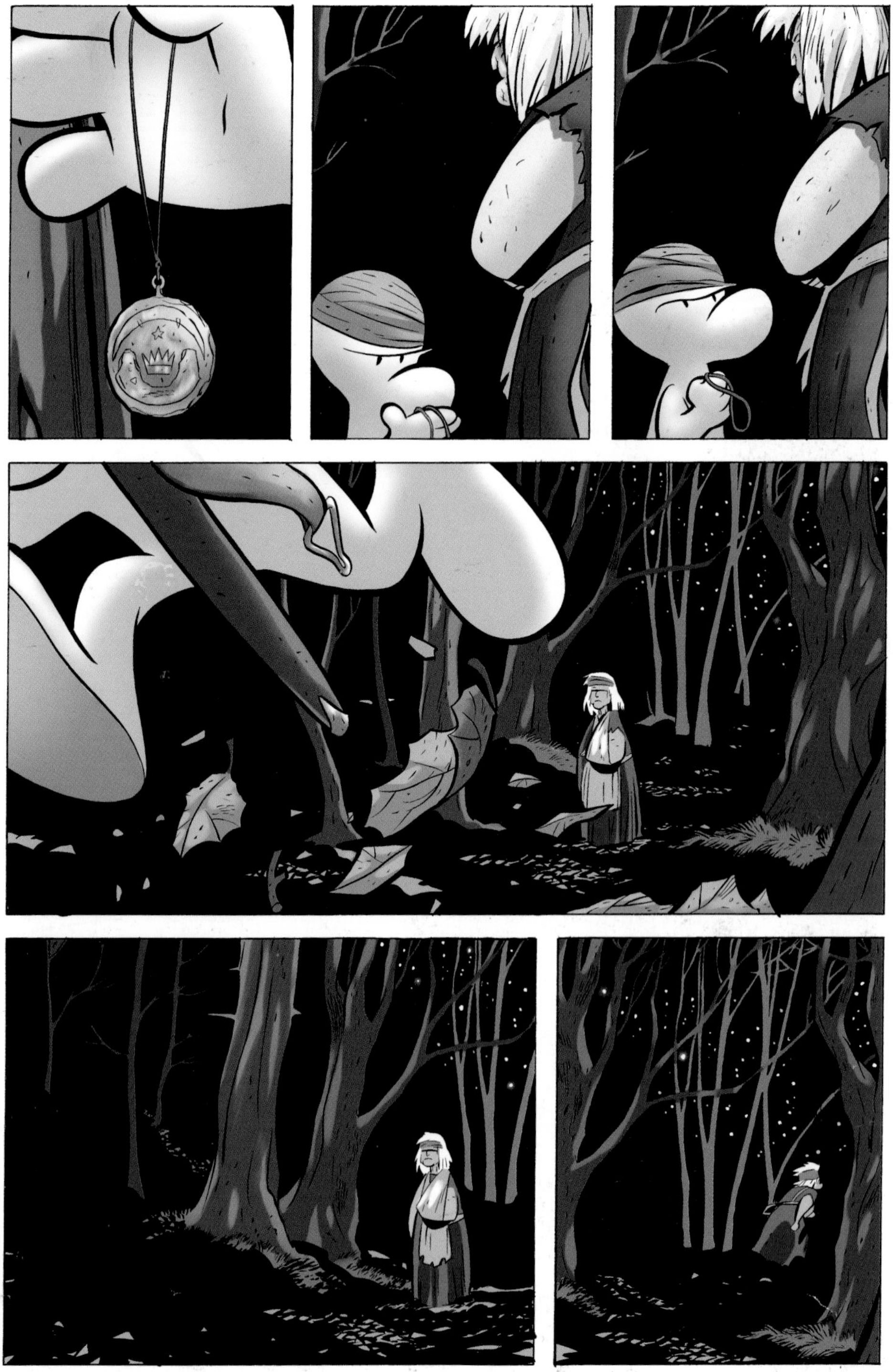

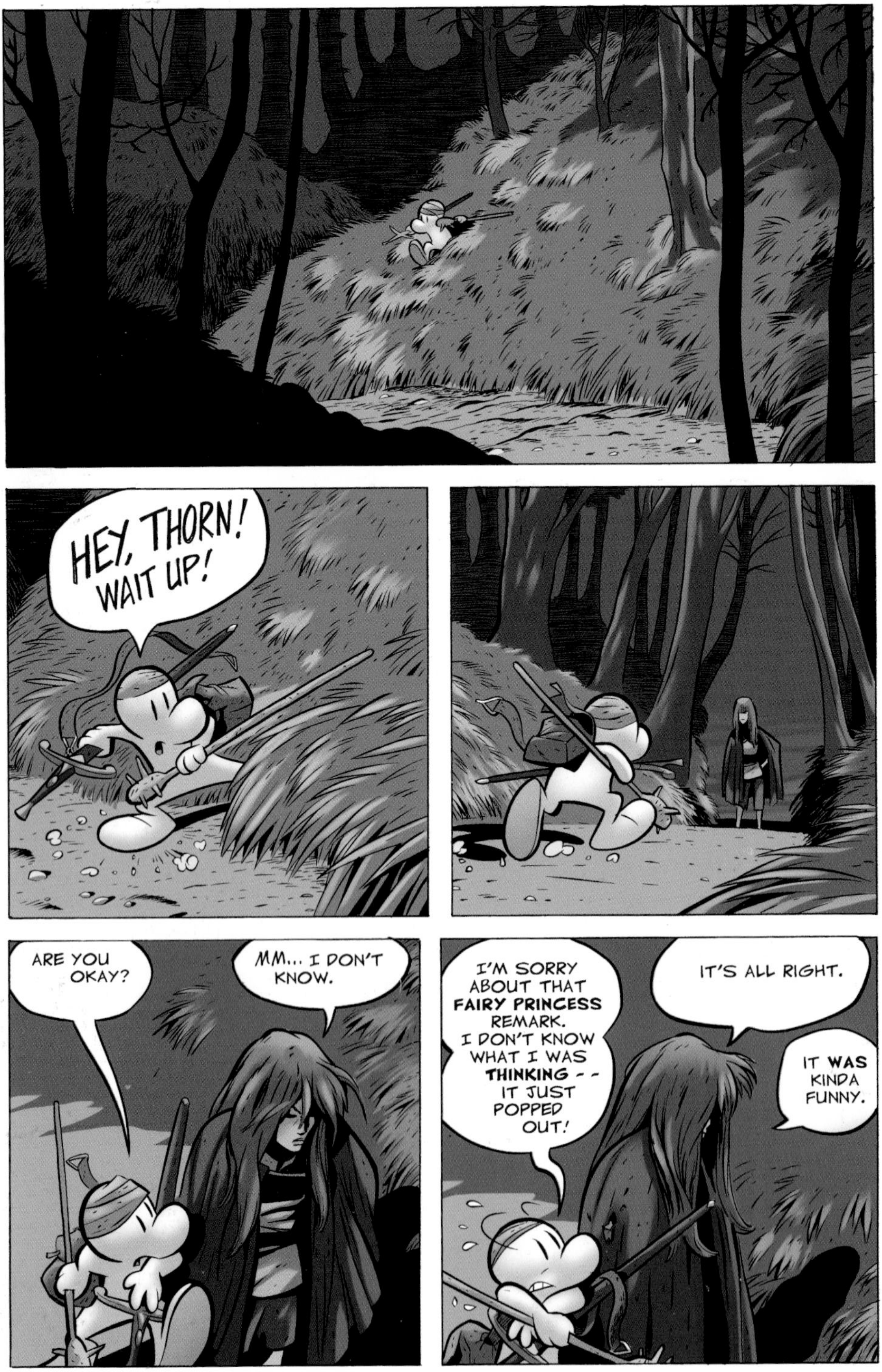
HEY, THORN! WAIT UP!
ARE YOU OKAY?
MM... I DON'T KNOW.
I'M SORRY ABOUT THAT FAIRY PRINCESS REMARK. I DON'T KNOW WHAT I WAS THINKING -- IT JUST POPPED OUT!
IT'S ALL RIGHT.
IT WAS KINDA FUNNY.

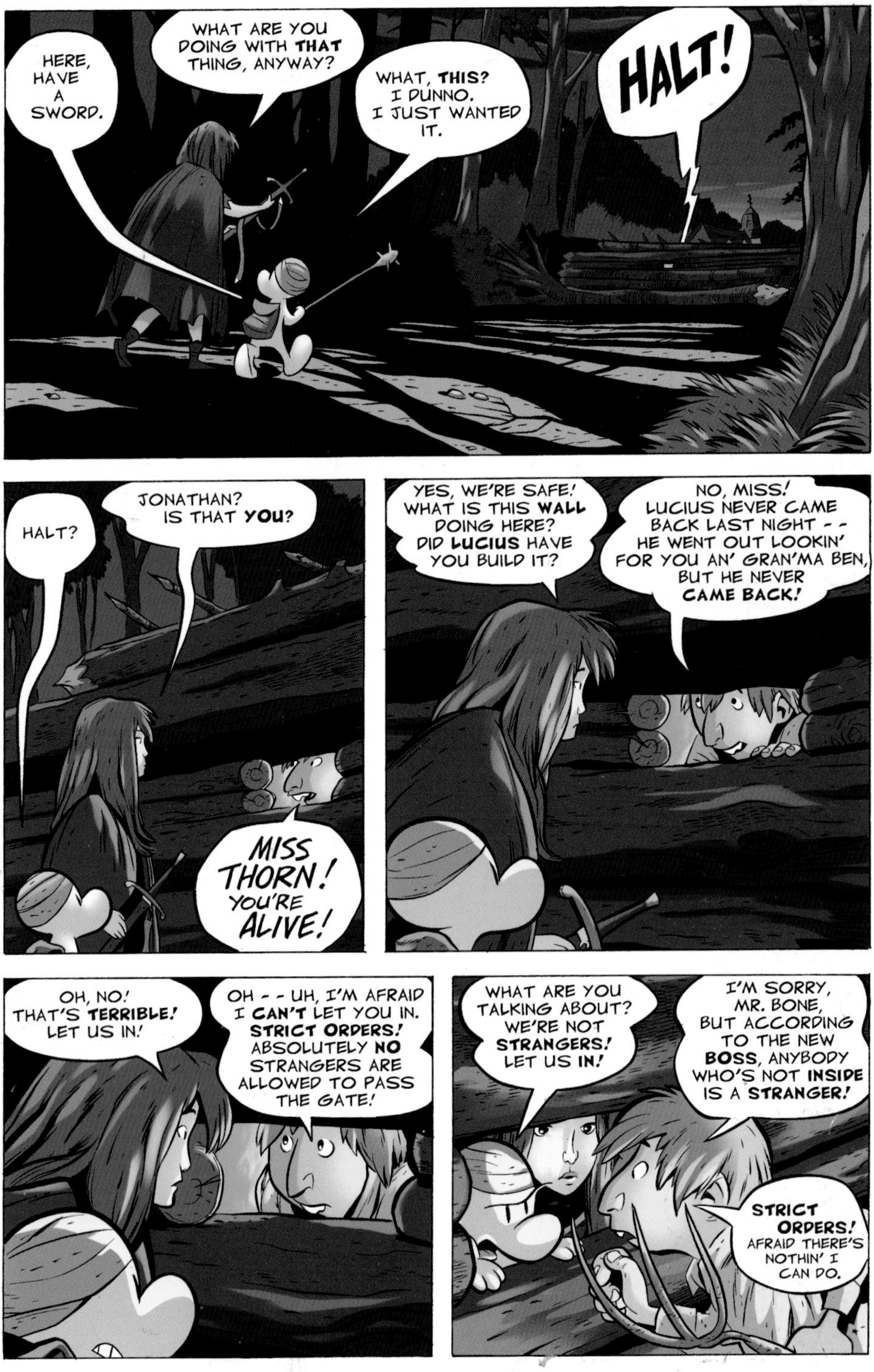
HERE, HAVE A SWORD.
WHAT ARE YOU DOING WITH **THAT** THING, ANYWAY?
WHAT, **THIS?** I DUNNO. I JUST WANTED IT.
HALT!
HALT?
JONATHAN? IS THAT **YOU?**
MISS THORN! YOU'RE ALIVE!
YES, WE'RE SAFE! WHAT IS THIS **WALL** DOING HERE? DID **LUCIUS** HAVE YOU BUILD IT?
NO, MISS! LUCIUS NEVER CAME BACK LAST NIGHT -- HE WENT OUT LOOKIN' FOR YOU AN' GRAN'MA BEN, BUT HE NEVER **CAME BACK!**
OH, NO! THAT'S **TERRIBLE!** LET US IN!
OH -- UH, I'M AFRAID I **CAN'T** LET YOU IN. **STRICT ORDERS!** ABSOLUTELY **NO** STRANGERS ARE ALLOWED TO PASS THE GATE!
WHAT ARE YOU TALKING ABOUT? WE'RE NOT **STRANGERS!** LET US **IN!**
I'M SORRY, MR. BONE, BUT ACCORDING TO THE NEW **BOSS**, ANYBODY WHO'S NOT **INSIDE** IS A **STRANGER!**
STRICT ORDERS! AFRAID THERE'S NOTHIN' I CAN DO.

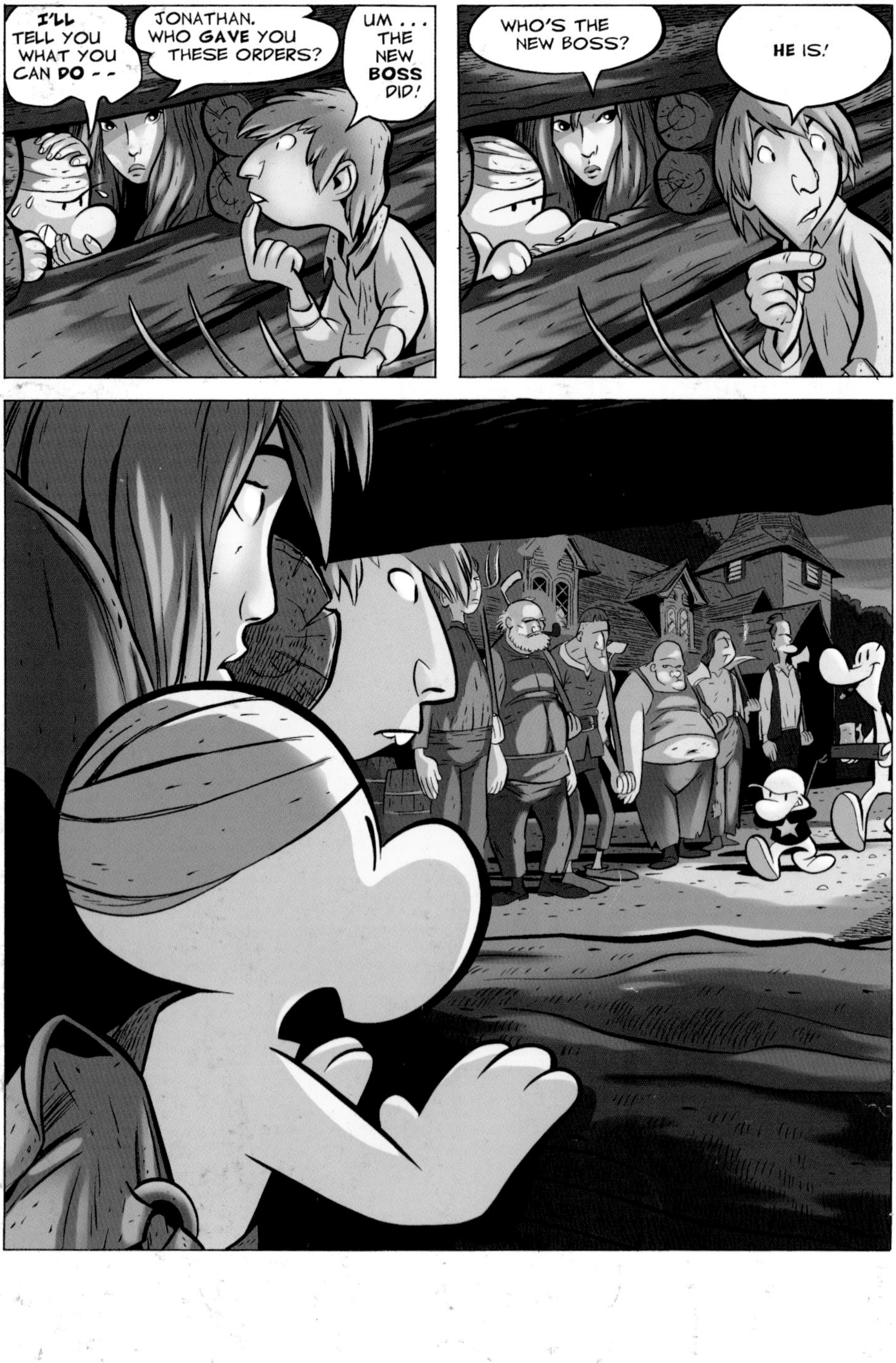
I'LL TELL YOU WHAT YOU CAN **DO** - -
JONATHAN. WHO **GAVE** YOU THESE ORDERS?
UM . . . THE NEW **BOSS** DID!
WHO'S THE NEW BOSS?
HE IS!

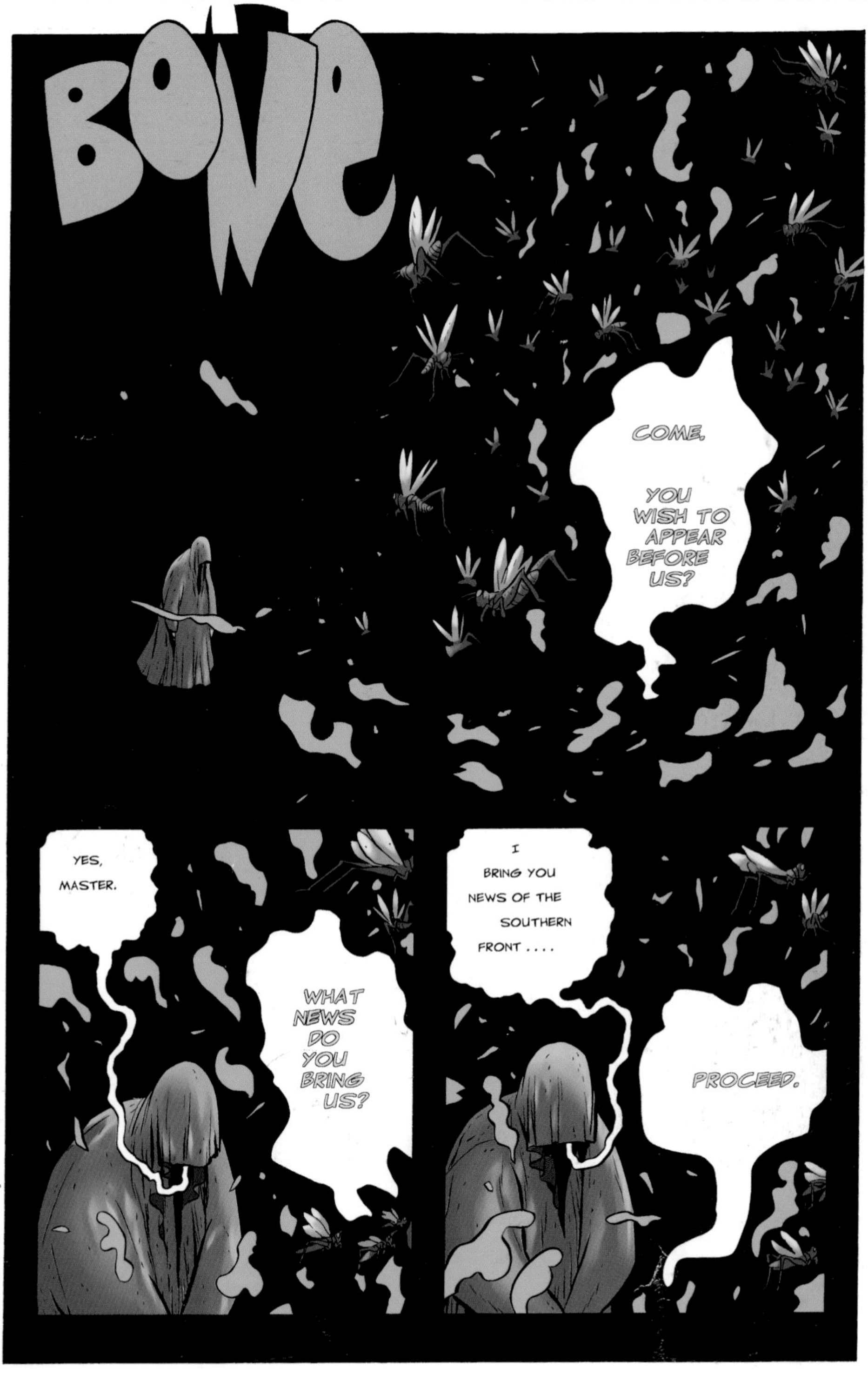
BONE
COME.
YOU WISH TO APPEAR BEFORE US?
YES, MASTER.
WHAT NEWS DO YOU BRING US?
I BRING YOU NEWS OF THE SOUTHERN FRONT . . . .
PROCEED.

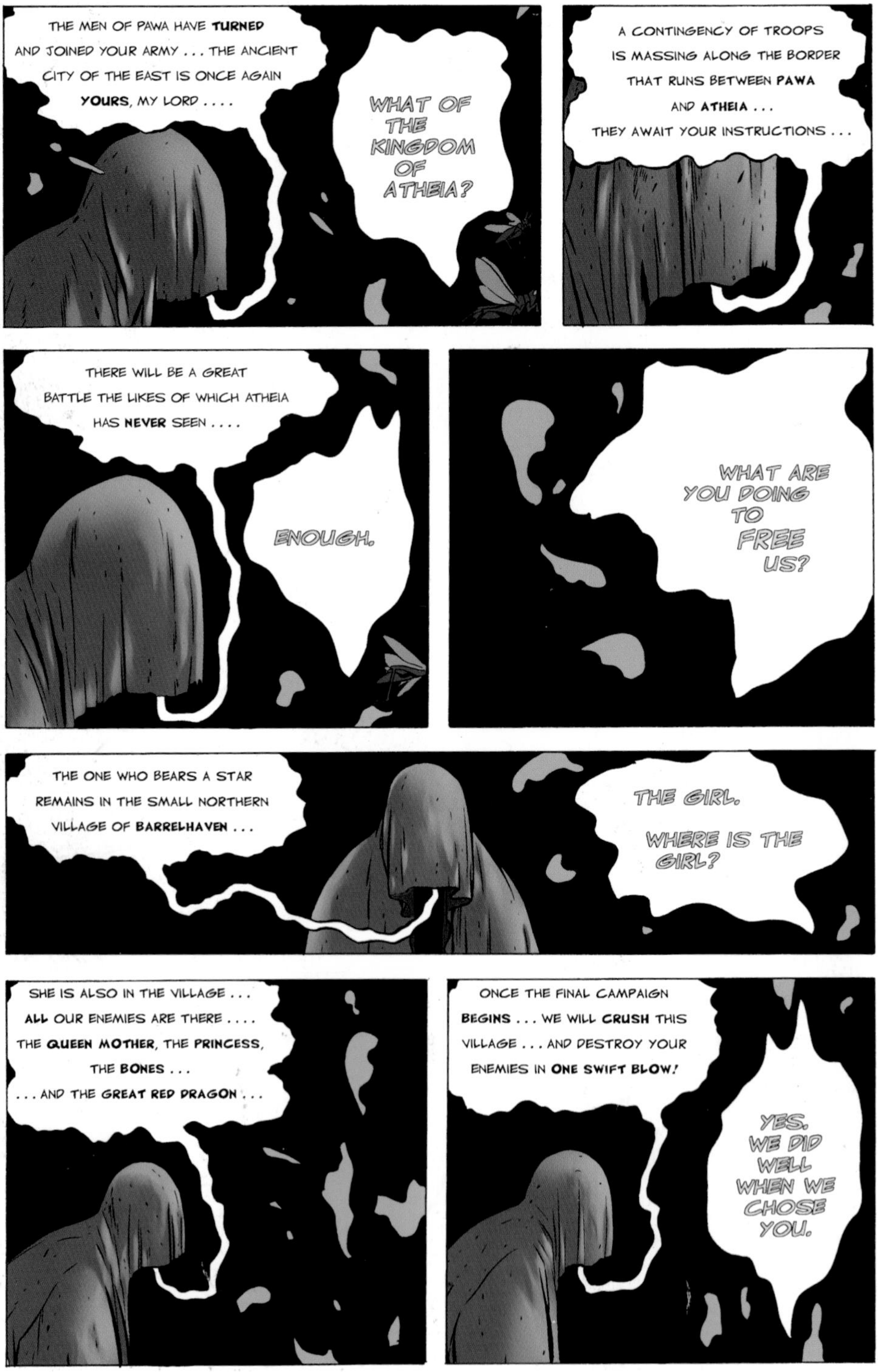
THE MEN OF PAWA HAVE TURNED AND JOINED YOUR ARMY . . . THE ANCIENT CITY OF THE EAST IS ONCE AGAIN YOURS, MY LORD . . . .
WHAT OF THE KINGDOM OF ATHEIA?
A CONTINGENCY OF TROOPS IS MASSING ALONG THE BORDER THAT RUNS BETWEEN PAWA AND ATHEIA . . . THEY AWAIT YOUR INSTRUCTIONS . . .
THERE WILL BE A GREAT BATTLE THE LIKES OF WHICH ATHEIA HAS NEVER SEEN . . . .
ENOUGH.
WHAT ARE YOU DOING TO FREE US?
THE ONE WHO BEARS A STAR REMAINS IN THE SMALL NORTHERN VILLAGE OF BARRELHAVEN . . .
THE GIRL.
WHERE IS THE GIRL?
SHE IS ALSO IN THE VILLAGE . . . ALL OUR ENEMIES ARE THERE . . . . THE QUEEN MOTHER, THE PRINCESS, THE BONES . . . . . . AND THE GREAT RED DRAGON . . .
ONCE THE FINAL CAMPAIGN BEGINS . . . WE WILL CRUSH THIS VILLAGE . . . AND DESTROY YOUR ENEMIES IN ONE SWIFT BLOW!
YES. WE DID WELL WHEN WE CHOSE YOU.

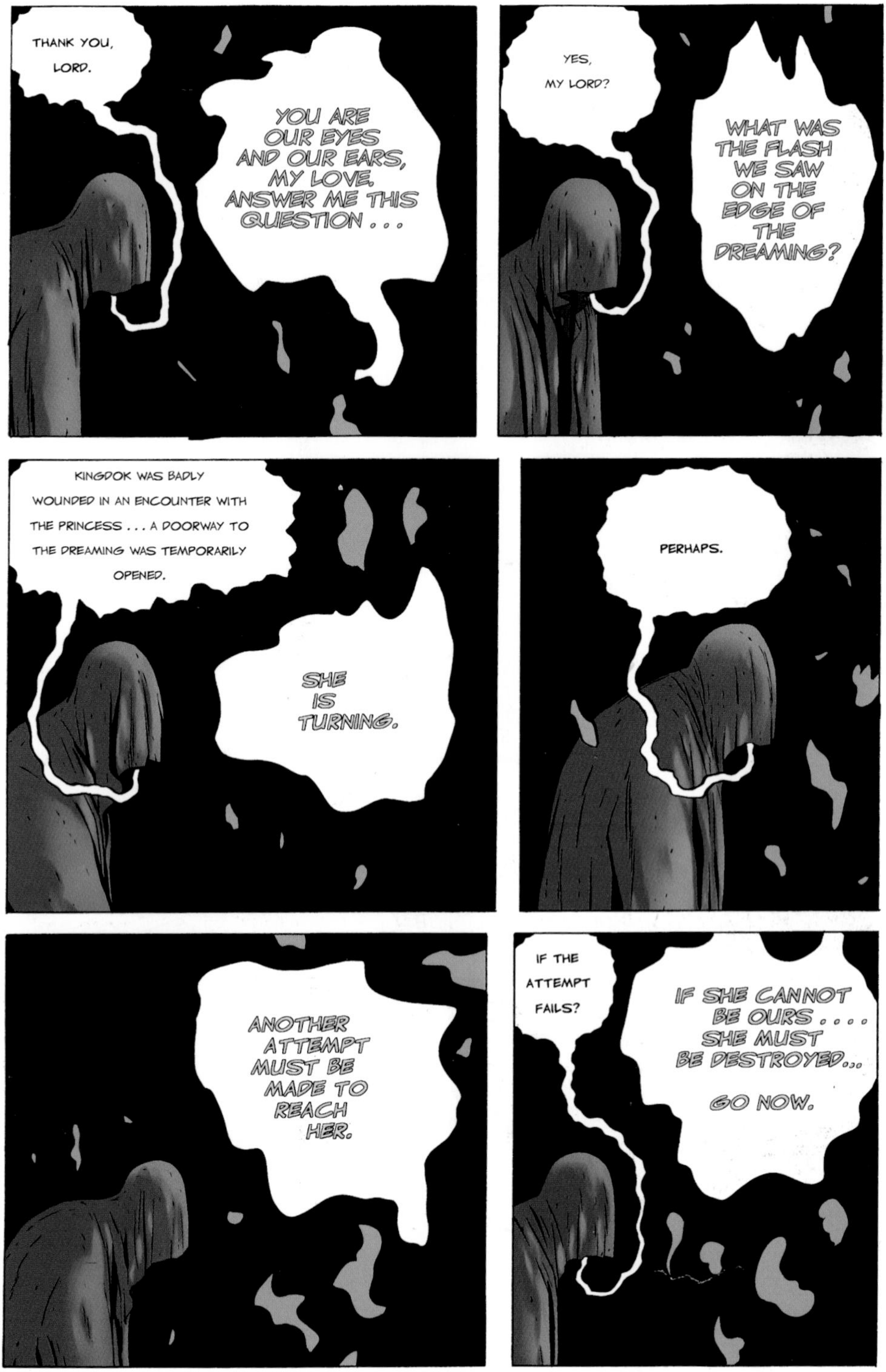
THANK YOU, LORD.
YOU ARE OUR EYES AND OUR EARS, MY LOVE. ANSWER ME THIS QUESTION . . .
YES, MY LORD?
WHAT WAS THE FLASH WE SAW ON THE EDGE OF THE DREAMING?
KINGDOK WAS BADLY WOUNDED IN AN ENCOUNTER WITH THE PRINCESS . . . A DOORWAY TO THE DREAMING WAS TEMPORARILY OPENED.
SHE IS TURNING.
PERHAPS.
ANOTHER ATTEMPT MUST BE MADE TO REACH HER.
IF THE ATTEMPT FAILS?
IF SHE CANNOT BE OURS . . . . SHE MUST BE DESTROYED...
GO NOW.

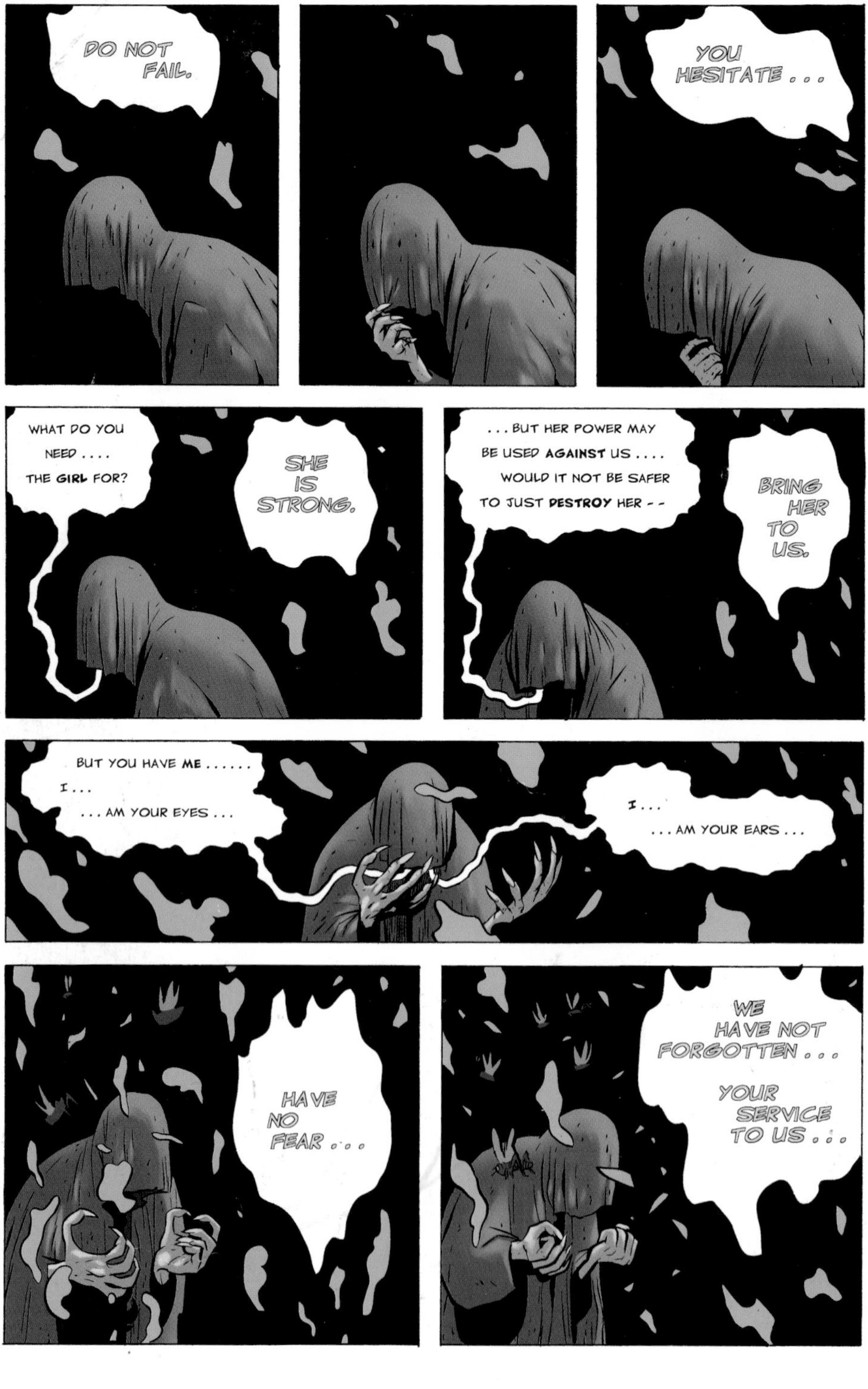
DO NOT FAIL.
YOU HESITATE . . .
WHAT DO YOU NEED . . . . THE GIRL FOR?
SHE IS STRONG.
. . . BUT HER POWER MAY BE USED AGAINST US . . . . WOULD IT NOT BE SAFER TO JUST DESTROY HER - -
BRING HER TO US.
BUT YOU HAVE ME . . . . . . I . . . . . . AM YOUR EYES . . .
I . . . . . . AM YOUR EARS . . .
HAVE NO FEAR . . .
WE HAVE NOT FORGOTTEN . . . YOUR SERVICE TO US . . .

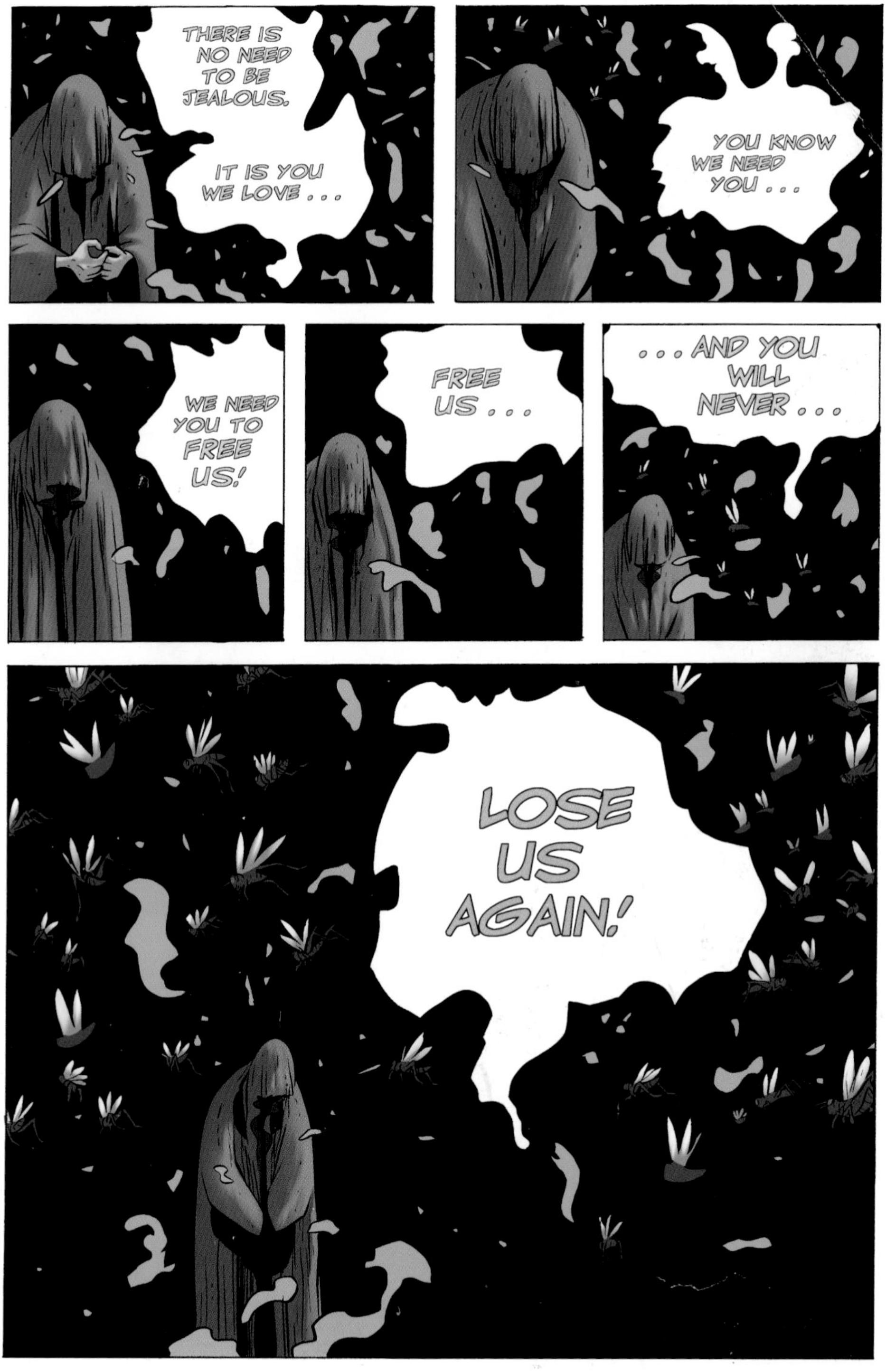
THERE IS NO NEED TO BE JEALOUS.
IT IS YOU WE LOVE . . .
YOU KNOW WE NEED YOU . . .
WE NEED YOU TO FREE US!
FREE US . . .
. . . AND YOU WILL NEVER . . .
LOSE US AGAIN!

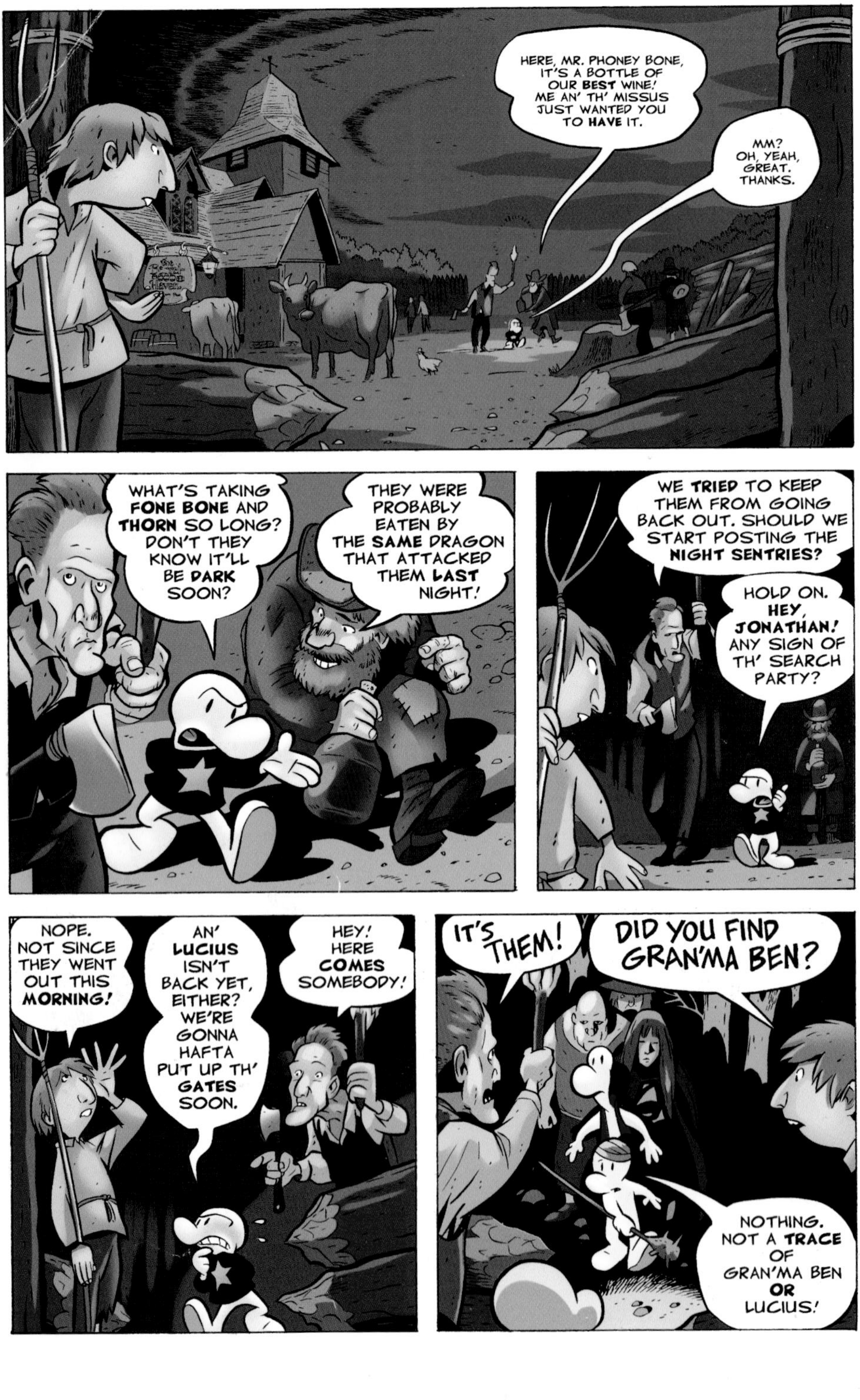
HERE, MR. PHONEY BONE, IT'S A BOTTLE OF OUR BEST WINE! ME AN' TH' MISSUS JUST WANTED YOU TO HAVE IT.
MM? OH, YEAH, GREAT. THANKS.
WHAT'S TAKING FONE BONE AND THORN SO LONG? DON'T THEY KNOW IT'LL BE DARK SOON?
THEY WERE PROBABLY EATEN BY THE SAME DRAGON THAT ATTACKED THEM LAST NIGHT!
WE TRIED TO KEEP THEM FROM GOING BACK OUT. SHOULD WE START POSTING THE NIGHT SENTRIES?
HOLD ON. HEY, JONATHAN! ANY SIGN OF TH' SEARCH PARTY?
NOPE. NOT SINCE THEY WENT OUT THIS MORNING!
AN' LUCIUS ISN'T BACK YET, EITHER? WE'RE GONNA HAFTA PUT UP TH' GATES SOON.
HEY! HERE COMES SOMEBODY!
IT'S THEM!
DID YOU FIND GRAN'MA BEN?
NOTHING. NOT A TRACE OF GRAN'MA BEN OR LUCIUS!

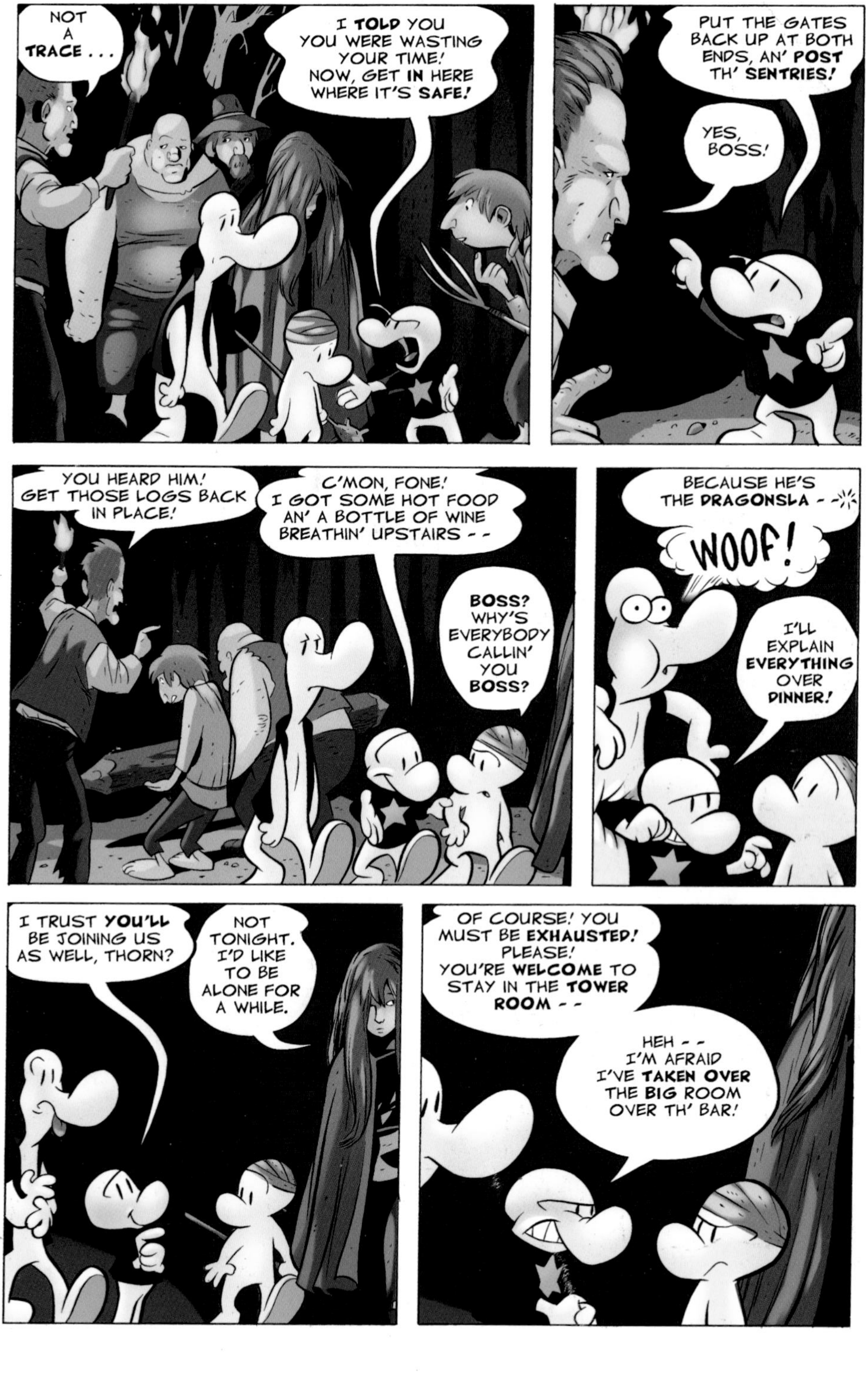
NOT A TRACE . . .
I TOLD YOU YOU WERE WASTING YOUR TIME! NOW, GET IN HERE WHERE IT'S SAFE!
PUT THE GATES BACK UP AT BOTH ENDS, AN' POST TH' SENTRIES!
YES, BOSS!
YOU HEARD HIM! GET THOSE LOGS BACK IN PLACE!
C'MON, FONE! I GOT SOME HOT FOOD AN' A BOTTLE OF WINE BREATHIN' UPSTAIRS - -
BOSS? WHY'S EVERYBODY CALLIN' YOU BOSS?
BECAUSE HE'S THE DRAGONSLA - -
WOOF!
I'LL EXPLAIN EVERYTHING OVER DINNER!
I TRUST YOU'LL BE JOINING US AS WELL, THORN?
NOT TONIGHT. I'D LIKE TO BE ALONE FOR A WHILE.
OF COURSE! YOU MUST BE EXHAUSTED! PLEASE! YOU'RE WELCOME TO STAY IN THE TOWER ROOM - -
HEH - - I'M AFRAID I'VE TAKEN OVER THE BIG ROOM OVER TH' BAR!

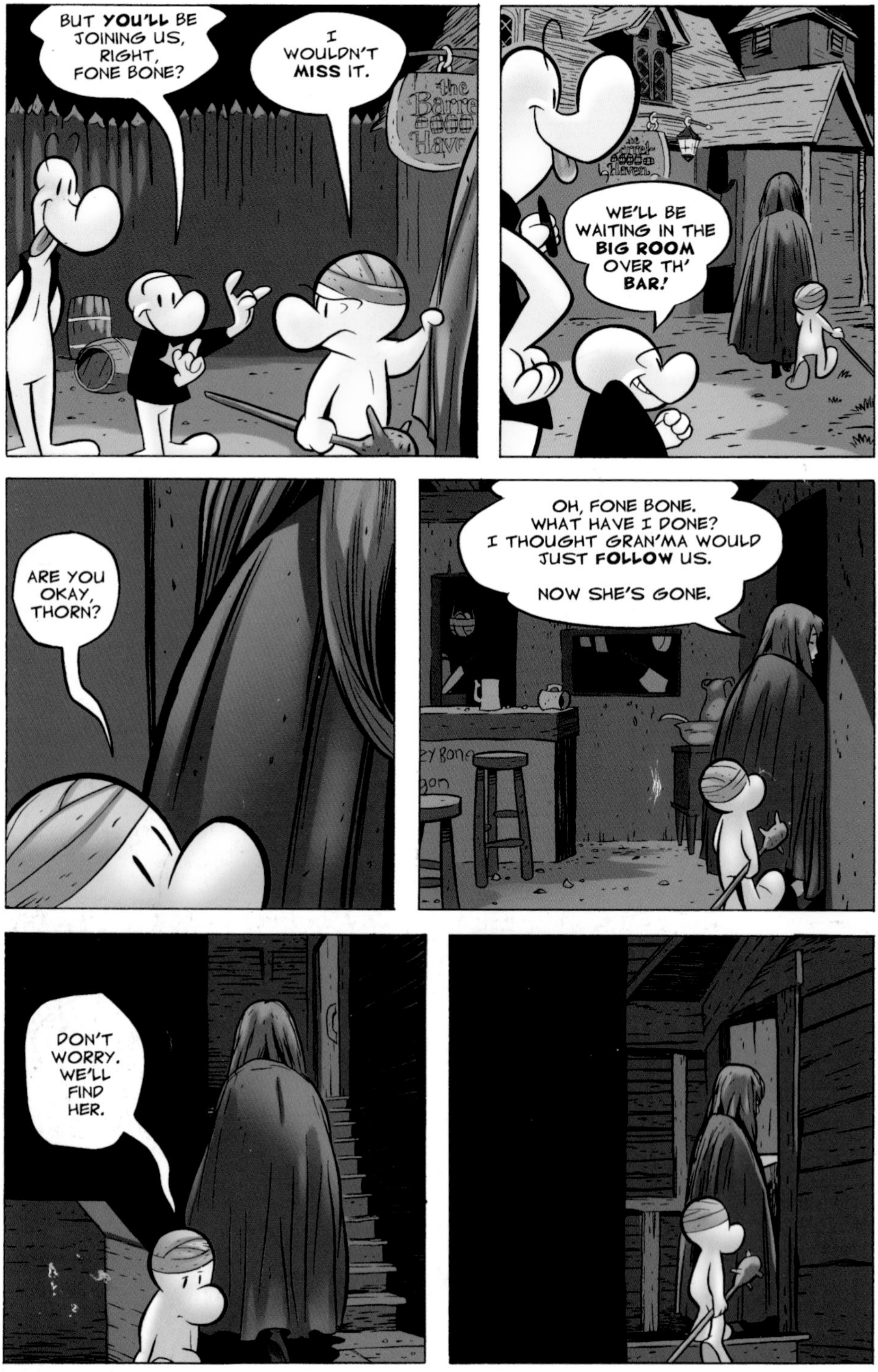
BUT YOU'LL BE JOINING US, RIGHT, FONE BONE?
I WOULDN'T MISS IT.
WE'LL BE WAITING IN THE BIG ROOM OVER TH' BAR!
ARE YOU OKAY, THORN?
OH, FONE BONE. WHAT HAVE I DONE? I THOUGHT GRAN'MA WOULD JUST FOLLOW US.
NOW SHE'S GONE.
DON'T WORRY. WE'LL FIND HER.

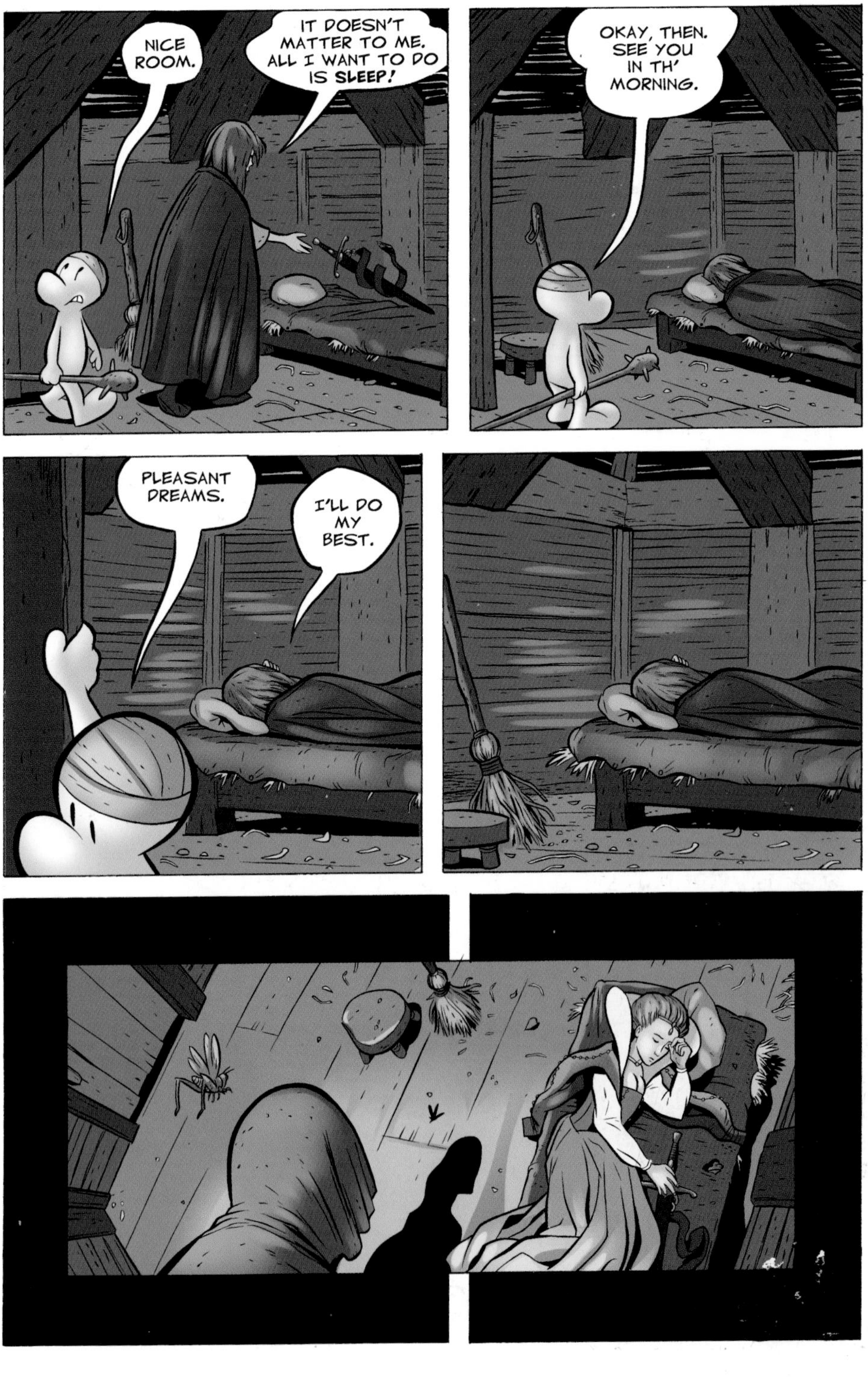
NICE ROOM.
IT DOESN'T MATTER TO ME. ALL I WANT TO DO IS **SLEEP!**
OKAY, THEN. SEE YOU IN TH' MORNING.
PLEASANT DREAMS.
I'LL DO MY BEST.

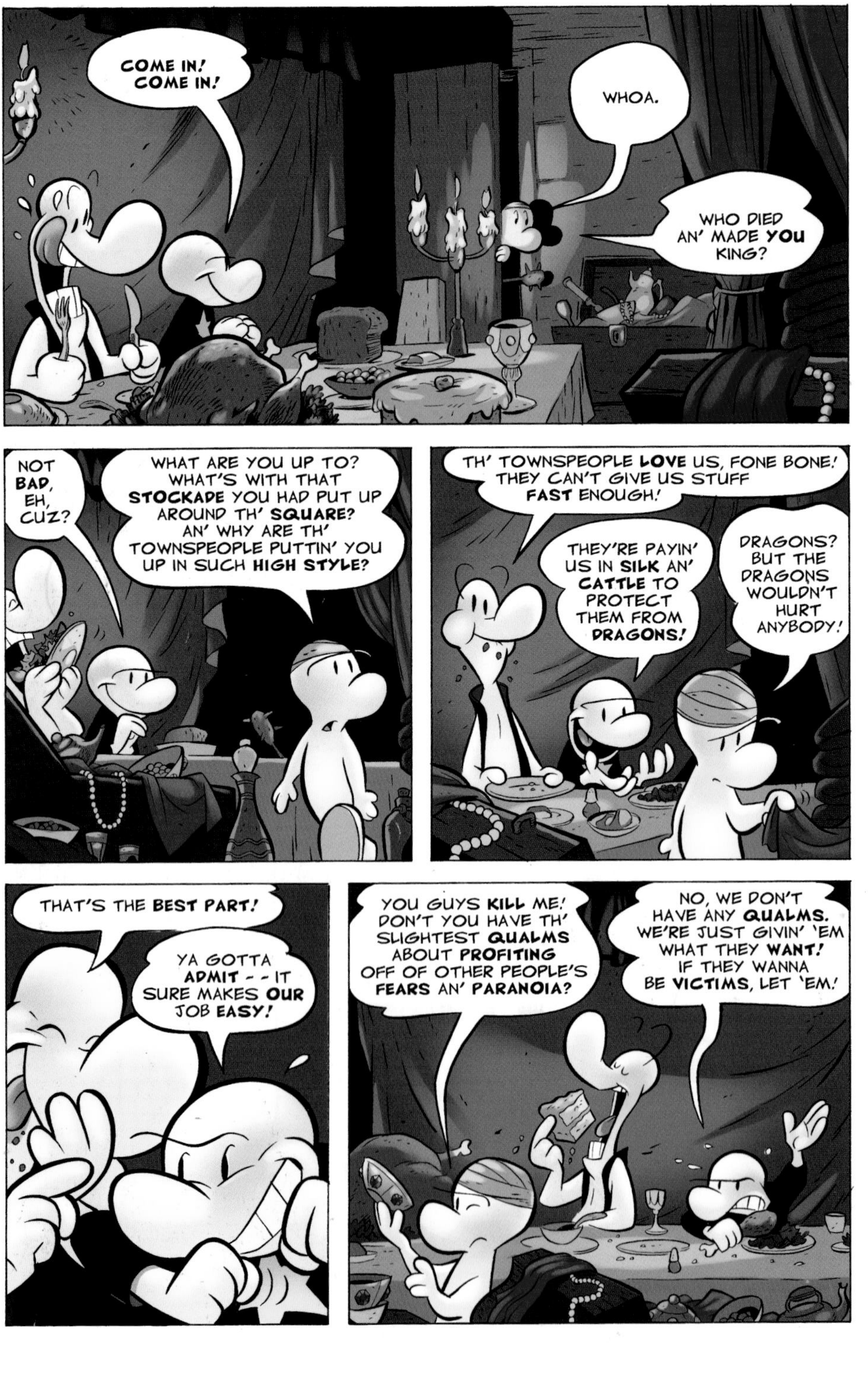
COME IN! COME IN!
WHOA.
WHO DIED AN' MADE YOU KING?
NOT BAD, EH, CUZ?
WHAT ARE YOU UP TO? WHAT'S WITH THAT STOCKADE YOU HAD PUT UP AROUND TH' SQUARE? AN' WHY ARE TH' TOWNSPEOPLE PUTTIN' YOU UP IN SUCH HIGH STYLE?
TH' TOWNSPEOPLE LOVE US, FONE BONE! THEY CAN'T GIVE US STUFF FAST ENOUGH!
THEY'RE PAYIN' US IN SILK AN' CATTLE TO PROTECT THEM FROM DRAGONS!
DRAGONS? BUT THE DRAGONS WOULDN'T HURT ANYBODY!
THAT'S THE BEST PART!
YA GOTTA ADMIT - - IT SURE MAKES OUR JOB EASY!
YOU GUYS KILL ME! DON'T YOU HAVE TH' SLIGHTEST QUALMS ABOUT PROFITING OFF OF OTHER PEOPLE'S FEARS AN' PARANOIA?
NO, WE DON'T HAVE ANY QUALMS. WE'RE JUST GIVIN' 'EM WHAT THEY WANT! IF THEY WANNA BE VICTIMS, LET 'EM!

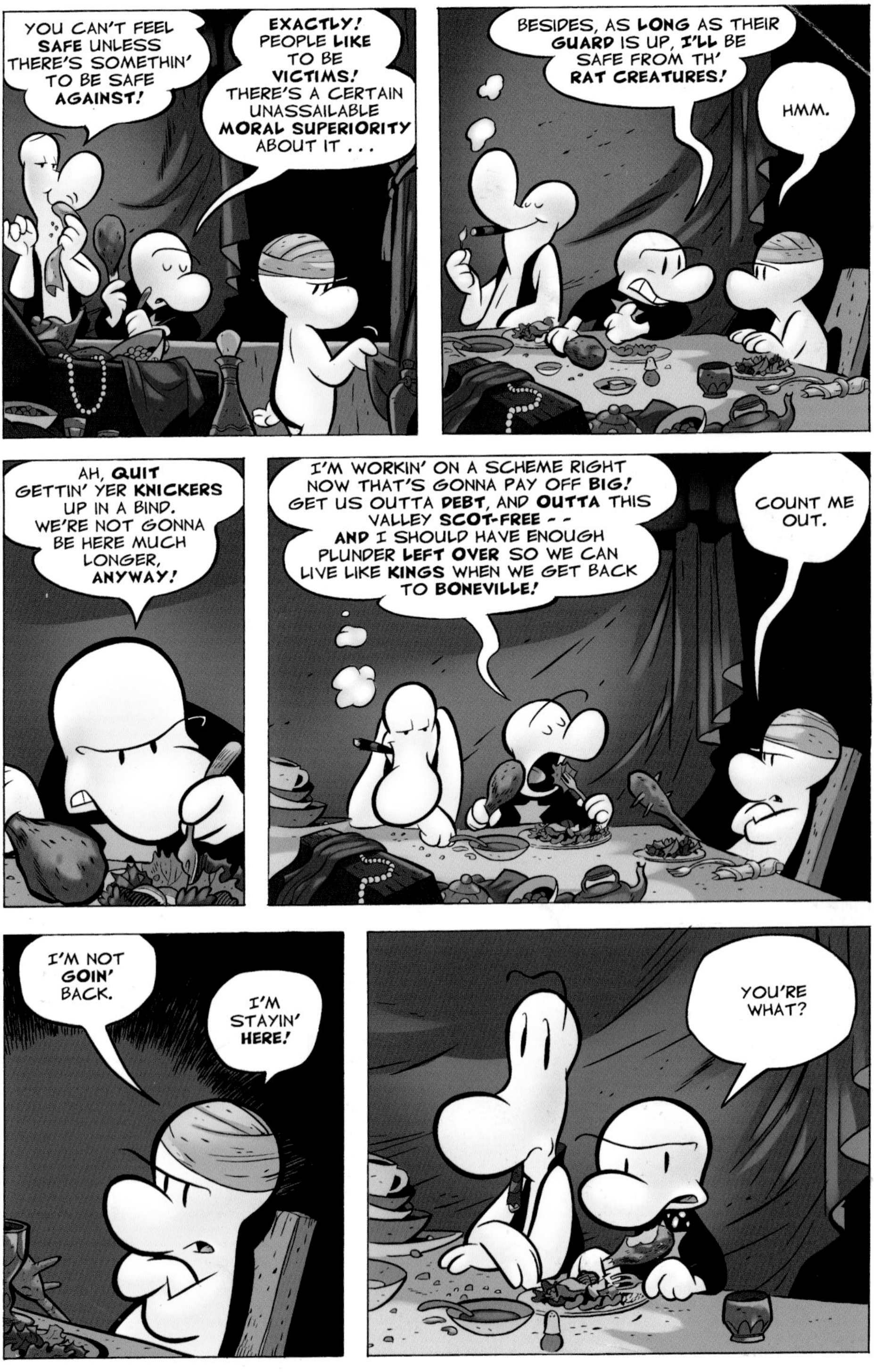
YOU CAN'T FEEL SAFE UNLESS THERE'S SOMETHIN' TO BE SAFE AGAINST!
EXACTLY! PEOPLE LIKE TO BE VICTIMS! THERE'S A CERTAIN UNASSAILABLE MORAL SUPERIORITY ABOUT IT . . .
BESIDES, AS LONG AS THEIR GUARD IS UP, I'LL BE SAFE FROM TH' RAT CREATURES!
HMM.
AH, QUIT GETTIN' YER KNICKERS UP IN A BIND. WE'RE NOT GONNA BE HERE MUCH LONGER, ANYWAY!
I'M WORKIN' ON A SCHEME RIGHT NOW THAT'S GONNA PAY OFF BIG! GET US OUTTA DEBT, AND OUTTA THIS VALLEY SCOT-FREE - - AND I SHOULD HAVE ENOUGH PLUNDER LEFT OVER SO WE CAN LIVE LIKE KINGS WHEN WE GET BACK TO BONEVILLE!
COUNT ME OUT.
I'M NOT GOIN' BACK.
I'M STAYIN' HERE!
YOU'RE WHAT?

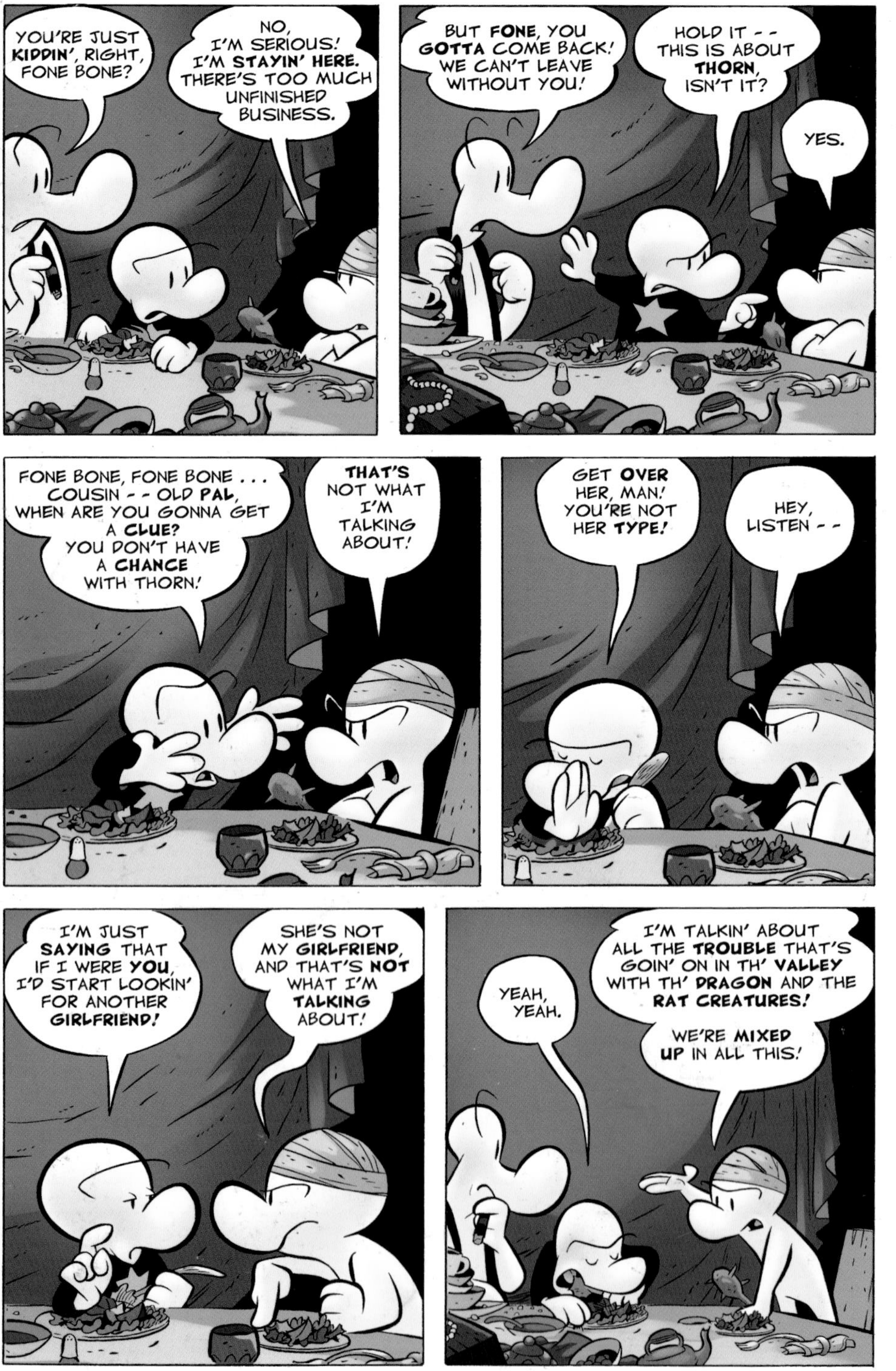
YOU'RE JUST KIDDIN', RIGHT, FONE BONE?
NO, I'M SERIOUS! I'M STAYIN' HERE. THERE'S TOO MUCH UNFINISHED BUSINESS.
BUT FONE, YOU GOTTA COME BACK! WE CAN'T LEAVE WITHOUT YOU!
HOLD IT - - THIS IS ABOUT THORN, ISN'T IT?
YES.
FONE BONE, FONE BONE . . . COUSIN - - OLD PAL, WHEN ARE YOU GONNA GET A CLUE? YOU DON'T HAVE A CHANCE WITH THORN!
THAT'S NOT WHAT I'M TALKING ABOUT!
GET OVER HER, MAN! YOU'RE NOT HER TYPE!
HEY, LISTEN - -
I'M JUST SAYING THAT IF I WERE YOU, I'D START LOOKIN' FOR ANOTHER GIRLFRIEND!
SHE'S NOT MY GIRLFRIEND, AND THAT'S NOT WHAT I'M TALKING ABOUT!
YEAH, YEAH.
I'M TALKIN' ABOUT ALL THE TROUBLE THAT'S GOIN' ON IN TH' VALLEY WITH TH' DRAGON AND THE RAT CREATURES!
WE'RE MIXED UP IN ALL THIS!

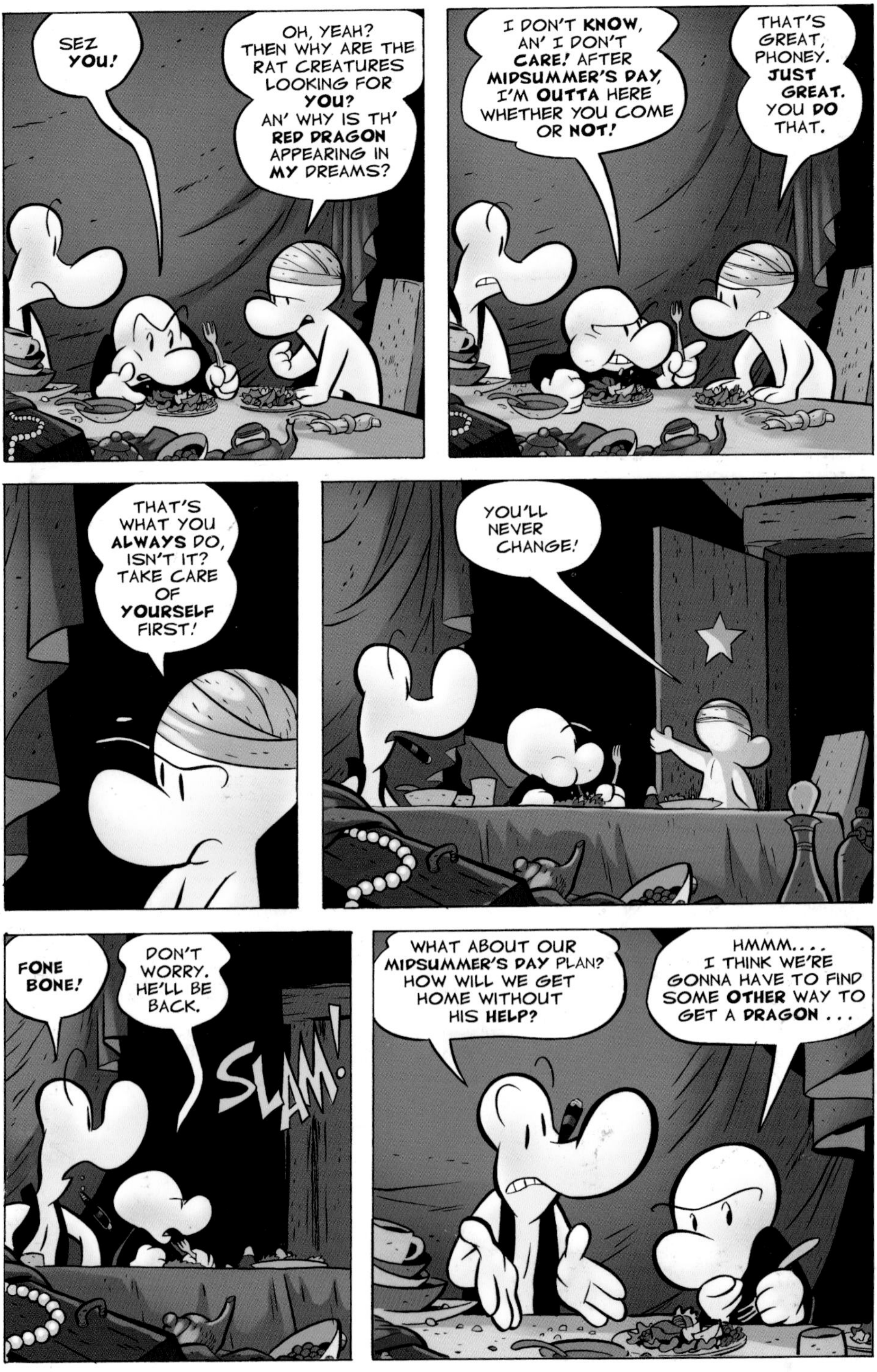
SEZ YOU!
OH, YEAH? THEN WHY ARE THE RAT CREATURES LOOKING FOR YOU? AN' WHY IS TH' RED DRAGON APPEARING IN MY DREAMS?
I DON'T KNOW, AN' I DON'T CARE! AFTER MIDSUMMER'S DAY, I'M OUTTA HERE WHETHER YOU COME OR NOT!
THAT'S GREAT, PHONEY. JUST GREAT. YOU DO THAT.
THAT'S WHAT YOU ALWAYS DO, ISN'T IT? TAKE CARE OF YOURSELF FIRST!
YOU'LL NEVER CHANGE!
FONE BONE!
DON'T WORRY. HE'LL BE BACK.
SLAM!
WHAT ABOUT OUR MIDSUMMER'S DAY PLAN? HOW WILL WE GET HOME WITHOUT HIS HELP?
HMMM. . . . I THINK WE'RE GONNA HAVE TO FIND SOME OTHER WAY TO GET A DRAGON . . .

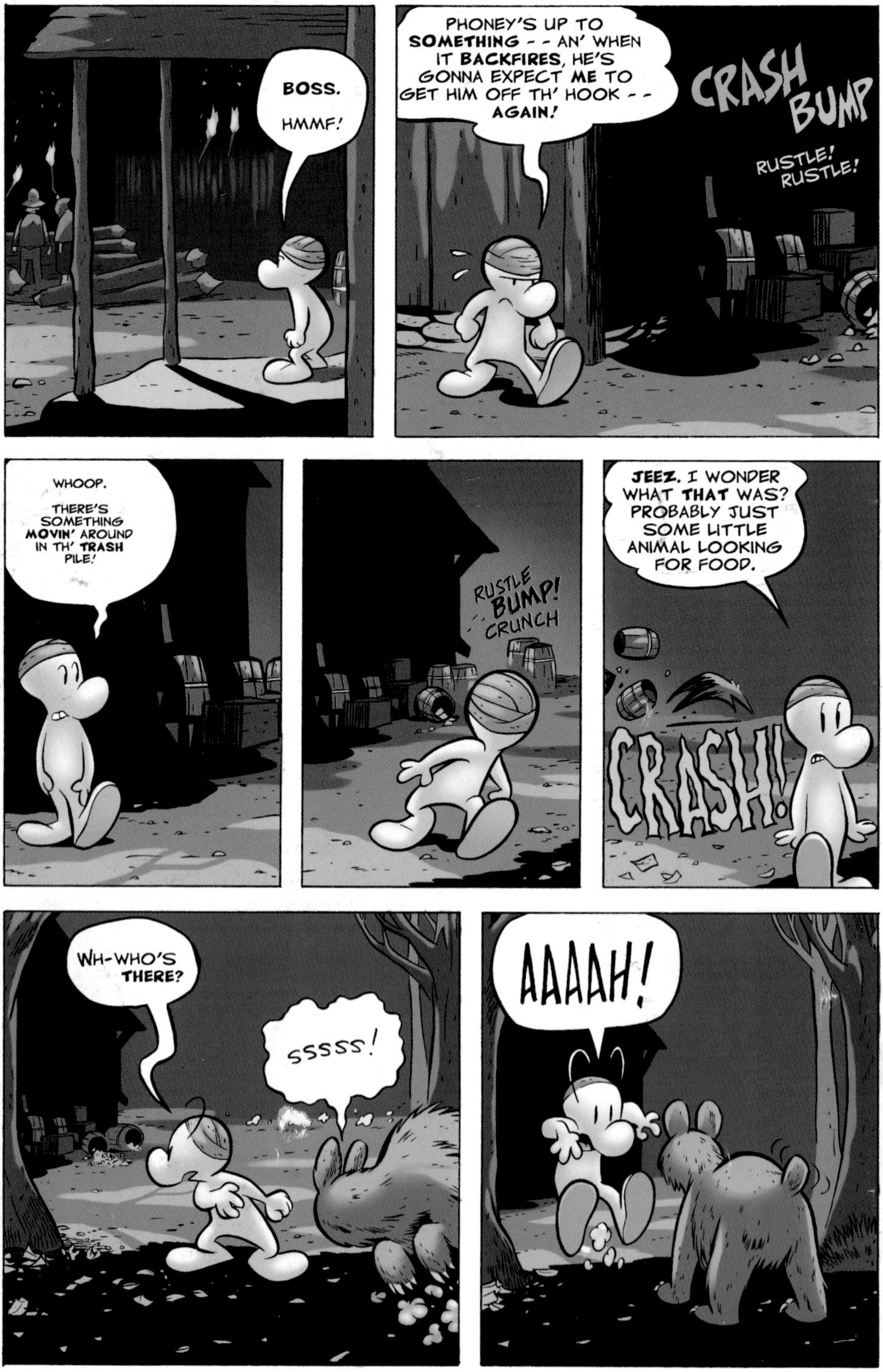
BOSS.
HMMF!
PHONEY'S UP TO SOMETHING - - AN' WHEN IT BACKFIRES, HE'S GONNA EXPECT ME TO GET HIM OFF TH' HOOK - - AGAIN!
CRASH
BUMP
RUSTLE! RUSTLE!
WHOOP.
THERE'S SOMETHING MOVIN' AROUND IN TH' TRASH PILE!
RUSTLE
BUMP!
CRUNCH
JEEZ. I WONDER WHAT THAT WAS? PROBABLY JUST SOME LITTLE ANIMAL LOOKING FOR FOOD.
CRASH!
WH-WHO'S THERE?
SSSSS!
AAAAH!

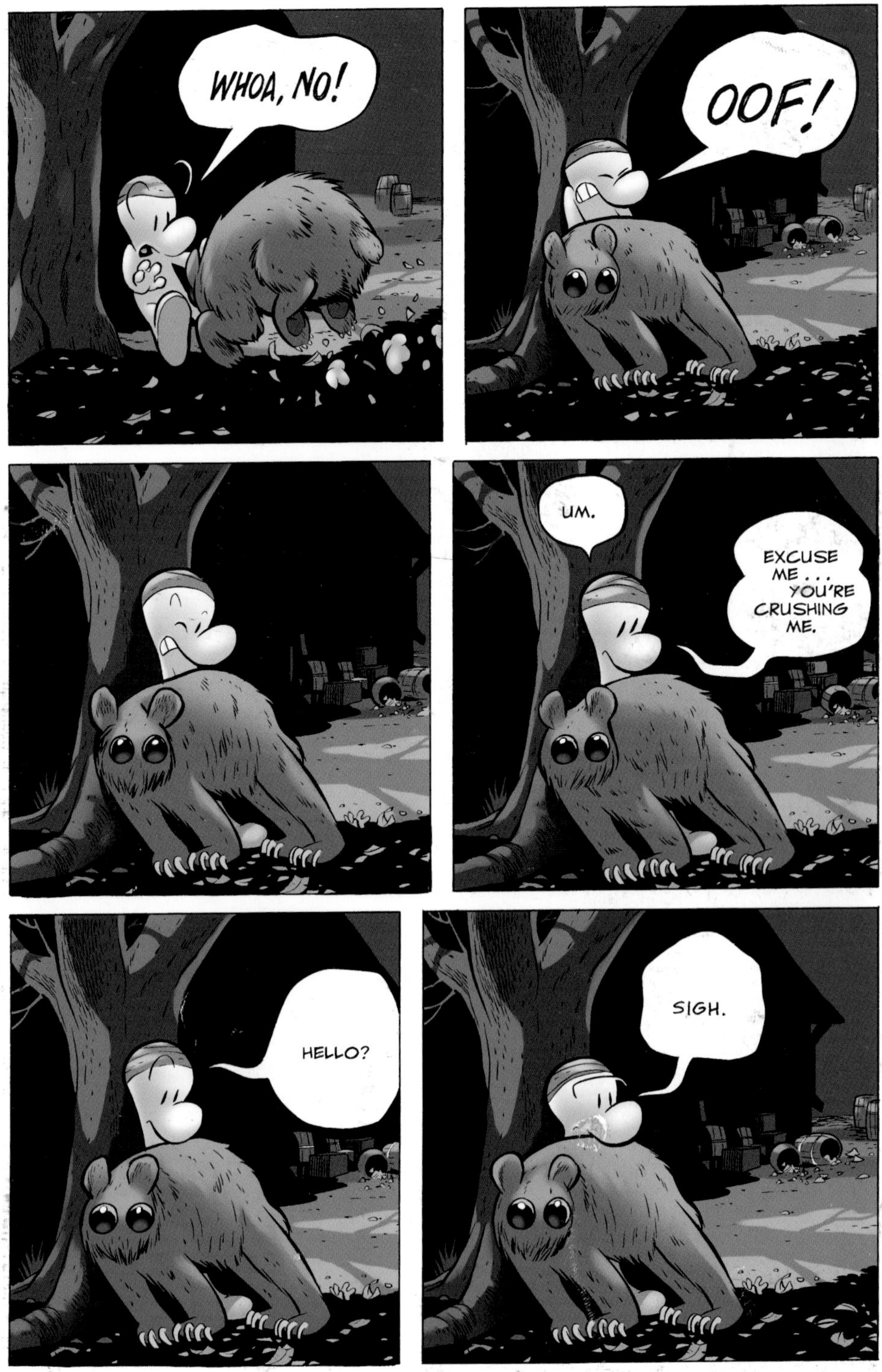
WHOA, NO!
OOF!
UM.
EXCUSE ME . . . YOU'RE CRUSHING ME.
HELLO?
SIGH.

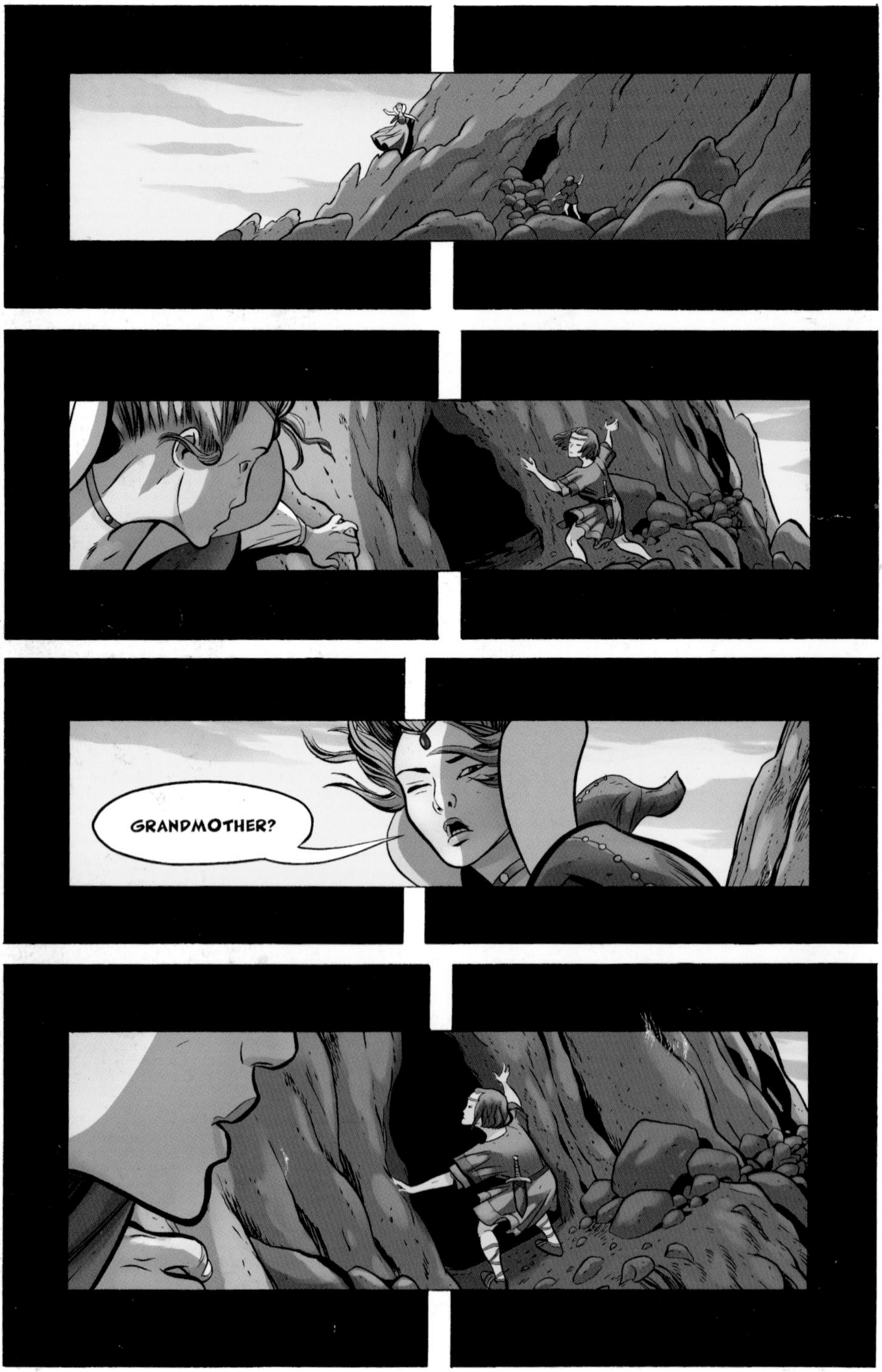
GRANDMOTHER?

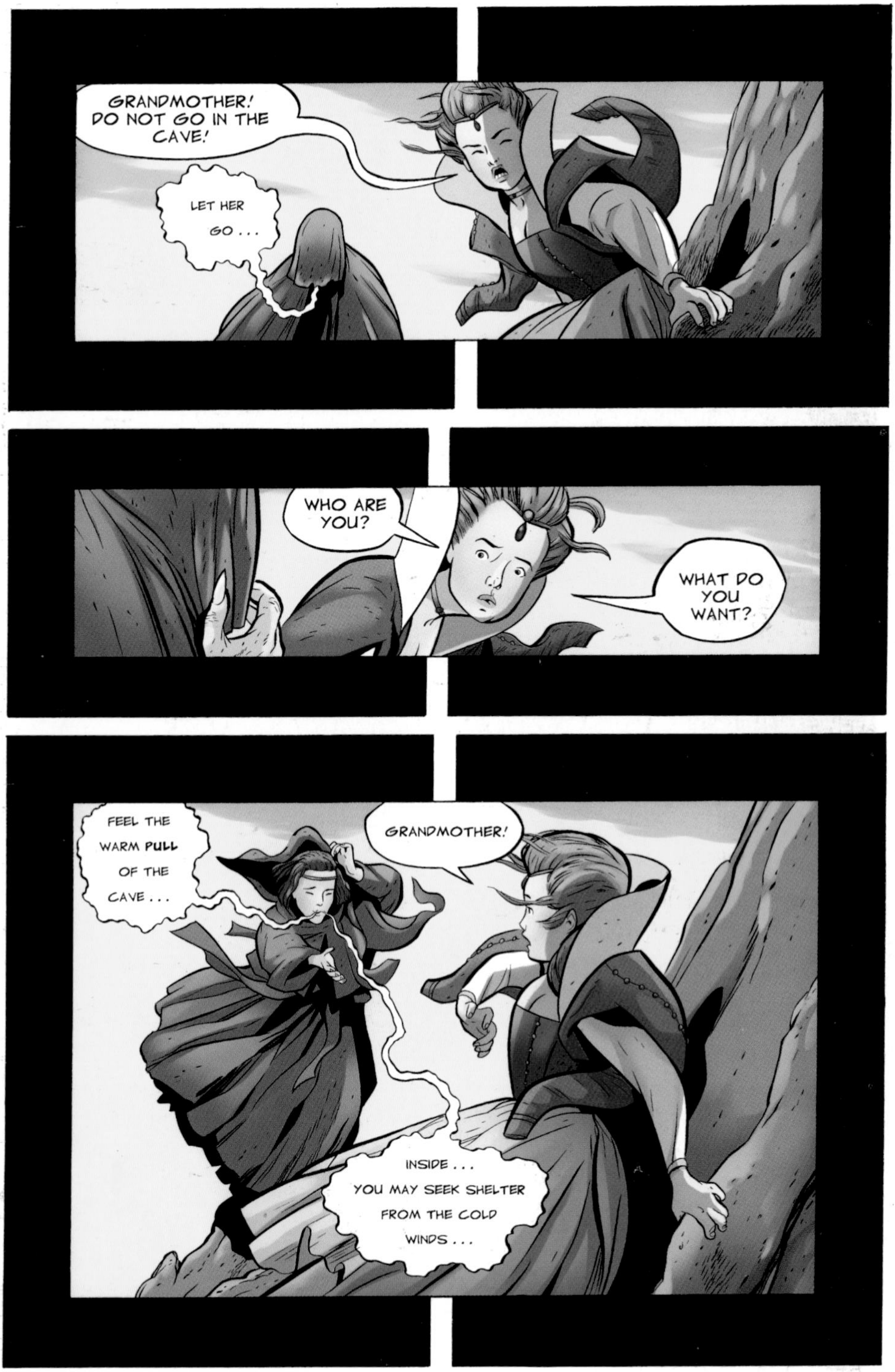
GRANDMOTHER! DO NOT GO IN THE CAVE!
LET HER GO . . .
WHO ARE YOU?
WHAT DO YOU WANT?
FEEL THE WARM **PULL** OF THE CAVE . . .
GRANDMOTHER!
INSIDE . . . YOU MAY SEEK SHELTER FROM THE COLD WINDS . . .

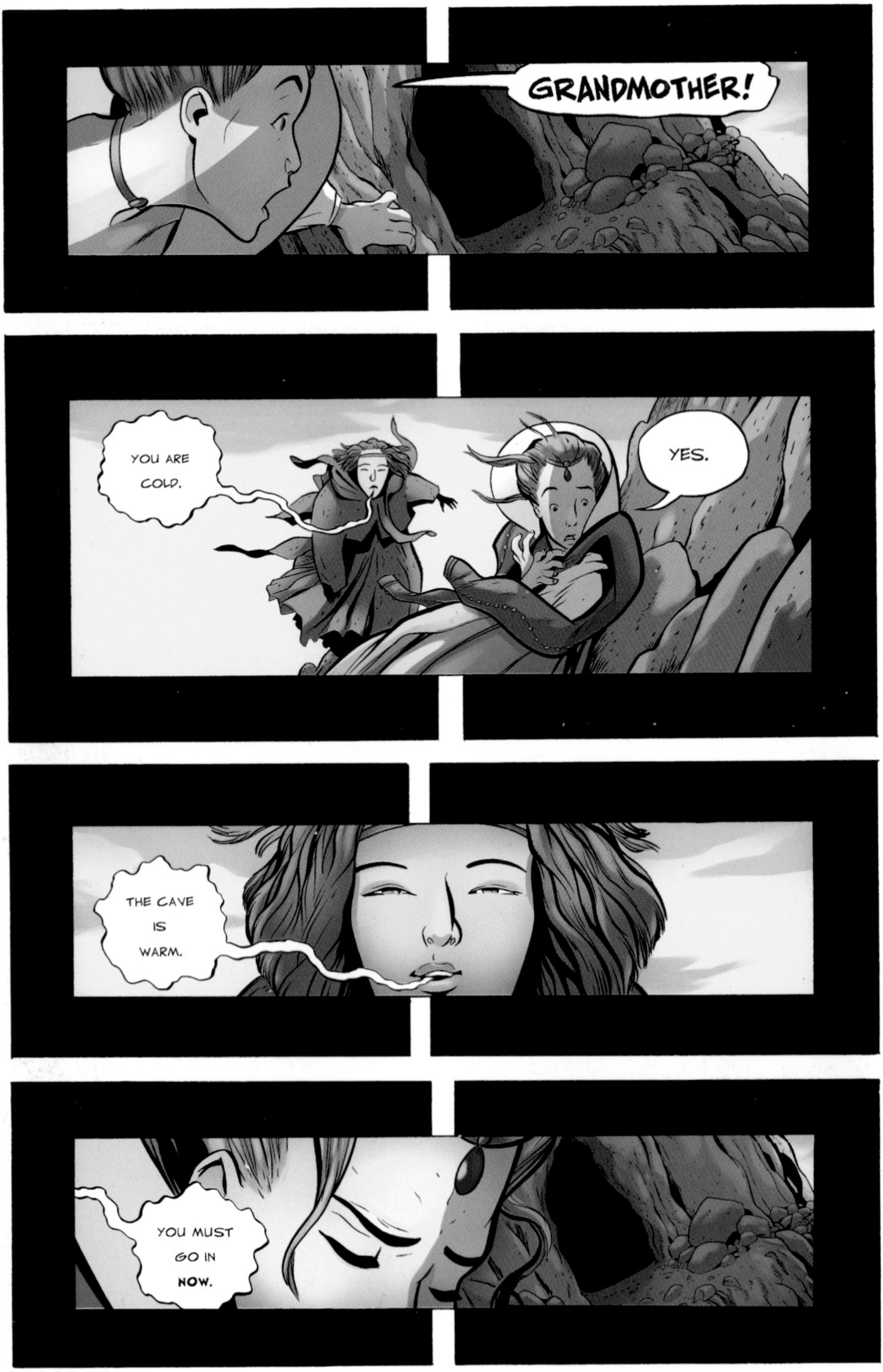
GRANDMOTHER!
YOU ARE COLD.
YES.
THE CAVE IS WARM.
YOU MUST GO IN NOW.

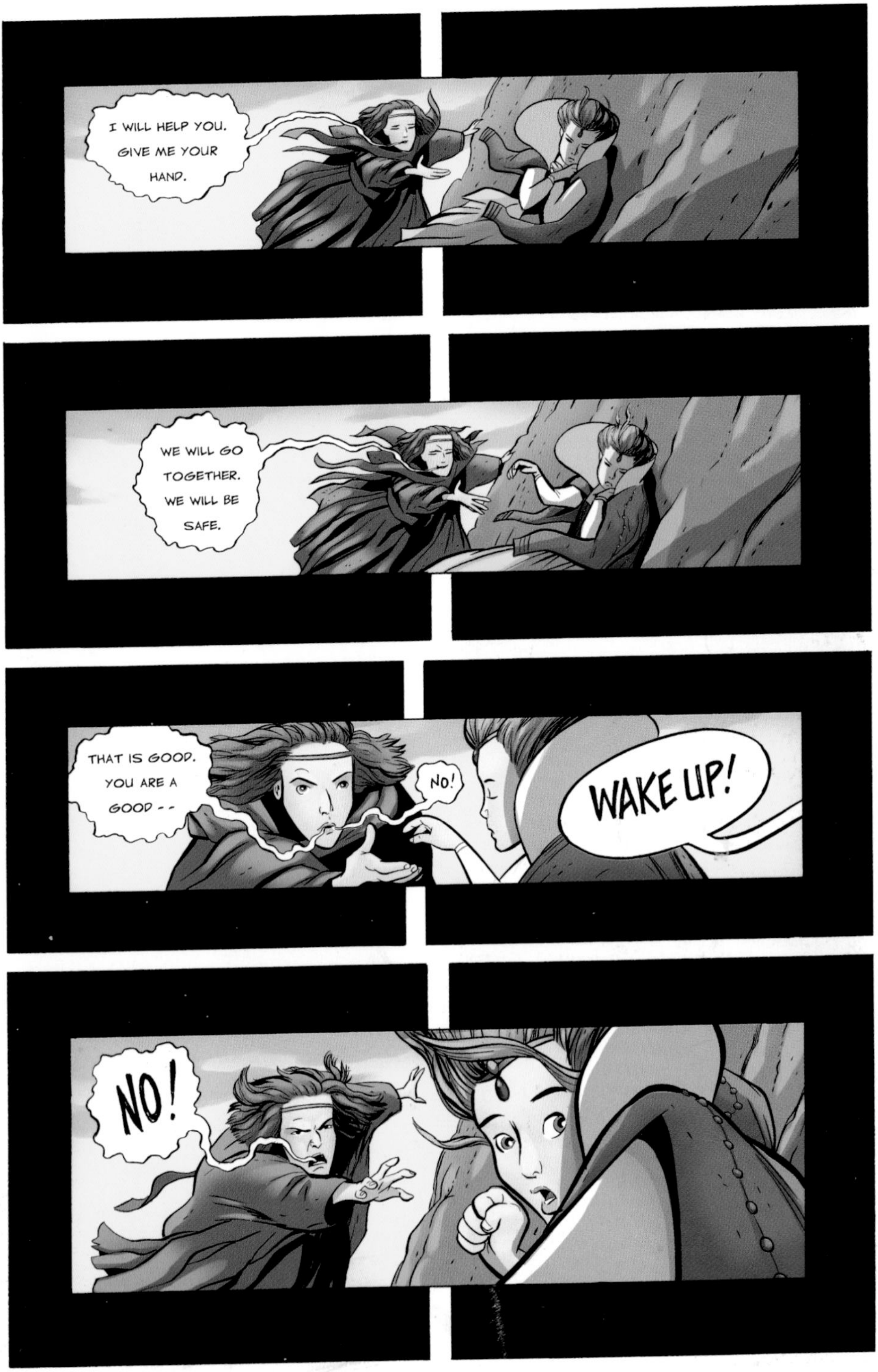
I WILL HELP YOU. GIVE ME YOUR HAND.
WE WILL GO TOGETHER. WE WILL BE SAFE.
THAT IS GOOD. YOU ARE A GOOD - -
NO!
WAKE UP!
NO!

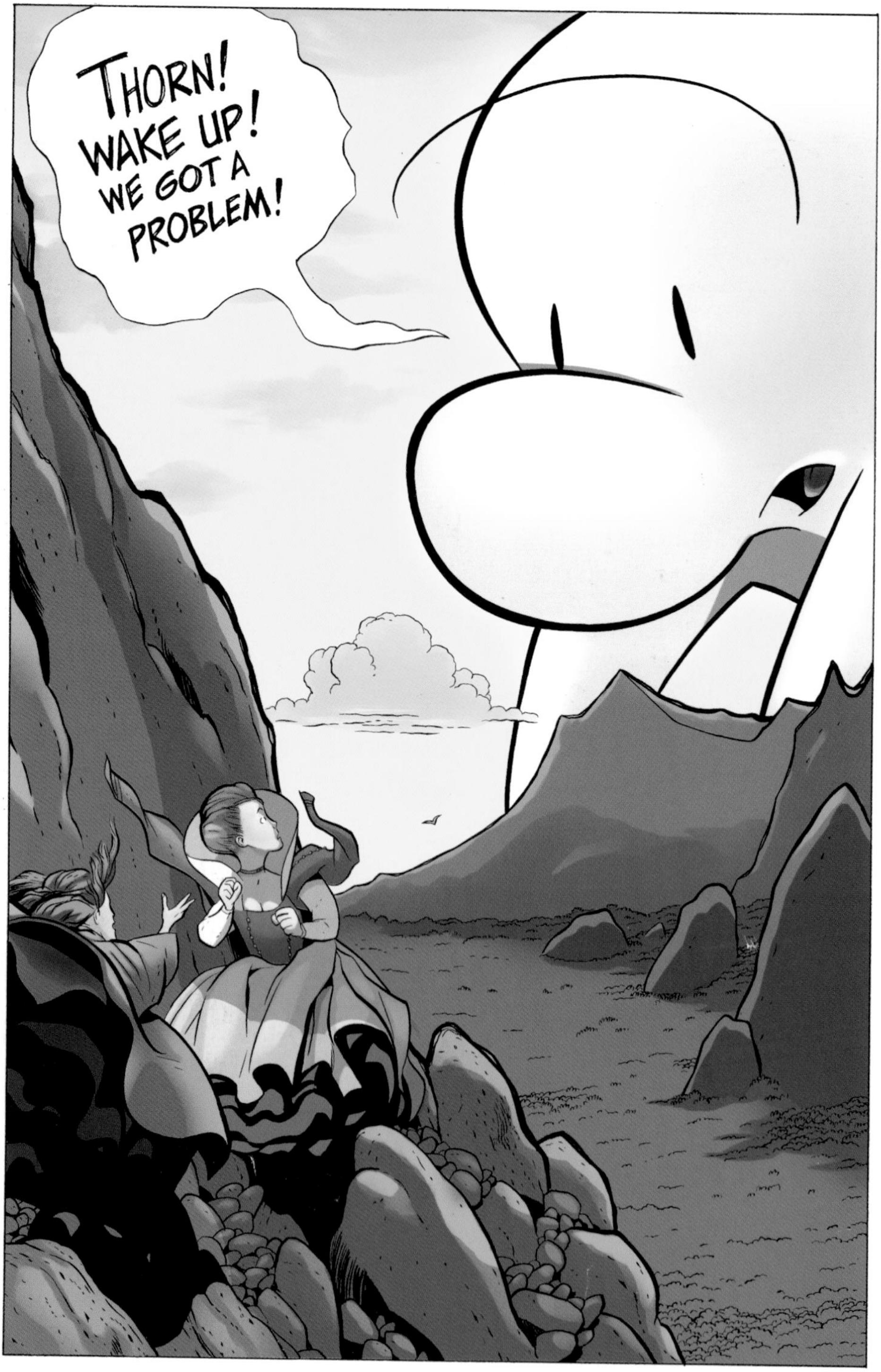
THORN! WAKE UP! WE GOT A PROBLEM!

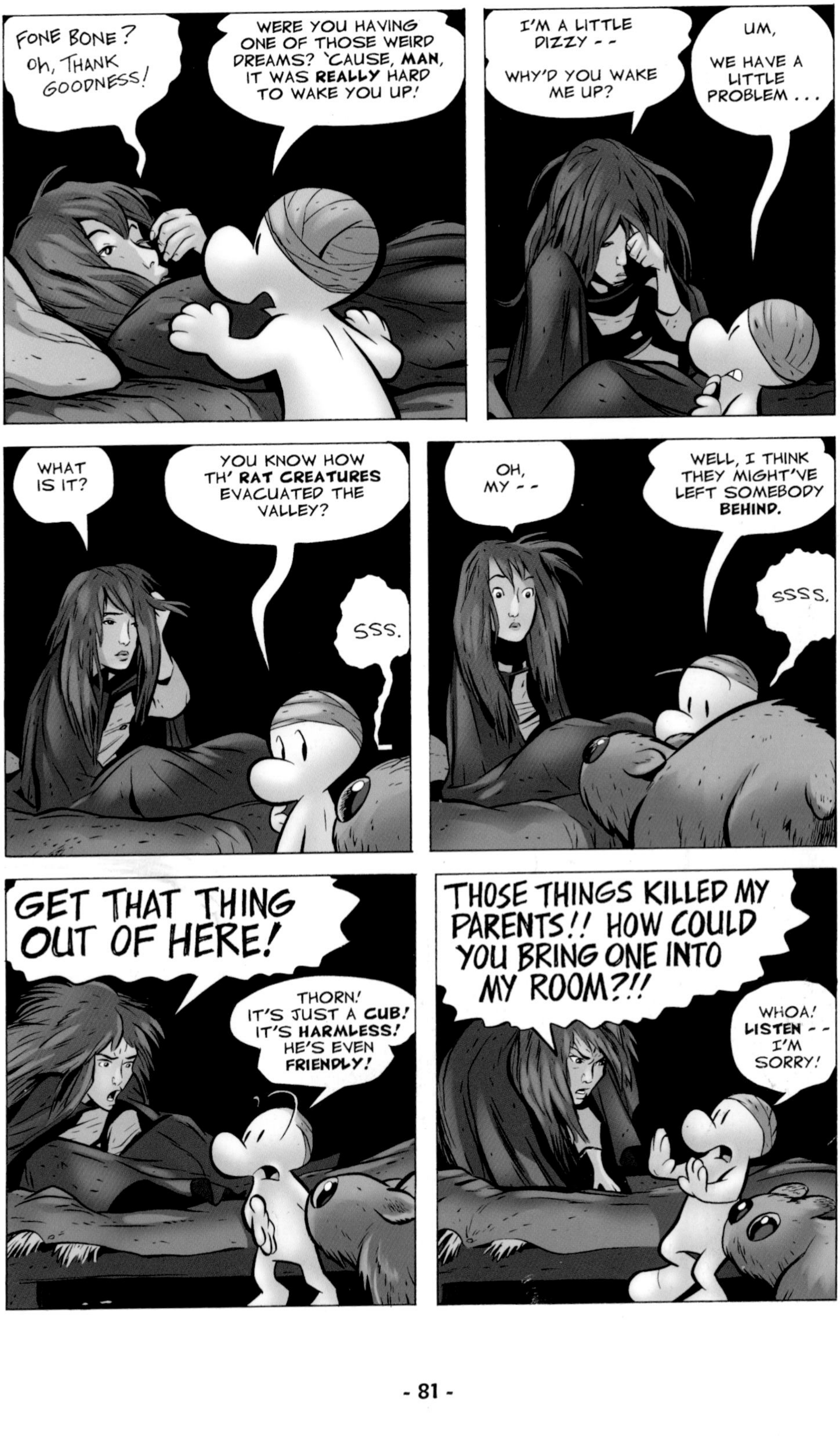
FONE BONE? Oh, THANK GOODNESS!
WERE YOU HAVING ONE OF THOSE WEIRD DREAMS? 'CAUSE, MAN, IT WAS REALLY HARD TO WAKE YOU UP!
I'M A LITTLE DIZZY - -
WHY'D YOU WAKE ME UP?
UM,
WE HAVE A LITTLE PROBLEM . . .
WHAT IS IT?
YOU KNOW HOW TH' RAT CREATURES EVACUATED THE VALLEY?
SSS.
OH, MY - -
WELL, I THINK THEY MIGHT'VE LEFT SOMEBODY BEHIND.
SSSS.
GET THAT THING OUT OF HERE!
THORN! IT'S JUST A CUB! IT'S HARMLESS! HE'S EVEN FRIENDLY!
THOSE THINGS KILLED MY PARENTS!! HOW COULD YOU BRING ONE INTO MY ROOM?!!
WHOA! LISTEN - - I'M SORRY!

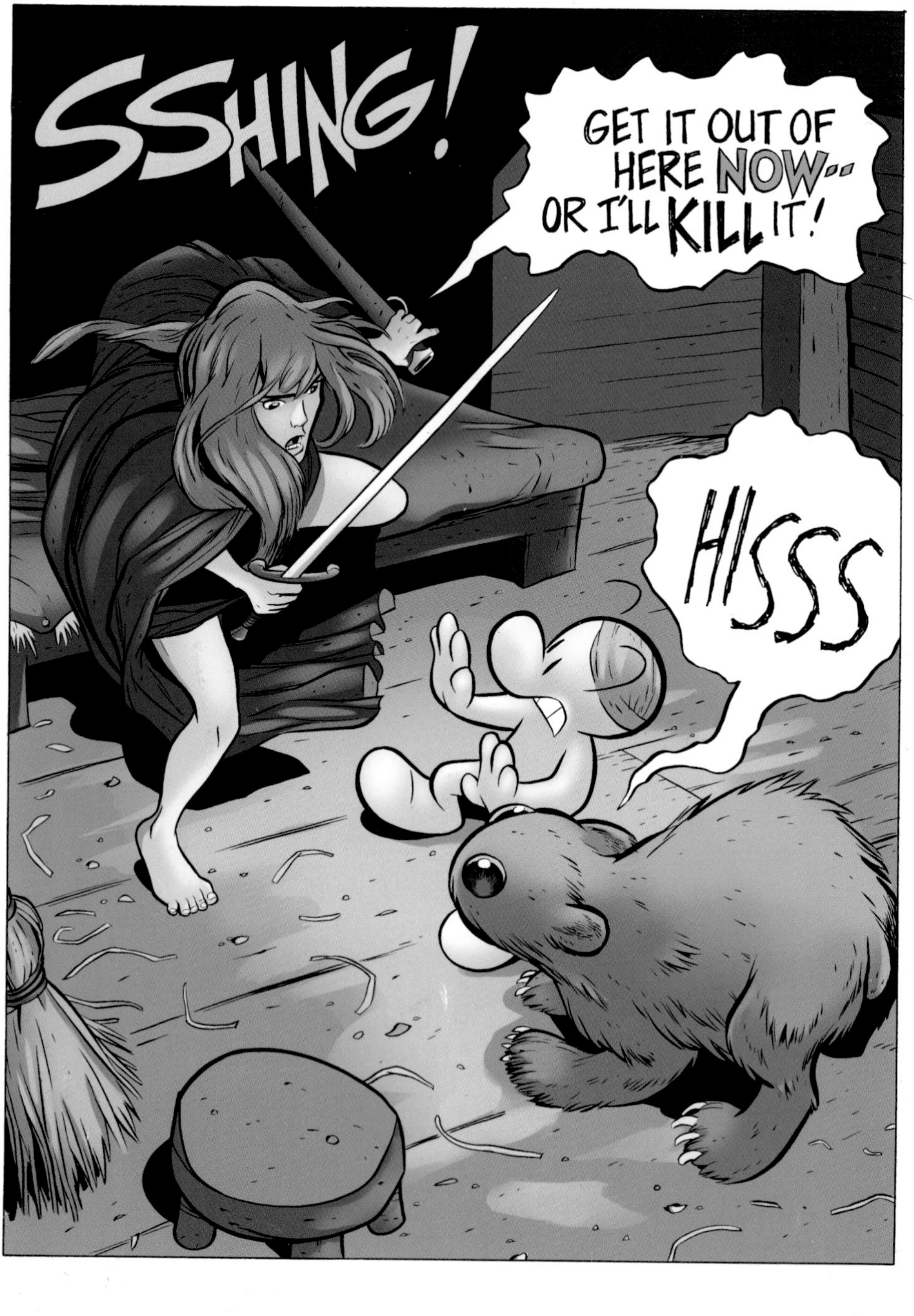
SSHING!
GET IT OUT OF HERE NOW.. OR I'LL KILL IT!
HISSS

CHAPTER FIVE DELIVER US THESE LAWS

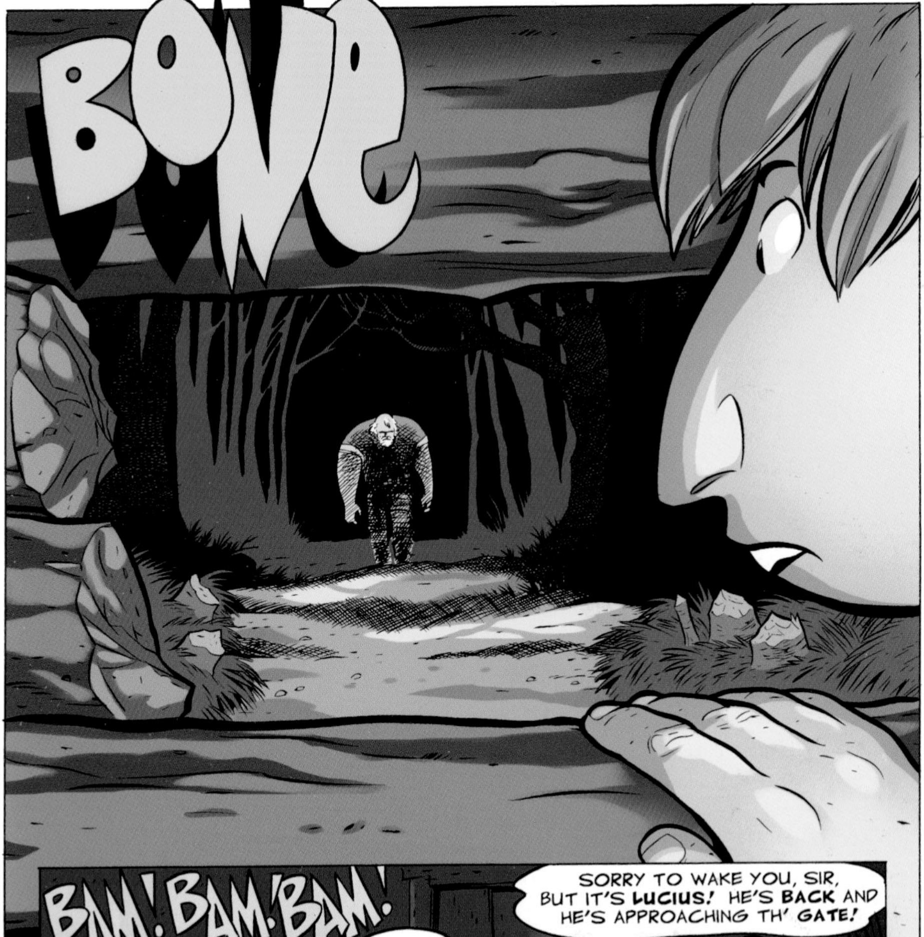
BONE
BAM! BAM! BAM!
WHAT? WHAT IS IT?
SORRY TO WAKE YOU, SIR, BUT IT'S LUCIUS! HE'S BACK AND HE'S APPROACHING TH' GATE!
HOLY--!
OKAY... LET HIM IN! AND GIVE HIM ANYTHING HE WANTS! I'LL BE RIGHT OUT!
GOT IT!
SMILEY! GET DRESSED AN' GO ROUND UP TH' MILITIA!
AYE, AYE, CAP'N!

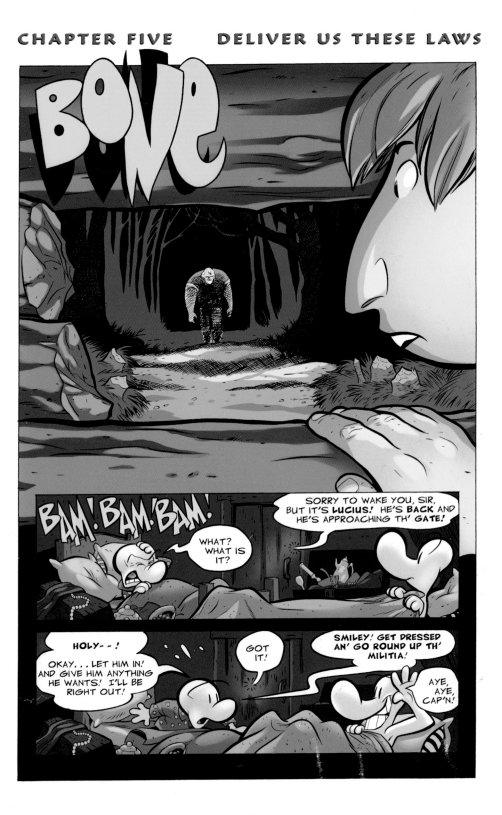

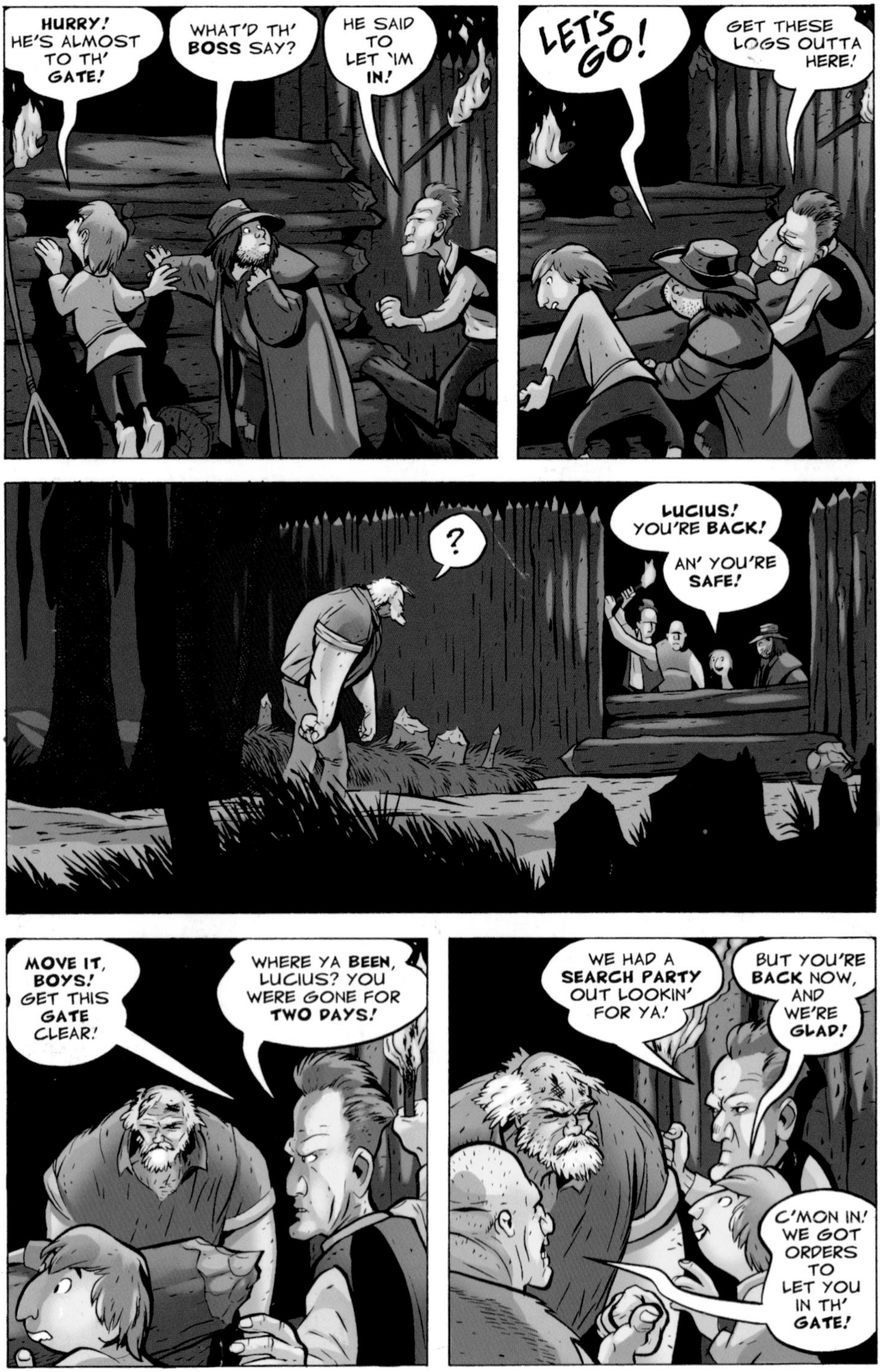
HURRY! HE'S ALMOST TO TH' GATE!
WHAT'D TH' BOSS SAY?
HE SAID TO LET 'IM IN!
LET'S GO!
GET THESE LOGS OUTTA HERE!
?
LUCIUS! YOU'RE BACK!
AN' YOU'RE SAFE!
MOVE IT, BOYS! GET THIS GATE CLEAR!
WHERE YA BEEN, LUCIUS? YOU WERE GONE FOR TWO DAYS!
WE HAD A SEARCH PARTY OUT LOOKIN' FOR YA!
BUT YOU'RE BACK NOW, AND WE'RE GLAD!
C'MON IN! WE GOT ORDERS TO LET YOU IN TH' GATE!

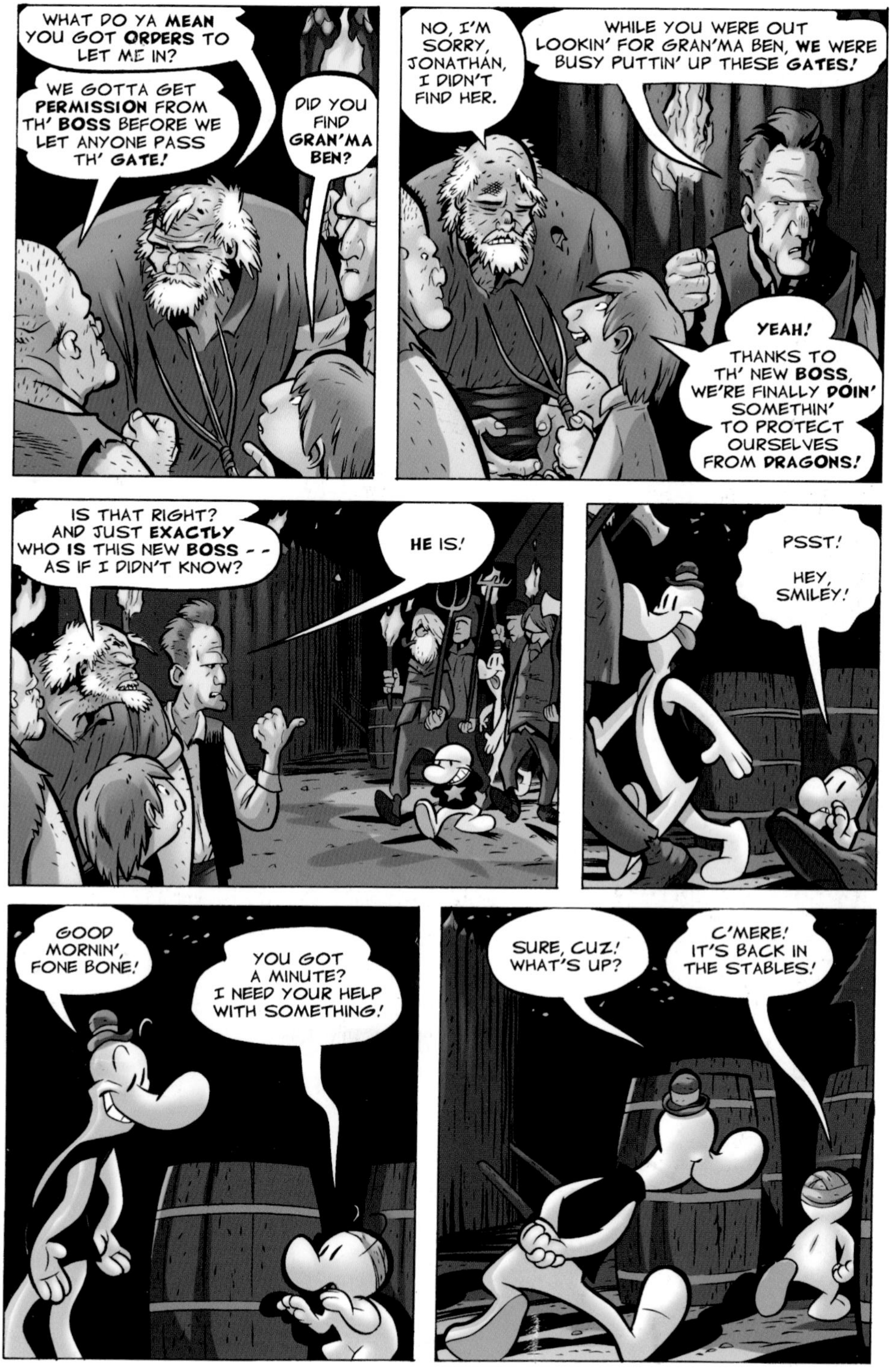
WHAT DO YA MEAN YOU GOT ORDERS TO LET ME IN?
WE GOTTA GET PERMISSION FROM TH' BOSS BEFORE WE LET ANYONE PASS TH' GATE!
DID YOU FIND GRAN'MA BEN?
NO, I'M SORRY, JONATHAN, I DIDN'T FIND HER.
WHILE YOU WERE OUT LOOKIN' FOR GRAN'MA BEN, WE WERE BUSY PUTTIN' UP THESE GATES!
YEAH!
THANKS TO TH' NEW BOSS, WE'RE FINALLY DOIN' SOMETHIN' TO PROTECT OURSELVES FROM DRAGONS!
IS THAT RIGHT? AND JUST EXACTLY WHO IS THIS NEW BOSS - - AS IF I DIDN'T KNOW?
HE IS!
PSST!
HEY, SMILEY!
GOOD MORNIN', FONE BONE!
YOU GOT A MINUTE? I NEED YOUR HELP WITH SOMETHING!
SURE, CUZ! WHAT'S UP?
C'MERE! IT'S BACK IN THE STABLES!

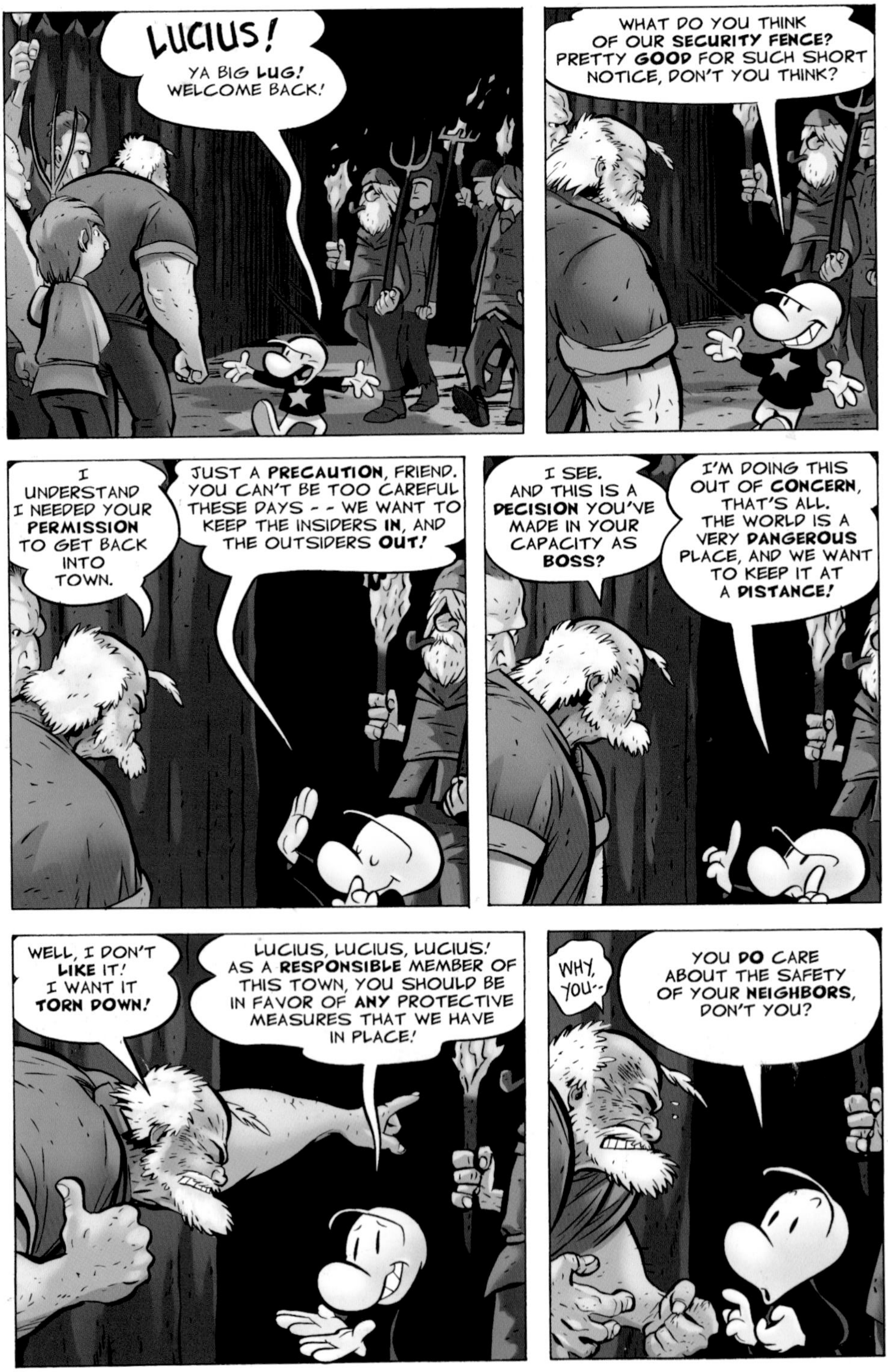
LUCIUS! YA BIG LUG! WELCOME BACK!
WHAT DO YOU THINK OF OUR SECURITY FENCE? PRETTY GOOD FOR SUCH SHORT NOTICE, DON'T YOU THINK?
I UNDERSTAND I NEEDED YOUR PERMISSION TO GET BACK INTO TOWN.
JUST A PRECAUTION, FRIEND. YOU CAN'T BE TOO CAREFUL THESE DAYS - - WE WANT TO KEEP THE INSIDERS IN, AND THE OUTSIDERS OUT!
I SEE. AND THIS IS A DECISION YOU'VE MADE IN YOUR CAPACITY AS BOSS?
I'M DOING THIS OUT OF CONCERN, THAT'S ALL. THE WORLD IS A VERY DANGEROUS PLACE, AND WE WANT TO KEEP IT AT A DISTANCE!
WELL, I DON'T LIKE IT! I WANT IT TORN DOWN!
LUCIUS, LUCIUS, LUCIUS! AS A RESPONSIBLE MEMBER OF THIS TOWN, YOU SHOULD BE IN FAVOR OF ANY PROTECTIVE MEASURES THAT WE HAVE IN PLACE!
WHY, YOU--
YOU DO CARE ABOUT THE SAFETY OF YOUR NEIGHBORS, DON'T YOU?

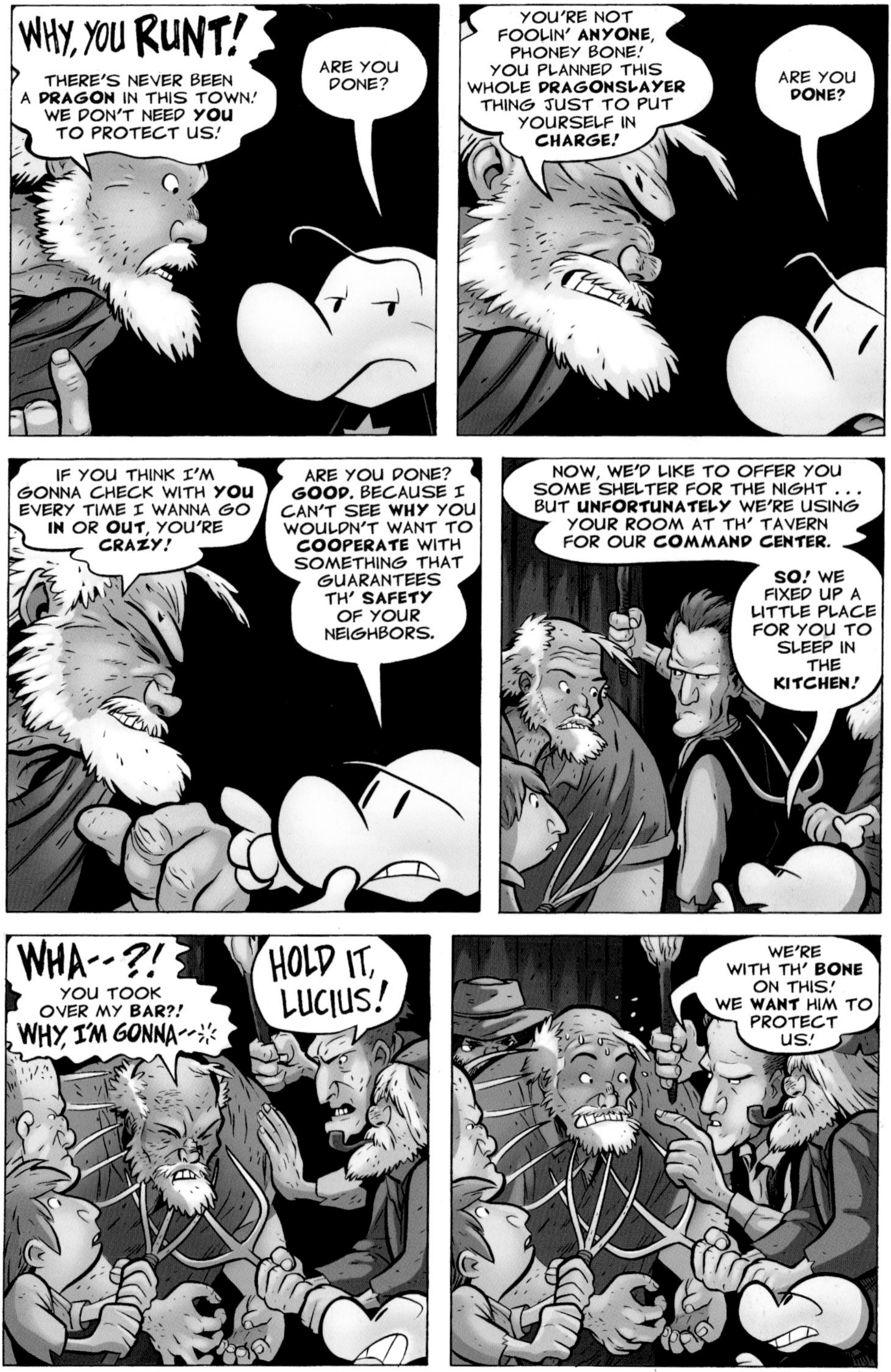
WHY, YOU RUNT!
THERE'S NEVER BEEN A DRAGON IN THIS TOWN! WE DON'T NEED YOU TO PROTECT US!
ARE YOU DONE?
YOU'RE NOT FOOLIN' ANYONE, PHONEY BONE! YOU PLANNED THIS WHOLE DRAGONSLAYER THING JUST TO PUT YOURSELF IN CHARGE!
ARE YOU DONE?
IF YOU THINK I'M GONNA CHECK WITH YOU EVERY TIME I WANNA GO IN OR OUT, YOU'RE CRAZY!
ARE YOU DONE? GOOD. BECAUSE I CAN'T SEE WHY YOU WOULDN'T WANT TO COOPERATE WITH SOMETHING THAT GUARANTEES TH' SAFETY OF YOUR NEIGHBORS.
NOW, WE'D LIKE TO OFFER YOU SOME SHELTER FOR THE NIGHT . . . BUT UNFORTUNATELY WE'RE USING YOUR ROOM AT TH' TAVERN FOR OUR COMMAND CENTER.
SO! WE FIXED UP A LITTLE PLACE FOR YOU TO SLEEP IN THE KITCHEN!
WHA--?! YOU TOOK OVER MY BAR?! WHY, I'M GONNA--
HOLD IT, LUCIUS!
WE'RE WITH TH' BONE ON THIS! WE WANT HIM TO PROTECT US!

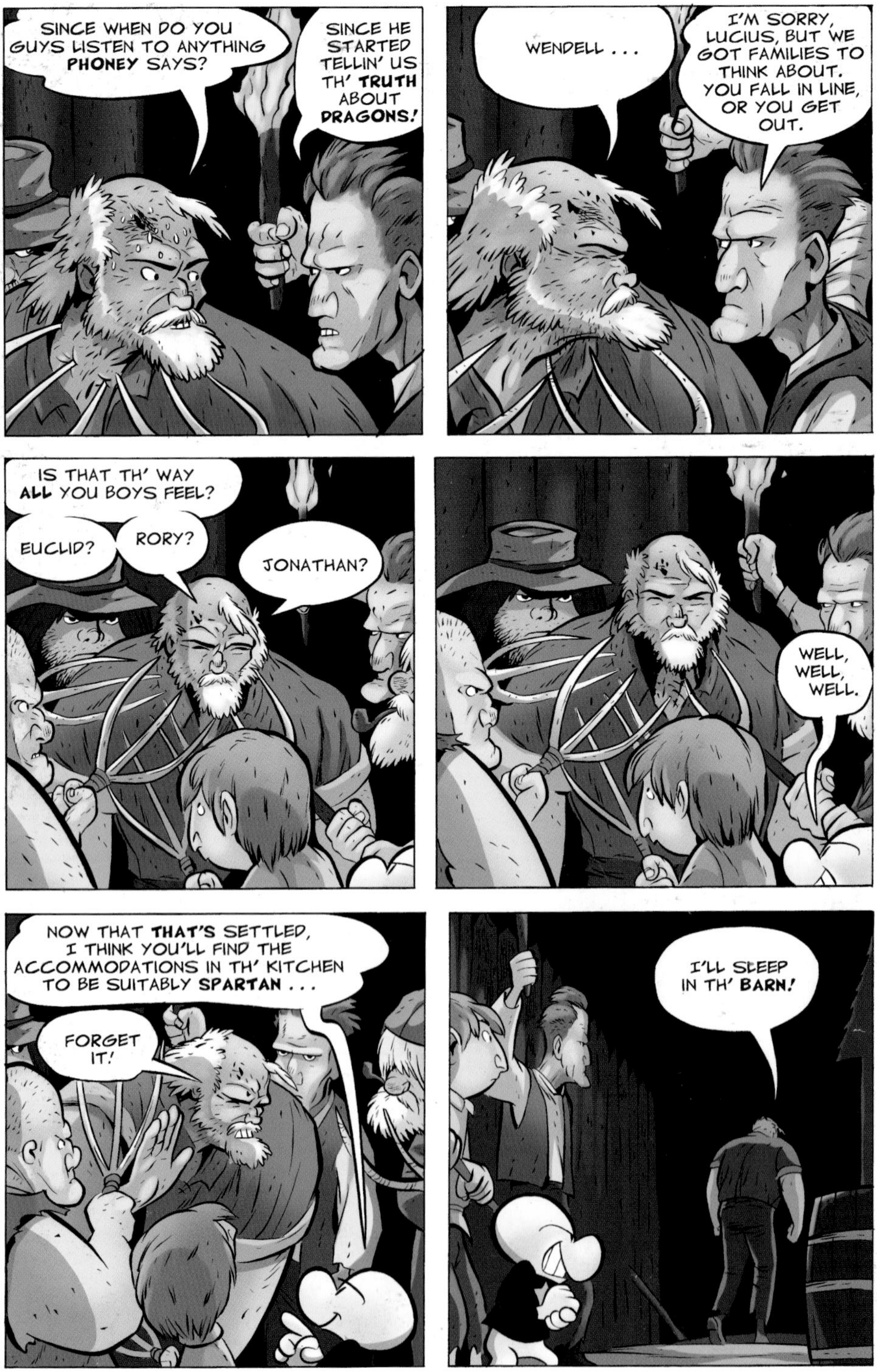
SINCE WHEN DO YOU GUYS LISTEN TO ANYTHING PHONEY SAYS?
SINCE HE STARTED TELLIN' US TH' TRUTH ABOUT DRAGONS!
WENDELL . . .
I'M SORRY, LUCIUS, BUT WE GOT FAMILIES TO THINK ABOUT. YOU FALL IN LINE, OR YOU GET OUT.
IS THAT TH' WAY ALL YOU BOYS FEEL?
EUCLID?
RORY?
JONATHAN?
WELL, WELL, WELL.
NOW THAT THAT'S SETTLED, I THINK YOU'LL FIND THE ACCOMMODATIONS IN TH' KITCHEN TO BE SUITABLY SPARTAN . . .
FORGET IT!
I'LL SLEEP IN TH' BARN!

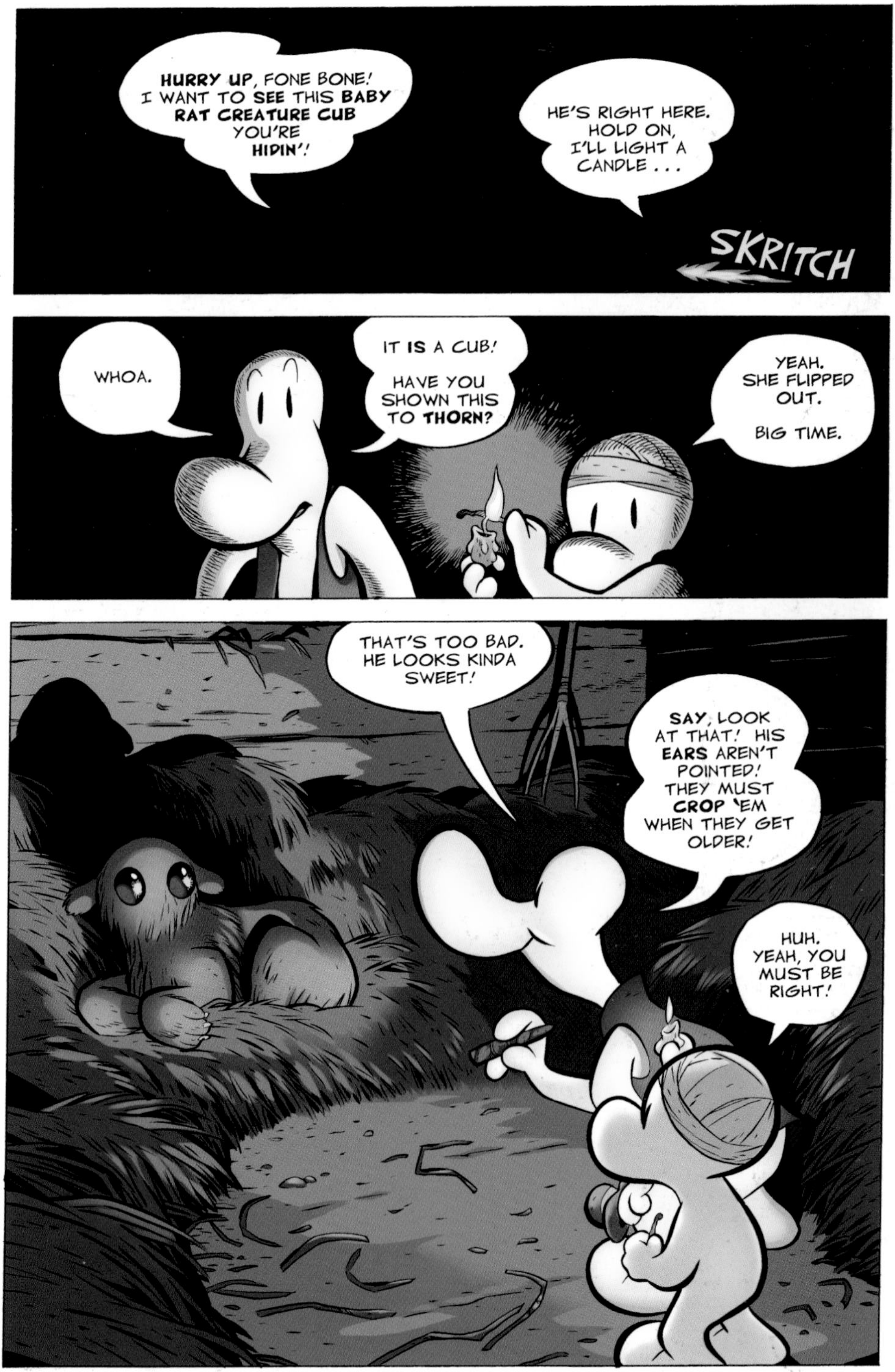
HURRY UP, FONE BONE! I WANT TO SEE THIS BABY RAT CREATURE CUB YOU'RE HIDIN'!
HE'S RIGHT HERE. HOLD ON, I'LL LIGHT A CANDLE . . .
SKRITCH
WHOA.
IT IS A CUB! HAVE YOU SHOWN THIS TO THORN?
YEAH. SHE FLIPPED OUT. BIG TIME.
THAT'S TOO BAD. HE LOOKS KINDA SWEET!
SAY, LOOK AT THAT! HIS EARS AREN'T POINTED! THEY MUST CROP 'EM WHEN THEY GET OLDER!
HUH. YEAH, YOU MUST BE RIGHT!

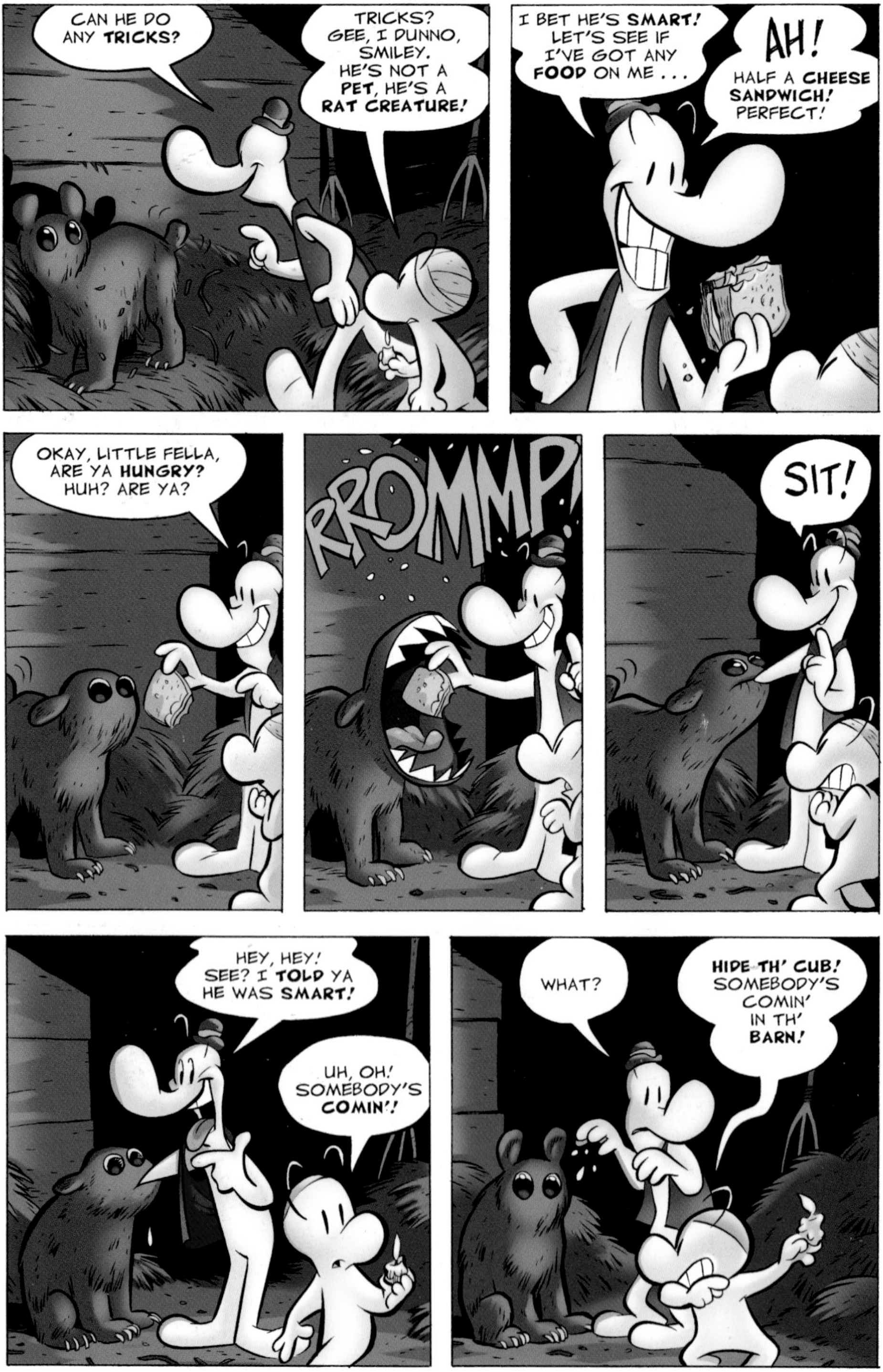
CAN HE DO ANY TRICKS?
TRICKS? GEE, I DUNNO, SMILEY. HE'S NOT A PET, HE'S A RAT CREATURE!
I BET HE'S SMART! LET'S SEE IF I'VE GOT ANY FOOD ON ME . . .
AH!
HALF A CHEESE SANDWICH! PERFECT!
OKAY, LITTLE FELLA, ARE YA HUNGRY? HUH? ARE YA?
RROMMP!
SIT!
HEY, HEY! SEE? I TOLD YA HE WAS SMART!
UH, OH! SOMEBODY'S COMIN'!
WHAT?
HIDE TH' CUB! SOMEBODY'S COMIN' IN TH' BARN!

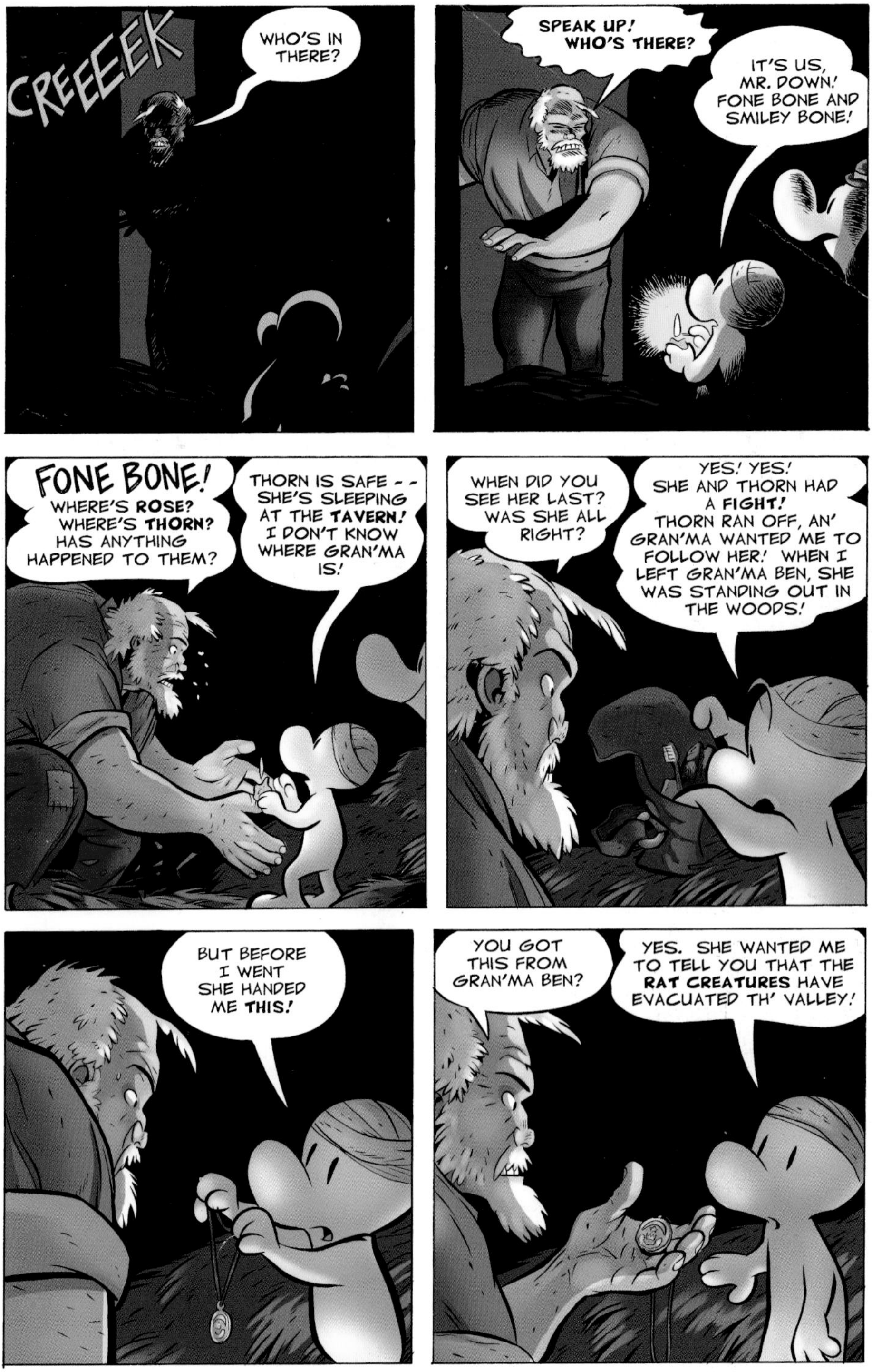
CREEEEK
WHO'S IN THERE?
SPEAK UP! WHO'S THERE?
IT'S US, MR. DOWN! FONE BONE AND SMILEY BONE!
FONE BONE! WHERE'S ROSE? WHERE'S THORN? HAS ANYTHING HAPPENED TO THEM?
THORN IS SAFE -- SHE'S SLEEPING AT THE TAVERN! I DON'T KNOW WHERE GRAN'MA IS!
WHEN DID YOU SEE HER LAST? WAS SHE ALL RIGHT?
YES! YES! SHE AND THORN HAD A FIGHT! THORN RAN OFF, AN' GRAN'MA WANTED ME TO FOLLOW HER! WHEN I LEFT GRAN'MA BEN, SHE WAS STANDING OUT IN THE WOODS!
BUT BEFORE I WENT SHE HANDED ME THIS!
YOU GOT THIS FROM GRAN'MA BEN?
YES. SHE WANTED ME TO TELL YOU THAT THE RAT CREATURES HAVE EVACUATED TH' VALLEY!

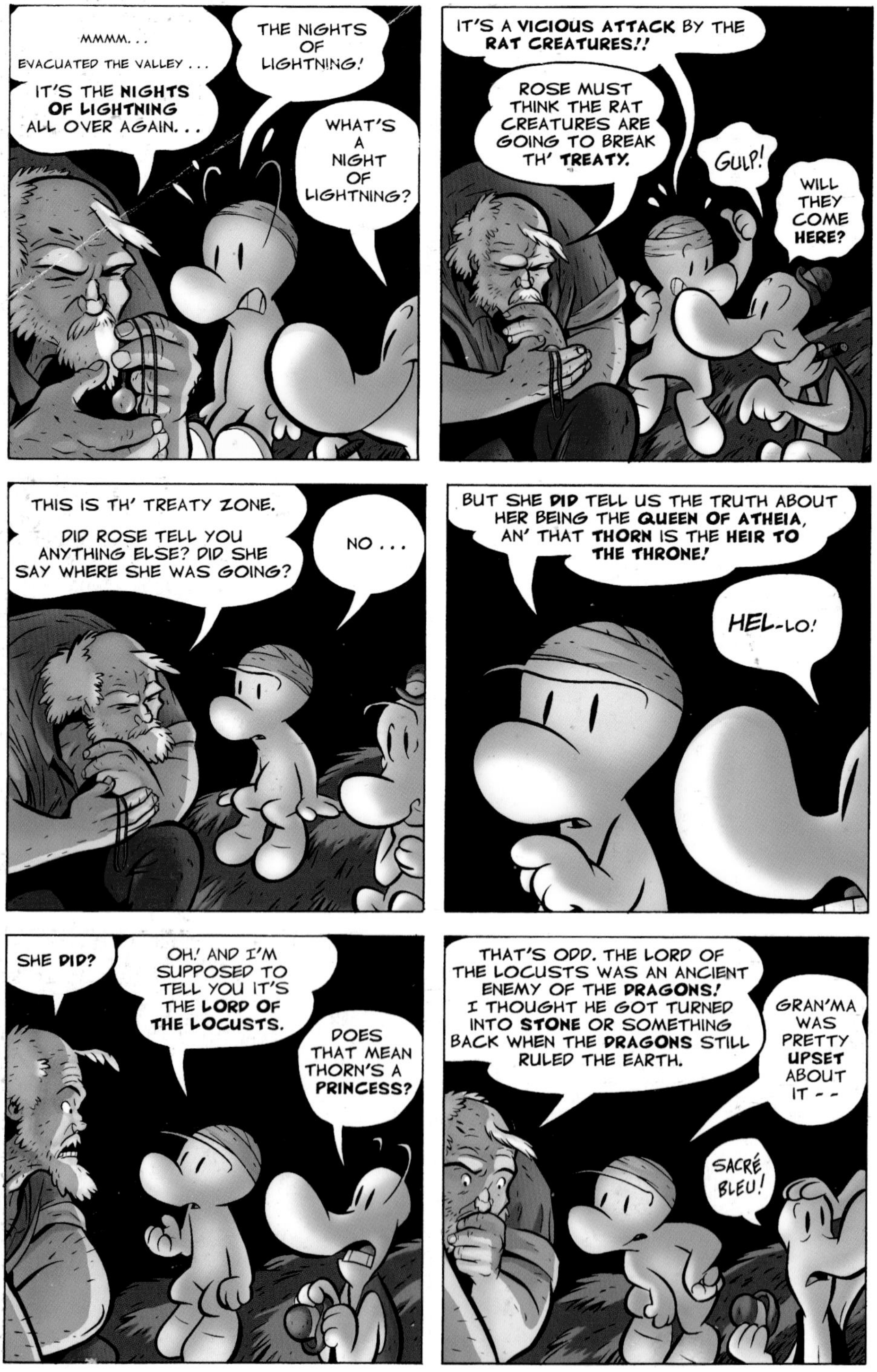
MMMM. . .
EVACUATED THE VALLEY . . .
IT'S THE NIGHTS OF LIGHTNING ALL OVER AGAIN. . .
THE NIGHTS OF LIGHTNING!
WHAT'S A NIGHT OF LIGHTNING?
IT'S A VICIOUS ATTACK BY THE RAT CREATURES!!
ROSE MUST THINK THE RAT CREATURES ARE GOING TO BREAK TH' TREATY.
GULP!
WILL THEY COME HERE?
THIS IS TH' TREATY ZONE.
DID ROSE TELL YOU ANYTHING ELSE? DID SHE SAY WHERE SHE WAS GOING?
NO . . .
BUT SHE DID TELL US THE TRUTH ABOUT HER BEING THE QUEEN OF ATHEIA, AN' THAT THORN IS THE HEIR TO THE THRONE!
HEL-LO!
SHE DID?
OH! AND I'M SUPPOSED TO TELL YOU IT'S THE LORD OF THE LOCUSTS.
DOES THAT MEAN THORN'S A PRINCESS?
THAT'S ODD. THE LORD OF THE LOCUSTS WAS AN ANCIENT ENEMY OF THE DRAGONS! I THOUGHT HE GOT TURNED INTO STONE OR SOMETHING BACK WHEN THE DRAGONS STILL RULED THE EARTH.
GRAN'MA WAS PRETTY UPSET ABOUT IT - -
SACRÉ BLEU!

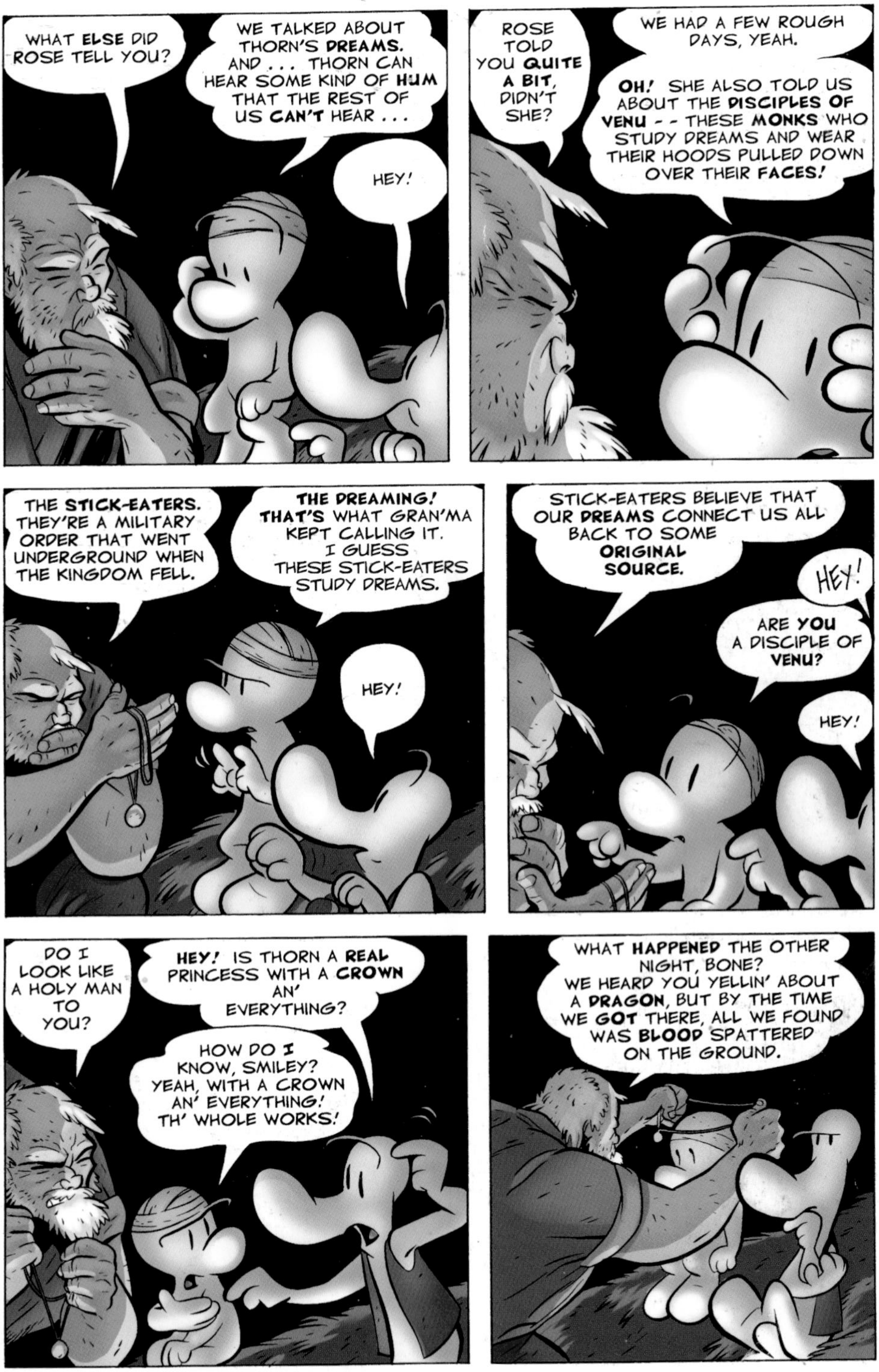
WHAT ELSE DID ROSE TELL YOU?
WE TALKED ABOUT THORN'S DREAMS. AND . . . THORN CAN HEAR SOME KIND OF HUM THAT THE REST OF US CAN'T HEAR . . .
HEY!
ROSE TOLD YOU QUITE A BIT, DIDN'T SHE?
WE HAD A FEW ROUGH DAYS, YEAH.
OH! SHE ALSO TOLD US ABOUT THE DISCIPLES OF VENU -- THESE MONKS WHO STUDY DREAMS AND WEAR THEIR HOODS PULLED DOWN OVER THEIR FACES!
THE STICK-EATERS. THEY'RE A MILITARY ORDER THAT WENT UNDERGROUND WHEN THE KINGDOM FELL.
THE DREAMING! THAT'S WHAT GRAN'MA KEPT CALLING IT. I GUESS THESE STICK-EATERS STUDY DREAMS.
HEY!
STICK-EATERS BELIEVE THAT OUR DREAMS CONNECT US ALL BACK TO SOME ORIGINAL SOURCE.
HEY!
ARE YOU A DISCIPLE OF VENU?
HEY!
DO I LOOK LIKE A HOLY MAN TO YOU?
HEY! IS THORN A REAL PRINCESS WITH A CROWN AN' EVERYTHING?
HOW DO I KNOW, SMILEY? YEAH, WITH A CROWN AN' EVERYTHING! TH' WHOLE WORKS!
WHAT HAPPENED THE OTHER NIGHT, BONE? WE HEARD YOU YELLIN' ABOUT A DRAGON, BUT BY THE TIME WE GOT THERE, ALL WE FOUND WAS BLOOD SPATTERED ON THE GROUND.

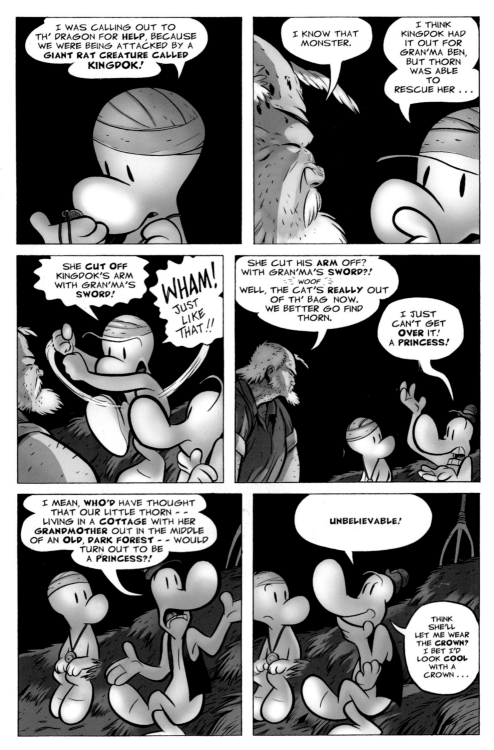

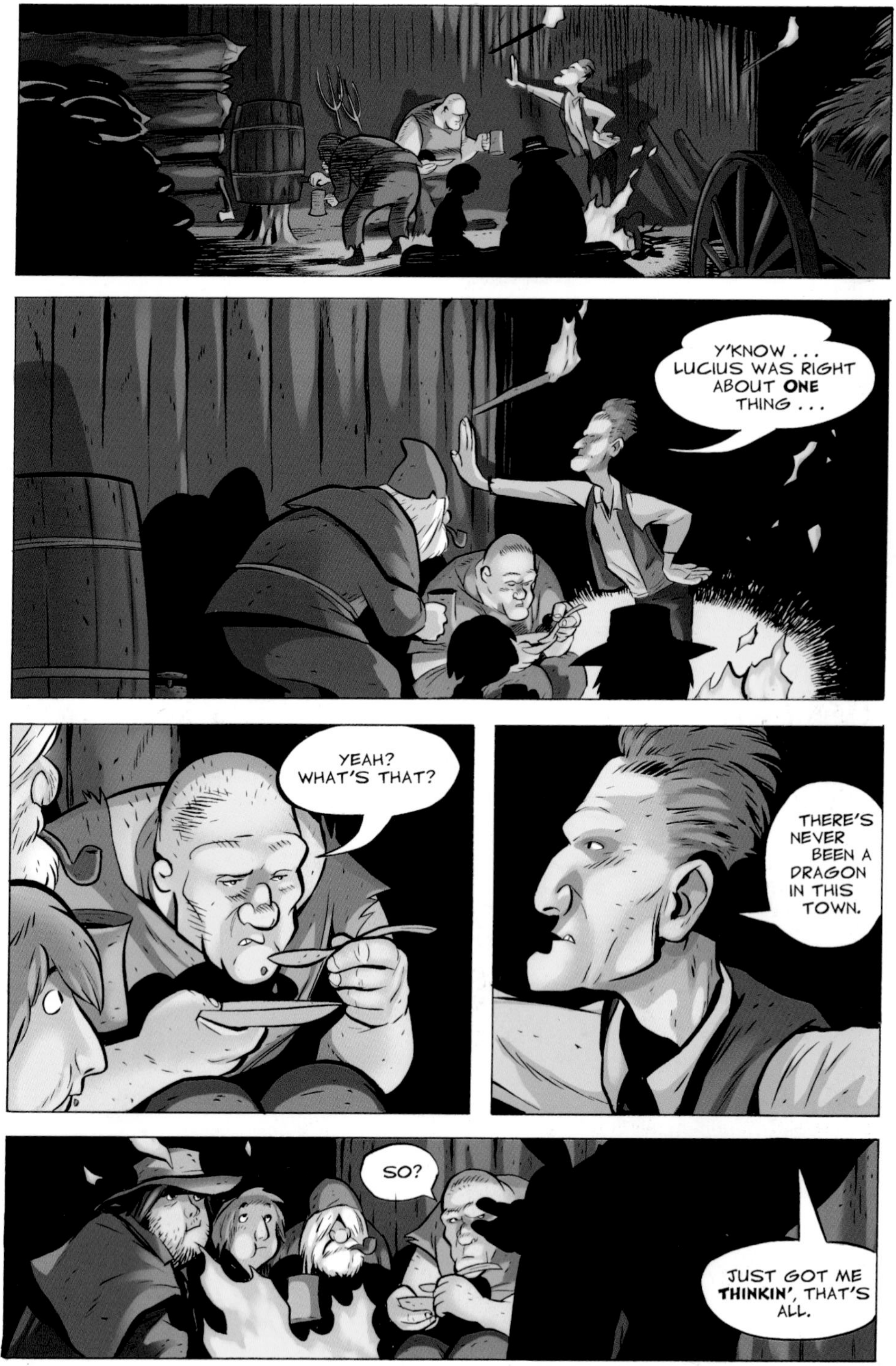
Y'KNOW . . . LUCIUS WAS RIGHT ABOUT **ONE** THING . . .
YEAH? WHAT'S THAT?
THERE'S NEVER BEEN A DRAGON IN THIS TOWN.
SO?
JUST GOT ME **THINKIN'**, THAT'S ALL.

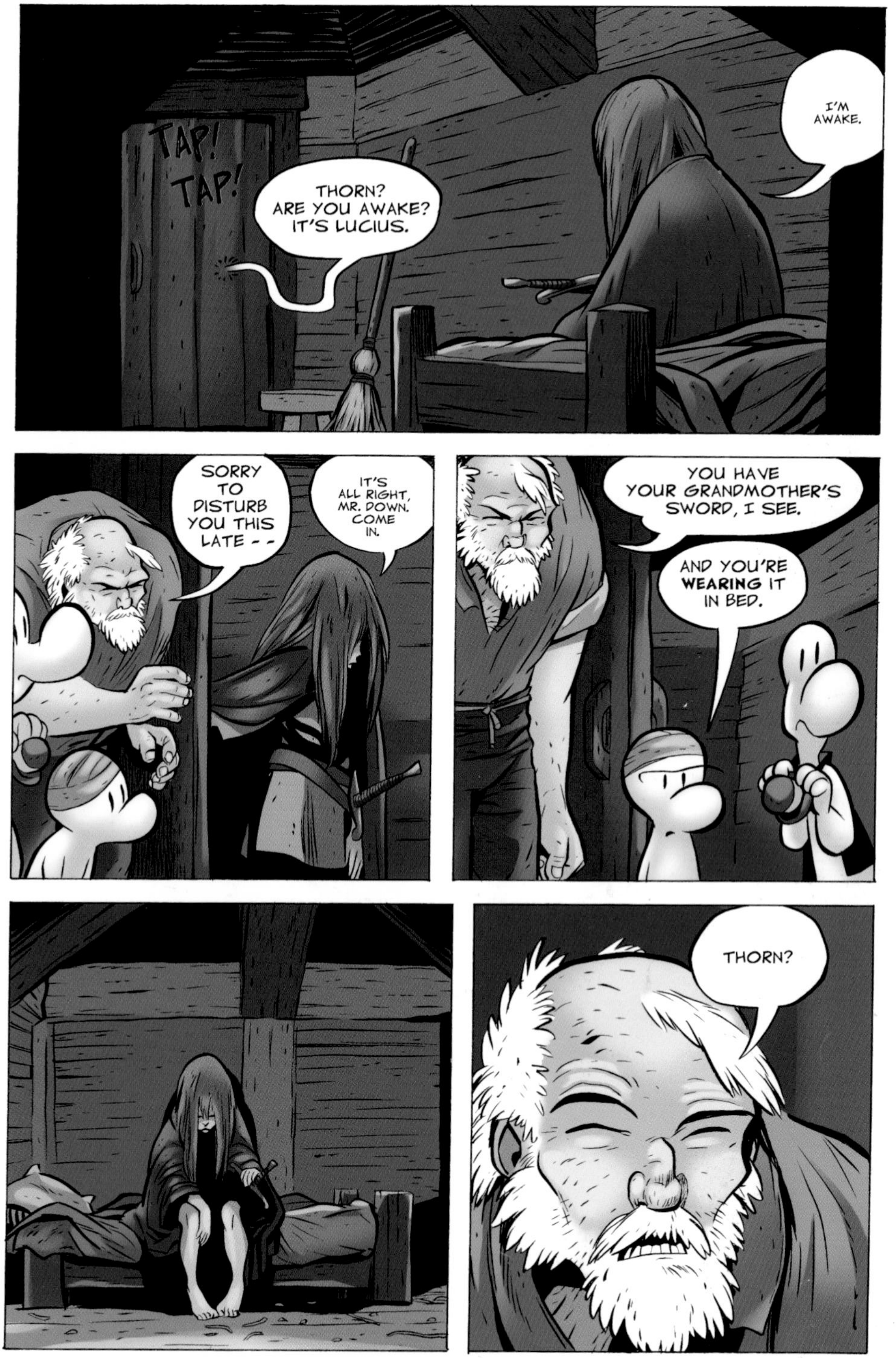
TAP! TAP!
THORN? ARE YOU AWAKE? IT'S LUCIUS.
I'M AWAKE.
SORRY TO DISTURB YOU THIS LATE - -
IT'S ALL RIGHT, MR. DOWN. COME IN.
YOU HAVE YOUR GRANDMOTHER'S SWORD, I SEE.
AND YOU'RE **WEARING** IT IN BED.
THORN?

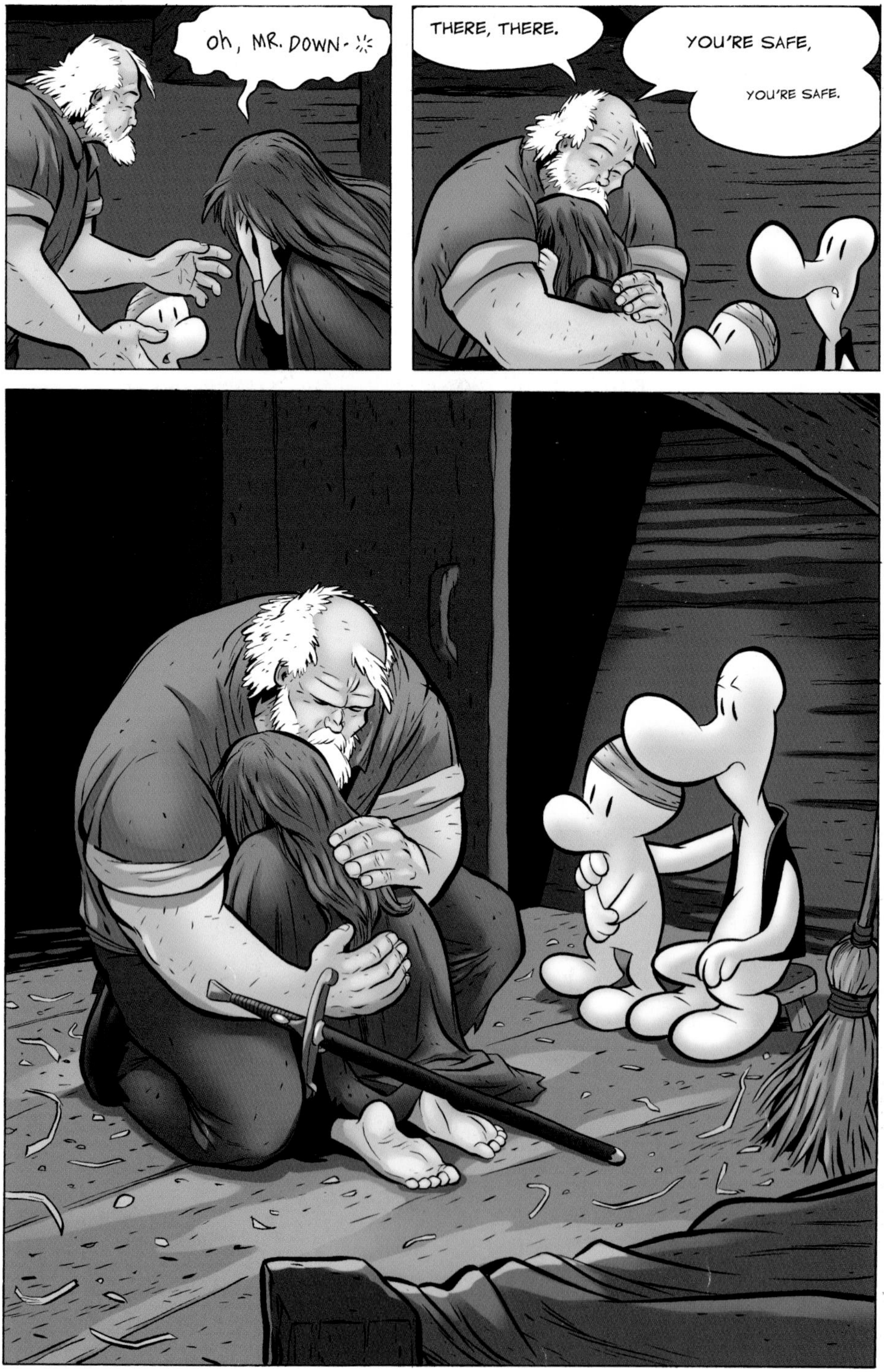
Oh, MR. DOWN-
THERE, THERE.
YOU'RE SAFE,
YOU'RE SAFE.

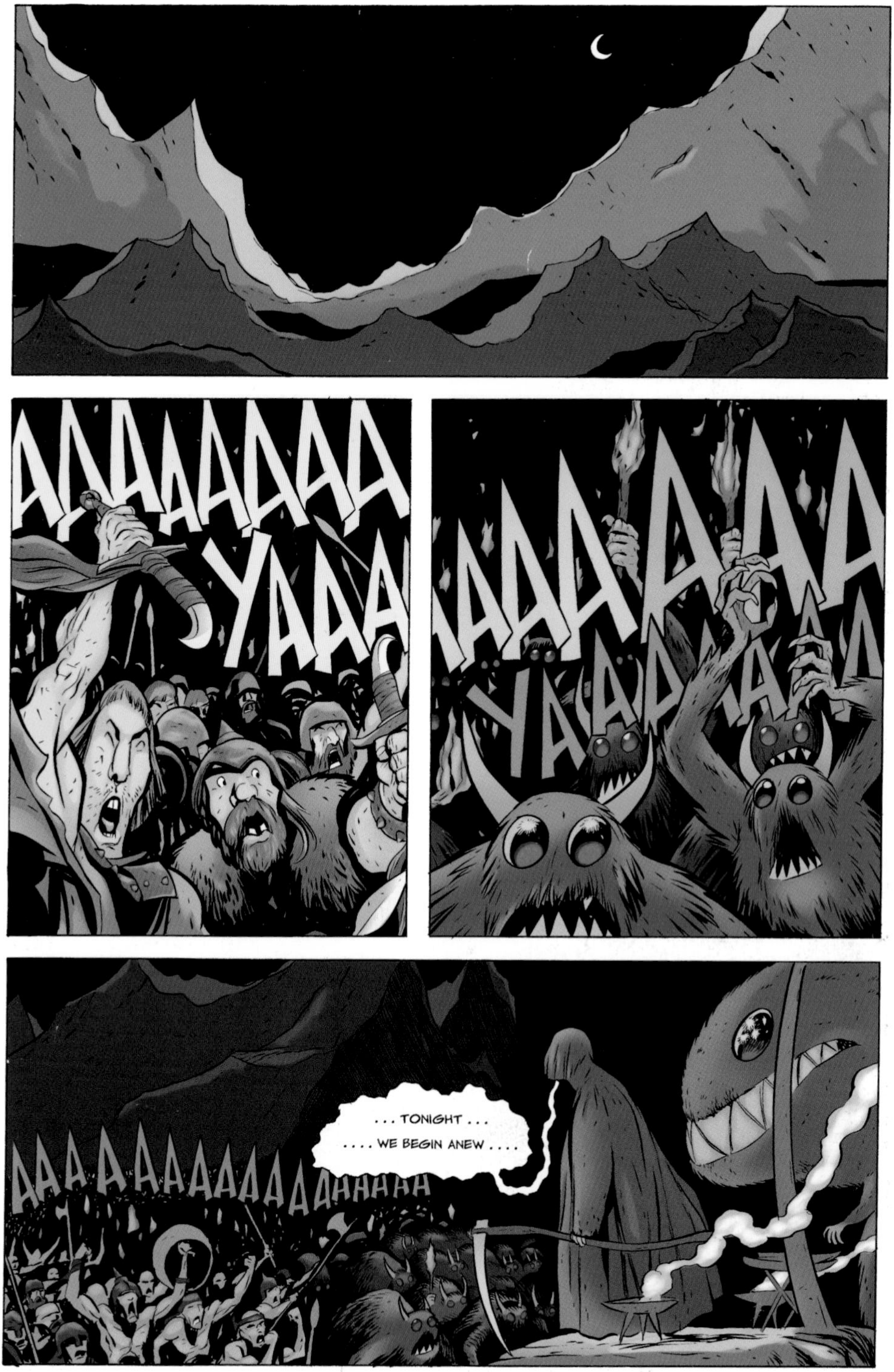
. . . TONIGHT . . .
. . . . WE BEGIN ANEW . . . .

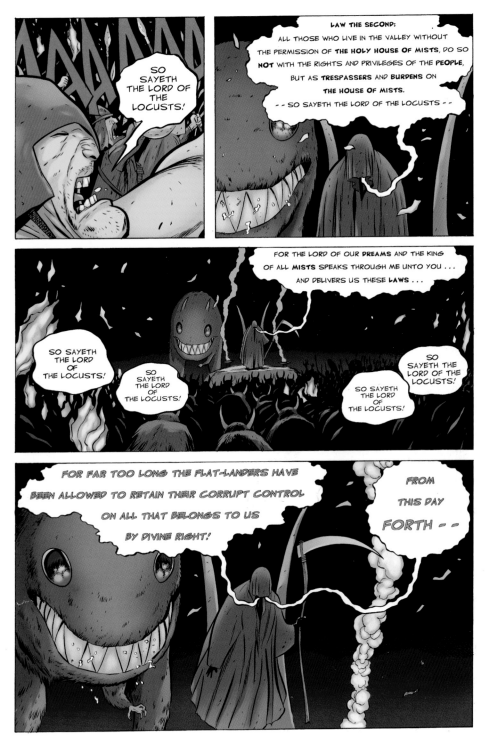

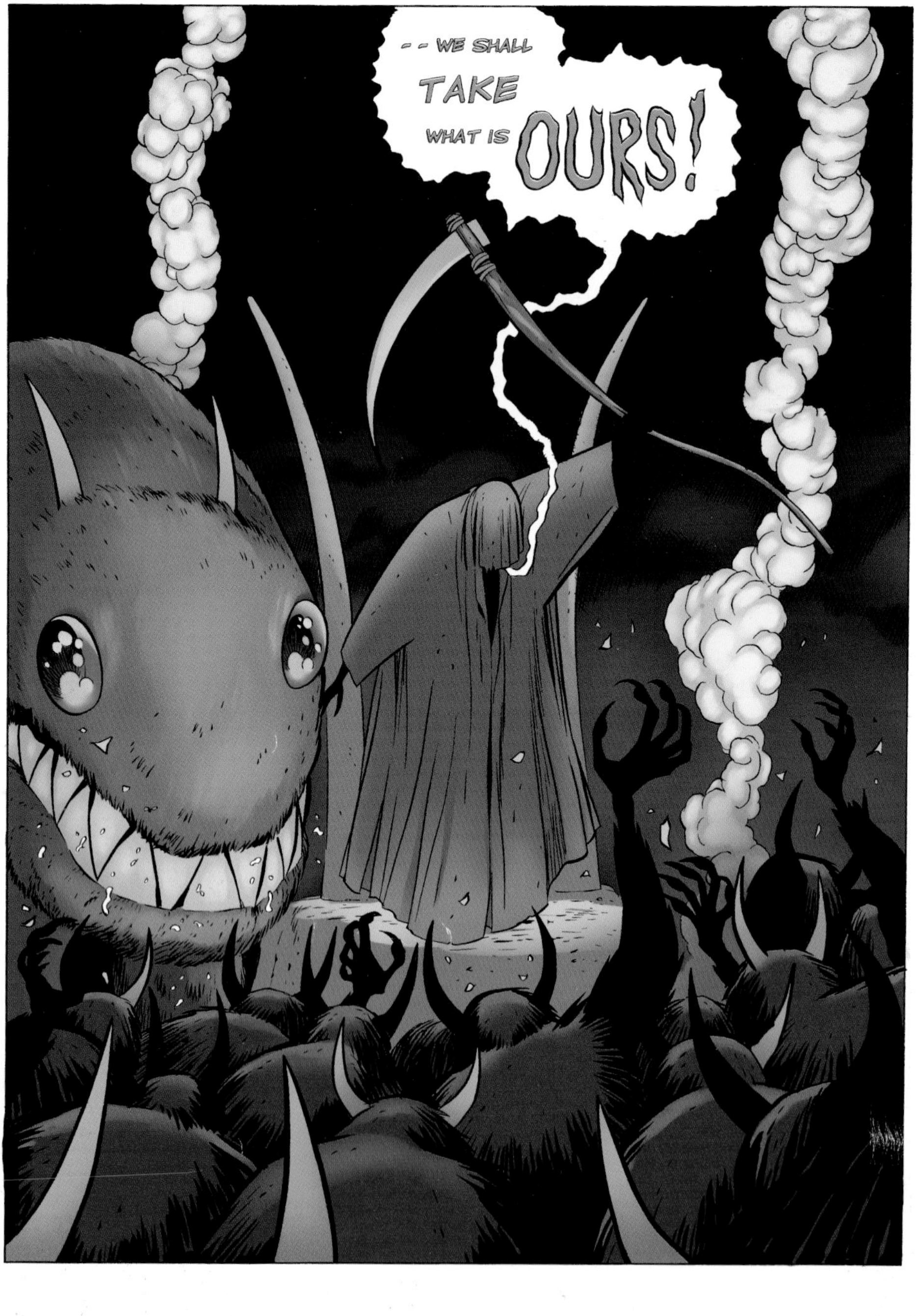
-- WE SHALL TAKE WHAT IS OURS!

CHAPTER SIX

THE MIDSUMMER'S DAY PLAN

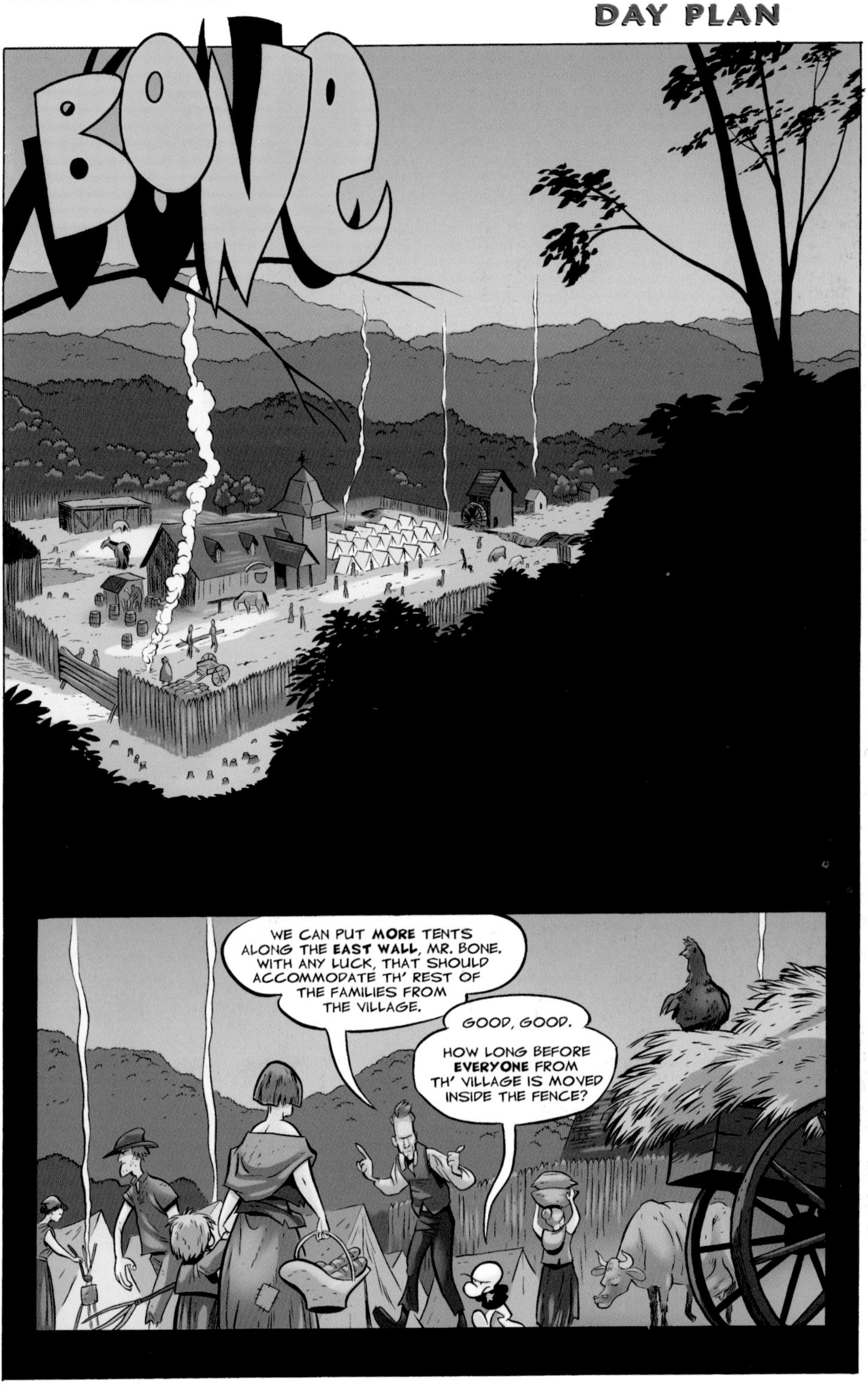

BONE
WE CAN PUT MORE TENTS ALONG THE EAST WALL, MR. BONE. WITH ANY LUCK, THAT SHOULD ACCOMMODATE TH' REST OF THE FAMILIES FROM THE VILLAGE.
GOOD, GOOD.
HOW LONG BEFORE EVERYONE FROM TH' VILLAGE IS MOVED INSIDE THE FENCE?

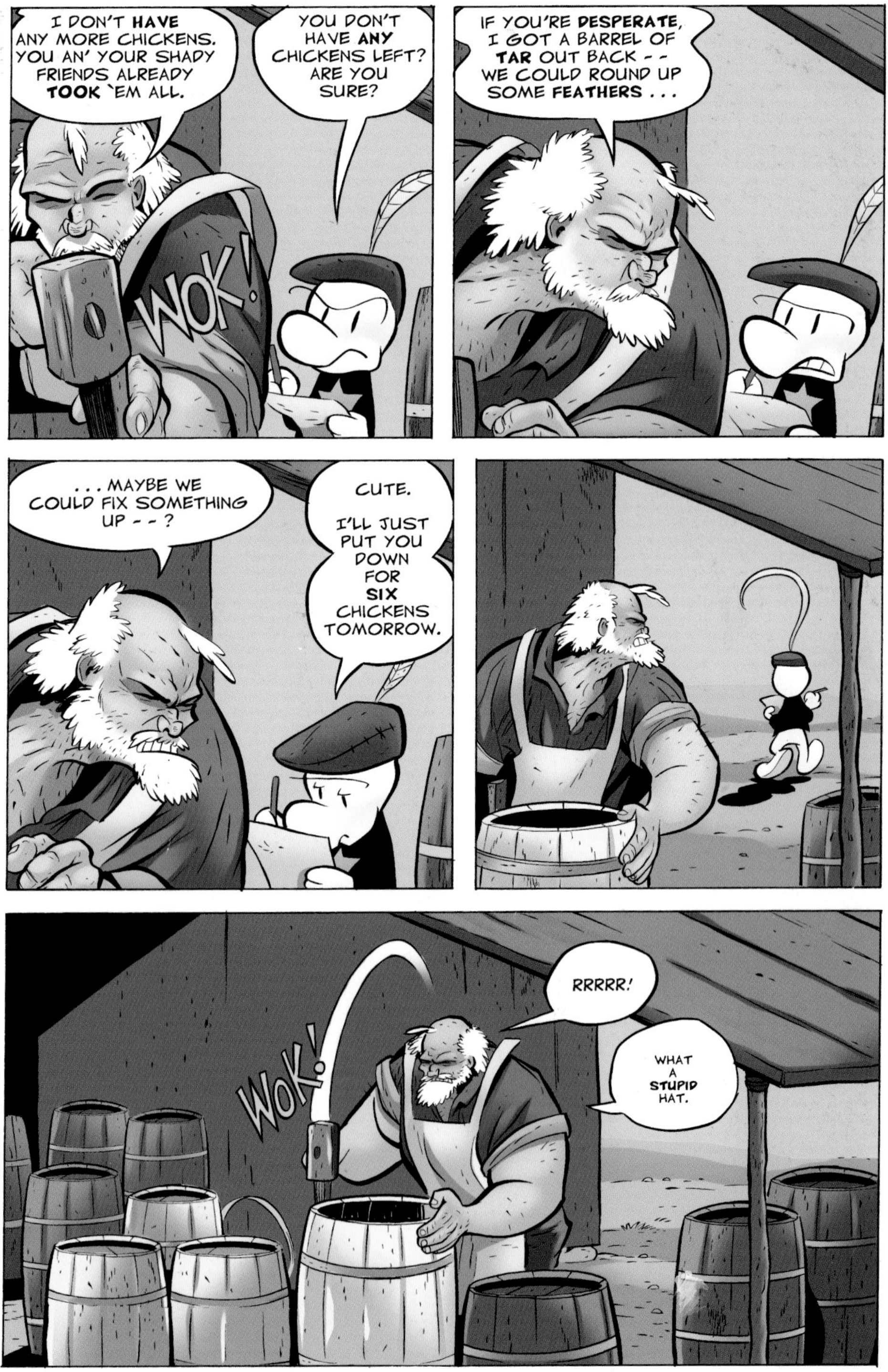
I DON'T HAVE ANY MORE CHICKENS. YOU AN' YOUR SHADY FRIENDS ALREADY TOOK 'EM ALL.
WOK!
YOU DON'T HAVE ANY CHICKENS LEFT? ARE YOU SURE?
IF YOU'RE DESPERATE, I GOT A BARREL OF TAR OUT BACK - - WE COULD ROUND UP SOME FEATHERS . . .
. . . MAYBE WE COULD FIX SOMETHING UP - - ?
CUTE.
I'LL JUST PUT YOU DOWN FOR SIX CHICKENS TOMORROW.
RRRRR!
WOK!
WHAT A STUPID HAT.

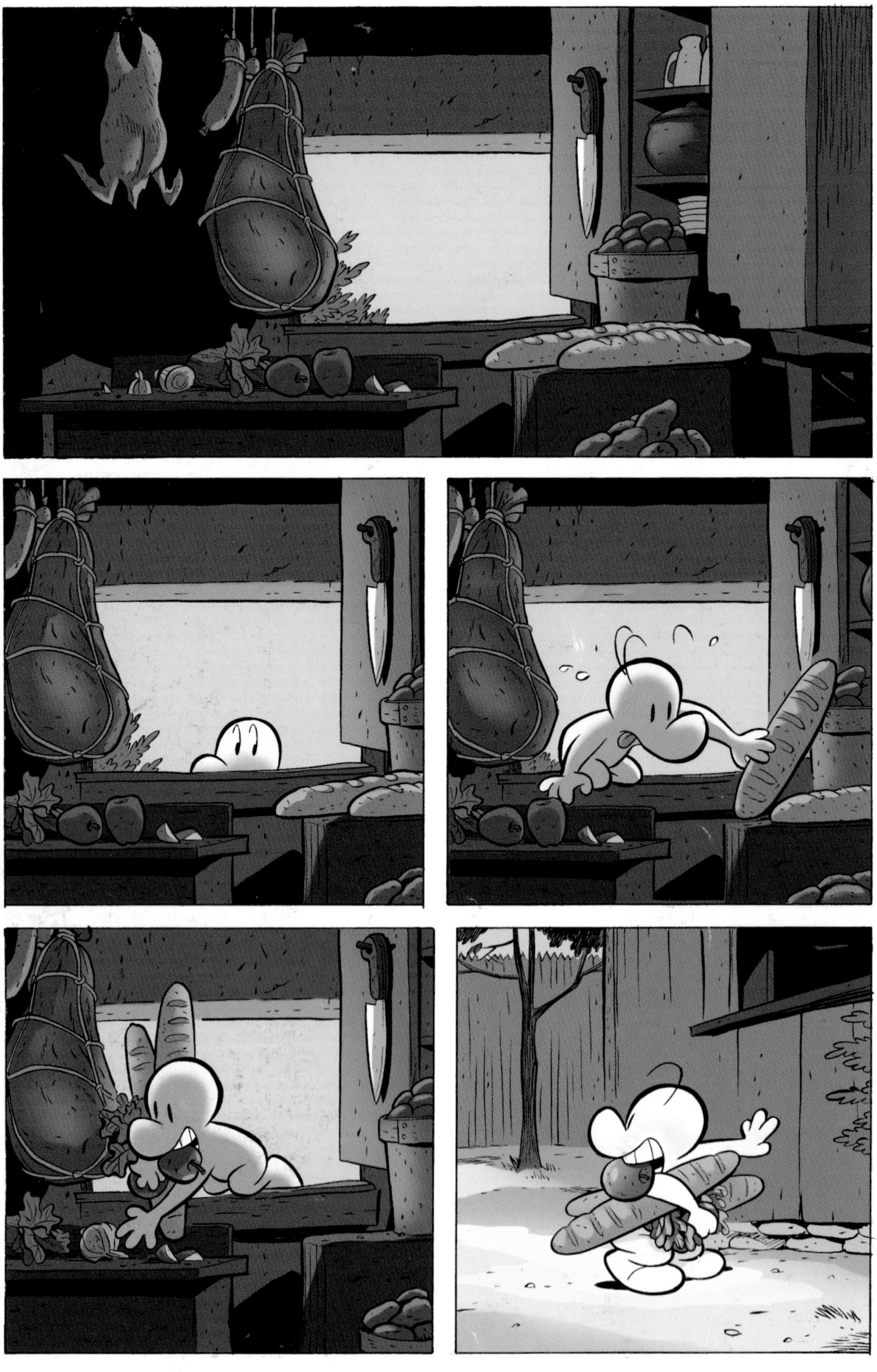

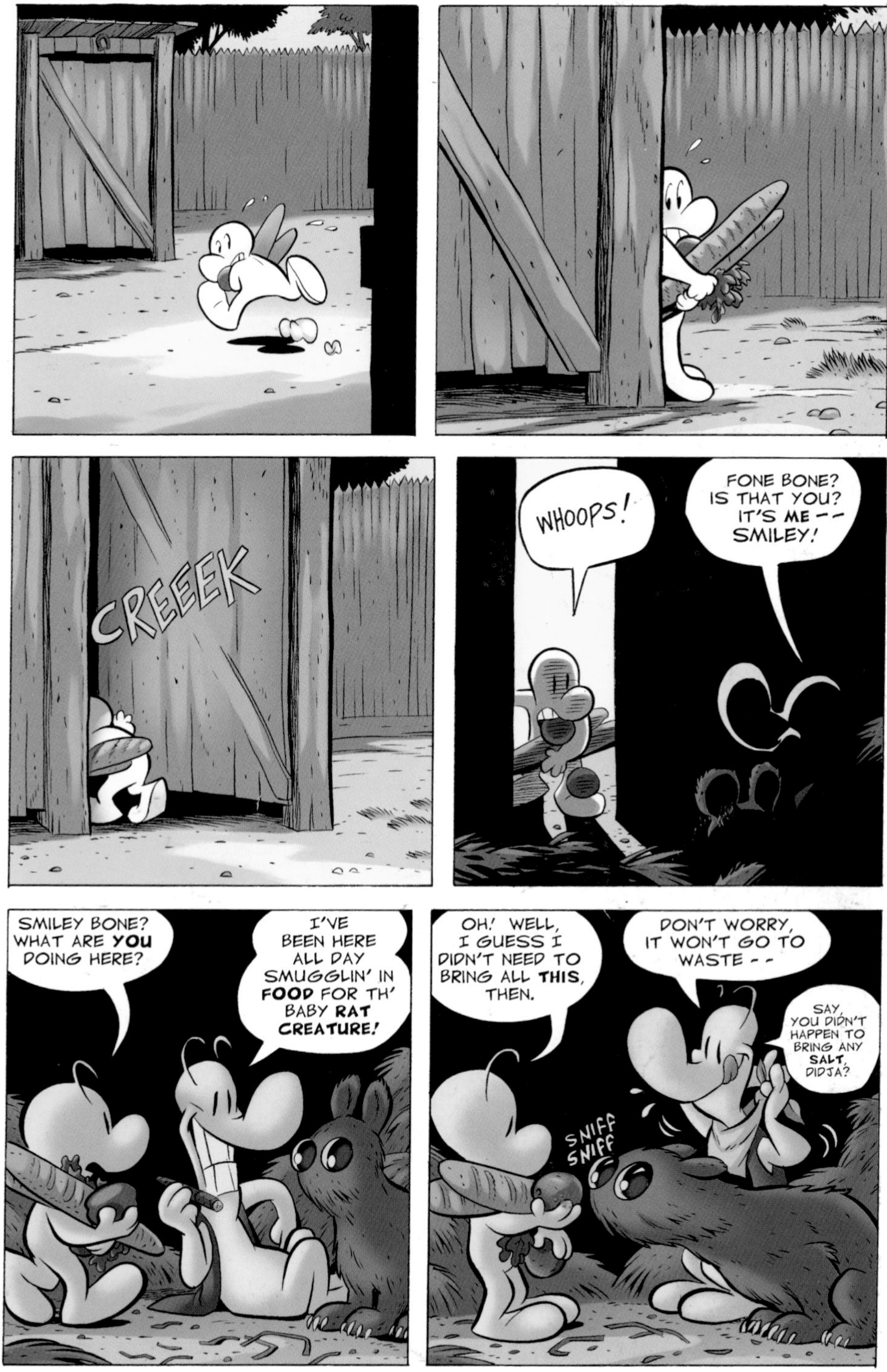
CREEEK
WHOOPS!
FONE BONE? IS THAT YOU? IT'S ME -- SMILEY!
SMILEY BONE? WHAT ARE YOU DOING HERE?
I'VE BEEN HERE ALL DAY SMUGGLIN' IN FOOD FOR TH' BABY RAT CREATURE!
OH! WELL, I GUESS I DIDN'T NEED TO BRING ALL THIS, THEN.
DON'T WORRY, IT WON'T GO TO WASTE --
SAY, YOU DIDN'T HAPPEN TO BRING ANY SALT, DIDJA?
SNIFF SNIFF

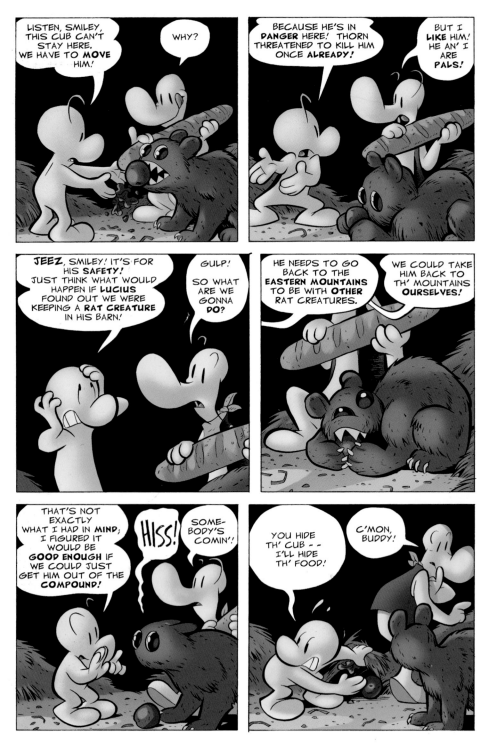

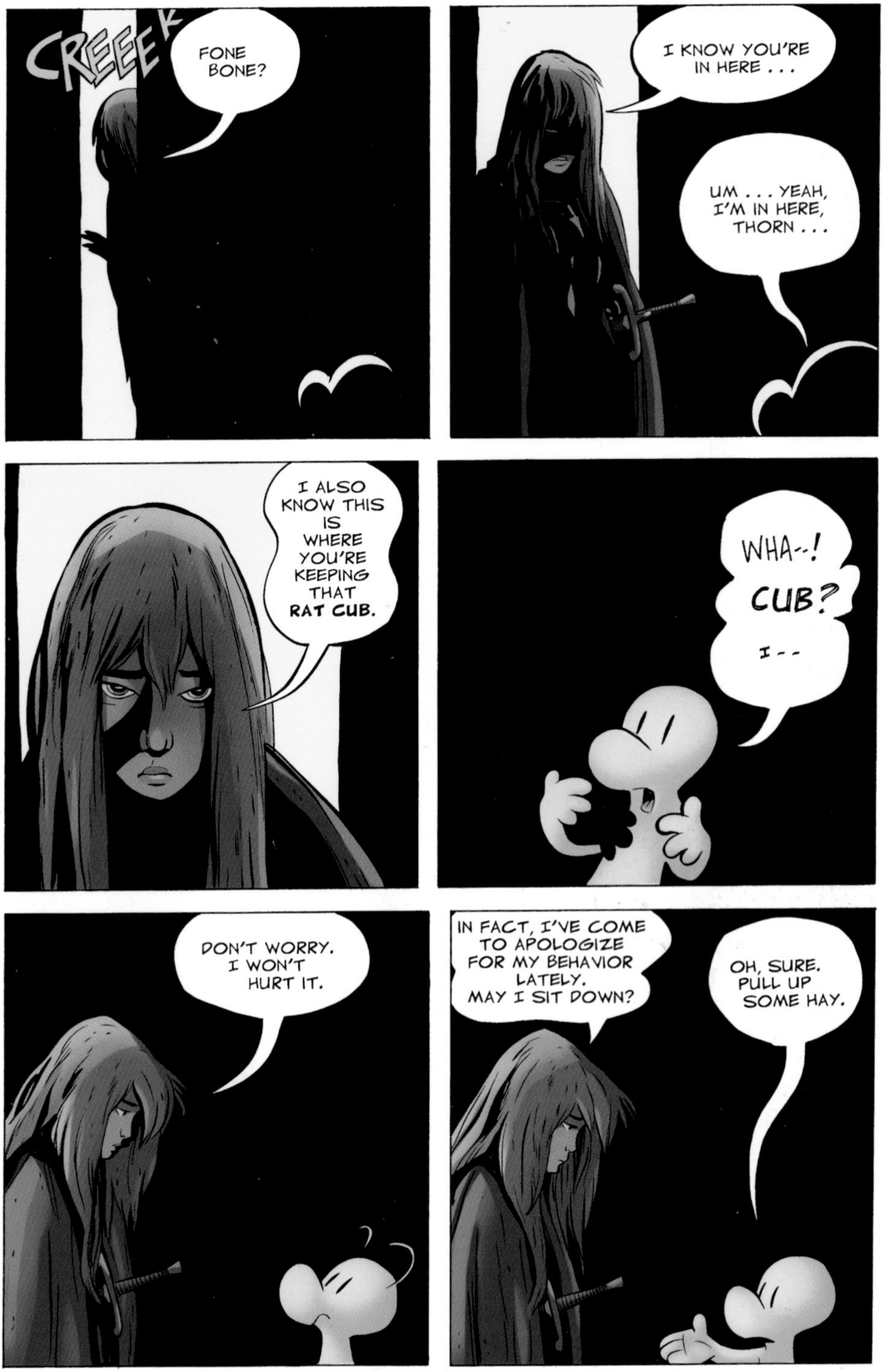
CREEEK
FONE BONE?
I KNOW YOU'RE IN HERE . . .
UM . . . YEAH, I'M IN HERE, THORN . . .
I ALSO KNOW THIS IS WHERE YOU'RE KEEPING THAT RAT CUB.
WHA--! CUB? I--
DON'T WORRY. I WON'T HURT IT.
IN FACT, I'VE COME TO APOLOGIZE FOR MY BEHAVIOR LATELY. MAY I SIT DOWN?
OH, SURE. PULL UP SOME HAY.

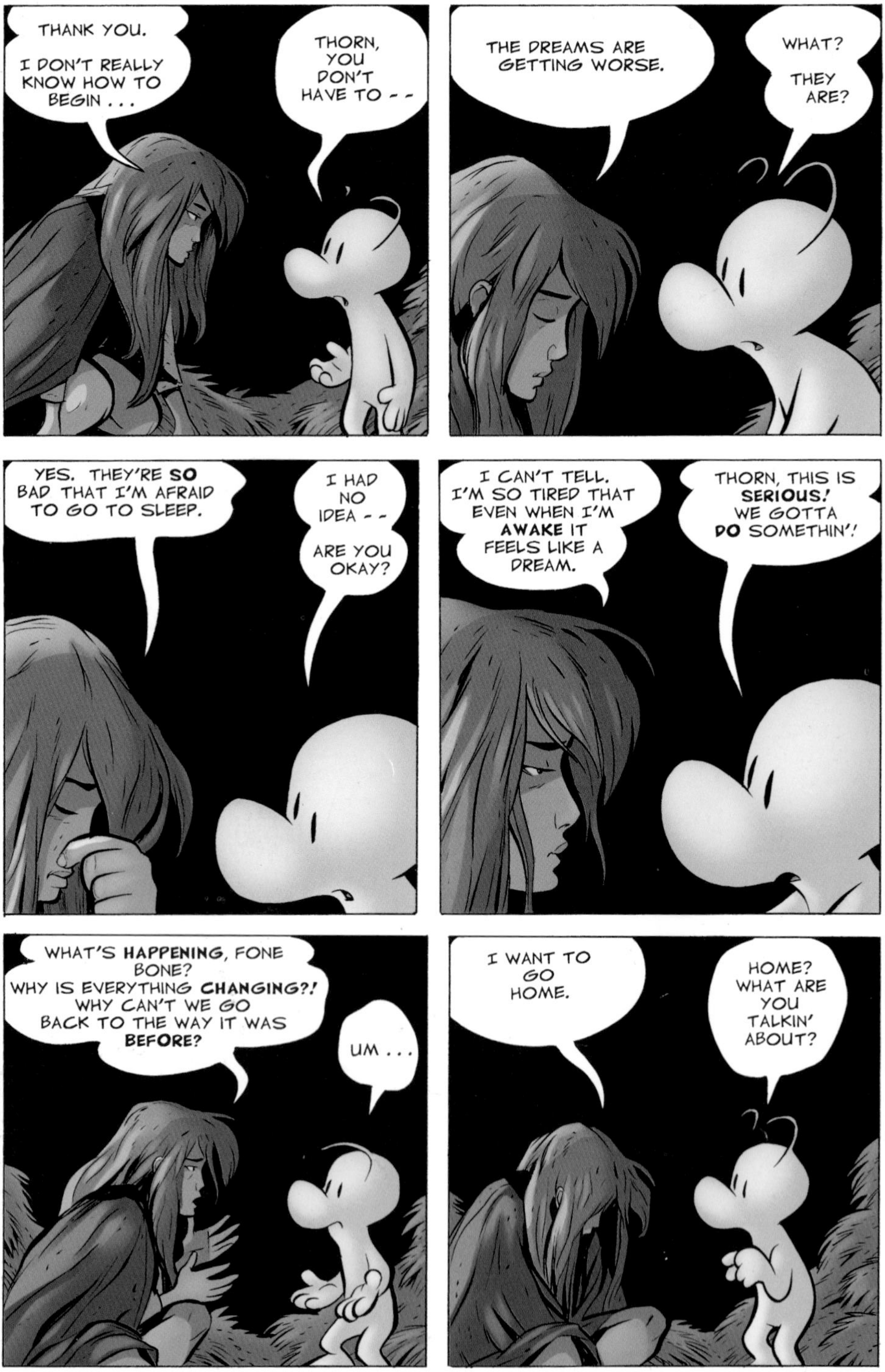
THANK YOU.
I DON'T REALLY KNOW HOW TO BEGIN . . .
THORN, YOU DON'T HAVE TO - -
THE DREAMS ARE GETTING WORSE.
WHAT?
THEY ARE?
YES. THEY'RE SO BAD THAT I'M AFRAID TO GO TO SLEEP.
I HAD NO IDEA - -
ARE YOU OKAY?
I CAN'T TELL. I'M SO TIRED THAT EVEN WHEN I'M AWAKE IT FEELS LIKE A DREAM.
THORN, THIS IS SERIOUS! WE GOTTA DO SOMETHIN'!
WHAT'S HAPPENING, FONE BONE? WHY IS EVERYTHING CHANGING?! WHY CAN'T WE GO BACK TO THE WAY IT WAS BEFORE?
UM . . .
I WANT TO GO HOME.
HOME? WHAT ARE YOU TALKIN' ABOUT?

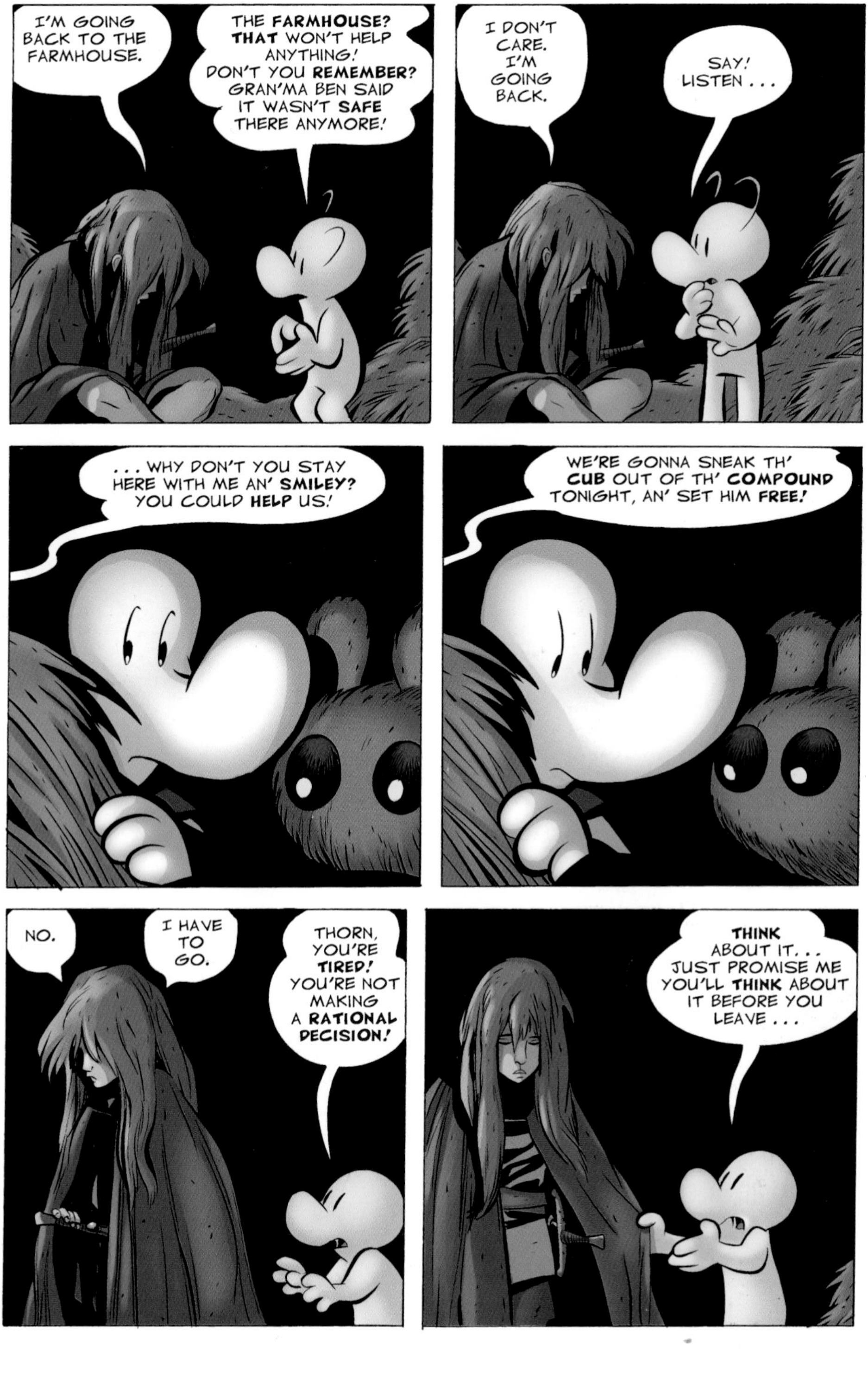
I'M GOING BACK TO THE FARMHOUSE.
THE FARMHOUSE? THAT WON'T HELP ANYTHING! DON'T YOU REMEMBER? GRAN'MA BEN SAID IT WASN'T SAFE THERE ANYMORE!
I DON'T CARE. I'M GOING BACK.
SAY! LISTEN . . .
. . . WHY DON'T YOU STAY HERE WITH ME AN' SMILEY? YOU COULD HELP US!
WE'RE GONNA SNEAK TH' CUB OUT OF TH' COMPOUND TONIGHT, AN' SET HIM FREE!
NO.
I HAVE TO GO.
THORN, YOU'RE TIRED! YOU'RE NOT MAKING A RATIONAL DECISION!
THINK ABOUT IT. . . JUST PROMISE ME YOU'LL THINK ABOUT IT BEFORE YOU LEAVE . . .

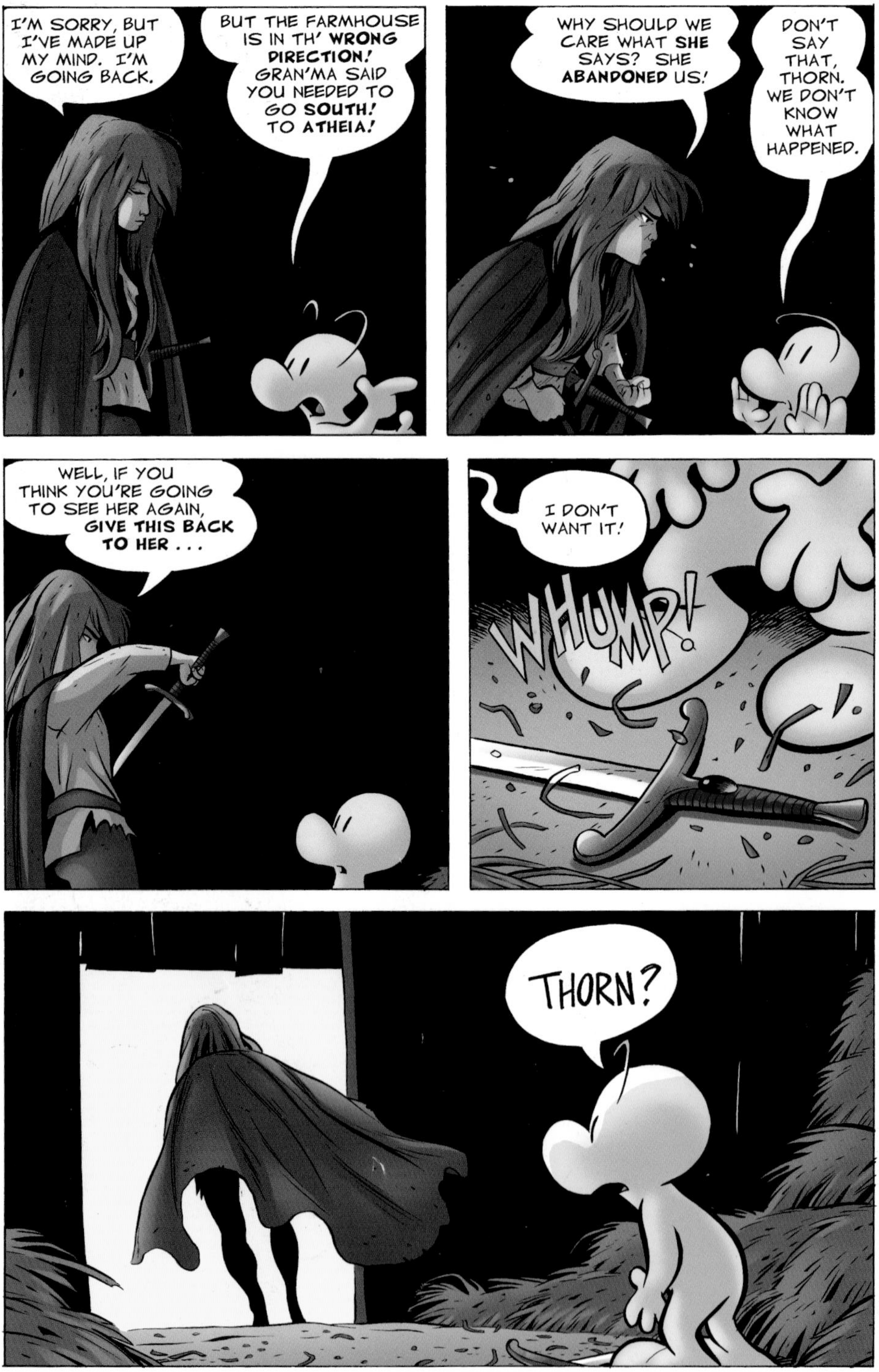
I'M SORRY, BUT I'VE MADE UP MY MIND. I'M GOING BACK.
BUT THE FARMHOUSE IS IN TH' WRONG DIRECTION! GRAN'MA SAID YOU NEEDED TO GO SOUTH! TO ATHEIA!
WHY SHOULD WE CARE WHAT SHE SAYS? SHE ABANDONED US!
DON'T SAY THAT, THORN. WE DON'T KNOW WHAT HAPPENED.
WELL, IF YOU THINK YOU'RE GOING TO SEE HER AGAIN, GIVE THIS BACK TO HER . . .
I DON'T WANT IT!
WHUMP!
THORN?

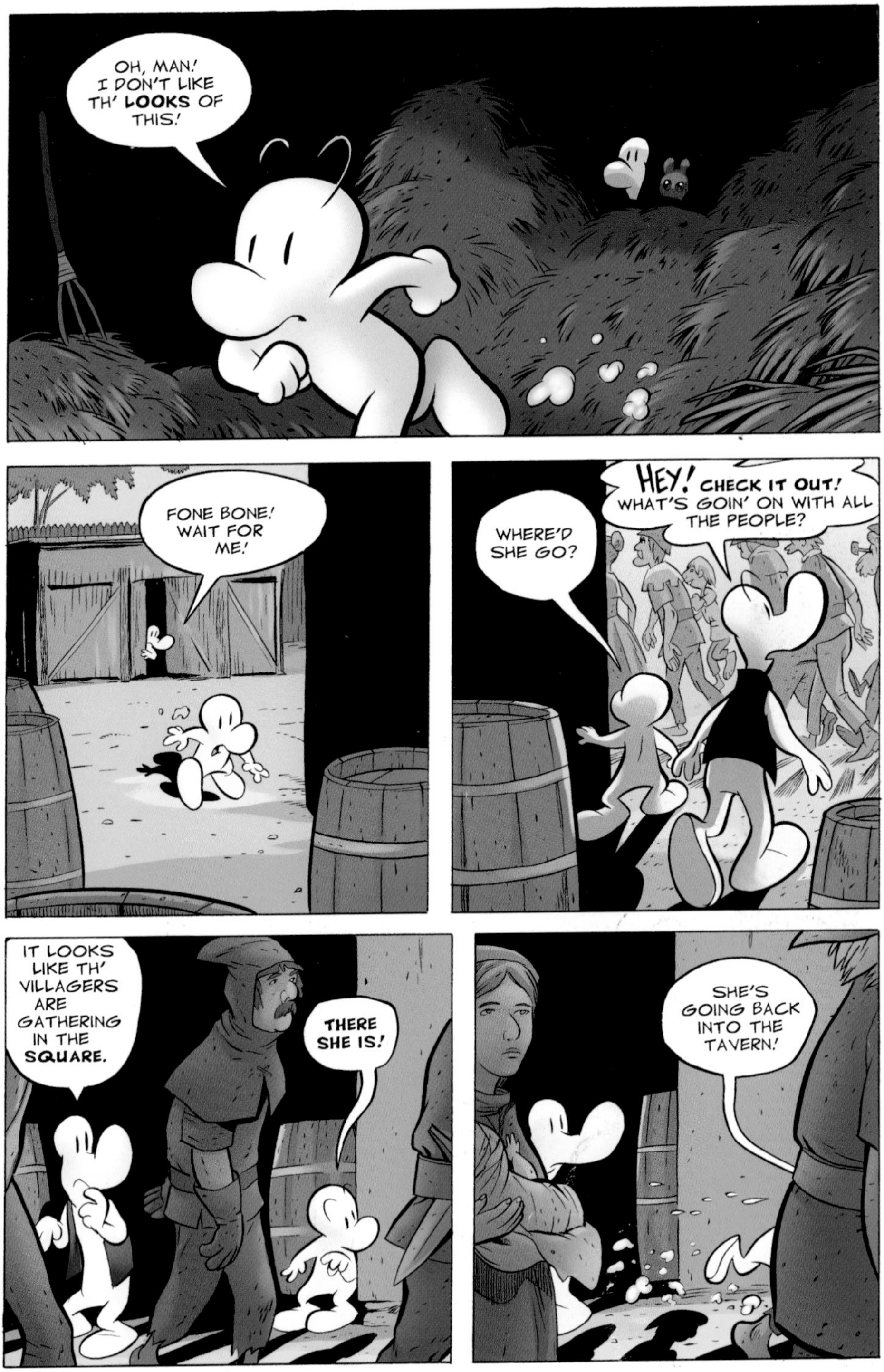
OH, MAN! I DON'T LIKE TH' LOOKS OF THIS!
FONE BONE! WAIT FOR ME!
WHERE'D SHE GO?
HEY! CHECK IT OUT! WHAT'S GOIN' ON WITH ALL THE PEOPLE?
IT LOOKS LIKE TH' VILLAGERS ARE GATHERING IN THE SQUARE.
THERE SHE IS!
SHE'S GOING BACK INTO THE TAVERN!

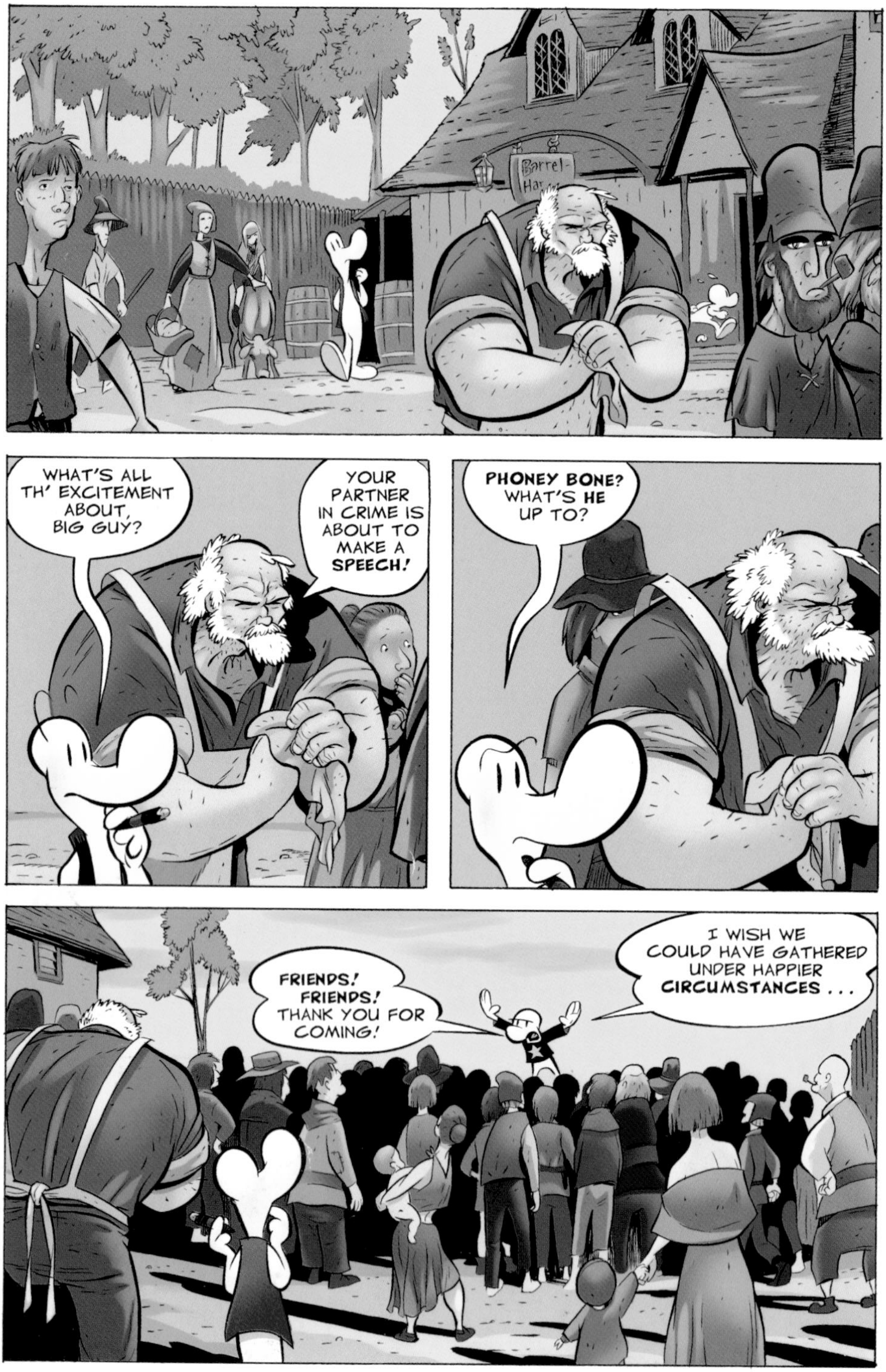
Barrel-Har
WHAT'S ALL TH' EXCITEMENT ABOUT, BIG GUY?
YOUR PARTNER IN CRIME IS ABOUT TO MAKE A **SPEECH!**
PHONEY BONE? WHAT'S **HE** UP TO?
FRIENDS! FRIENDS! THANK YOU FOR COMING!
I WISH WE COULD HAVE GATHERED UNDER HAPPIER **CIRCUMSTANCES . . .**

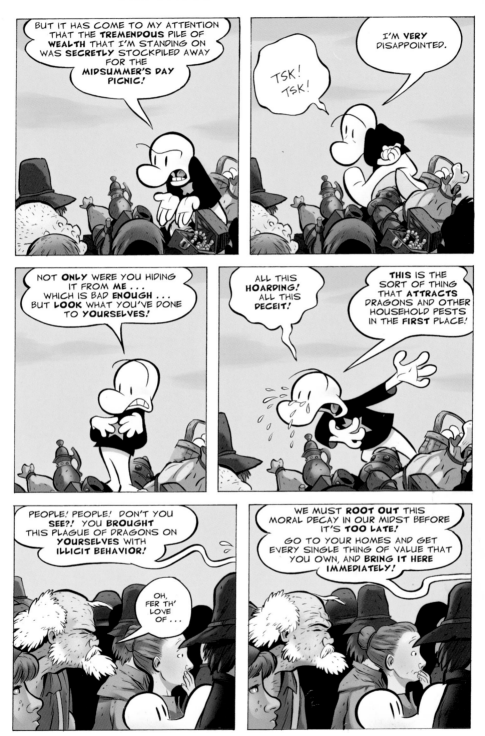

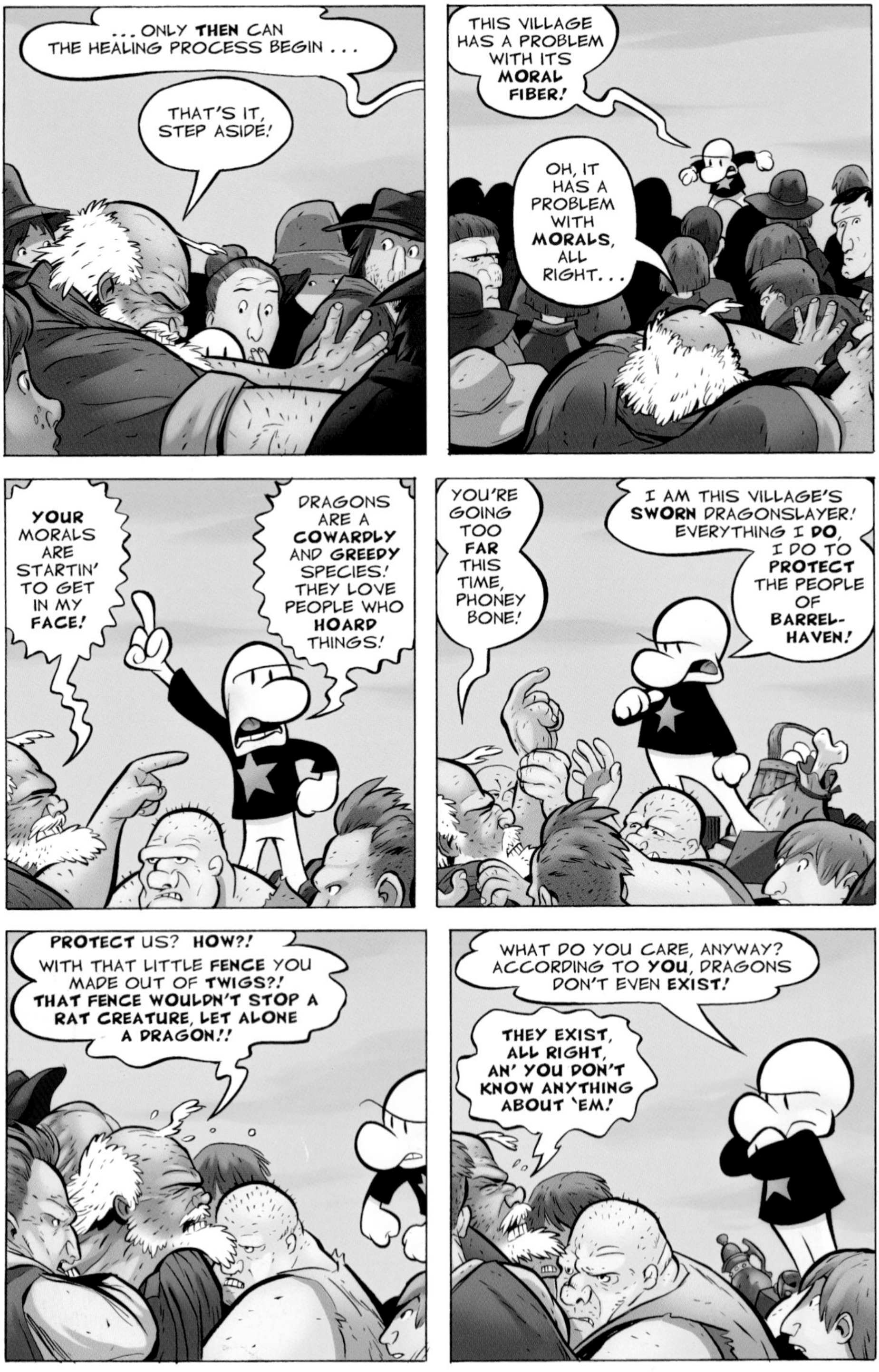
...ONLY THEN CAN THE HEALING PROCESS BEGIN...
THAT'S IT, STEP ASIDE!
THIS VILLAGE HAS A PROBLEM WITH ITS MORAL FIBER!
OH, IT HAS A PROBLEM WITH MORALS, ALL RIGHT...
DRAGONS ARE A COWARDLY AND GREEDY SPECIES! THEY LOVE PEOPLE WHO HOARD THINGS!
YOUR MORALS ARE STARTIN' TO GET IN MY FACE!
YOU'RE GOING TOO FAR THIS TIME, PHONEY BONE!
I AM THIS VILLAGE'S SWORN DRAGONSLAYER! EVERYTHING I DO, I DO TO PROTECT THE PEOPLE OF BARREL-HAVEN!
PROTECT US? HOW?! WITH THAT LITTLE FENCE YOU MADE OUT OF TWIGS?! THAT FENCE WOULDN'T STOP A RAT CREATURE, LET ALONE A DRAGON!!
WHAT DO YOU CARE, ANYWAY? ACCORDING TO YOU, DRAGONS DON'T EVEN EXIST!
THEY EXIST, ALL RIGHT, AN' YOU DON'T KNOW ANYTHING ABOUT 'EM!

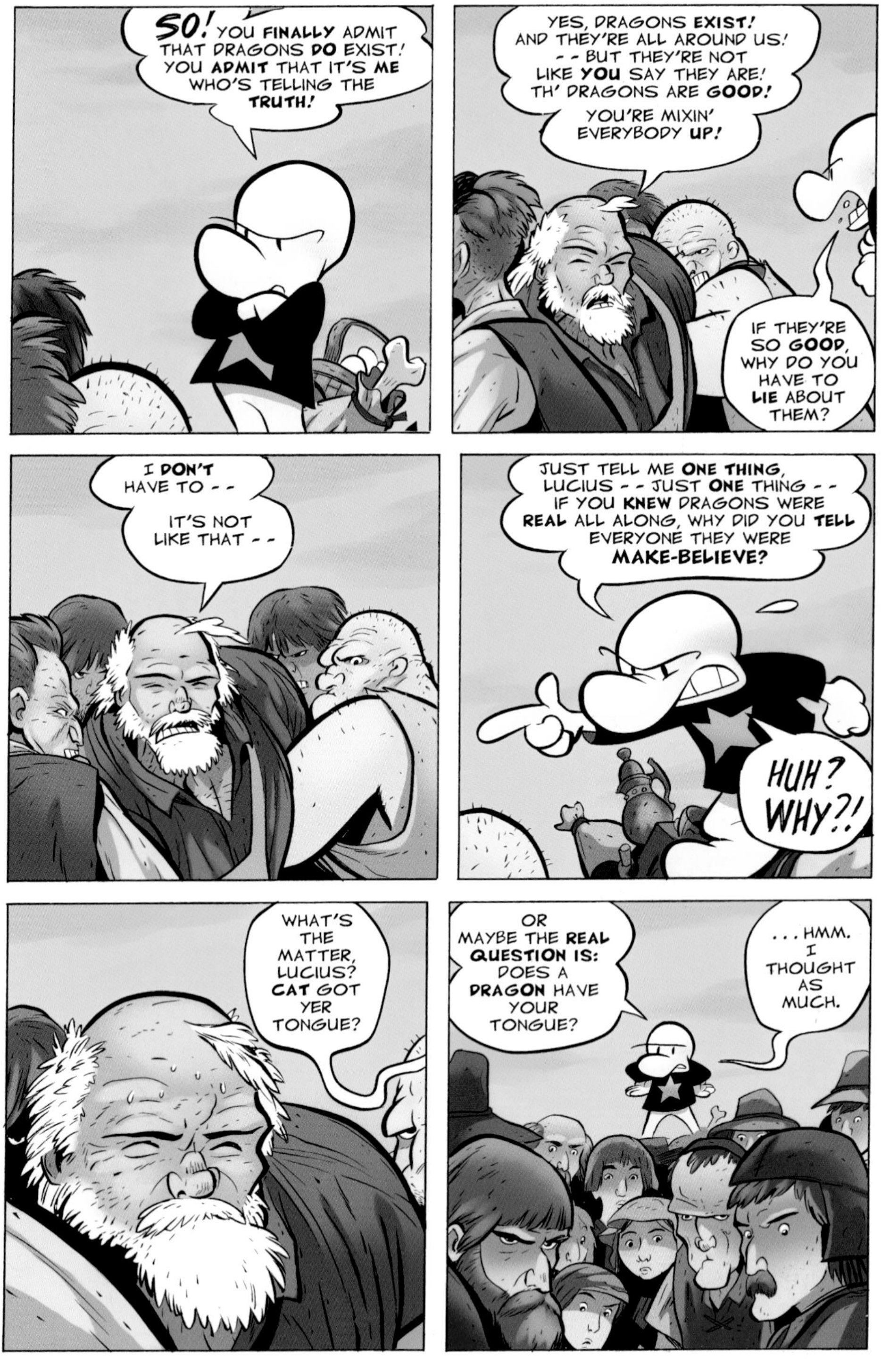
SO! YOU FINALLY ADMIT THAT DRAGONS DO EXIST! YOU ADMIT THAT IT'S ME WHO'S TELLING THE TRUTH!
YES, DRAGONS EXIST! AND THEY'RE ALL AROUND US! - - BUT THEY'RE NOT LIKE YOU SAY THEY ARE! TH' DRAGONS ARE GOOD!
YOU'RE MIXIN' EVERYBODY UP!
IF THEY'RE SO GOOD, WHY DO YOU HAVE TO LIE ABOUT THEM?
I DON'T HAVE TO - -
IT'S NOT LIKE THAT - -
JUST TELL ME ONE THING, LUCIUS - - JUST ONE THING - - IF YOU KNEW DRAGONS WERE REAL ALL ALONG, WHY DID YOU TELL EVERYONE THEY WERE MAKE-BELIEVE?
HUH? WHY?!
WHAT'S THE MATTER, LUCIUS? CAT GOT YER TONGUE?
OR MAYBE THE REAL QUESTION IS: DOES A DRAGON HAVE YOUR TONGUE?
. . . HMM. I THOUGHT AS MUCH.

THE DRAGONSLAYER

THE MIDSUMMER'S DAY PLAN

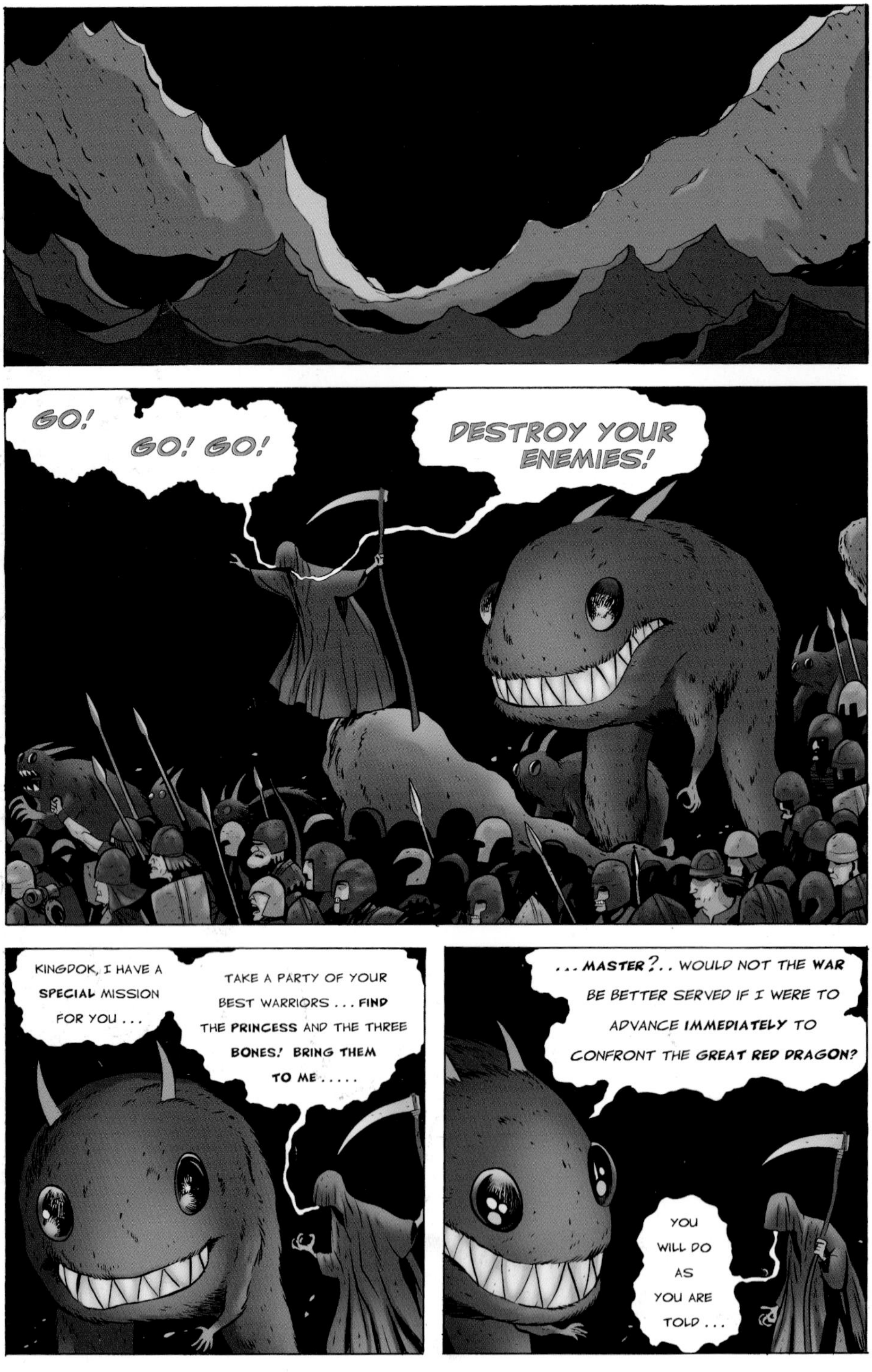
GO! GO! GO!
DESTROY YOUR ENEMIES!
KINGDOK, I HAVE A SPECIAL MISSION FOR YOU . . .
TAKE A PARTY OF YOUR BEST WARRIORS . . . FIND THE PRINCESS AND THE THREE BONES! BRING THEM TO ME . . . . .
. . . MASTER? . . WOULD NOT THE WAR BE BETTER SERVED IF I WERE TO ADVANCE IMMEDIATELY TO CONFRONT THE GREAT RED DRAGON?
YOU WILL DO AS YOU ARE TOLD . . .

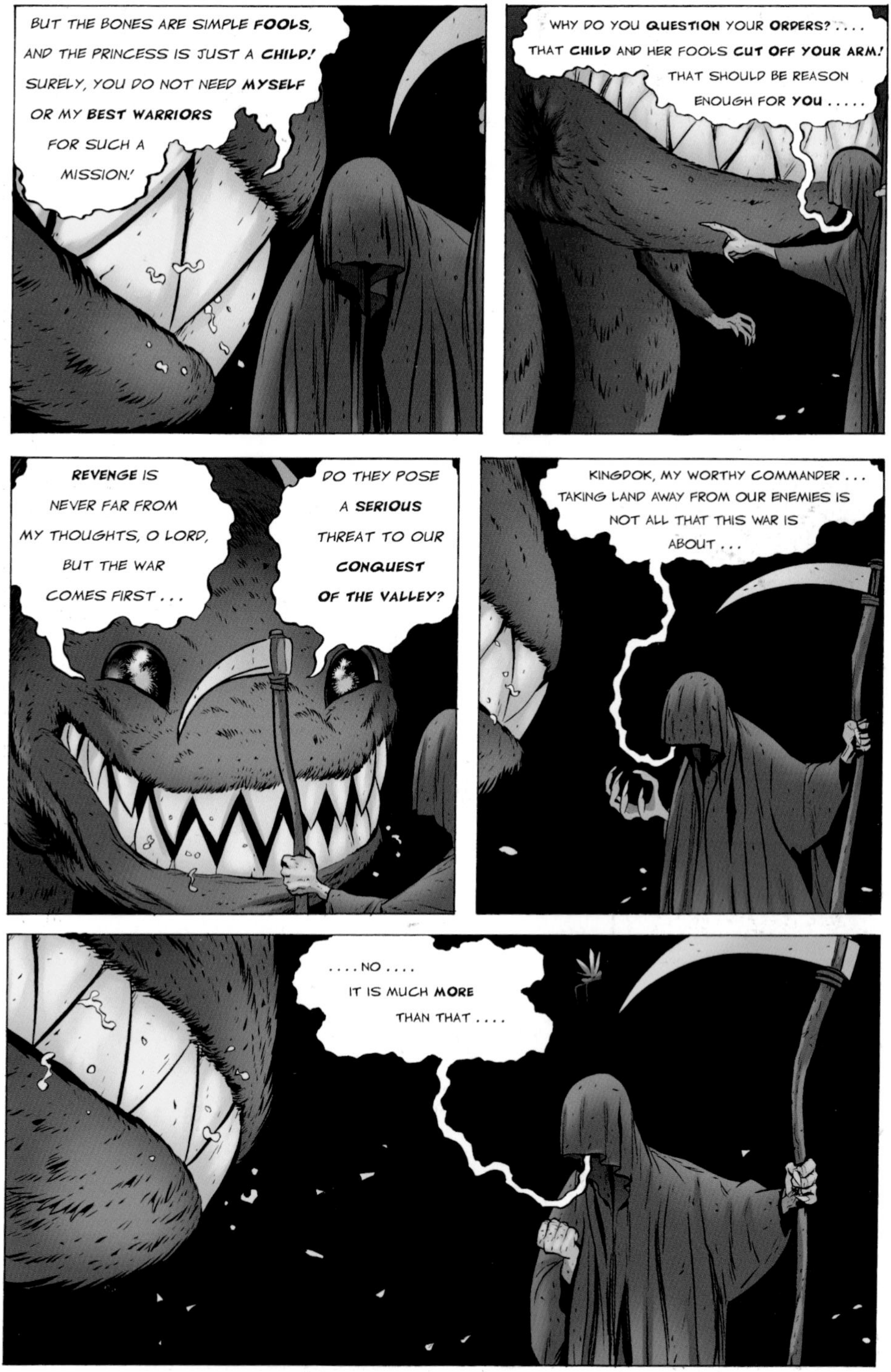
BUT THE BONES ARE SIMPLE FOOLS, AND THE PRINCESS IS JUST A CHILD! SURELY, YOU DO NOT NEED MYSELF OR MY BEST WARRIORS FOR SUCH A MISSION!
WHY DO YOU QUESTION YOUR ORDERS? . . . . THAT CHILD AND HER FOOLS CUT OFF YOUR ARM! THAT SHOULD BE REASON ENOUGH FOR YOU . . . . .
REVENGE IS NEVER FAR FROM MY THOUGHTS, O LORD, BUT THE WAR COMES FIRST . . .
DO THEY POSE A SERIOUS THREAT TO OUR CONQUEST OF THE VALLEY?
KINGDOK, MY WORTHY COMMANDER . . . TAKING LAND AWAY FROM OUR ENEMIES IS NOT ALL THAT THIS WAR IS ABOUT . . .
. . . . NO . . . . IT IS MUCH MORE THAN THAT . . . .

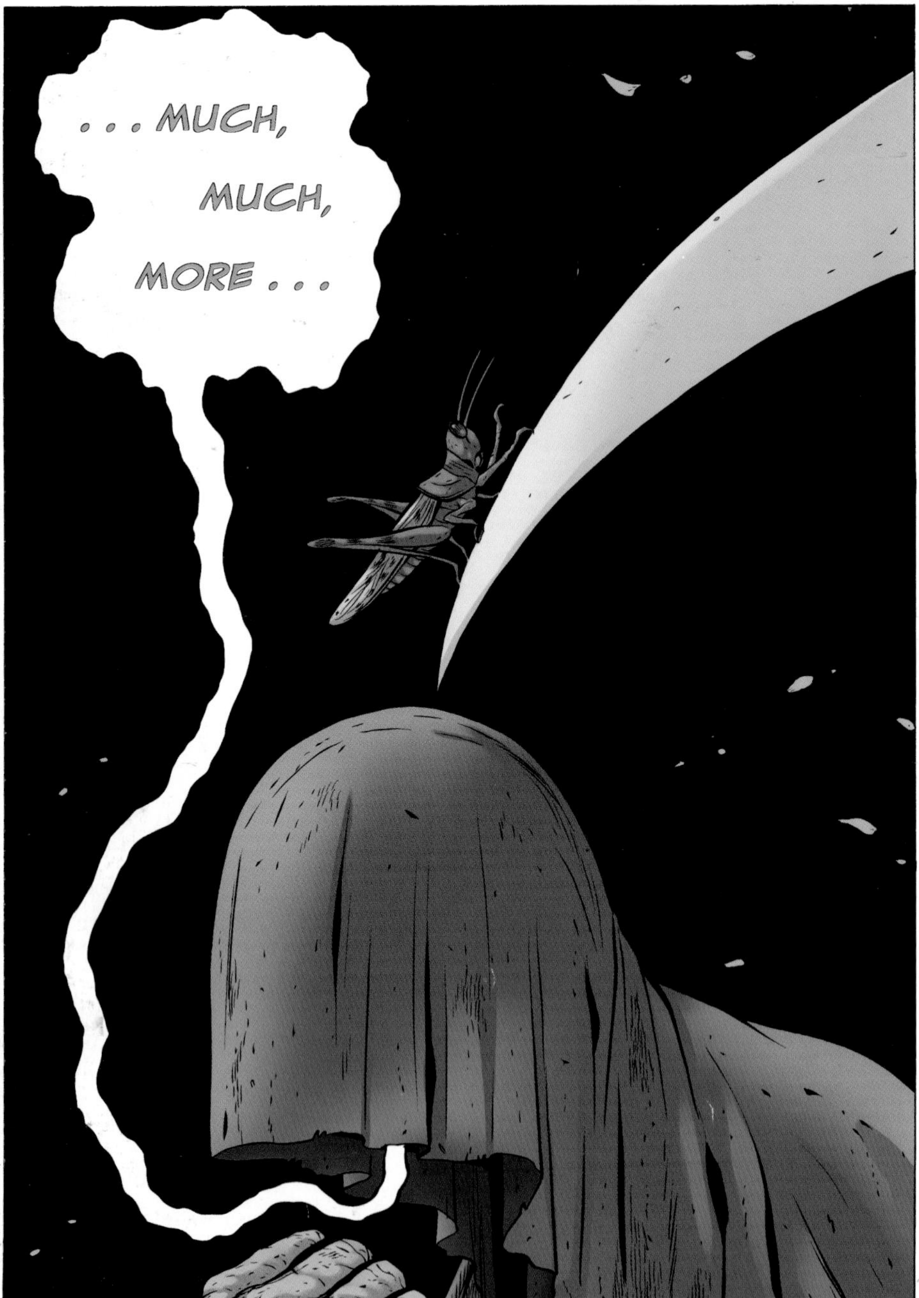
. . . MUCH,
MUCH,
MORE . . .

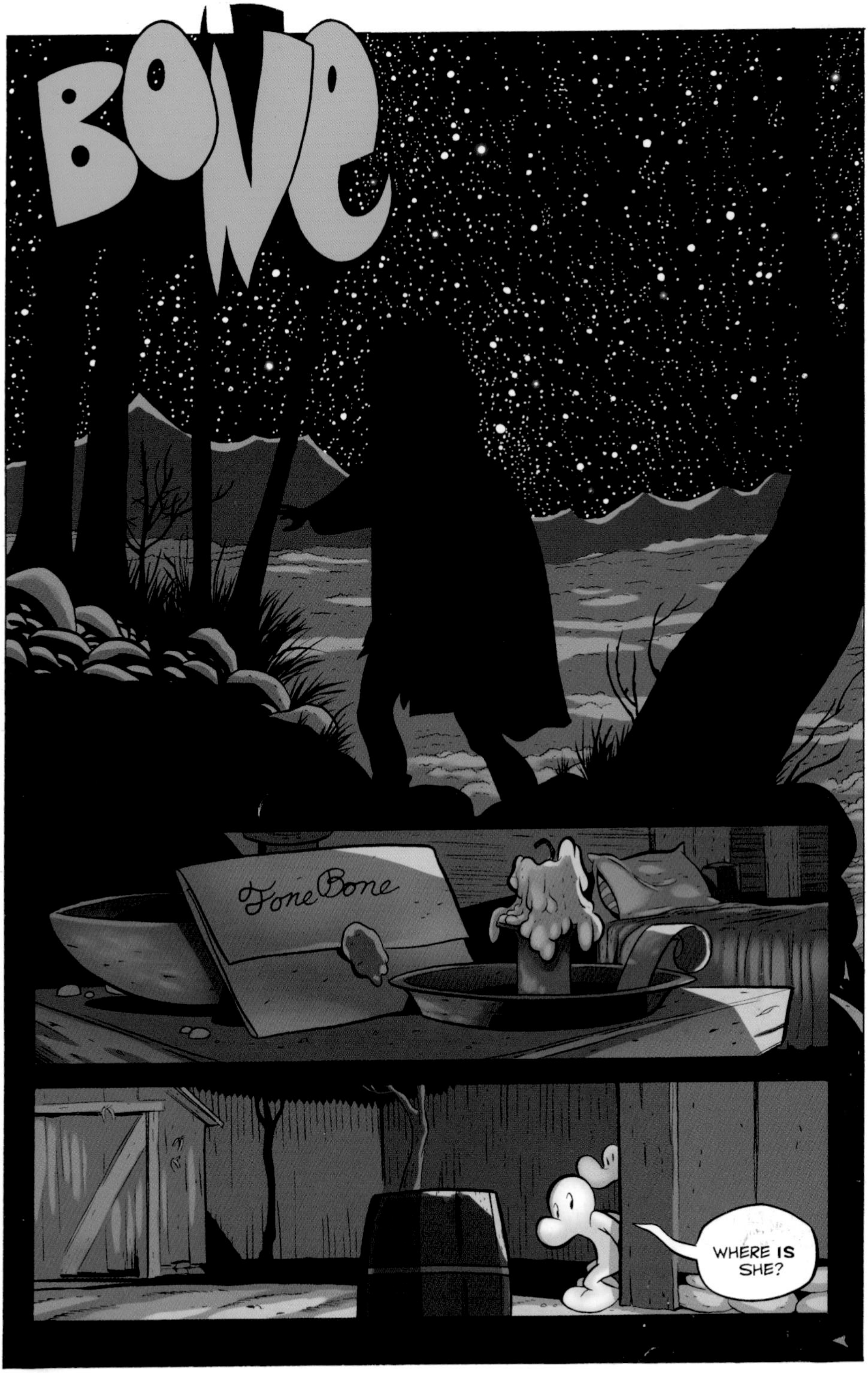
BONE
Fone Bone
WHERE IS SHE?

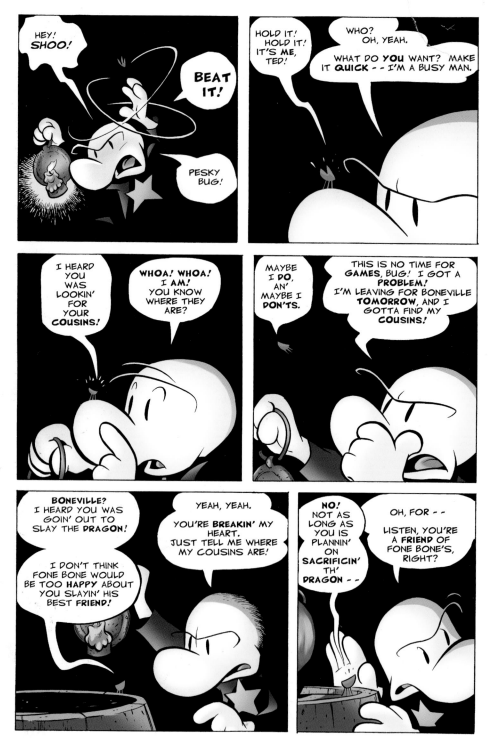

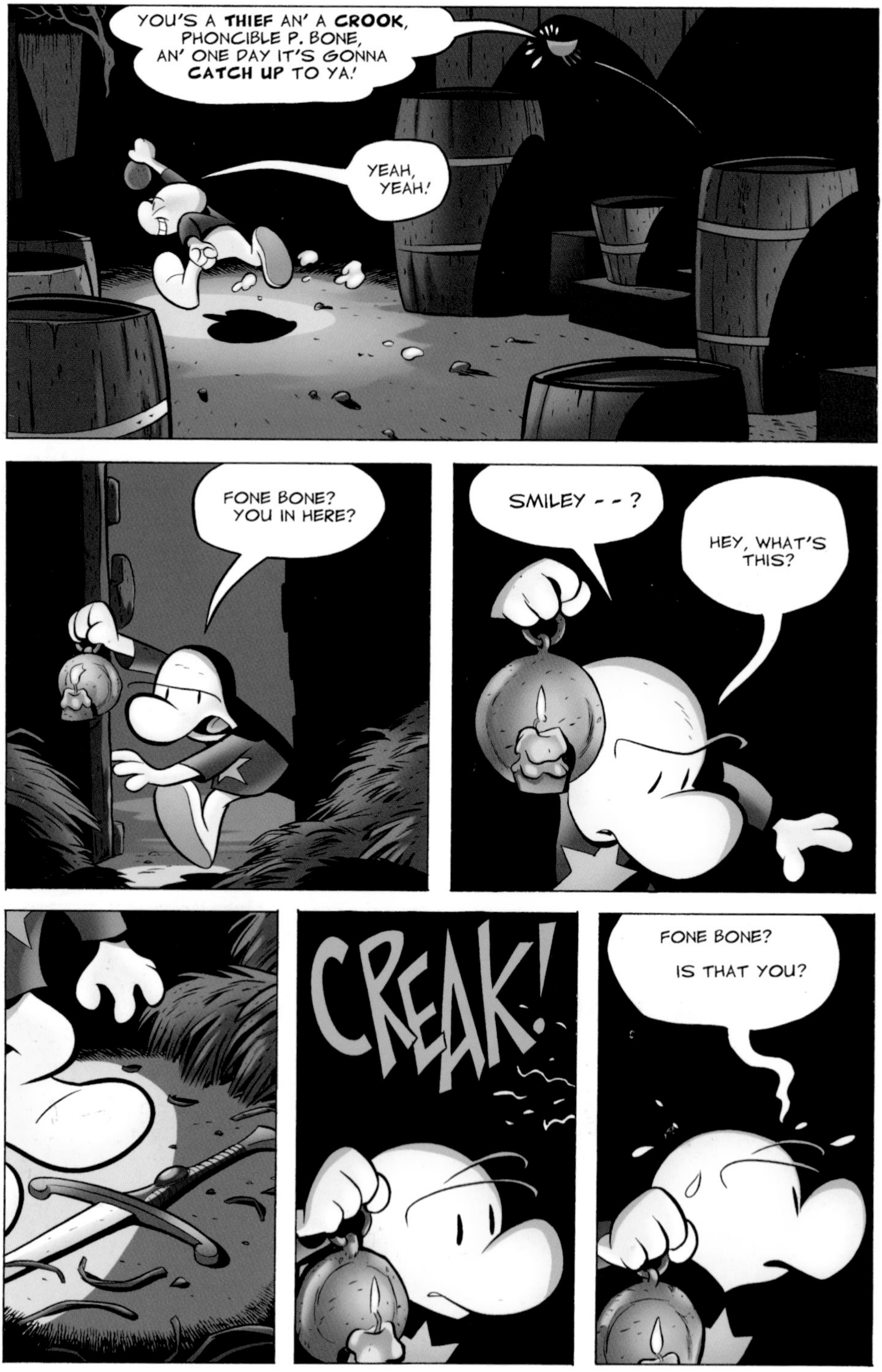
YOU'S A **THIEF** AN' A **CROOK**, PHONCIBLE P. BONE, AN' ONE DAY IT'S GONNA **CATCH UP** TO YA!
YEAH, YEAH!
FONE BONE? YOU IN HERE?
SMILEY - - ?
HEY, WHAT'S THIS?
CREAK!
FONE BONE?
IS THAT YOU?

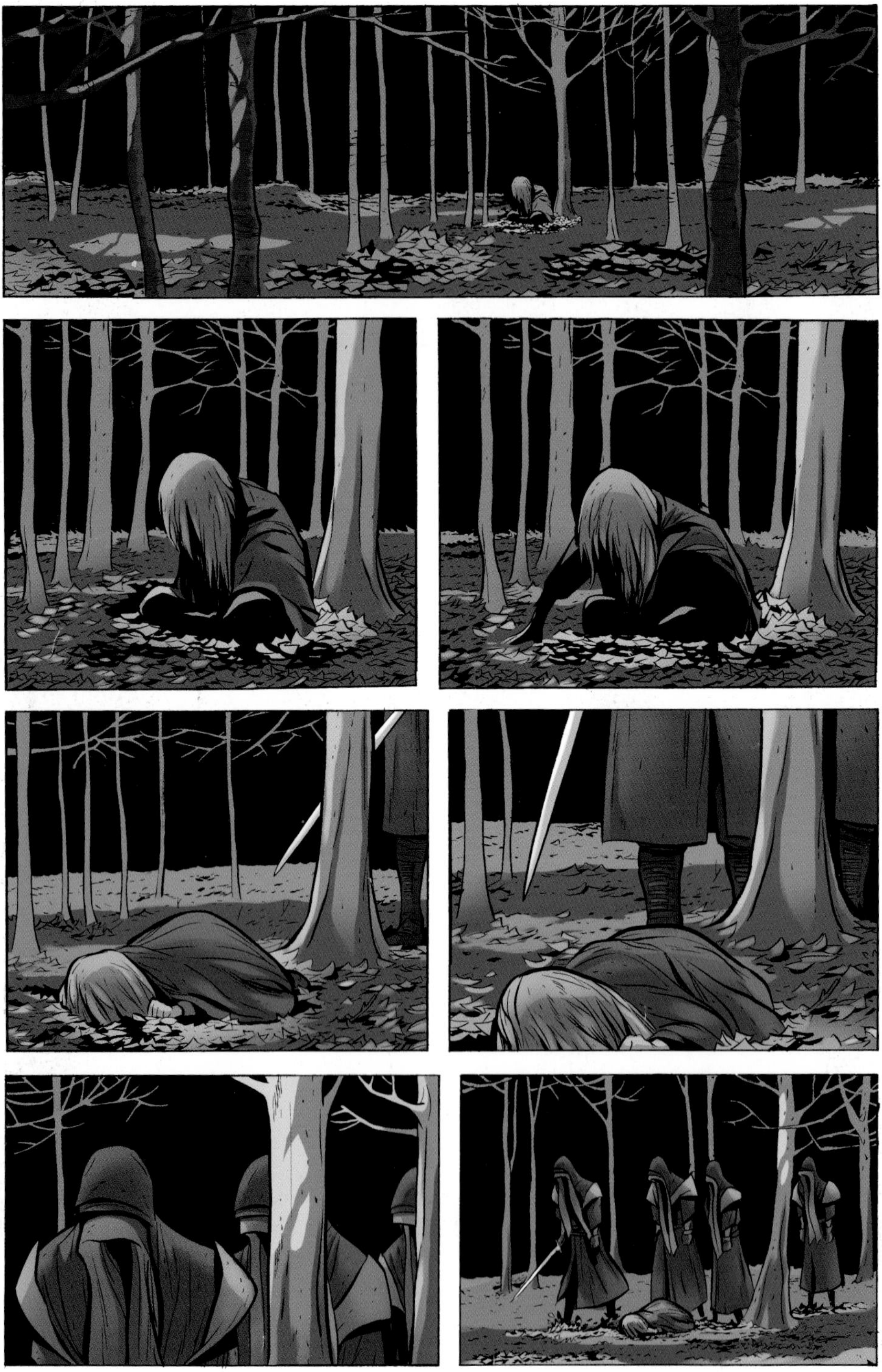

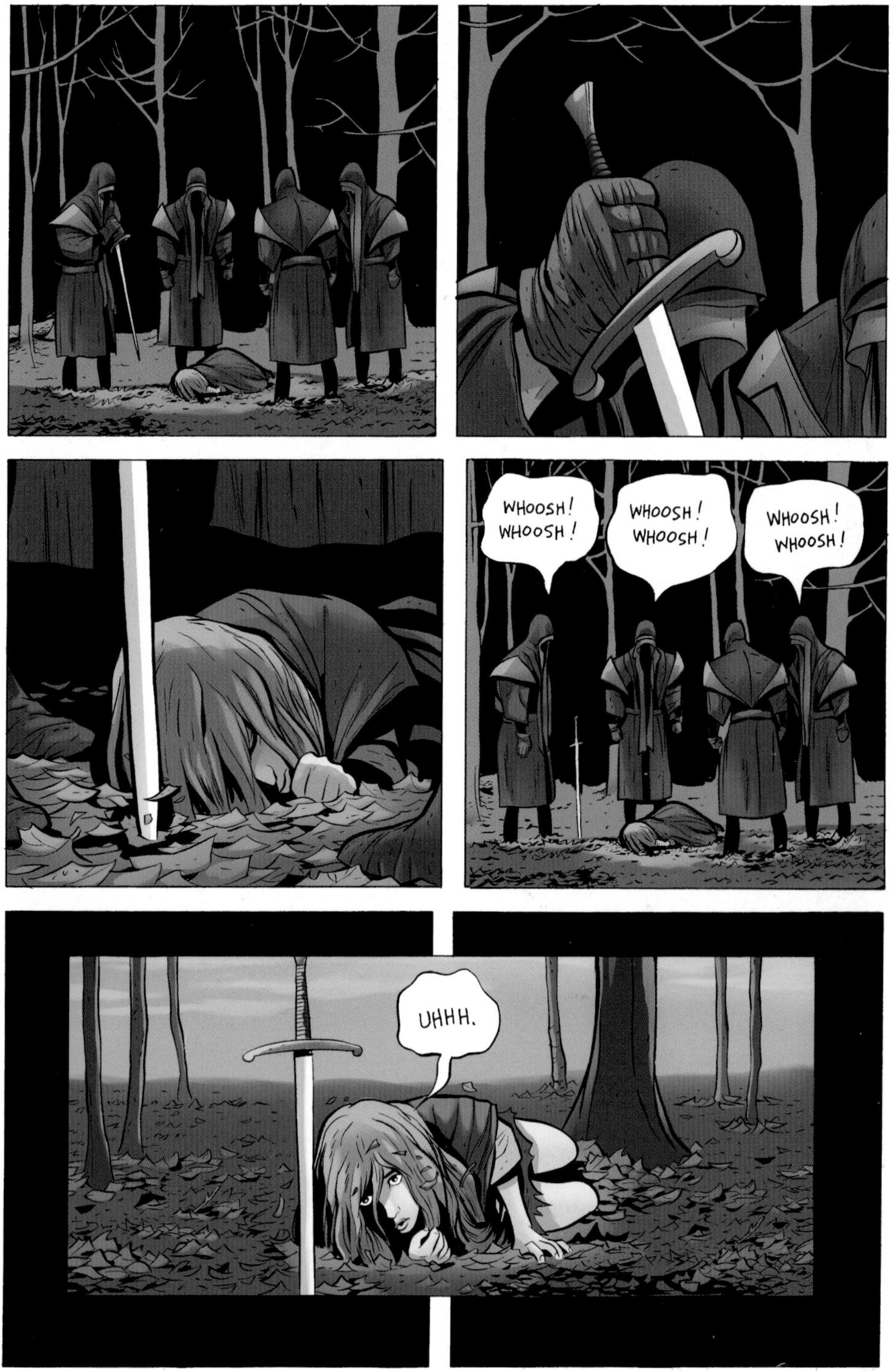
WHOOSH! WHOOSH!
WHOOSH! WHOOSH!
WHOOSH! WHOOSH!
UHHH.

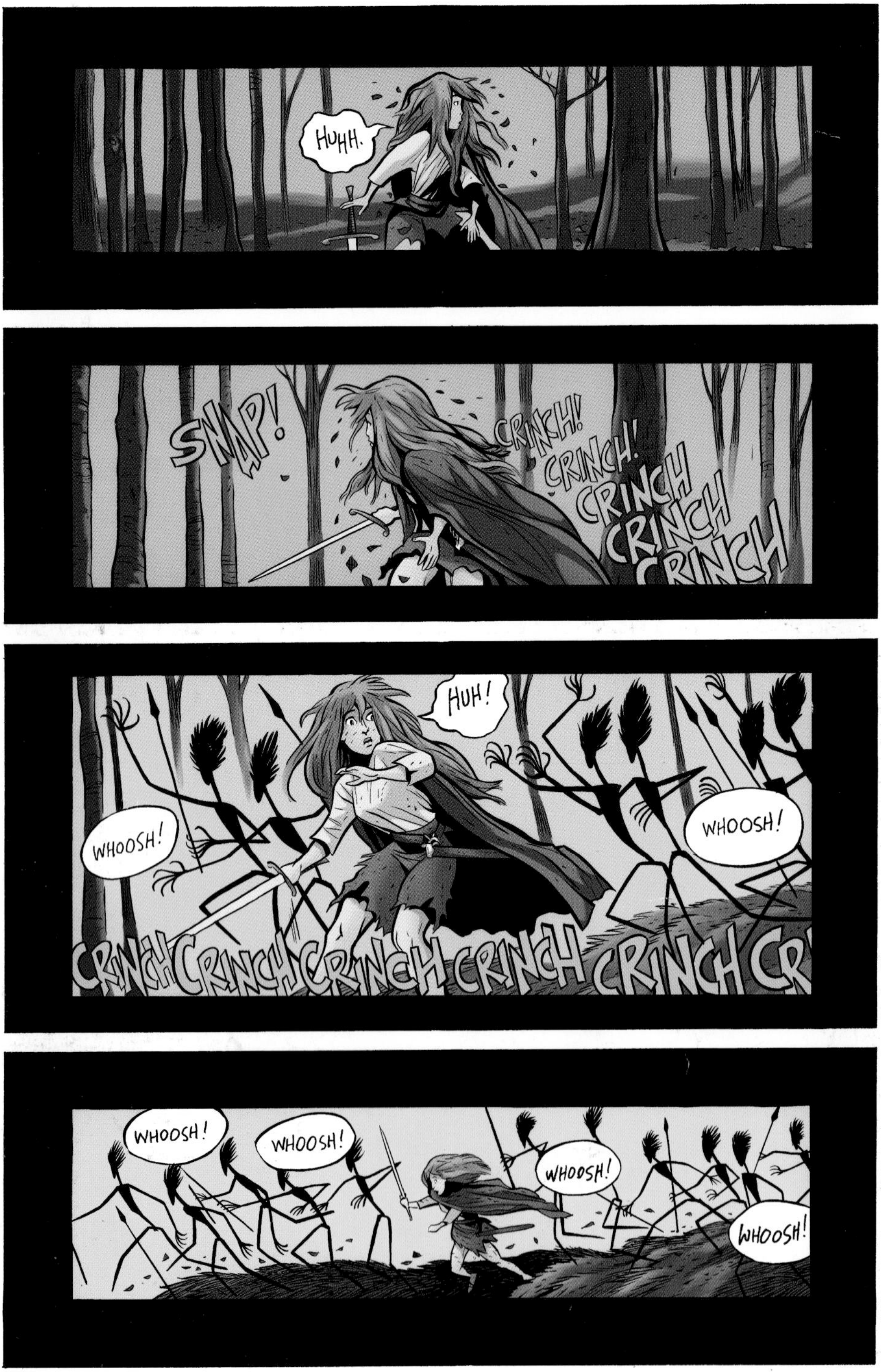
HUHH.
SNAP!
CRINCH!
CRINCH!
CRINCH
CRINCH
CRINCH
HUH!
WHOOSH!
WHOOSH!
CRINCH CRINCH CRINCH CRINCH CRINCH CR
WHOOSH!
WHOOSH!
WHOOSH!
WHOOSH!

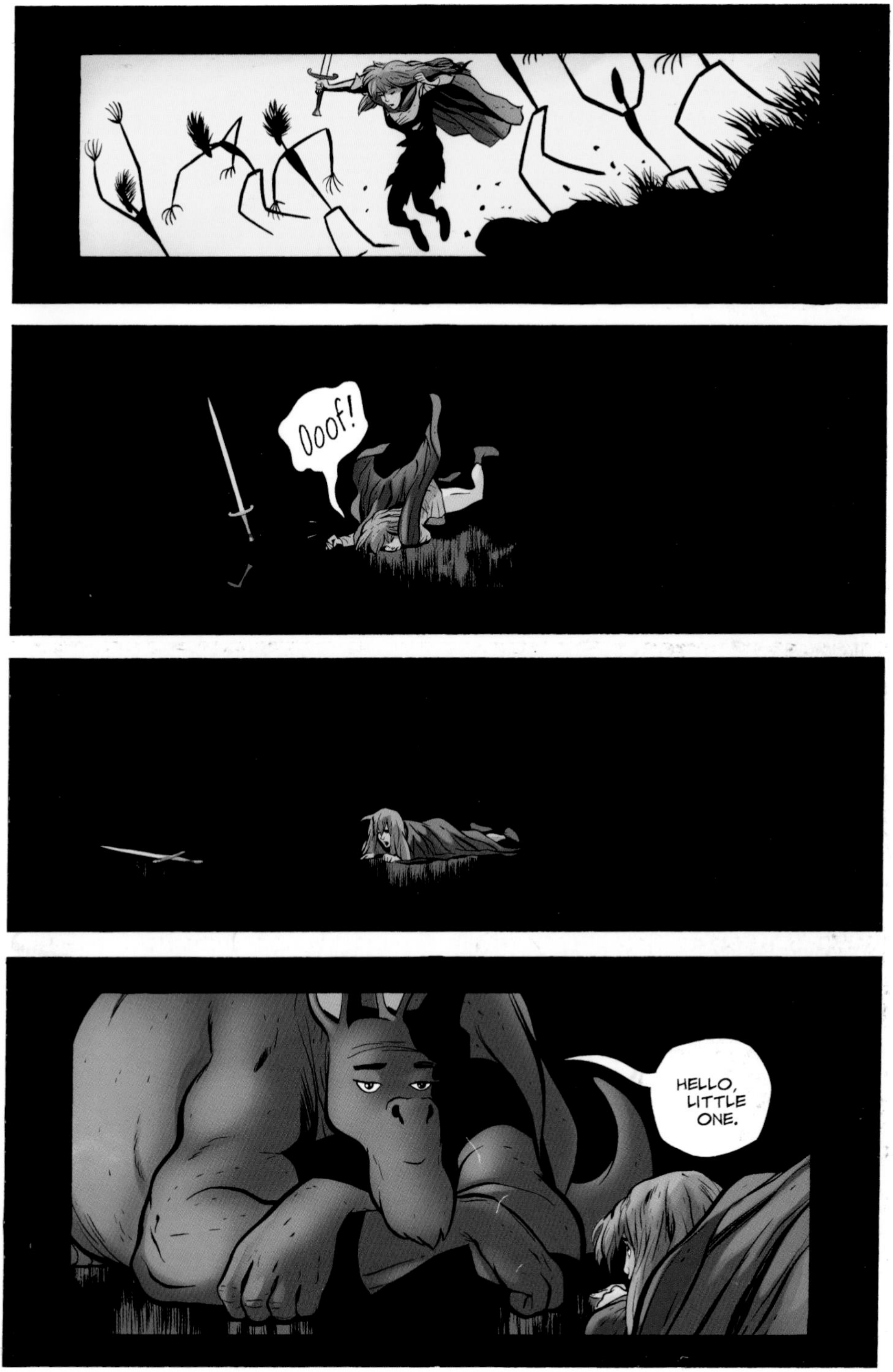
Ooof!
HELLO, LITTLE ONE.

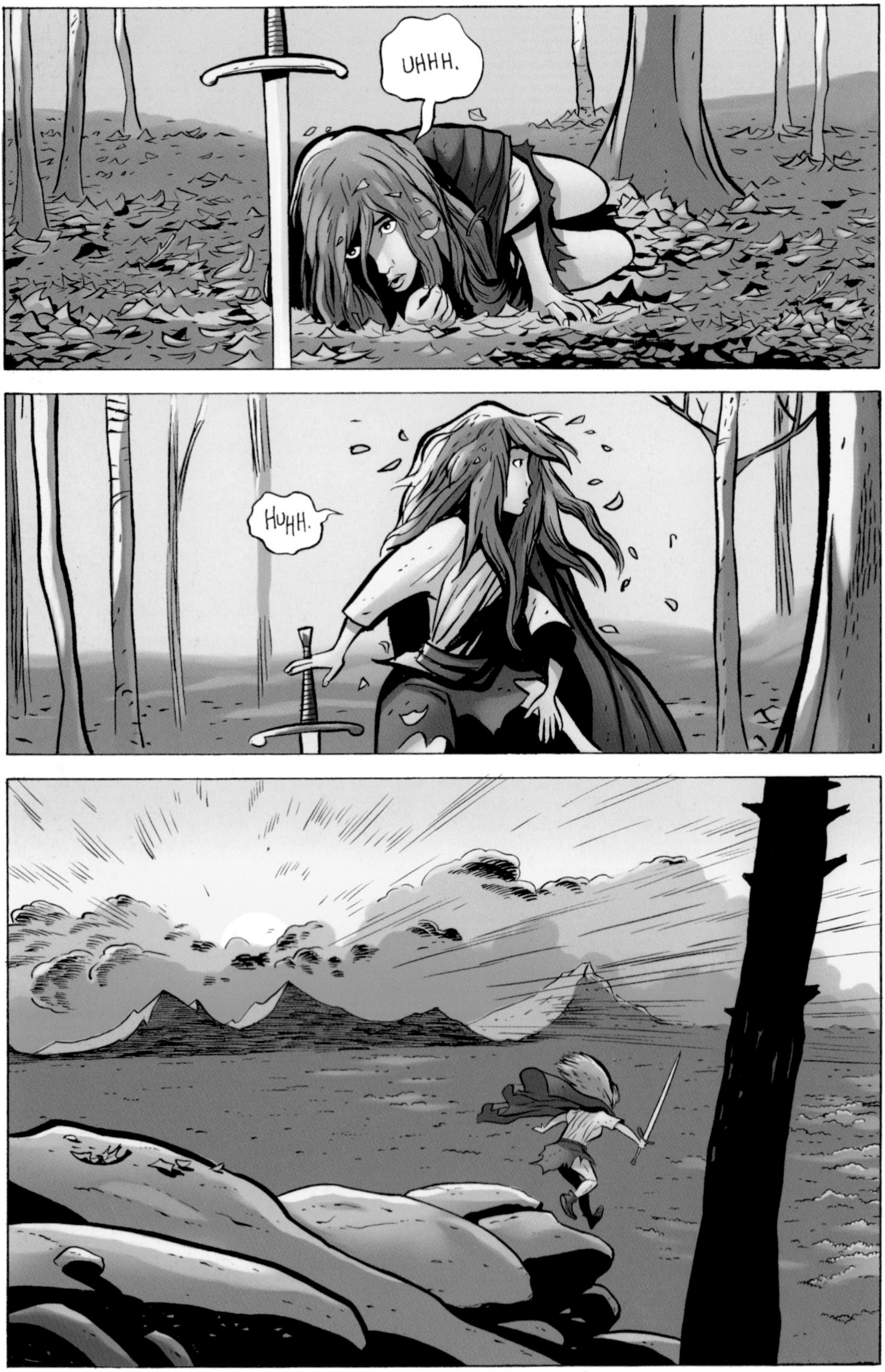
UHHH.
HUHH.

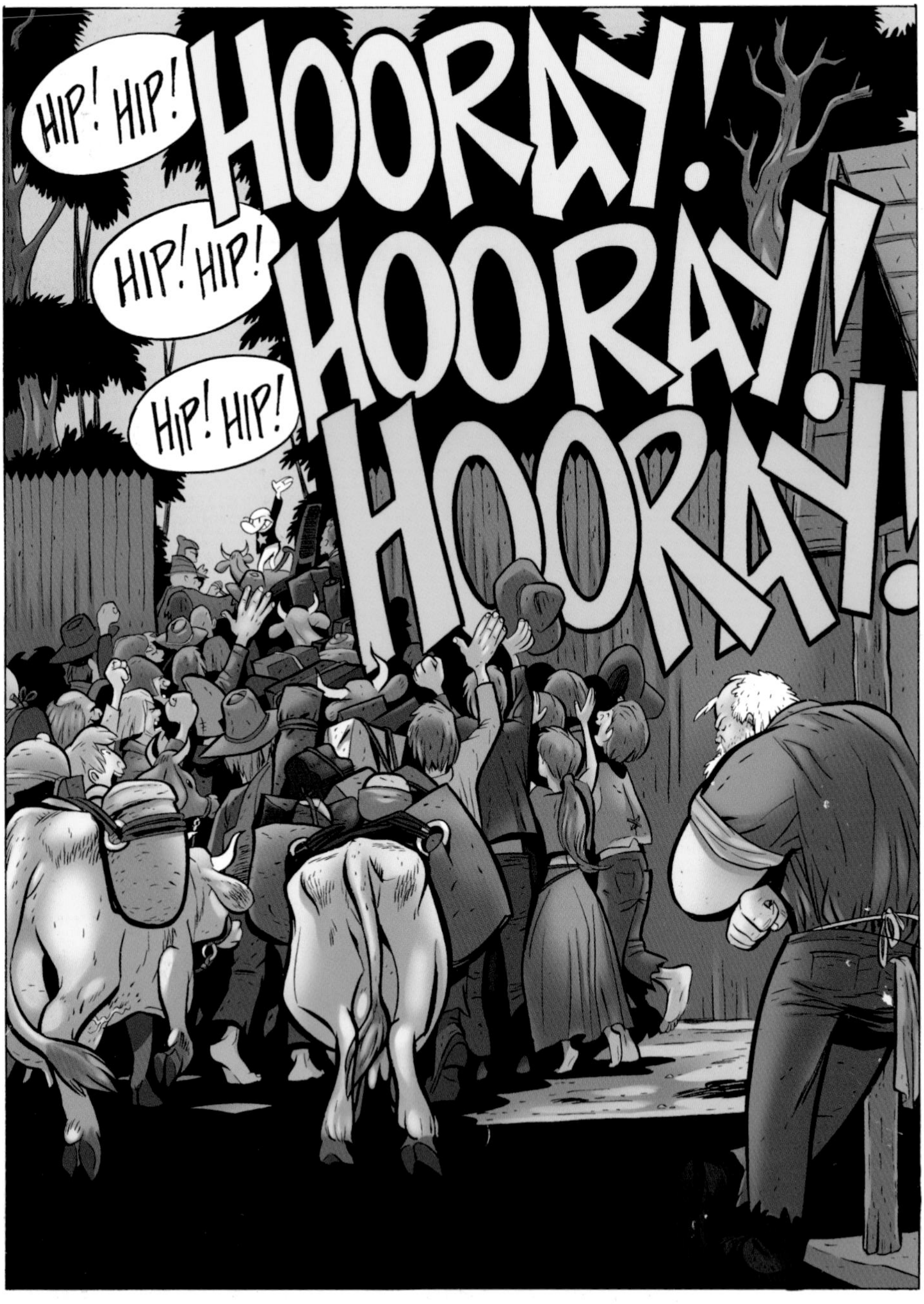
HIP! HIP!
HOORAY!
HIP! HIP!
HOORAY!
HIP! HIP!
HOORAY!

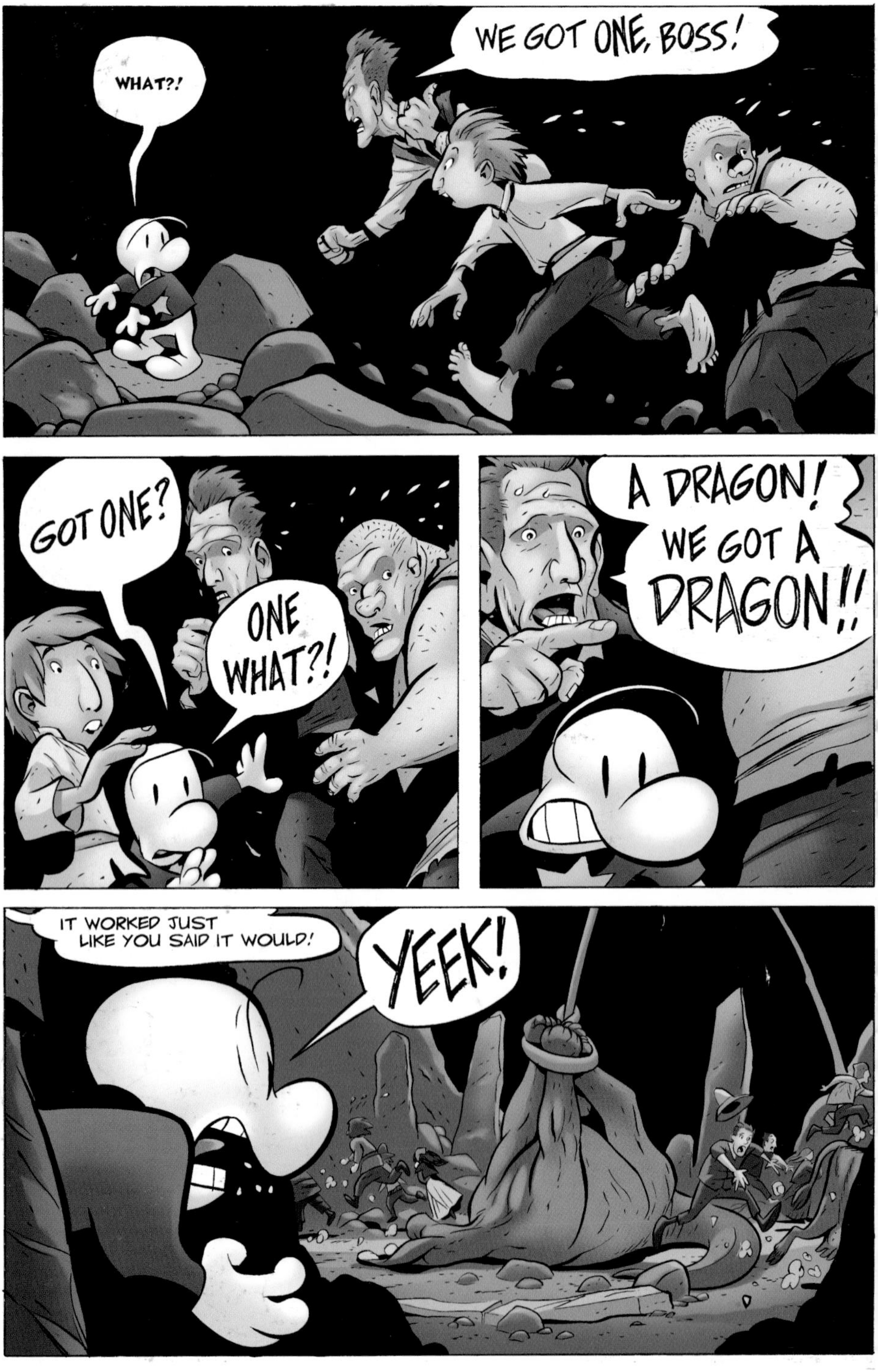
WHAT?!
WE GOT ONE, BOSS!
GOT ONE?
ONE WHAT?!
A DRAGON! WE GOT A DRAGON!!
IT WORKED JUST LIKE YOU SAID IT WOULD!
YEEK!

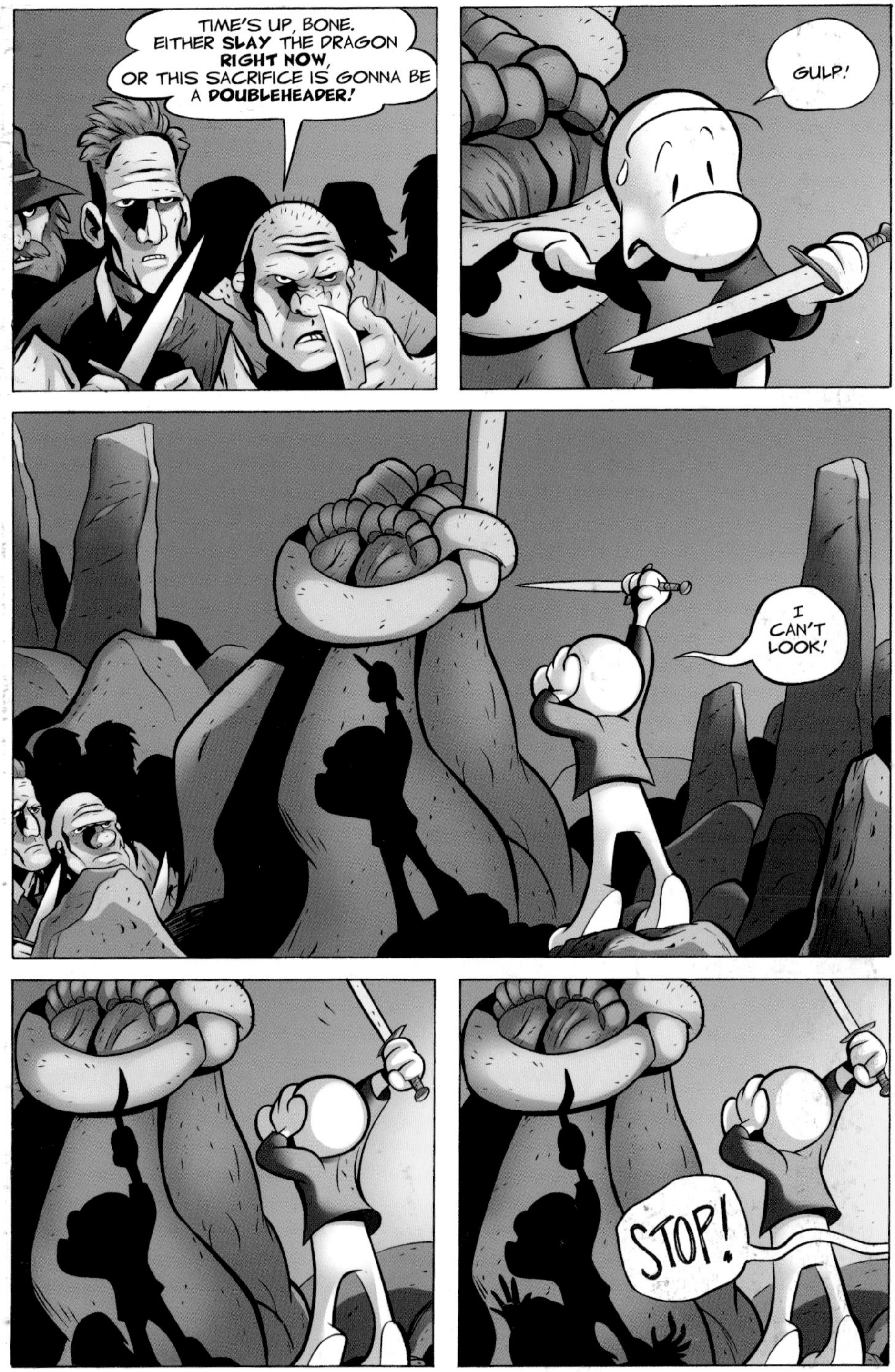
TIME'S UP, BONE. EITHER **SLAY** THE DRAGON **RIGHT NOW**, OR THIS SACRIFICE IS GONNA BE A **DOUBLEHEADER!**
GULP!
I CAN'T LOOK!
STOP!

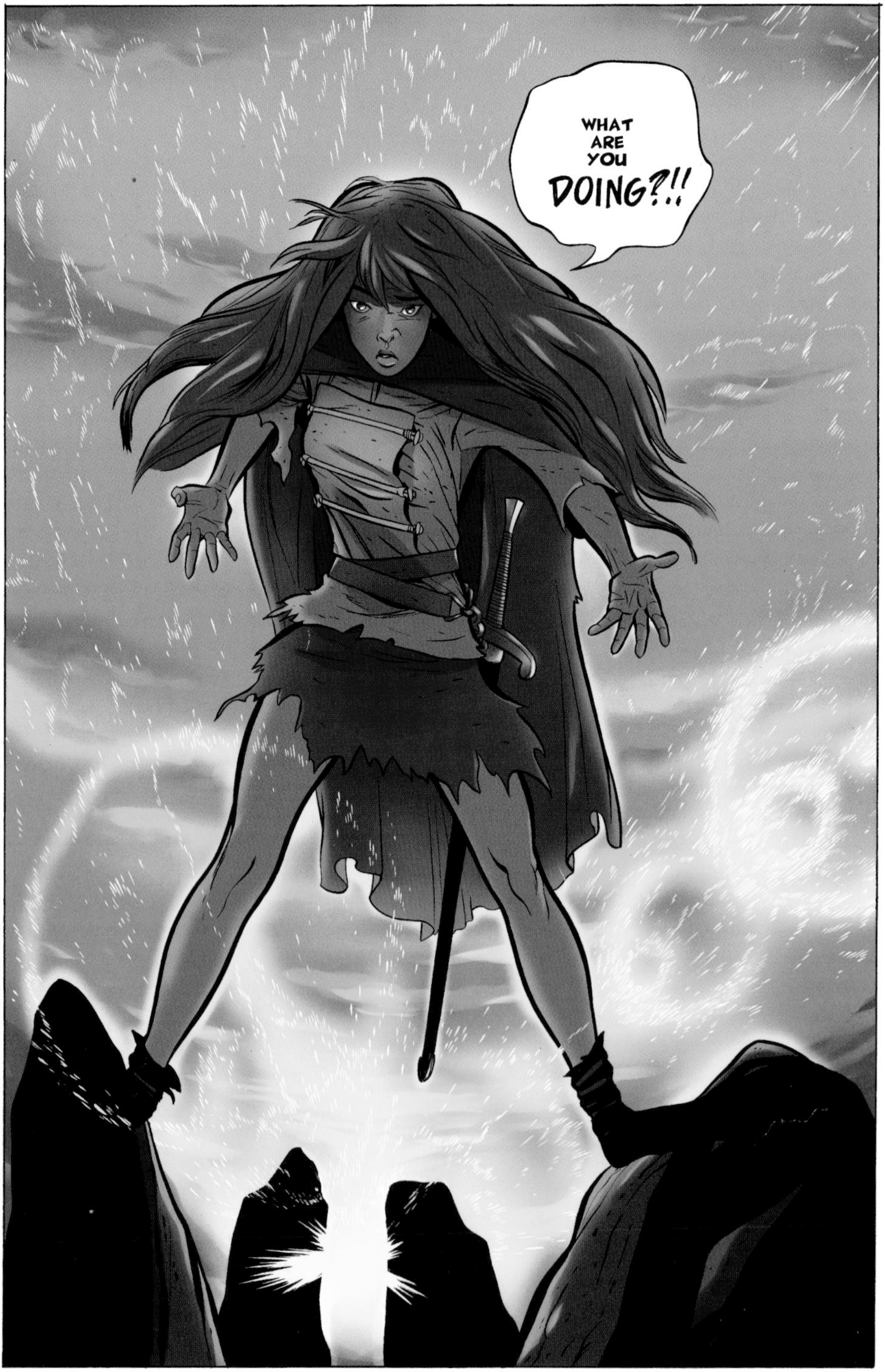
WHAT ARE YOU DOING?!!

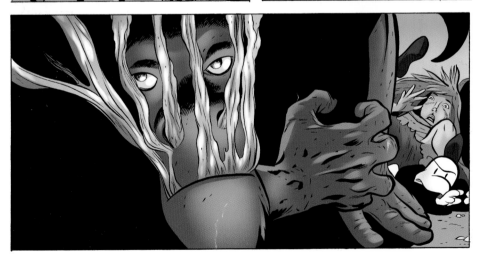

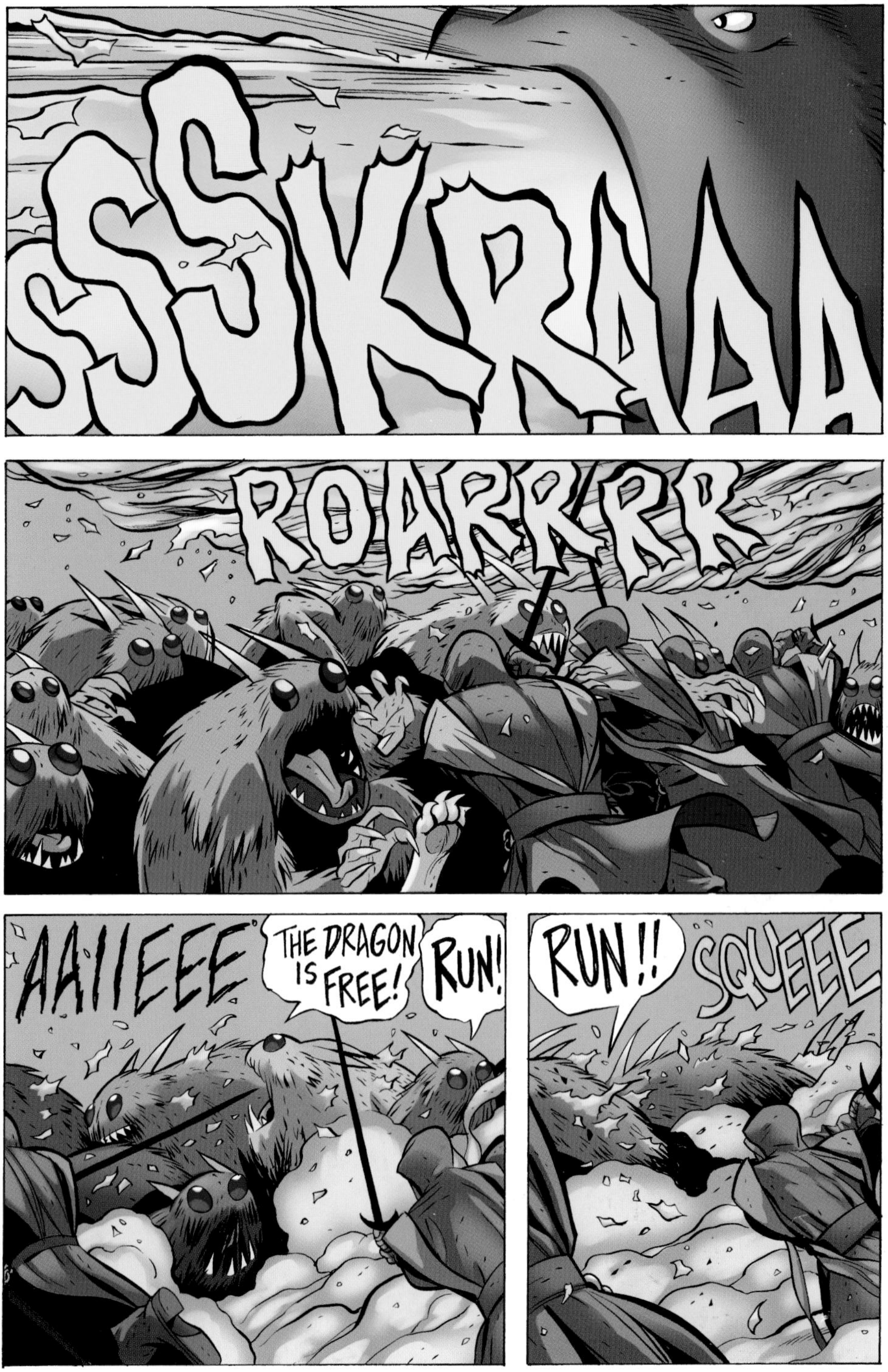
SSSKRAAA
ROARRRR
AAIIEEE
THE DRAGON IS FREE!
RUN!
RUN!!
SQUEEE

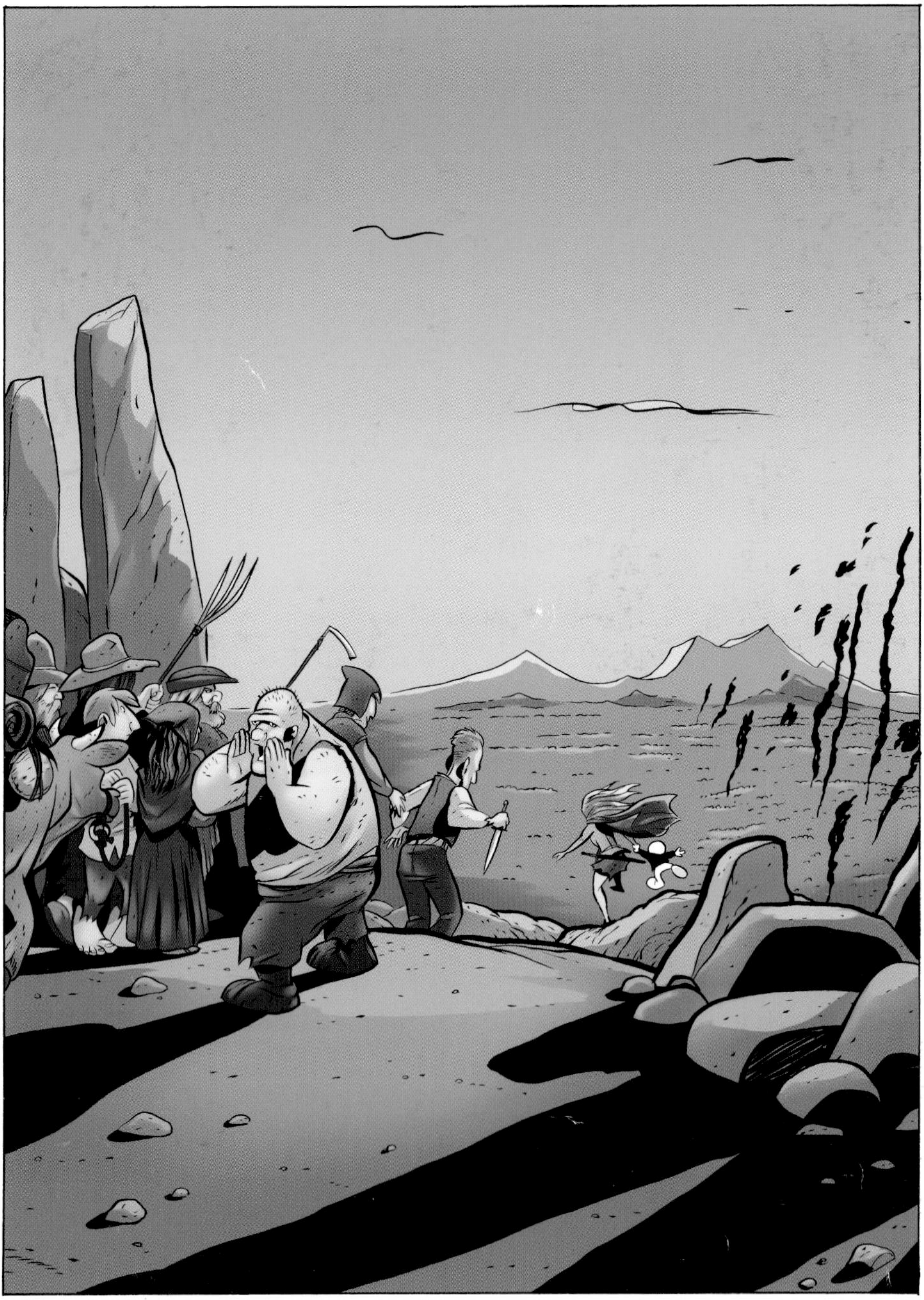

...TO BE CONTINUED.

About JEFF SMITH

JEFF SMITH was born and raised in the American Midwest and learned about cartooning from comic strips, comic books, and watching animated shorts on TV. After four years of drawing comic strips for The Ohio State University's student newspaper and co-founding Character Builders animation studio in 1986, Smith launched the comic book *BONE* in 1991. Between *BONE* and other comics projects, Smith spends much of his time on the international guest circuit promoting comics and the art of graphic novels.

More about BONE

An instant classic when it first appeared in the U.S. as an underground comic book in 1991, Bone has since garnered 38 international awards and sold a million copies in 15 languages. Now, Scholastic's GRAPHIX imprint is publishing full-color graphic novel editions of the nine-book *BONE* series. Look for the continuing adventures of the Bone cousins in *Rock Jaw: Master of the Eastern Border*.

Dreaming of Harvestar

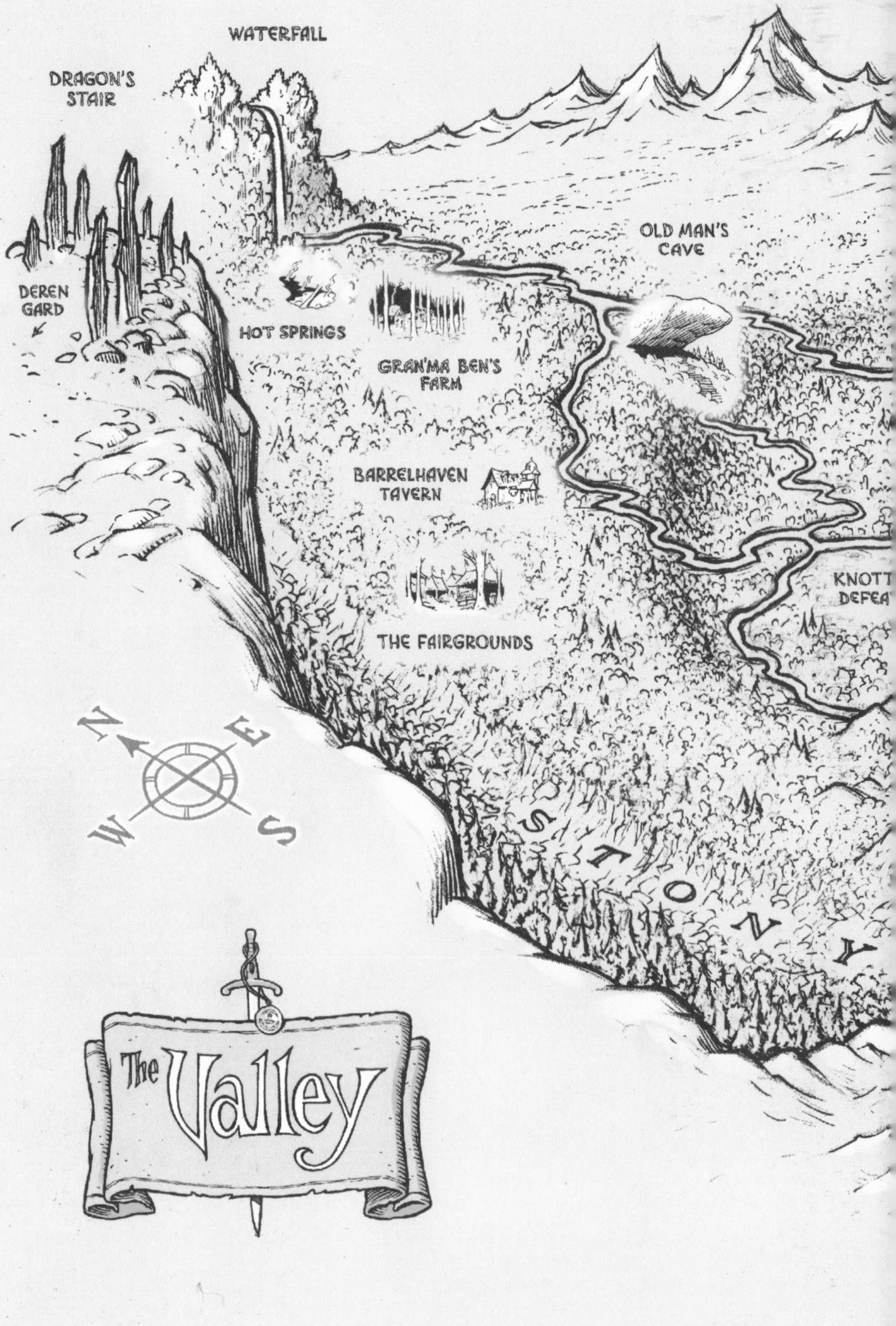

WATERFALL
DRAGON'S STAIR
DEREN GARD
HOT SPRINGS
OLD MAN'S CAVE
GRAN'MA BEN'S FARM
BARRELHAVEN TAVERN
THE FAIRGROUNDS
KNOTT
DEFEA
STONY
N
E
S
W
The Valley